Love You Dead

Love You Dead

Peter James

W F HOWES LTD

This large print edition published in 2017 by
W F Howes Ltd
Unit 5, St George's House, Rearsby Business Park,
Gaddesby Lane, Rearsby, Leicester LE7 4YH

1 3 5 7 9 10 8 6 4 2

First published in the United Kingdom in 2016
by Macmillan

A CIP catalogue record for this book is available
from the British Library

ISBN 978 1 51006 525 3

Typeset by Palimpsest Book Production Limited,
Falkirk, Stirlingshire

Printed and bound by
T J International in the UK
Printforce Nederland b.v. in the Netherlands
Ligare in Australia

FOR SUE ANSELL
My very dear friend who has read
every book since my very first, giving me
her sound wisdom and advice.

CHAPTER 1

Tuesday 10 February

The two lovers peered out of the hotel bedroom window, smiling with glee, but each for a very different reason.

The heavy snowfall that had been forecast for almost a week had finally arrived overnight, and fat, thick flakes of the white stuff were still tumbling down this morning. A few cars, chains clanking, slithered up the narrow mountain road, and others, parked outside the hotels, were now large white mounds.

Everyone in the smart French ski resort of Courchevel 1850 was relieved – the resort managers, the hoteliers, the restaurateurs, the seasonnaires, the ski-rental shops, the lift companies, and all the others who relied on the ski season for much of their livelihood. And, most importantly of all, the winter-sporters themselves. After days of blue skies, searing sunshine and melting snow, which meant treacherous ice in the mornings and slush and exposed rocks in the afternoons, finally the skiers and snowboarders, who had paid top money

1

for their precious annual few days on the slopes, now had great conditions to look forward to.

As Jodie Bentley and her elderly American fiancé, Walt, put on their skis outside the boot-room entrance of the Chabichou Hotel, the falling snow tickled exposed parts of their faces beneath their helmets and visors.

Although a seasoned skier and powder hound, this was the financier's first time skiing in Europe and he had been relying all week on his much younger fiancée, who seemed to know the resort like the back of her hand, to guide him.

They skied down carefully in the poor visibility to the Biollay lift, just a couple of minutes below the hotel, went through the electronic turnstiles, and joined the short queue to the chairlift. A couple of minutes later, clutching their ski poles, the wide chair scooped them up and forward.

Walt pulled down the safety bar, then they settled back, snug in their cosy outfits, for the seven minutes it took for the lift to carry them to the top. As they alighted, the wind was blowing fiercely, and without hanging around, Jodie led the way down an easy red then blue run to the Croisette, the central lift station for the resort.

They removed their skis, and Walt, despite suffering from a prolapsed disc, insisted on carrying Jodie's skis as well as his own up the ramp to the lift. As a red eight-seater gondola came slowly round, he jammed their skis into two of the outside holders, then followed Jodie in. They sat down and pushed up their visors. They were followed by another couple and, moments later, just before the doors closed, a short man in his fifties clambered in after them, wearing a smart Spyder ski outfit and a flashy leather helmet with a mirrored visor.

'*Bonjour!*' he said in a bad French accent. Then added, 'Hope you don't mind my joining you?' He settled down opposite them as the gondola lurched forward.

'Not at all,' Walt said.

Jodie smiled politely. The other two strangers, both busy texting on their phones, said nothing.

'*Ah bien, vous parlez Anglais!*' The stranger unclipped his helmet and removed it for an instant to scratch the top of his bald head. 'American?' he said, pulling off his gloves, then removing a tissue from his pocket and starting to wipe his glasses.

'I'm from California, but my fiancée's a Brit,' Walt said, amicably.

'Jolly good! Beastly weather but the powder at the top should be to die for,' the man said.

Jodie smiled politely again. 'Where are you from?' she asked.

'The south – Brighton,' the stranger replied.

'Good lord, what a coincidence! So am I!' Jodie said.

'Small world,' he muttered, and suddenly looked uncomfortable.

'So what line of business are you in?' Walt asked him.

'Oh, in the medical world. Just recently retired and moved to France. And yourselves?'

'I have a group of investment trusts,' the American replied.

'I was a legal secretary,' Jodie said.

As the small gondola climbed, rocked by the wind, the snow was turning into a blizzard and the visibility deteriorating by the minute. Walt put his arm round Jodie and hugged her. 'Maybe we shouldn't go too high this morning, hon, it's going to be very windy at the top,' he said.

'The powder's going to be awesome up there,' she replied, 'and there won't be too many people this early. There are some really fabulous runs, trust me!'

'Well, OK,' he said, peering dubiously through the misted-up windows.

'Oh, absolutely,' the Englishman said. 'Trust your beautiful young lady – and the forecast is improving!' As the gondola reached the first stage, he waited politely for them to alight first. 'Nice meeting you,' he said. 'Bye for now.'

The other couple, still texting, remained on the gondola.

With Walt again insisting on carrying Jodie's skis, they trudged the short distance to the cable car. Normally jam-packed with skiers squashed together like sardines, this morning the huge cabin was three-quarters empty. Along with themselves there were just a few die-hards. Several boarders in their baggy outfits, two rugged-looking, bearded men in bobble hats, wearing rucksacks, who were sharing swigs from a hip flask, and a small assortment of other skiers, one wearing a GoPro camera on his helmet. Walt raised his visor and smiled at Jodie. She raised hers and smiled back.

He removed a glove, jamming it between his skis, produced a chocolate bar from his breast pocket and offered it to Jodie.

'I'm fine, thanks, still stuffed from breakfast!'

'You hardly ate anything!' He broke a piece off, put the bar back in his pocket and zipped it shut, then chewed, peering out anxiously. The cable car rocked in the wind, then swayed alarmingly, causing everyone to shriek, some out of fear, others for fun. He put an arm round Jodie again and she snuggled up against him. 'Maybe we should get a coffee at the top and wait to see if the visibility improves?' he said.

'Let's do a couple of runs first, my love,' she replied. 'We'll find some fresh powder before it gets ruined by other skiers.'

He shrugged. 'OK.' But he didn't sound particularly enthusiastic. He stared at her for some moments. 'You know,' he said, 'you're incredible. Not many people can look beautiful in a helmet and visor, but you do.'

'And you look every inch my handsome prince!' she replied.

He tried to kiss her but the top of his helmet bashed against her visor. She giggled, then leaned closer to him and whispered, 'Too bad there's other people on here,' running her gloved hand down his crotch.

He squirmed. 'Jeez, you're making me horny!'

'You make me horny all the time.'

He grinned. Then he looked serious again, and a tad nervous. He peered through a window into the blizzard, and the car yawed in the wind, then swung, almost throwing him off balance. 'You have your cell with you, hon?' he asked.

'Yes.'

'You know – just in case we lose each other in this white-out.'

'We won't,' she said, confidently.

He patted his chest and frowned. Patted it again, then tugged open another zipper. 'Jeez,' he said, and began to pat all over the front of his stylish black Bogner ski jacket. 'I can't believe it, how stupid. I must have left mine back in the room.'

'I'm sure I saw you put it in – your top right-hand pocket – before we left,' she said.

He checked all over again, and his trouser pockets. 'Goddammit, must have fallen out some-where – maybe when we were putting our skis on.'

'We're going to stay close. Just in case we do get separated, then plan B is we both ski back down to the Croisette and meet there. Just follow the signs for Courchevel 1850 – it's well posted all the way.'

'Maybe we should ski straight back down and go and check it's not lying in the snow outside the hotel.'

'Someone'll find it if it is, darling. No one's going to steal it, not at that lovely hotel.'

'We'd better go back down, I need it. I have a couple of important calls to make this afternoon.'

'OK,' she said. 'Sure, fine, we'll ski fast!'

Five minutes later the cable car slowed right down, and a shadow loomed ahead. The car rocked from side to side, bumping against the buffered sides of the station, slowly sliding in, before stopping. Then the doors opened and they stepped out in their heavy ski boots, onto the gridded metal walkway.

They shuffled along it, then carefully down the steps and out into the ferocious blizzard, their faces stinging from snow as hard as hailstones. They could barely see a few feet in front of them, and the group ahead, ducking down and clipping into their boards, were little more than shadowy silhouettes.

As they stood beside a sign mostly obscured with snow, Walt laid their skis down on the ground, kicked the ice away from the bottom of his boots, tapping them with his ski poles to make extra sure there were no lumps of snow stuck there, then stepped into his bindings and snapped them shut.

As the silhouettes began to move away, Jodie said, 'Hang on a sec, darling, I need to clean my visor.'

Walt waited, turning his face away from the wind as best he could, while Jodie tugged down one of her zippers, produced a tissue and wiped the inside of her visor, then the outside.

'This is horrible!' He had to shout to make his voice heard.

'We're almost at the highest point in the whole resort,' she said. 'As soon as we get off this ridge we'll be out of the wind!'

'I hope you're right! Maybe we should start with something easy – is there a blue run back down? I don't fancy anything too challenging in this goddam visibility!'

'There is and it's lovely. There's one tiny steep bit to get into it, then it'll be a glorious cruise. It's my favourite run!'

He watched the last of the silhouettes disappearing as Jodie pulled her gloves back on, then stepped into her skis.

'Ready?' she asked.

'Uh-huh.'

She pointed to the right. 'We go down here.'

'Are you sure? Everyone else has gone that way.' He pointed in the direction that the others who had been in the cable car with them had taken.

'You want the hardcore black run down or a gentle blue?'

'Blue!' he said emphatically.

'That crazy lot have all taken the black.' She glanced over her shoulder and could just make out the cable car leaving the station for its return journey. It would be around fifteen minutes before the next load of skiers arrived. Right now, they were alone. 'Blue?' she said. 'Are you sure? I'm sure you'd cope with the black.'

'Not in this visibility.'

'Then we go this way,' she said.

'I can't see any sign pointing this way, hon. There must be a signpost up here, surely?'

With one ski pole, she began to brush away the fresh powder snow from the ground beside her. After a moment, tracks were revealed beneath it, frozen into the cruddy, icy surface beneath. 'See?' she said.

He peered at them. They led straight ahead for a couple of yards before disappearing into the swirling white blizzard. Looking relieved, he smiled. 'Clever girl! I'll follow you.'

'No, you go first in case you fall over – I can help you up. Just follow the tracks. Bend your knees and brace yourself because the first fifty yards or so are a bit steep, then it levels out. Just let yourself go!' She shot an anxious glance around her to make absolutely sure no one was watching.

'OK!' he said with a sudden burst of enthusiasm. 'Here goes! Yeee-ha!'

He launched himself forward on his poles, like a racer out of the gate, and whooped again. 'Yeee-ha!'

Then his voice turned into a terrible scream. Just for one fleeting second before it was swallowed by the wind.

Then silence.

Jodie turned round, then pushing with her poles, headed off in the direction all the other skiers had taken, oblivious to the wind and the stinging snow on her cheeks.

CHAPTER 2

Tuesday 10 February

Jodie did what she and Walt had agreed if they lost each other, which was to ski down to the Croisette and wait in front of the entrance to the ski school.

It was much warmer down here than it had been up at the top of the Saulire, and just as the Englishman they'd met in the gondola had predicted, the weather was now improving. The falling snow had turned to flecks of sleet, and the sun was trying to break through. And apart from that man, no one in either of the lifts in which they had travelled to the top had taken any notice of them.

She removed her helmet so that, maybe later, someone would recognize her and be able to back up her story. That guy from Brighton might even prove useful. He'd be able to verify she and Walt had both set off skiing together in the poor visibility. A shame she hadn't asked him his name.

She glanced at her watch, wondering just how long would be considered a respectable waiting time. An hour, she decided. An hour would be a perfectly reasonable time before she headed into a bar for a nice warm coffee and an Eau de Vie schnapps – maybe a double – to take the edge off her nerves. Somewhere to sit and plan her story carefully.

She pushed back her sleeve and glanced at her watch. 11.05 a.m. The day was still young, and more skiers were venturing out of their hotels and chalets now that the weather was clearing, and heading into the lift stations around her. Suddenly an idiot on a snowboard ran over her skis and grabbed hold of her, trying to prevent them both falling over.

'Awfully sorry! Pardonnay-moi!' His apology was as clumsy as his actions.

'Dickhead,' she said, freeing herself from his clutches.

'There's no need to be rude.'

'Oh, right, I'm just standing here minding my own business and you crash into me. What do you want me to do – dance?'

She stepped away from him, huffily, and resumed staring up at the slopes, clocking anyone in a black jacket and trousers who might, possibly, be her fiancé. Not that she was expecting to see him. But she continued watching, her story prepared just in case – however unlikely it was – he appeared.

An hour and a half later Jodie stepped out of the bar, pulled on her fur-lined Cornelia James gloves, hoisted her skis onto her shoulder and trudged the short distance up the steep incline towards the Chabichou Hotel. Above her she heard the *wokka . . . wokka . . . wokka* sound of a helicopter and looked up at it. Maybe it was taking a group heli-skiing up to some off-piste powder. Or maybe it belonged to the local emergency services.

Had someone found his body already? A bit sooner than she had planned – damn the weather, she'd hoped for the white-out to last a bit longer. But no matter.

Popping a piece of mint chewing gum into her mouth to mask the smell of alcohol, she placed the skis and poles in the rack by the ski-room entrance and went inside and into the ski shop. There were rows of new skis lining one wall, a rack of helmets on another and several manne-quins clad in the latest in skiing chic dotted around.

The young, handsome Frenchman who was the ski-shop manager, and had kitted them out with their rental skis, greeted her with a smile. In a charming French accent Simon Place said, 'You're not skiing? We have the best conditions here in the mountains in weeks – beautiful powder – and I think this afternoon the weather will be sunshine!'

'I've lost my fiancé – it was a white-out at the top when we went up. I don't like skiing on my own. Stupidly left my phone in our room – I'm going to call him to try to find him. That's one problem with this resort, it's so big.'

13

As he helped her off with her boots, he asked, 'You liked the skis?'

'Yes, they're good.'

'Stockli skis – they are – you know – the Rolls-Royce skis.'

'Too bad they don't come with a chauffeur,' she said and walked out into the corridor, leaving him puzzling over the remark.

She picked her key up from the hotel's reception desk, telling the receptionist she'd become separated from her fiancé out skiing, and was worried because she'd waited for him at the bottom for an hour and he hadn't turned up. She added that he was an experienced skier and she was sure he would be fine, and asked the receptionist, when Walt eventually turned up, to tell him she'd be in the spa if she wasn't in their room. Then she took the lift up to the third floor.

The room had already been cleaned; it looked neat and tidy, and there was a faint, pleasant smell of pine. She removed her phone from the back of the shelf where she had placed her underwear and dialled Walt's number, wanting to be sure that if the police were subsequently to check her phone, she had done what she had said.

She heard Walt's phone buzz and then begin warbling as well. She ended the call, removed his phone from under the pile of his clothes in the drawer where she had hidden it, and placed it on the desk beside his laptop. Then she peeled off her wet jacket, hung it over a radiator, dumped her gum into the waste bin and sat down on the freshly plumped duvet, thinking hard.

So far so good. She felt hungry. And the large schnapps had gone to her head a little. She had a witness that she'd travelled up to the top with her fiancé. She had another witness in the ski shop that she had returned without him, having become separated in the white-out, and that she'd gone back to the hotel to get her phone.

And no witness to what had happened at the top of the Saulire.

When they had got engaged, Walt had told her that he had written her into his will. So sweet of him.

There was a nice spa downstairs, with a swimming pool. She'd check her emails, have some lunch in the restaurant and check with the receptionist again. Then, if no update, she'd have a relaxing afternoon in the spa and perhaps get a massage. Around 5.30 p.m., a good hour after the lifts had closed, she'd go back to the reception desk and reiterate her concerns about her fiancé not having returned – and ask if they could check with the police and clinics.

Just like any anxious loved one might do.

She was feeling pretty happy with herself.

CHAPTER 3

Tuesday 10 February

Roy Grace was feeling pretty happy with himself, too, as he slid off the physiotherapist's table in her small Brighton consulting room. And looking forward to Saturday, Valentine's Day. He'd booked a table at his and Cleo's favourite Brighton restaurant, English's, and he was already thinking, with anticipation, about what he was going to have. Oysters Kilpatrick – grilled, with bacon – and then either lobster or a Dover sole – with mushy peas. A glass of champagne to start with and then a nice bottle of their Pouilly-Fuissé white burgundy, his favourite wine, when he could afford it.

Buying their new house, a cottage in the country on the outskirts of Henfield, had stretched them both financially, but they'd still kept a small amount aside for spoiling each other on special occasions, and this was one. They'd already had a great house-warming party with family and friends, and he was delighted that his sister was becoming close friends with Cleo's sister, Charlie.

16

His first wife, Sandy, had had no siblings, and relations with her odd parents had always been strained, at best. So this was really nice to see.

'That's it!' Anita Lane said. 'We're done! I don't think I need to see you again, unless your leg starts giving you any grief, in which case call me.'

'Thanks,' he said. 'Brilliant!'

He'd been coming here twice a week since early January, after a surgeon at the Royal Sussex County Hospital had removed eleven shotgun pellets from his right leg just before Christmas. He had been shot at close range by a suspected serial killer he'd been attempting to arrest in a bunker beneath a house in Hove. The surgeon had breezily told him he'd been very lucky not to lose his leg.

To begin with, recovery had been agony, with several of the nerves damaged, and he'd woken many times during the nights that followed with the sensation that his leg was on fire. But he'd stuck rigidly to the exercise programme the physio had given him, in between their sessions; finally the pain had eased and the mobility was returning.

'Keep up the exercises for a few more weeks,' she said.

'How soon can I start running again, Anita?'

'You can start now but build it up slowly. Don't try and do a marathon, OK?'

'I won't!'

'If you get pain, come straight back to see me. That's an order!'

'You're quite the bully, aren't you?' He grinned.

'It's because I can see you're chomping at the bit. You've had a massive trauma to that leg, and just because you've thrown your walking stick away and I'm discharging you doesn't mean you can start going mad. *Comprende?*'

'*Comprende!*'

'And try not to get into any *bundles* with any villains for a while.'

'I'm a detective superintendent, I don't get into many fights with suspects.'

'Oh, right, being a detective *superintendent* means you just get shot by them?'

He grimaced. 'Yep, well, hopefully not too often.'

'I hope not. A lot of people only get shot once, and it's not a physiotherapist they need afterwards but an undertaker. Stay safe, isn't that what you say?'

'I'm impressed with your police lingo!' He shook her hand, went out to the receptionist and paid the bill, carefully sticking the receipt in his wallet. Treatment for injuries sustained whilst on duty were reimbursed out of police funds.

Twenty minutes later he arrived back at his office in Sussex House, feeling a sense of an era passing. Although in part a lateral, out-of-the-box thinker, Roy Grace was at heart an extremely methodical man, the quality he had always admired and respected in those he had learned from in the past, and which he sought in anyone he selected to work with him. He was a creature of habit, and didn't like change, which he always found unsettling. And thanks to the government's swingeing budget cuts to the police, massive changes had already happened and there were more afoot.

The effect on morale was palpable. A decade ago he could guarantee that almost everyone in the force loved their job. Now, too many people were leaving before their retirement time, fed up with the freezes on promotion, or with the alterations to their pensions foisted on them midstream in their careers, or with walking on eggshells in fear of the political correctness zealots. Being a police officer had become a job where you were afraid to speak your mind or tell a joke. Yet, Grace knew only too well from his own experience, it was precisely that gallows humour the police were so famous for that enabled officers to cope with the horrors they sometimes saw.

In truth, many of the changes had helped to create more tolerant, less corrupt, less sexist and less racist police forces than when Roy Grace had begun his career. There were many pluses. He did still love his job and he tried not to let the negatives get to him, but there were moments, too, for the first time in the two decades he had served, that he had found himself contemplating alternatives. Particularly during his month off in January convalescing, when he'd had time to think. But in his heart he knew nothing could ever give him the satisfaction that solving murders did, despite all the changes.

And there was one very big change happening right here, to this building. Formerly the HQ CID, before the merger of the Major Crime Team with Surrey, this two-storey art deco building had been his base for the past decade. Once it had been a hive of activity, filled with detectives, SOCOs, a forensic department, the Fingerprint, Imaging and High Tech Crime Units, and the hub for many homicide and other serious crime investigations. But in a few months it would be no more, thanks to the brutal – and in his view highly short-sighted – government budget cuts inflicted on his and other police forces in the UK.

The Imaging Unit had already moved to Surrey. Soon the High Tech Crime Unit would be moved a few miles north of Brighton to Haywards Heath. And while nothing was confirmed yet, the rumour was that his branch of the Major Crime Team would be moved to the Sussex Police headquarters in Lewes.

Like most of the officers and support staff here, he had never really liked this building. Stuck on an industrial estate on the edge of the city, with no canteen, far too many people crammed into it, and a heating and air-conditioning system that was unable to cope in any weather conditions, he should have been glad of the impending move. But now, with the building beginning to take on the air of a ghost town, he was starting to feel nostalgic for it. All that would remain on this site, by this coming autumn, would be the custody block right behind it.

He walked through the large, deserted open-plan first-floor office that had until recently been the Detectives' Room, passing the cleared desks of officers and civilian staff who had already moved elsewhere, then entered his own office, one of the few enclosed ones.

He closed the door and sat behind his desk, staring out through the drizzle at the Asda super-store across the road which served as their canteen, thinking about Cleo's first Mother's Day which was just a few weeks away. He needed to get her a present from Noah. Roy had an ongoing list on his phone of gifts to get Cleo for her birthday and for Christmas, one of which was turquoise earrings – she loved the colour – and a rollerball pen. He added *book*, to remind himself to get down to City Books to pick up a novel she wanted, although he had forgotten the title. He would have to tease it out of her, somehow.

Then he logged on to his computer terminal and checked the serials and emails that had come in since he'd been at the physio, noting an email trail that referred to the Sussex Police rugby team. It reminded him he needed to find a new captain, as the current one was being sent to work on anti-terrorist training at the FBI's base in Quantico, Virginia. He was also pleased to see that the bread-making machine Cleo and he had ordered for the house was on its way.

He fired off some quick responses and forwarded the rugby emails to one of his predecessors, a retired former detective chief superintendent, David Gaylor, who had continued to be the team manager. Next he turned his attention back to the case that had been consuming him ever since his return to work.

His assailant, Dr Edward Crisp.

He glanced at the photograph of the Hove general practitioner, who appeared to be staring back at him with a smug grin.

Crisp had murdered five women in their early twenties – or rather, five that they knew about. His tally could quite possibly be higher. Maybe a lot higher. They'd had him cornered in an underground lair, but after shooting Grace in the leg with a shotgun, the man had made a seemingly impossible escape. No one knew how. One theory was that Crisp, an experienced potholer and caver, had gone through the Brighton and Hove sewer system, and had emerged through one of the manholes in the complex network.

Southern Water, who controlled it, were initially adamant that it would not have been possible for anyone to have survived. If Crisp hadn't drowned, he'd have ended up in one of the filters that prevented objects larger than a fraction of an inch reaching the open sea. Yet their searches found no trace of a body. They'd been forced to admit, reluctantly, that it was possible, however unlikely, that Crisp had survived.

One thing that Roy Grace was certain of was Crisp's cunning. The man's estranged wife, Sandra, had been interviewed exhaustively, and exonerated from any complicity. She seemed very happy – and relieved – to be away from him. The only one who appeared to be missing the doctor was the family dog, Smut, now living with her and apparently pining. Incredible though it was, for all the years that they had lived together, she'd had no idea that the derelict house next door to their Brighton mansion, where Crisp had carried out some, if not all, of his atrocities, had been owned by an offshore company set up by her husband.

Very recently the police had received possible evidence that Crisp had survived.

It was in the form of a sinister email that the doctor had subsequently sent to one of Roy's team, some weeks after his disappearance – and presumed death.

The source of the email was apparently untraceable. An anonymous Hotmail account that could have come from anywhere in the world. And which, just possibly, could have been sent, on a time delay, weeks earlier.

Fortunately, so far February had been a calm time, with no reported homicides in Sussex, leaving

Roy Grace free to work, doggedly, through contacts at police forces throughout Europe, the USA, Australia, Africa and the Far East for any signs of the doctor. He had also spent some time with a desk officer at Interpol, ensuring that Crisp's details and photograph were circulated around the world.

Crisp's MO was to target women in their early twenties with long brown hair. Summaries of every unsolved murder matching this profile, from within the UK and overseas, were stacked all round Roy and filled numerous folders on his computer.

And he was still no further forward. There were around two hundred countries in the world, and right now Dr Edward Crisp could be sitting in a hotel room, with his bald head and big glasses and smug grin, in any one of them.

Although a few, especially Syria and North Korea, could probably be safely eliminated.

'So where the hell are you, you bastard?' Grace said aloud in frustration.

'Right here, O master!'

He looked up, startled, to see his mate DI Glenn Branson, a black, shaven-headed man-mountain, standing in front of him with a broad smile.

'You're not looking a happy bunny,' Branson said.

'Yeah, you know why not? Because every time I start to feel a happy bunny, I see Edward bloody Crisp's face grinning at me.'

'Well, I've got some news for you.'

'Tell me.'

Branson reached over and placed an email printout on Grace's desk.

Grace read it, then looked up at his mate. 'Shit.'

CHAPTER 4

Tuesday 10 February

Shortly before 6 p.m., Jodie woke up with a start, on the big soft duvet in her Courchevel hotel room, to the sound of a helicopter flying low and fast over the resort. She could see through the window it was almost dark outside. Her mouth was dry and she had a slight headache.

She drank some water, went over to the desk and flipped open the lid of her Mac laptop. She tapped in her password, then checked her emails. Immediately she smiled. Another one from him!

My dearest Jodie,

I trust you are having a good time, wherever in the world this finds you on your travels. For too long you've been tantalizing me with your lovely messages. I love that very very sexy picture you sent me yesterday. I feel a truly wonderful connection between us and cannot wait to finally meet you! When do you think that might be? I'm now

26

settled into my glorious new beachfront house in Brighton where I have some very lovely celebrity neighbours. Please tell me it won't be long?

Fondest love, Rowley

She typed her reply.

My very sexy Rowley!

I agree, even though we've not yet met I feel massively in touch with you, too, and just love how you think. I really do! And I love how you make me feel just by reading your words! I plan to be back in Brighton just as soon as I've finished my business commitments here in New York – or, as I've been told how to pronounce it like the locals, Nooo Yawk! Each time I think of you I think of a beautiful expression I once read, written by an Indian poet. 'The path of love is narrow, and there is not room for two people on it, so you must become one.' That's how I feel about us.

She signed it with a row of kisses and sent it. Then she carefully filed his email and her reply into a folder titled *Charities Local*, which was buried inside another folder marked *Charities*. Just in case, somehow, Walt had ever found his way

27

into her computer. Not that there had ever been much likelihood, as he wasn't particularly computer savvy.

She logged off, closed the lid and sat still for some minutes, gathering her thoughts, getting her story together. Slipping out of the dressing gown she'd worn back from the spa, she pulled on a sweater and jeans and tied back her hair. She decided against putting on make-up, wanting to look pale and distressed.

She took the lift down three floors and walked towards the reception desk. As she approached, she saw a young, fair-haired man standing by it, dressed in a blue fleece jacket with the word *Gendarmerie* in white across the back of it.

The receptionist, to whom she had spoken several times during their short stay, was holding a phone in her hand, and replaced it as she saw Jodie.

'Ah, Mademoiselle Bentley,' she said, looking uneasy. 'I was just calling your room.' She pointed to the police officer. 'This is Christophe Chmiel from the Courchevel Gendarmerie – he wishes to have a word with you.'

'What – what about?' She turned to the policeman, feeling a genuine prickle of anxiety.

He gave her a concerned smile and spoke in good English. 'Mademoiselle Bentley, is it possible please I have a private word with you?'

'Yes – yes, of course. Is this about my fiancé, Walt? I'm really worried about him – we got separated skiing this morning, up at the top in the white-out – and I've not seen him all day. Please tell me nothing's happened to him? I've been waiting all afternoon for some news, I'm at my wits' end.'

The receptionist spoke to the officer in French. '*Voulez-vous utiliser notre bureau?*'

'*Oui, bien, merci,*' he replied.

The receptionist led them behind the counter into a small office with two computer screens, several filing cabinets and two swivel chairs. Then she closed the door behind them.

The police officer gestured to one of the chairs and, looking as weak and anxious as she could, Jodie sat down. 'Please tell me Walt's safe, isn't he?' she asked.

He pulled out a small notepad and looked at it, briefly. 'Mademoiselle Bentley, is your fiancé's name Walt Klein?'

'Yes, it is.'

'And you last saw him at what time today?'

She shrugged. 'About ten o'clock this morning. We took the cable car up to the top of the Saulire. The visibility was terrible but he was keen for us to be up early to get the fresh powder before it was skied out.'

He gave her a dubious look. 'You are both good skiers?'

'Yes – he's better than I am – he's an expert – I'm a bit nervous because I don't know this resort very well yet. But we were told the weather was improving. We couldn't see a damned thing at the top, but there were some other skiers who were in the cable car with us. I saw them ski off and thought the best thing would be to follow them. Walt told me to go first, in case I fell and he could help me. So I set off, trying to keep up with the others, but they shot off ahead of me, going too quickly. I stopped and waited for Walt but he never appeared. Do you know where he is? I've been terrified he's had an accident. Please tell me he's all right.' She began crying.

Chmiel waited for her to compose herself. 'We are just trying to establish exactly what has happened,' he said, then asked, 'What did you do when your fiancé did not appear?'

'We'd agreed to phone each other and, if we couldn't get through, we'd head down to the Croisette and wait for each other there, and in a worst case, we'd come back to the hotel and meet here. Then I realized that, stupidly, I'd not brought my phone, so I skied on down to the Croisette.' She sniffed and dabbed her eyes.

'And you waited for him?'

'I waited an hour.'

'And you weren't concerned?'

'Not at that point, no. It's pretty easy to lose someone in a white-out, and he and I come from rather different skiing cultures.'

'Cultures?'

She took some moments to compose herself. 'I'm so worried about him. He's always skied in places like Park City and Aspen – American resorts where they have powder all the time. I don't like skiing in zero visibility but it didn't bother him, so long as there was fresh powder. He knew I hadn't been that keen to go out today, so I figured he'd found himself some great virgin snow, and reckoned I'd be just as happy to come back here and enjoy the pool and have a massage.'

The officer nodded. 'Mademoiselle Bentley, I am very afraid to tell you, but this afternoon a body was found at the bottom of the sheer side of the Saulire—'

'Oh God, no!' she cried out. 'No, please no, please no! No, no, tell me it's not Walt. Please tell me!'

'This face – this is not possible to ski – not even for off-piste experts – it is only used by the paragliders. The identification we have is two credit cards and the gentleman's ski-lift pass. It is looking to us as if he must have perhaps mistaken the tracks. The name on the credit cards is Walter Klein. The ski-lift pass was issued by this hotel.'

'Can you describe him?' she asked, tears rolling down her cheeks.

'I have not myself seen him yet. I am told he is a gentleman perhaps in his seventies, with white hair, quite tall and a little heavy build.' He looked at her quizzically.

She began sobbing. 'Oh God, oh God, oh God, no.'

31

'I'm sorry to ask you this, but would you come with me to Moûtiers to identify the body?'

She crumpled, burying her face in her arms. After some moments she fell silent, wary of overdoing it.

CHAPTER 5

Tuesday 10 February

R oy Grace had been hoping to get home early, in time to help Cleo bath Noah and put him to bed with his favourite picture-book story. Instead he had been chained to his desk all day, with Glenn Branson, exchanging phone calls and emails with an English-speaking police officer, Bernard Viguet, in the Lyon, France, office of Interpol.

On his desk in front of him lay the email Glenn had brought in earlier, that had come from an officer in the Lyon Gendarmerie addressed to the Senior Investigating Officer of Operation Haywain, the continuing enquiry into the missing suspected serial killer, Dr Edward Crisp.

It stated that a sex worker in the city had gone missing two days ago, after being seen getting into a car late at night in the red-light district. A fellow prostitute, who had been shy to come forward at first, had raised the alarm. She had caught a glimpse of the man in the car, and he resembled the image of Crisp that Grace had circulated

33

through Interpol. The colleague had given a description of the car, and the part of its registration plate that she could recall. It matched a rental car that had been hired from Hertz, and subsequently returned, by an Englishman called Tony Suter.

Something that had piqued Grace's interest was that Tony Suter was one of the numerous aliases that Crisp had used in past years. Of course, it could have been coincidence. What could also have been coincidence was the appearance of the sex worker. She was in her early twenties, with long brown hair.

The exact profile of every single one of Crisp's known female victims to date.

The car had been valeted and already gone out with another customer. The French police were now urgently looking for it. In response to Roy Grace's confirmation that this could indeed be his suspect, they were currently in the process of obtaining the CCTV footage from the rental company's premises, and a manhunt was under way for the young woman.

'A big place, Lyon.'

'I've been there.'

'One of the largest metropolitan areas in France,' Branson said, helpfully.

'Thanks for the geography lesson.'

'You're welcome. Here's one for you – *The French Connection*, with Gene Hackman, remember that?'

'Yes, why?'

'That was partly set in Marseilles. The second largest city.'

'What's that got to do with anything?'

'Nothing. Just trying to use any opportunity to educate you. And it had a great ending.'

'You trying to tell me something?'

Branson was hesitant suddenly. 'Oh, yeah, right,' he said. 'I forgot. Maybe not so tactful.'

'You could say that,' Grace said. 'Unless you're trying to give me some kind of message?'

Branson grinned, then raised his hands submissively. 'No message.'

'I'm glad about that, because the bad guy got away.'

CHAPTER 6

Tuesday 17 February

After a week of hanging around, dealing with French officialdom, before Walt Klein's body was finally released after the post-mortem, Jodie accompanied her fiancé back to New York. She travelled up at the pointed end, sipping vintage bubbly in First Class, appearing to the cabin crew every inch a grieving lover consoling herself with alcohol. Walt travelled in less style, in the rear cargo hold of the plane. Although to be fair, she reasoned at one point, drifting off into a pleasant doze, he had more legroom in his coffin than those poor bastards back in economy.

And also, to be fair, she had not scrimped on the coffin. It was a top-of-the-range hand-carved rosewood affair, with a satin taffeta border and genuine brass handles. There was no finer coffin to be had anywhere in the Alps, the undertaker in Moûtiers had assured her. And certainly, when she saw the price, none that could possibly have been more expensive.

That would have been fine by her late fiancé, had he been in a position to help with the decision. Walt was dismissive of bargains. 'You buy cheap, you buy twice,' he had told her on more than one occasion. He'd have been proud of just how expensive this beauty had been, she thought. His final little treat to himself! She would present the bill to his lawyer, who would reimburse her.

The champagne she had been quaffing throughout the journey, from her constantly topped-up glass, was still in her system, maintaining her pleasantly woozy haze through the lengthy immigration queue. Although she hoped she did not reek too much of alcohol when, questioned by the immigration officer at passport control as to the reason for her visit, she had replied, trying to look and sound suitably grief-stricken, 'To bury my fiancé.'

She collected her bags and entered the arrivals hall, then instantly felt in need of another top-up of alcohol when she saw the frosty faces of Walt's two children – Don, his tall, serious, forty-year-old son, and Carla, his softer, warmer, thirty-five-year-old daughter, who had come to the airport more out of respect for their deceased father than any love for their gold-digger of a potential stepmother.

'Carla,' Jodie said, throwing her arms round her. 'Oh my God, this is so terrible. So terrible.' She burst into tears.

'Dad was an expert skier,' Don said, drily. 'He's skied off-piste for years. He wouldn't make a mistake.'

'It was a white-out, in a blizzard,' Jodie sobbed. 'We couldn't see our hands in front of our faces.'

'Dad wouldn't have made a mistake,' he repeated.

'We're staying at Dad's apartment until the funeral,' Carla said. 'Hope that's OK with you?'

'But as we figured you might want to be alone, to grieve for our father, and avoid all the hassle from the press, we took the precaution of booking you into a hotel,' Don said. 'Your choice.'

Suddenly she heard a male voice call out, 'Jodie!'

She turned, saw the strobe of a flashgun and heard the whirr of a camera motor. Another voice called her name and, as she glanced to the right, another flashgun went. Then another.

There were a dozen paparazzi lined up, all now shouting her name.

'Jodie, did you know about Walt?'

'How much did you know about Walt's finances?'

Jodie had met Walt in Las Vegas just over six months earlier. He'd been sitting at a table on his own, in a smoking bar at the Bellagio, drinking a Martini and lighting a cigar. She'd sat a few tables away, smoking a cigarette and drinking a margarita, eyeing potentials. This was one of the city's most expensive hotels; people who stayed here or even just came in for a drink were likely to be reasonably well off at worst, seriously loaded at best.

She'd travelled from Brighton, arriving the day before, to have a break, play some blackjack at the high-stakes tables, and try to find a new man. Her kind of man. A nice, lonely, elderly man. Someone who would be grateful for her attentions. But, most importantly of all, someone rich. Very rich.

This trip was an investment, just like her profiles on the high-end dating agencies were.

She chose blackjack because it was sociable, you got a chance to talk to your fellow gamblers and there was a steady turnover of players. She'd made a study of it, read books and knew all the tricks of the game. There was no strategy that could guarantee winning, but there was one that enabled her to stay at a high-rollers table for hours on end, losing very little money. A small cost for the opportunities it gave her to size up the men who perched beside her at the table.

And you could get married in this city, with no fuss at all, any time from 8 a.m. to midnight, on any day.

It looked like she was getting lucky sooner on this trip than she had expected. The jackpot on day one?

A little overweight and flabby, in his mid-seventies, she guessed, with a thick head of wavy silver hair. He was dressed in a yellow Gucci cardigan over a shirt with gold buttons, and blue suede Tod's loafers.

He looked lonely.

And sad.

And had no wedding ring on his finger.

Hunched up over the table, he was peering at his phone, reading something. Wall Street prices?

After a while he put it down, ate the olive from his Martini, then drained the drink and signalled to a waiter for another. Then he puffed on his cigar – a Cohiba, she could tell from the yellow and black band.

She stared at him, holding her cigarette between her fingers, the smoke rising. It took some moments before he finally looked up and caught her eye. She smiled. He gave her a brief, slightly embarrassed nod of acknowledgement, blinked his heavy-lidded eyes, then made a play of looking back down at his phone and tapping the keys, as if to show he wasn't any kind of Billy-No-Mates, but a busy man.

Instantly she made her move, crushing out her cigarette, scooping up her glass and her bag. Then she strode across to his table, in her silky Ted Baker dress and red Jimmy Choos, and sat down opposite him. Putting on her poshest, cut-glass English accent, she said, 'You look as lonely as I feel.'

'That so?'

He lifted his eyes from his phone, and gave her a melancholic stare. She raised her glass. 'Cheers!'

Obligingly, at that moment, the waiter produced a fresh Martini for him. He raised it and they clinked glasses. 'Cheers,' he said back to her, a little hesitant, as if unsure whether he'd just been hit on by a hooker.

'Jodie Bentley,' she said. 'I'm from Brighton, England.'

'Walt Klein.' He set his glass down and folded his arms.

Mirroring him, deliberately, she set her glass down and folded her arms, too. 'So what brings you to Vegas?' she asked.

'You want the trailer or the full three hours with intermission?'

She laughed. 'I don't have a train to catch. So as long as there's ice cream, popcorn and alcohol involved, the intermission version is fine by me!'

He grinned. 'Yeah, well, right, I'm here to try to forget for a while.' He opened his arms and placed his hands either side of his thighs. Instantly, but subtly, she did the same.

'Forget?'

'I went through a pretty bad divorce. Married forty-four years.' He shrugged and his heavy eyelids lowered, like theatre curtains, then raised again.

Once more she mirrored him. 'Forty-four years – you don't look old enough! Married in your teens, did you?'

'Very flattering of you! I'm probably a bit older than you think. What do you reckon?'

'Fifty-five?'

'You're being too kind. I like your accent. Love the British accent!'

'Well, thenk yew,' she said, exaggerating it even more. 'OK, fifty-seven?'

'Try seventy-seven.'

'No way!'

'Uh-huh.'

'You look twenty years younger! You must take good care of yourself.'

He held up the cigar then nodded at his Martini. 'These things take good care of me. Only kidding! Yep, I work out daily. Play tennis regularly, and I like to ski in winter.'

'I like to keep fit, too,' she said. 'I belong to a health club back home. And I ski whenever I can. Where do you like to go?'

'Mostly Aspen, Jackson Hole, Wyoming and Park City in Utah.'

'No kidding? Those are resorts I've always wanted to go to, particularly Aspen.' She opened her handbag and pulled out her cigarettes, took one out and held it up, mirroring him again.

'You know the place I'd really like to go is Courchevel in France!'

'It's the best skiing in the world,' she said.

'You know it, do you?'

'Really well.'

'So maybe I should take you there?'

'Tonight?'

He raised his eyebrows. 'If you want.' He looked at his watch. 'OK, so it's eight thirty. France is – if I'm working it out right – nine hours ahead of us, so five thirty in the morning. If I chartered a jet now we could be there in time for dinner tomorrow night.'

'There's just one problem,' she said.

'Which is?'

'There's no snow there right now. It's August!'

'Good point.'

'How about a nice dinner here instead?' she suggested.

'That would mean cancelling my dinner plans,' he said.

'Which were?'

'There was a famous gourmet in your country, back in the 1950s, way before you were born, a multi-millionaire Armenian called Nubar Gulbenkian. He once said, "The best number for dinner is two – myself and a good waiter."'

'I'm not sure I would totally agree.' She gave him a mischievous look. 'So you were going to have dinner with yourself?'

'Yep.'

'I waited tables once,' she said. 'When I was a student.'

'You did?'

'Didn't last very long. I poured someone's very expensive wine into a water glass by mistake, and it still had water in it!'

He laughed. 'Hope they didn't take it from your wages.'

'Luckily not, but they fired me.' She smiled. 'So,' she asked. 'Your divorce – what happened?'

Walt Klein looked sheepish. 'Well, after my divorce I married my second wife, Karin, who was much younger than me. I thought we had a good relationship and that we'd be together forever. My kids and my five grandkids adored her. Then one day, I guess about two years back, she suddenly said to me, in a restaurant, "You make me feel old."' He shrugged. 'That was kind of it. She told me she wanted a divorce. I asked her if there was anyone else and she denied it.'

'And was there?'

'She was into art and had been bored for some while. I'd bought her an art gallery down in the West Village. I heard through a friend she was screwing a sculptor whose work she was exhibiting.'

'I'm sorry,' Jodie said.

'Shit happens.'

'It does.'

'So what's your story?'

'Do you want the trailer or the full three hours, with intermission?'

He laughed. 'Give me the trailer now – then the full three hours over dinner.'

'OK.' She gave him a wan smile. 'I was married to a wife beater.'

'That's terrible. Poor you.'

'It was, it's been a nightmare. A total nightmare. I'm not sure I could ever trust a man again.'

'You want to start from the beginning?'

Jodie nodded. 'Sure. If you don't mind listening?'

'I have all evening,' he said. 'Another drink?'

'Yes, thank you,' she said, seeing the way he was looking at her. Knowing she already had him in the palm of her hand.

She made an excuse that she had to visit the

Ladies. Locked in a cubicle there, she googled 'Walt Klein'.

He was a stockbroker, investment adviser and financier, with a Wall Street securities company, bearing his name, and an estimated eight billion dollars under management.

Smiling happily, she slipped her phone back into her handbag and went back out. Walt Klein would do very nicely.

Very nicely indeed.

CHAPTER 7

The past

Jodie Danforth had a ton of homework to do. But she wasn't able to concentrate. Instead she sat cross-legged on her bed, barefoot in jeans and a Blur T-shirt, holding her diary in her hand, sobbing, in her perfectly untidy bedroom upstairs in her parents' perfect house. It was a square, white-painted mock-Georgian villa, with green shutters, set in an immaculate garden, still bathed in late-evening May sunlight, in a tree-lined street of almost identical houses on the outskirts of Burgess Hill, a town a few miles to the north of Brighton.

Everything was always in its place. Her mother cleaned the house obsessively. Her father cleaned their cars obsessively, and proudly. Out at the front on the drive sat her father's immaculate new black Jaguar and her mother's Saab convertible. Perfect parents, with one perfect daughter – her elder sister, Cassie. And one big embarrassment. Their problem daughter. Herself.

Posters of Jodie's icons were on her bedroom

walls. Madonna; Nicole Kidman and Tom Cruise; Kylie Minogue; Take That; Blur and Oasis. All of them perfect, too. With perfect noses.

Unlike her own.

Through her tears, she wrote in her diary:

Everywhere I go people are pointing at me and laughing, because I'm so ugly. Telling me I'm a freak. My nose is ridiculous. I watched my reflection in the window of the bus taking me to school this morning. It's not a nose, it's a great big hooked beak. A snozzle. A snout. Some bitch left a picture of the aeroplane Concorde on my desk this morning, with a Post-it note attached, on which she had written that my nose was like the front of the plane. Hooked and dipped.

My eyes are too big, also. When I look in the mirror they are all swollen – and it's not just from crying. They're too big for my face. Fact. And my lips are too fat – like someone's punched me in the mouth and made them swell up. And my ears are too big. It's like someone put my face together using all the wrong parts. Like they took them from the wrong box.

And my breasts are ridiculous. I'm flat. I've got a chest like a boy's. Cassie's, of course, are perfectly formed.

Earlier in the day in the English class everyone had to stand up and read aloud to the class a Shakespeare sonnet they had chosen. Trudy Byrne read out one, staring pointedly at me all the time.

'My mistress' eyes are nothing like the sun;
Coral is far more red than her lips' red;
If snow be white, why then her breasts are dun;
If hairs be wires, black wires grow on her head.
I have seen roses damask'd, red and white,
But no such roses see I in her cheeks;
And in some perfumes is there more delight
Than in the breath that from my mistress reeks.'
And so on. So <u>bloody</u> on.

It's true. My hair is like a bunch of black wires. They sprout all over my head like pubes or a scouring pad. Why don't I have the same blonde straight hair that my bloody sister, Cassie, has?

I've just been dealt a really shitty hand.

Dad dotes on Cassie. She is always playing around and joking with him. But when he looks at me I can see the disappointment in his face. Like, I'm not really his daughter at all. Not the second daughter he always promised himself. Not much of a substitute for the son he was really hankering for. And if he couldn't have a son, at least he could have had a second stunner of a daughter.

Instead he got me.

Mum and Dad are arguing again downstairs. I can hear their voices above the sound of the television. Dad's angry because he's worried about losing his job. They're making a lot of redundancies in his company, although Mum assures him he's too important, they could never let him go. Sounds like he's been drinking again. That's not unusual. He gets drunk most nights. He's worried about money. About the mortgage payments on this house. The finance on the fancy cars. That at fifty he's over the hill and might never get another job.

Jodie heard a slam. The front door? Often when her parents argued her father went out and down to the pub. She listened for the sound of his car starting, but heard nothing. Maybe he was being sensible for once and walking.

She opened her bedroom door to listen, and could hear music coming from her sister's room. She could talk to her mother. She wanted right now to curl up on the sofa in her mother's arms and maybe watch some television with her. Her mother was the only person who ever told her she was beautiful. Even though Jodie knew that was a lie. The television was on, loudly. An American couple shouting at each other.

She made her way downstairs, then stopped shortly before the bottom as she heard another slam. Her father coming back in?

'That bloody cat!' he shouted. 'Why can't it shit in its own garden?' He looked up at Jodie coming down the stairs as if it was her fault.

She stared back at him as he stormed into the living room.

Her mother said something Jodie could not hear above the din of the television. It sounded like she was trying to pacify him.

'How great is that? All I've got in the world is a neighbour's sodding cat that uses our garden as a toilet, a wife who drives me to drink and one daughter who's a total nightmare!'

The television was suddenly muted and she could hear both their voices clearly.

'You've got to realize she's going through a difficult time of life,' her mother said. 'Mid-teens is hard for girls.'

'Bollocks – Cassie was never like this.'

'Ssshhh! Keep your voice down! You dote on Cassie because she's pretty. Jodie can't help her looks. She'll blossom in a couple of years.'

'It's not just her looks, it's her attitude – she's a miserable little cow.'

'Maybe she'd be less miserable if you tried a little harder with her.'

'I have tried. If I give her a hug she shrinks away like some slippery reptile. Which she *is*.'

'Alastair! That's no way to speak about your daughter.'

'If she is my daughter.'

'What's that supposed to mean?'

'She doesn't look like you, and she sure as hell doesn't look like me. So who were you shagging to get pregnant with her? Someone from a travelling circus freak show?'

Jodie heard a thud, like a slap, followed by a howl of pain from her father.

'You bitch!' he shouted.

'Don't ever speak about our daughter like that. Do you hear me?'

'She's a freak and you know it. Hit me again and I'll tear your bloody head off.'

'Take it back or I will hit you again, you bastard. Jesus, what did I ever see in you to marry you?'

'She's an embarrassment. She's fat, she's ugly and she's got an ugly mind. If she was something I'd bought in Poundland I'd take her back and demand a replacement. Too bad we can't.'

'Alastair, I'm warning you. She's already got a complex, poor kid, always living in her sister's shadow – and whose fault is that? Yes, we both know she's got unfortunate looks. Give it a couple of years, I really do think she'll blossom,' she snapped.

'See that, out of the window?' my father said.

'See what?'

'That pig out there – flying across the horizon. That pig's prettier than our daughter.'

CHAPTER 8

Tuesday 17 February

The little squirrel monkey, astride the slender branch of a tree, stared at them through the window of the enclosure at Drusillas zoo. Its coat was a patchwork of grey, ginger and white, and it had sad, inquisitive eyes. Suddenly it began gnawing a chunk of carrot it was holding in its front paws.

Noah, who had been staring back at it, wide-eyed, as if unsure what to make of the creature, suddenly giggled.

It was a fine day, unseasonably warm. 'Like the monkey, do you?' Roy Grace said to his son, who was cradled in front of his chest in a baby sling. 'Want monkeys on your wallpaper – or a monkey mobile?'

Noah beamed and dribbled. Then as the monkey continued eating, he chuckled, dribbling some more.

God, it was the most beautiful thing, to hear his son laughing, Grace thought, wiping Noah's chin with a tissue. Then, peering down, he made monkey faces and noises at his son.

Noah giggled again.

Roy Grace grinned and put his arm round Cleo, who leaned in to him. He was taking a precious day off work to be with his loved ones, and wished he did this more often. He was able to, he knew; he had so many days of accrued leave owing to him. Yet he couldn't help feeling a slight cloud of guilt, having already had all of January off. He remembered a quote from somewhere: 'What man on his deathbed ever said, "Gosh, I wish I had spent more time in the office."'

Yes, it was true, but at the same time, much as he was loving being with Cleo and his son, his thoughts kept returning to work. He was lucky, he knew. He had the best wife in the world, and the best son, who had brought him a change of perspective and priorities. And on good days, the best job in the world. After years of darkness, in the shadow of his long-missing first wife Sandy, life was really great again. He was happy. Happier than he had ever known.

And that worried him. Could any human sustain being this happy?

There was so much darkness in the world. The ever-present threat of terrorism. The scrotes out there intent on committing harm. He just wanted these two people he loved so much to be safe forever.

His phone rang.

As he answered it he saw Cleo's knowing but understanding expression.

'Roy Grace,' he said.

He heard the French accent of the Interpol officer Bernard Viguet.

The body of the prostitute who had been missing for several days had been found in a ditch on the outskirts of Lyon. Further, the Hertz rental car that she had been seen entering had been found and forensically searched. Crisp's DNA had been present in it.

A sharp-eyed Lyon customs officer had detained a man boarding an international flight at Lyon Airport, from the description Sussex Police had circulated, with his left arm in plaster from an apparent skiing accident. A DNA swab taken from him confirmed him as Dr Edward Crisp.

Suggesting Cleo take Noah on to see the fruit bats, he phoned DS Potting and updated him. 'Norman, I'm going to be sending you to Lyon with Glenn. The French police will need an intelligence package on Crisp. Can you liaise with the team so I can send it to them?'

'Right away, chief. Good news!'

Next he phoned Glenn Branson.

'Gourmet capital of France, Lyon,' Branson said, sounding hopeful. 'Happy to go down there and liaise with the French police.'

'You want to go to Lyon, be my guest. I was there once with Sandy and I ate the most disgusting thing I've ever put in my mouth.'

'Yeah?'

'Andouillette. The local sausage. It's basically a

pig's colon stuffed with bits of its intestine. It smells like bad breath.'

'Yeccchhhh!'

'A lot of French people love it,' Grace went on. 'It's an acquired taste. I'll insist you try one.'

'You're a closet sadist, aren't you?'

'Nope, I just believe in the maxim, *I look and I see, I listen and I hear, I do and I understand.*'

'What's to understand about eating a pig's colon?'

'All part of your education. And the *entente cordiale*. Never diss other people's cultures. I think a trip to France to liaise with the French police and see Crisp would be good. And you might enjoy the break, you've not really given yourself any time out since Ari died.'

Glenn Branson's estranged wife, Ari, had died after an allergic reaction to the anaesthetic in surgery, following a bicycle accident. Subsequently the detective inspector had begun dating a bright young reporter on the local paper, the *Argus*, and was now going to marry her. Glenn had given him the news while Roy had been in hospital. At first he'd been cautious for his mate, marrying a news-paper reporter, but he liked her, and having seen the chemistry between them he felt they seemed right together.

'Yeah, right.'

'I'm serious.'

'And come home to Siobhan with that on my breath?'

'So you've gone off Lyon now, have you?' Grace chided.

'No, I'll go.'

'We'll apply for an extradition order, but almost certainly they're going to want to keep him in France at least until that trial is over. And there'll be a ton of bureaucracy to work through for the extradition procedure. There are various protocols involved with a European Arrest Warrant. First we need to get the Crown Prosecution Service to agree that he will face charges, prior to starting the whole process. He'll have to appear in front of a French magistrate before being released to the British police. The National Extradition Unit will be responsible for bringing him back to the UK, but the French police want you to travel to Lyon to share the intelligence we have on Crisp. They've informed me there's been a development in Crisp's involvement. I've got a pile of paperwork that's arrived from France, in French, which we'll need to get translated, so we'll need to find out who the preferred external translation company is.'

'That's good,' Glenn Branson said.

'Why's that?'

'It'll give me time to go to a chemist and buy some breath freshener – for the sausage thing.'

'Yeah, from past experience dealing with French police bureaucracy, you'll have plenty of time.'

CHAPTER 9

Wednesday 18 February

Jodie sat, tearfully, in the huge, old-fashioned office of Paul Muscutt, the senior partner of the Manhattan law firm of Muscutt, Williams and Wooding, and executor of the estate of the late Walter Irwin Klein. Twenty-seven storeys above Fifth Avenue, and with a glorious view through the window to her left directly down onto St Patrick's Cathedral, she was trying to mask her excitement. Warm sunshine streamed in. Jet lag was helping to take the edge off her skiing tan, making her look something of the pale, grieving widow she was trying to be.

Holding her lace-edged handkerchief, she sipped her strong coffee.

Muscutt, who had momentarily been called out of his office, strode back in through the door and headed towards her. In his forties, conservatively dressed, with neat brown hair, he had a no-nonsense businesslike air.

He shook her hand firmly. 'My deepest sympathy, Mrs Bentley.'

'Thank you,' she said, sounding as if she was stifling a sob.

'I'm afraid the media are really going for the suicide angle,' he said, slipping down into the black leather chair behind his uncluttered desk.

'Suicide? What do you mean?'

'It's only a theory, of course, from the French police in the Alps, but with all the financial trouble poor Walt had gotten himself into, it would fit.'

'I've read a bit on the internet, after the barrage of press at the airport when I arrived here, and caught some of the news stories, but I was hoping you'd tell me more – is any of it true?'

The lawyer frowned. 'Walt never told you? He didn't level with you?'

'Told me? No?'

'About his finances?'

'No, we never talked about money.' It was true, they didn't. 'Are you saying the French police think he might have committed suicide?'

'It's a possibility. Walt was in true Walter Mitty land, he believed right up until – I guess about a week before his death, when we last spoke – that somehow everything was going to come good for him. Maybe in that week he realized there was no way out. Walt was an experienced skier. He was following you in a white-out – why would he suddenly go off in a completely different direction?'

Suicide.

Her heart was pounding at the thought. So they

58

suspected maybe it wasn't an accident after all, but *suicide*!

For an instant she thought that would be great. But then, reflecting, it began to worry her.

Suicide? Trouble with finances? Shit, how is this going to affect things?

Muscutt peered for a moment at a stack of documents in front of him, which were held together by a single length of green tape, then looked back at her. 'Anyhow, Mrs Bentley,' he said in his strong, confident voice, 'I guess we might never know what was going on in Walt's mind.'

'He loved me – we adored each other. I can't believe he never talked to me about this. I mean – he told me he'd changed his will to include me. What do you mean, exactly, *financial troubles*?'

'You didn't find him looking a little worried just recently? A bit distracted?'

She shrugged. 'Not really, no – he was pretty much like he always was.'

'OK, well, I'm sure you are anxious to know the – ah – situation regarding the provisions for you in your late fiancé's will?'

She shrugged, trying to look nonchalant and not show her excitement. Her past husband had been a disappointment, leaving her far less than she had anticipated. Enough to buy her the Roedean house and to keep her comfortable, but nowhere near enough to pay for her dreams. But this time, she had been confident, she had struck gold. Just how many millions was she about to inherit from

Walt? Riches beyond her wildest dreams. Maybe it ran into billions!

'No, not at all,' she said, acting her heart out. 'I just loved Walt so much. I can't believe he's gone – we had such a short time together. Anything he might have left me is meaningless. I just want him back.'

'Is that so?' He gave her a dubious look.

She nodded, bleakly.

'I thought it would be better to see you alone, rather than have Walt's whole family present at this time.'

'I appreciate that,' she replied.

'I have to tell you that I don't have good news for you.'

She stiffened. Muscutt's whole demeanour seemed to have changed. It felt as if the sky had clouded over. She gave him a wide-eyed look.

'Walt's wealth came from a group of funds he ran – he had several billion under his management. But during recent months he was under investigation by the US Securities and Exchange Commission. Would you know what a so-called Ponzi scheme is?'

She frowned. 'I've heard of the expression.'

'Remember a shyster called Bernie Madoff? He's currently in a Federal Correctional Institution after defrauding investors in one of the biggest financial scams of recent years. Basically he used funds from new investors to give high returns, way above market rates, to earlier investors – and siphoned off a percentage for himself. I'm afraid it looks like that's what Walt was doing, too. All his bank accounts have been frozen and all his assets are being seized. If he was still alive, he could have been looking at a jail sentence equally as long as Madoff's, if not longer.' The sympathy seemed to have gone from the lawyer's voice and demeanour. 'And I guess the other problem will be to get any payout from his life policies – most companies don't pay out on suicide.'

She stared at the man, and could swear he was struggling to conceal a smirk.

'What are you actually saying?' she asked.

'What I'm saying is that it doesn't look like you will inherit one cent, Mrs Bentley. But that's not the worst of it. As his fiancée, you may well be investigated yourself as a possible accomplice. I imagine the police will be wanting to talk to you.'

'What?' She felt limp, as if all the energy had been sucked out of her. 'Accomplice? I knew nothing at all about his affairs.'

'But you enjoyed a nice lifestyle in your short time with him, right? Living high on the hog.'

'He never said a word to me about his business. I just assumed he was the successful businessman he seemed to be.'

'I have to remind you that all his credit cards have been stopped. I'm aware you used your own to pay for Walt's funeral expenses, including the casket, and for the flights back – but I'm afraid you are likely to be out of pocket – there is no way of reimbursing you.'

'God, that's why his credit cards were declined! What a fool – I thought – you know – he was just over his limit or something. This can't be true!'

He pushed a bundle of documents towards her. 'Have a look through these. They are all Grand Jury indictments against your late fiancé.'

She reached forward and ran her eyes over several pages without absorbing anything. It was all written in legal terminology she did not understand. A wintry chill rippled through her. At the same time, she felt anger rising. 'This is just bullshit!'

'I wish it was, Mrs Bentley, believe me. Walt has been one of this firm's biggest clients. He owes us many thousands of dollars – that we're unlikely to see now.'

'What a bastard,' she said. 'What a fucking bastard! He conned me! How many months have I—?' She fell silent for a moment.

'*Wasted?* Is that the word you are looking for?'

'He conned me!'

'Good to see you showing your true colours, finally, Mrs Bentley.'

'Just what the hell's that supposed to mean?'

'Oh, I think you know, Mrs Bentley. I think you know exactly what I mean.' He peered, hard and unsmiling, at her.

'I don't like your tone,' she said. 'I don't like what you are insinuating.'

He looked at his large, ornate watch. An Audemars Piguet, she could see. She knew all the top watch brands and their values – and this one was over $50,000. Then he stood up. 'I would be very happy to continue our discussion, but up until now my time has been on the late Mr Klein's account. I will require payment from you, in advance, for any further time you require from me.'

She also stood up, and scooped the Chanel handbag that Walt had bought her off the table beside her. 'I don't think there is anything more to discuss,' she said, tears of shock, anger and huge disappointment in her eyes.

As she reached Muscutt's office door, the lawyer said, 'See you at the funeral.'

'I don't think so.'

He smiled, remaining behind his desk. 'I didn't think so either. Nor did any of his family. Oh, and if there's anything you need when you're back in the UK, we do have a London office.'

She slammed the door behind her.

CHAPTER 10

Wednesday 18 February

Back in her suite in the Four Seasons, Jodie kicked off her shoes and sat down on a sofa, thinking hard. Weighing up the pros and cons of staying in the city for Walt's funeral.

Her room phone rang. It seemed like it hadn't stopped since she'd arrived in New York.

She answered it, hesitantly. 'Hello?'

'This is the front desk, Mrs Bentley. I have a Dave Silverson who'd like to speak to you.'

'Dave Silverson? I don't know anyone of that name.'

'From the *New York Post*.'

Her brain raced for a second. 'Er – no thanks. Thank you.'

She hung up.

The phone rang again almost immediately. It was a different voice this time. 'Mrs Bentley, I have a Jan Pink from the *National Enquirer*. Can I put her through?'

Shit. 'No,' Jodie said, emphatically. 'I did ask before, I want privacy, OK? No calls.'

Then her phone rang again. She let it ring on. Six rings then it fell silent and the red message alert began flashing. A few seconds later, it rang again. She sat on the bed, thinking. Someone had told the press where she was. Walt's snotty children? That arrogant lawyer?

She let it ring on until it stopped.

Should she go to the funeral?

She would only be attending for appearances' sake. And did they matter at the funeral of a man already totally discredited? There would be major press and media coverage, for sure, which she could do without. There was also the risk of her being arrested because of her association with Walt. The more distance she put between herself and New York, and the quicker she did it, the better, she decided.

Starting by getting out of this suite.

There was a hotel she'd stayed in a couple of years back, overlooking Central Park. She called them and to her relief they had availability. She checked out, and took the hotel's limousine the few blocks to the Park Royale West Hotel.

Twenty minutes later, checked in under a carefully created alias she used on occasion, Judith Forshaw, and giving her address as Western Road in Brighton, she was comfortably installed in a suite on the forty-second floor. She phoned down to the concierge for the number of British Airways, and booked herself on the day flight to Heathrow, leaving Kennedy Airport at 8 a.m. the next morning. She also booked a limousine for 5 a.m. to take her to the airport.

Then she went to the minibar, removed the half-bottle of champagne that was in there, opened it, poured some into a glass and, ignoring the no-smoking warnings, lit a cigarette with hands still shaking with rage at smug Muscutt. At that bastard Walt Klein.

At the world.

She shot a glance up at the smoke detector on the ceiling, knowing from experience that the smoke from a single cigarette was not usually enough to set the alarm off, then she downed the contents of the glass in one gulp, refilled it, and went over to the window. She stood beside the tripod-mounted telescope that was part of the décor and, using another glass as an ashtray, stared down at the people, the size of ants, strolling, jogging, cycling or walking their dogs in the late-afternoon sunshine in Central Park.

Right now she felt no sunshine in her heart.

Months wasted.

As the effects of the champagne began to kick in, she gradually began to cheer up a little. 'Never look back, girl. Only forward!' she said aloud, drained the second glass, then emptied the remainder of the bottle into it and drained that, too. She flushed the cigarette butt down the toilet and rinsed out the glass, then sat on the edge of the bed. Walt Klein was history. She was now totally focusing on her next target, Rowley Carmichael.

She liked the name Carmichael a lot. She could already visualize her signature. *Jodie Carmichael*. Much classier than Jodie *Klein* would have looked.

And she liked everything else about Rowley Carmichael a lot, too. Most of all his listing, at equal number 225, on the most recent *Sunday Times* Rich List.

She took an apple from the bowl of fruit on the table, cut it in half with the knife provided, and bit into it, hungrily. Then, chewing, she opened the lid of her laptop, and smiled as she saw that another email from Rowley had come in.

Several months ago she had spotted his online advertisement:

Mature widower. Seeks companion with love of fine art, opera, theatre, fine dining, wine, travel, adventure for companionship – and maybe more . . .

Even though she had been engaged to Walt Klein, Jodie had responded using her maiden name. She was registered, under different names, with several online dating agencies for wealthy singles. She had, electronically, kissed a lot of proverbial frogs. But it was that one on *Rich and Single* that had caught her attention, a couple of months back. She liked the 'and maybe more . . .' To her trained eye, it had a subtext of a certain element of desperation.

Desperation was good.

She'd read it through a couple of times more,

then pinged a carefully constructed email back, accompanied by a demure photograph, taken after she'd skilfully applied make-up, attached to the profile she had just created for herself:

Beautiful, raven-haired widow of a certain age seeks mature male with cultured tastes in arts, food and travel for friendship and perhaps a future.

Rowley Carmichael had replied less than an hour later.

Since then, in preparation for Walt's eventual demise, she had secretly and very carefully been reeling Rowley Carmichael in. Now he was ready. And she was free! She never kept all her eggs in the same basket; although Walt appeared vastly wealthy she'd always had a plan B, and that was to get rid of him as quickly as possible and move on.

She yawned. It was just after 4 p.m. and it would soon be growing dark outside. She was increasingly feeling the effects of jet lag – and the champagne. At the same time she didn't want to waste an evening in New York – you never knew what might happen. Maybe she'd meet someone for a one-night stand. Right now, she didn't much care who, so long as he was good-looking and not a slobbering geriatric like Walt. This was a city of single bars famed for one-night stands. That's what she fancied right now. A one-night stand with a hunk, who would screw her brains out for a few hours. God, she'd not had decent sex for – a year. More than a year.

And the good news was that one of the city's hottest singles bars was right here, downstairs in this hotel.

She set her alarm for 6 p.m., lay back on the bed and crashed out.

CHAPTER 11

Wednesday 18 February

Shortly before 7 p.m., showered and wearing the most revealing outfit she had with her – a short black dress and black leather ankle boots – Jodie perched on a red chair at the long, darkly lit bar and ordered a Manhattan. She was slender and beautiful, with all the confidence to go with it. She had styled her dark hair in ringlets and was classily – if just a tiny bit too revealingly – dressed.

But her best asset of all had always been her eyes. They were wide, cobalt blue and crystal clear. You-can-trust-me eyes. Come-to-bed eyes.

Dangerous eyes.

She sipped her drink slowly, pacing herself. But sooner than she had anticipated, all that was left of it was the maraschino cherry at the bottom. Already she was feeling a warm glow from the alcohol. As she raised a hand to signal one of the bartenders, she became aware of a figure beside her, a man easing himself onto the next chair.

'Allow me to buy you another?' he asked in a

richly charming voice that was part American, part mittel-European and part very drunk.

She shot him a glance. He was in his late thirties or early forties, with Latino good looks beneath short, black tousled hair and beautiful, almost impossibly white teeth. He wore a black jacket over a white shirt, with a gold chain round his neck. And he looked wasted, either on drugs or booze.

'Sure,' she said, smiling back. 'A Manhattan, straight up, with two cherries.'

He ordered two, then turned back to her. 'My name's Romeo,' he said.

'Juliet!' she replied, thinking on her feet.

'You are kidding?'

'Nope!'

His eyes widened in a smile. Large, hazelnut irises. With very dilated pupils, she noticed. He was definitely off his face on something.

'*But soft! What light through yonder window breaks? It is the east, and Juliet is the sun. Arise, fair sun, and kill the envious moon!*' he said, theatrically.

'*Who is already sick and pale with grief!*' she replied.

'You know it?' he said with astonishment. 'You know Shakespeare?'

'Of course!'

'Well, I am impressed. Romeo meets Juliet in a bar! How often is that going to happen?'

'Meant to be!' she replied, locking eyes with his. 'So what's your full name?'

'Romeo Munteanu.'

Their drinks arrived and he raised his glass. '*That thou, her maid, art far more fair than she.*'

'*Be not her maid, since she is envious.*' Jodie tilted her head.

'Well,' he said. 'I think anyone would be envious of us at this moment. The two most beautiful people in all of New York seated in a bar together.'

'So you're a modest man, are you, Romeo?'

'Truth before modesty!' He clinked his glass against hers and they drank. 'So what brings you to this city?'

'Family business,' she said. 'You?'

'Business, too.'

'What business are you in?'

'Oh, you know, import–export. That kind of thing.'

She picked up on his evasive tone. 'Sounds interesting. Where are you from?'

'Romania – Bucharest. Have you been there?'

Locking eyes with his again she said, provocatively, 'Not yet.'

Their drinks slipped down easily and quickly and he ordered a second round.

'So do you work for a Romanian company?' she asked.

'International,' he said. 'International company. I travel constantly. I like to travel.'

'Me too.'

He lifted one cherry out of his glass by the stalk, held it up in the air and moved it towards her mouth with a quizzical look.

She closed her lips around it, pulled it clear of the stalk and chewed it, tasting the sweetness of the marinated fruit and the tang of the bourbon and Martini Rosso.

Twenty minutes later, as he drained his third Manhattan – and Jodie hers, too – he said, suddenly, 'Do you do coke?'

She nodded, feeling reckless from the drink now. 'Uh-huh.'

'I've got the best stuff ever – like – I mean – the *best*, you know? Up in my room.' He nodded at the ceiling. 'That is – if you're brave enough to come to a stranger's room?'

'Fortune favours the brave, right?'

'Does that come from Shakespeare, too?'

She smiled. '*Fortune and men's eyes.*'

'Uh?'

'Sonnet Twenty-Nine. *When, in disgrace with fortune and men's eyes, I all alone beweep my outcast state.*'

He looked at her, bemused, for some moments. 'Not only are you very beautiful, you are a font of knowledge. What else do you know?'

She stared back into his eyes. 'I know how to drive a man I fancy wild in bed.'

'Indeed? And I believe I know how to satisfy a woman.'

'Is that so?'

'Yes, it is so.'

'So show me!'

CHAPTER 12

Wednesday 18 February

Ten minutes later, entwined in each other, Romeo and Juliet kissed passionately throughout the entire short journey of the elevator up to the fifty-second floor. Still partially entwined, they stumbled along the corridor to the door of his suite.

Inside, he led her to a sofa, then picked up the phone and ordered a bottle of vintage champagne from room service to be sent up urgently. He hung up and disappeared for several minutes through double doors into another room, then returned with a plastic bag full of white powder, a drinking straw and a knife.

He made several lines of cocaine on the glass surface of the coffee table, lifted the straw to his nose, ducked his head down and sniffed up one entire line. 'Whoohaaaaa!' he whooped. 'Whooohaaaaa! I tell you, this is the best! The best in this whole city!' He handed her the straw.

Just as she took a tentative sniff, the doorbell pinged.

'Don't worry, I won't let anyone in!'

As Romeo went to get the door, she heard the rustle of paper, then a voice saying, 'Thank you, sir, have a great evening!' Moments later Romeo reappeared holding a silver tray with the bottle of champagne in an ice bucket, two flutes, a bowl of nuts and another of olives. He set them down on the table, next to the cocaine, kissed the back of her neck and sat down beside her.

Then, without warning, he grabbed the straw from her and sucked up another line, followed by another. Shouting out 'Whooohaaaaa!' he hauled her to her feet and began kissing her wildly. So wildly it alarmed her.

She tried to back off. 'Hey!' she said. 'Hey! Gentle, OK?'

'Don't *gentle* me. I know what bitches like you want!' His voice was slurred. 'You like it rough, yes?'

'No.'

He pushed up her skirt and fumbled for her underwear.

'Hey!'

He shoved her back, violently. She stumbled and crashed into the wall. He was pressing himself against her, pulling her knickers down.

'Stop!' she said, increasingly frightened by his sudden mood switch.

He was grinning demonically now, his eyes glazed with alcohol and the drug. 'You want it, bitch. You want me to fuck you hard, don't you? You like it rough.'

75

With one hand he held her against the wall. With the other, he was unbuckling his belt. His eyes were crazed, he was scaring her.

She headbutted him, on the bridge of his nose. He staggered backwards and sank down onto his knees, blood spurting from his nostrils, his face a mask of confusion. Instantly, she lashed out as hard as she could with her right foot, the pointed toe of her Louboutin catching him beneath his chin, snapping his head sharply up and shooting a loud grunt from deep inside his throat.

His eyes stared, unfocused for an instant, then closed. He fell backwards and lay still.

Shaking, aware she had drunk far too much, she staggered forward and looked down at him. He was out of it, but still breathing. Blood streamed down his cheeks from his busted nose and onto the carpet. She grabbed her clutch bag from the sofa, rubbed her head which hurt and, glancing at him again, walked quickly over to the door.

Then she stopped, realizing the opportunity she now had. She turned and went through the double doors he had gone through some minutes earlier, into a large bedroom with a walk-in closet leading off it. She peered around in search of his wallet. There was an open, partially unpacked suitcase on a metal and leather stand close to the bed. She rummaged through it and at the bottom found another plastic bag full of white powder. It was sealed shut.

Her nerves jangling, she looked over her shoulder.

Might as well take it, she decided, and put it into her clutch bag. Then – and she had no idea what made her do it – she dropped to her knees, lifted the vallance of the bed and peered under it.

And saw a large Louis Vuitton suitcase.

She ran back to the doorway. Romeo was still totally out of it. She returned to the bed, pulled out the case, popped the two catches and lifted the lid.

Despite her drunken state, she began to shake with excitement.

It was packed with bundles of new $100 bills wrapped with paper bands.

Shit!

She looked over her shoulder again, closed the lid, snapped the catches shut, then picked up the case and went back cautiously to the doorway.

The Romanian hadn't moved.

She glanced at the opened bag of cocaine on the table, tempted to take that too. But he had slit it open messily and some of the powder had spilled onto the table and floor. She let herself out of the door as silently as possible and closed it behind her, then gripping the case tightly, sprinted along the deserted corridor towards the fire exit sign. She hurried, stumbling, down the bare concrete steps for ten floors until she saw the number on the door of her own floor.

42.

She pushed the fire door open. The corridor was empty. Stepping out, she strode along it as nonchalantly as she could.

Moments later, safely back in her suite, she switched on the lights, closed the door and slipped on the safety chain.

Her heart was hammering, her brain racing.

Music was playing on the television and the curtains were drawn. She looked around warily, her nerves all over the place. The turn-down service had been, she realized.

Hurriedly, she put the suitcase on the bed, then began to check the money. It was in bundles, each wrapped with a paper band marked $10,000. She counted twenty. Jesus! $200,000. A very nice surprise and sweet compensation after the shit she had been through in Muscutt's office today.

She removed the bundles of bills and stashed them, spreading them between her own three large suit-cases, interweaving them with her clothes, as well as putting some in her hand luggage. She was wondering whether to take his case with her, to avoid it being found here, then stopped and decided to check it for any tracking device that might be in it.

She unzipped the side pocket, but it was empty. Then she ran her hands round the interior lining. And felt a small lump.

She went over to the fruit bowl, which had already been replenished, the knife replaced with a clean one by the turn-down service; picking up the knife, she cut open the suitcase's lining, shooting a nervous glance towards the door every few moments. How long before Romeo woke up – and found out what was missing?

She slipped her hand inside the lining and pulled out a plain white envelope with a small object inside it. She slit it open and saw, inside, a shiny black USB memory stick.

Why was this hidden in the lining?

She looked at her watch. 9.40 p.m. Was it too late to get a night flight out of here?

She put the memory stick back in the envelope and zipped it securely in a pocket inside her handbag. She had a feeling that to have been so carefully hidden, it must have a value. She would call Romeo Munteanu when she got back to England, she decided, in her addled mind, and find out how much he would be willing to offer for the return of the memory stick.

Or maybe not.

After all, two hundred thousand greenbacks, at today's exchange rate, wasn't a bad return for one evening's work.

Hardly the millions she had been expecting from Walt Klein. But not to be sneered at.

She hastily finished packing her bags, transferred the packet of white powder from her clutch to her handbag, then looked at the suitcase, debating what to do with it. She stepped out, looking around cautiously, went a short distance down the corridor and put it in the laundry room, then hurried back and phoned down for a porter.

For the next few minutes she paced around, nervously waiting. When the doorbell pinged a few minutes later, she checked the spyhole before opening the door. She asked the porter to get her a taxi to Newark Airport, gave him a twenty-dollar bill and said she would see him outside.

Again, warily, she went out into the corridor and took the elevator down. She scanned the almost deserted lobby before she stepped out, feeling relieved it wasn't under siege from the paparazzi. She cancelled the limousine she had booked for the morning, checked out, fearful that Romeo Munteanu would appear at any moment, and hurried out through the revolving door into the bitterly cold Manhattan night.

The porter showed her the suitcases, safely stowed in the trunk of the yellow cab, before slamming the lid.

Moments later she sat back in the cramped rear, as the elderly, turbaned driver headed out across Columbus Circle.

'Newark?' he said. 'Which airline?'

'Change of plan, I'll tell you in a minute,' she said, tapping the Google app on her iPhone, searching for any flights out of here, on any airline, to the UK tonight. Or, alternatively, any flight out of here tonight to anywhere.

CHAPTER 13

Wednesday 18 February

Three minutes later, Jodie said to the cab driver, 'LaGuardia, please.'

A siren wailed.

Shit. Her nerves were jangling.

A police car screamed alongside them, Jodie held her breath. But it carried on past them down Central Park South and bullied its way through the stop lights at the junction with Fifth Avenue.

She pulled her laptop out of her handbag, opened it and inserted the memory stick she'd found in the suitcase. After some moments a new icon appeared on her desktop. She double-clicked to open it and, as she had suspected it might, a password request popped up.

She pulled the stick out and zipped it in an inside pocket in her bag. She knew someone in England who'd be able to discover its contents easily enough.

Then she looked at the bag of white powder. The high partition in front of her, with its television monitor showing the news, silently, and the

81

Perspex shield made it impossible for the driver to be able to see her. She looked around carefully to ensure there was no CCTV camera in the rear, then opened the seal, wetted her finger, dipped it in and put it in her mouth.

Cocaine.

Shame to waste it, she thought. Shame to chuck it, but she'd be mad to keep it. She balled her left hand and put a pinch of powder onto it, cursing as the cab braked sharply, nearly throwing the bag and the laptop out of her grasp. Then she sniffed hard, with each nostril in turn. And felt the instant rush.

It was good!

From past experience of buying cocaine she had some idea how much street value this bag contained. Thousands of pounds' worth.

Within moments of inhaling the drug, her nerves were steadying and she began to feel great. Really great! Oh yes! Result, lady!

She took another snort, and resealed the bag. She needed to get rid of it, she knew, but she was reluctant. This was good stuff. She was about to replace it in her handbag, to have a final hit at the airport and then bin it, when she had a sudden reality check. How long before Romeo Munteanu woke up? What would he do when he did and found the cash and his cocaine stash missing? It was pretty unlikely that anyone with that amount of cash in a suitcase hidden under a bed was likely to be engaged in something legal. Equally, in his drugged state, he might just be irrational enough to call the police and give them her description.

They had sniffer dogs at airports. Was it worth the risk for a final snort?

Of course, she could repack as soon as she got out of the taxi when they reached the airport, and put the drug at the bottom of her suitcase.

But should she?

She wasn't thinking straight, she knew.

She had still not decided when she saw, through her window, the first signpost for LaGuardia Airport flash past.

CHAPTER 14

Thursday 19 February

It was barbecue night at the Shark Bite Sports Bar. Which meant that in a while the regulars would be drunk and stuffing their faces with charred chicken, cremated steaks and disintegrating fish and crustaceans.

Tooth, a short, wiry man with a shaven head and an angry face, sat out on the deck area overlooking the creek at the south end of Turtle Cove Marina, accompanied by his associate, Yossarian. He was constantly slapping his exposed legs and arms, which were under assault from mosquitoes. Smoke from the barbecue was getting in his eyes and really pissing him off.

The Caribbean evening air was 36 degrees and the humidity was high. Dressed in khaki shorts, a singlet printed with a picture of Jim Morrison, and flip-flops, he was perspiring. He was smoking a Lucky Strike cigarette and drinking a Maker's Mark bourbon on the rocks. Yossarian sat beside him, twitching his nostrils at the smell of the meat, and occasionally lapping water from a bowl on the wooden decking.

The dog was an ugly mutt. It had different-coloured eyes, one bright red, the other grey, and looked like the progeny of a Dalmatian that had been shagged by a pug. It had started following Tooth along a street in Beverly Hills a few years back, when he was casing a house for a hit, and had ignored all his attempts to shoo it away. So he had ended up bringing it back to this island with him. He wasn't sure who had adopted who. And he didn't care.

It was getting to the end of Happy Hour right now, and the air-conditioned interior of the bar was full of ex-pat Brits, Americans and Canadians who mostly knew each other, and got drunk together in here every Thursday night – and most other nights, too. Tooth never talked to any of them. He didn't like drunks. He was content to be with his loyal, sober associate.

There was a roar of laughter from inside the bar. It was wild some nights. A few years ago two Haitians who had tried to rob the bar had been shot dead by a customer. It was that kind of a place.

This island that he had called home for the past decade was a paradise for tourists, and one of the assholes of the Caribbean to the US border authorities. Around seventeen miles long and five wide, Providenciales – or Provo, as it was known to the locals – sat midway between Haiti, Jamaica and the southern tip of the Florida Keys.

The British made a pretence of policing it, and had put in a puppet governor, but mostly they left it to the US Coastguard, who had a base there, to deal with – or ride roughshod over – the corrupt and inept local police.

It was why Tooth chose to live here. No one asked questions and no one gave a damn. They left Tooth and his associate alone and he left them alone. He lived in a ground-floor apartment in a complex on the far side of the creek, and his cleaning lady, Mama Missick, looked after the dog when he was away on business.

The mosquitoes were particularly bad tonight. He didn't do mosquitoes. Hated the critters. He'd long ago decided that if he ever met God – unlikely, as he didn't believe in Him – the first question he would ask was why He had created mosquitoes.

To piss everyone off?

He was pissed off right now. His right ankle, where he had been bitten a short while ago, was itching like hell. Given the chance, he would nuke every mosquito on the planet. But right now he had another more important issue. Business. Or rather the lack of it.

Tooth had left school early and eventually ended up in the army, where he had served two tours in Iraq. It had changed his life forever, because it was there he discovered his real expertise as a killer – and in particular as a sniper. It had served him well.

He drank two more bourbons and smoked four more cigarettes, then headed home along the dark, deserted road with Yossarian, to grill some bonefish he had caught earlier on his boat, *Long Shot*.

He could do with another good contract. Two of his primary sources, both American, had gone – one doing life without parole, the other shot dead – he had executed the man himself. Now he had two new sources of business, but he hadn't heard from either in several months. His stash, in his Swiss bank account, was running low. Fuelling his thirty-five-foot launch, with its thirsty twin Mercedes engines, which took him out hunting for his food most days, was expensive.

And one day he might need the boat to make a fast exit from this place. With a top speed of fifty-four knots, not much at sea could catch it. Besides, his days out on *Long Shot* were his life.

And he never knew how they were numbered. He just lived each year to see if he would get past his next birthday, which was not for several weeks. He had developed a kind of ritual on each birthday. He would leave the Shark Bite and drive to Kew Town, to visit his regular hooker. There were no drink-driving laws on the island. Afterwards he would drive home and play Russian Roulette.

The same .38 bullet had been in the chamber for the past ten years. He had dum-dummed it himself. Two deep cuts in the nose. These would cause the bullet to rip open on impact, punching a hole the size of a tennis ball in whatever it hit. He would have no possible chance of survival.

Tooth inserted the bullet back into the barrel, and spun the chamber. The gamble was where the bullet ended up. Would it be an empty chamber behind the firing pin or the loaded one?

Physics worked for plays of this game. The bullet weighed the chamber down. So it wasn't a six-to-one chance. Most likely the bullet would end up at the bottom of the chamber. But one day, and that could be today, it would be different.

Bang.

Oblivion.

Although it wasn't his birthday, he decided what the hell. Birthdays were just numbers. He pressed the barrel of the revolver to the side of his head. To the exact part of his temple he knew would have maximum destructive effect.

Then his phone rang.

He hesitated. Answer or ignore it? Could be business. And he couldn't pull the trigger with his fucking phone ringing. He answered it.

And heard the harsh accent.

In recent years his paymasters had changed from American mobsters, who all sounded like they had chewing gum jammed up their nostrils, to these Eastern Europeans who were humourless but precise.

'Call you back,' he said, and instantly hung up.

He went over to a locked closet, selected a

fresh pay-as-you-go phone from the ten that he had bought on his last trip to mainland USA, and returned the call to his contact. He listened to the instructions carefully, committing them to memory, reminded his client of his terms – one hundred per cent of the cash now to his Swiss bank account – then hung up. He didn't do negotiation.

Then he picked up his gun again and pressed it to his temple.

Yossarian looked at his master and barked, balefully.

'You want the bullet?' Tooth asked. 'That what you're telling me? You don't need to worry about me dying, you'll be all right when I've gone. Got you taken care of. Mama Missick likes you. Dunno why, but she said she'd take care of you if anything happened to me. My lawyers have my will. I've left everything to you. You'll be taken care of.'

Yossarian looked at him with his one grey and one red eye, staring him out.

'Playing mind games with me?'

He put the gun back to his temple and, still staring at the dog, pulled the trigger.

Click.

As he lowered the gun, he could swear the goddam creature was grinning at him.

'Think that's funny, do you?' He aimed the gun at the dog's head and tightened his grip on the trigger. The dog continued to grin.

Then he raised the gun in the air and pulled the trigger all the way back.

There was a loud bang. Plaster from the ceiling showered down on him. Yossarian continued grinning. Like his master, the dog didn't do fear.

CHAPTER 15

Thursday 19 February

Jodie had plenty of time to think on her journey back to England. She'd caught a late flight at LaGuardia to Washington and checked into an airport hotel before returning to the airport first thing and buying a ticket on another internal flight, to Atlanta, using another alias, Jemma Smith.

From there she bought a ticket on a Virgin flight to London. She figured people would be less likely to be looking out for her here in Atlanta, although due to the US immigration system, she would have to leave under the same name that she came in on, Jodie Bentley.

She had bought a thriller by a British writer called Simon Toyne, because she had liked the cover. It helped to distract her, but with all the thoughts going through her mind it was hard to concentrate for any length of time.

She had made use of her enforced stay in Washington, having her hair dyed blonde at a salon she found in the airport. And she bought some new clothes. Several times she'd thought about phoning Romeo Munteanu through the hotel, to see how much he'd pay to have the memory stick returned, but held back. She needed to know what was on it before making a move – if she made one at all.

One thing she knew for sure was that it had a value to someone, otherwise he would not have gone to such trouble to conceal it in his suitcase. And she knew for sure, too, he would be trying to track her down, although she was pretty certain, with what she had done, that she'd bought a time advantage.

On the plane to London whilst waiting for boarding to be completed, she flicked through the airline magazine. There was a travel article on Venezuela. It brought back a memory.

Emira.

Emira del Carmen Socorro! Her Venezuelan-born best friend at the posh school Jodie's parents had sent her to – but could barely afford – The Towers Convent. Unlike Jodie, Emira Socorro was genuinely posh. Like Cassie, she was beautiful. And like Cassie, boys flocked around Emira at parties, charmed by her exotic accent. Emira's parents had a huge Georgian country house, with both an indoor and outdoor swimming pool, a tennis court, a lake and a butler.

Emira had taken an instant shine to Jodie and they had become firm friends, smoking secretly together, getting drunk, occasionally taking drugs. It wasn't until some years later that Jodie realized quite why it was that Emira stuck to her so closely. It was because she was useful to her in many ways. Her plain looks made Emira shine. She lost count of the times that she played gooseberry to Emira's endless conquests with guys. And she learned, at the age of sixteen, that the one way she could keep up with Emira was to put herself out to guys.

She became a regular one-night-stand merchant. The easy shag for drunken guys at parties who'd failed to pull the girls they were actually after. Unceremonious humps behind sofas, on piles of coats in a spare room, in the back of their mummy or daddy's cars. And once in a potting shed that smelled of mushrooms.

She found she actually enjoyed her reputation as the local bike. She enjoyed it a lot more than the sex itself, which she didn't mind. She carried a stash of condoms in her handbag and used to delight in boasting of her own conquests to an often-astonished Emira.

When they were eighteen they lost almost all contact. Emira went off to finishing school in Austria. Jodie went to Southampton University to study Sociology – and to get away from her parents.

The last time she saw Emira was at her friend's twenty-first birthday party – a swanky affair at her parents' Sussex mansion, filled with beautiful people, and where the band The Manfreds had been hired to play. Hardly anyone she knew was there and Jodie wandered around getting increasingly pissed and aggressive. Eventually she'd found herself staggering up the driveway to her family home, sometime after dawn had begun to break, unsure whether she had just shagged the guy who'd given her a lift or not.

Two years later she'd opened a copy of *Hello!* and seen a six-page spread of Emira's society wedding to a young, gorgeous aristocratic rock promoter who owned a chunk of prime London real estate, a stately home in Scotland, a clifftop mansion in Barbados and a villa on Cap Ferrat.

'It's just so nice having a private jet. It means not having to share one's plane journey anywhere with a bunch of strangers,' Emira was quoted as saying. Then she was further quoted, making Jodie cringe: 'I'm really not a snob. I have friends from all walks of life. Those are the kinds of people I grew up with, you know. Just ordinary people.'

CHAPTER 16

Friday 20 February

Landing at Heathrow at 6.30 a.m. on Friday, Jodie had a slight hangover and was red-eyed from tiredness. She'd been too wired to sleep, so instead had watched a couple of movies, but had been unable to concentrate on them.

Now, after a shower and breakfast in the arrivals lounge, her top priority was to go home, get into her Mercedes and drive to the cattery at Coriecollies Kennels, near Lewes, to collect her beloved cat.

Her second was business.

Graham Parsons had been waiting for her at the rear of Marrocco's, on Hove seafront, seated beneath a huge painting, almost the width of the wall, of a happy-looking fat man tucking into a lobster.

The front part of the establishment was a colourful ice-cream parlour. The rear, smart and subdued, with comfortable seating and modern art on the walls, was a seafood restaurant. A bottle of champagne sat in an ice bucket, and he had a plate of oysters in front of him.

He was a solidly built, hard-looking man, just shy of his sixtieth birthday – so he had told her the first time they met, in the downstairs bar one Saturday night in Bohemia. It was one of the few cool places in Brighton for middle-aged singles, and he was drunk, having gone out after an argument with his wife. He had poured his life story out to her. A career villain, Parsons had spent the first half of his criminal life as a professional armed robber, for which he had clocked a total of eighteen years behind bars before 'seeing the light'.

Cybercrime.

For the past twenty years – both in prison and out – he'd been an internet criminal mastermind, running a ring that made millions out of mortgage frauds with non-existent properties, and further millions by cloning credit and debit card details from cashpoint machines.

But as with so many criminal masterminds, Proceeds of Crimes legislation had clawed back much of his gain. He was comfortably off but needed an income to maintain his lifestyle – which came in the form of a number of lucrative side-lines. One of these was creating identities to accompany the highly authentic passports he could provide – thanks to five years of sharing a cell with a master forger at the maximum security prison, Parkhurst, on the Isle of Wight. Jodie was a good customer.

Parsons was living testimony to the old saw that British prisons were Universities of Crime. He was smartly dressed as always – today in a pinstriped suit, shirt and tie, sporting a gold wedding band, a rhinestone ring on the opposite hand and a fancy watch. His hair was jet black – from a bottle, she deduced from the grey roots that were showing. Yet he wore a permanent slightly lost expression – as if freedom never really agreed with him and the only place he had been truly comfortable in his life was behind bars, running prison rackets.

'Jodie, doll! How are you?' He stood up, embraced her and gave her a smacker on both cheeks.

As she settled into the chair opposite him, he tugged the bottle out of the ice bucket, wiped the drips with the cloth and filled her glass. 'Have one!' He indicated the oysters.

She eyed them dubiously. 'Thanks, I'm good.'

He shook some Tabasco onto an oyster, squeezed some lemon, then spooned some vinaigrette on, lifted the shell and tipped the bivalve into his mouth. 'They're in season!'

She smiled. 'I'm told they make you randy.'

'Probably why they never served 'em in prison,' he said and grinned. 'So, you wanted to see me urgently?'

Even though she knew they were in a safe environment, Graham never chose the same place twice to meet, she looked around discreetly before slipping the envelope across the table to him. 'Yes.'

In an almost magician-like sleight of hand

movement, it disappeared into his inside pocket. 'So what can you tell me about it?'

'I was given it by a friend in the States. He thought I might find it interesting. But it's password protected.'

'Leave it with me, doll.' Then he shoved a menu at her. 'Great seafood here. I like this place. Been here before?'

'Bought an ice cream once, years ago.'

'Pistachio – I recommend the pistachio. So you found yourself *Mr Right* yet?'

She sipped the champagne. 'I thought I had. But it seems not.'

'Yeah? When all else fails, bell me, right?'

Jodie smiled. Then she raised her glass. 'I don't think your wife would be too impressed, would she?'

'Charlaine? You know what, doll – she'd get over it!'

CHAPTER 17

Saturday 21 February

It was 5 p.m. and growing dark. The yellow Nissan cab stopped to drop off a passenger outside Macy's department store in Herald Square, New York City, then switched on its *Off Duty* lights. But before it could move away, the rear door opened.

A short, shaven-headed man, carrying two Macy's bags, head bowed against the falling snow, gave a silent *job-done* acknowledgement to the exiting passenger, clambered into the warmth of the rear and pulled the door shut behind him. Shit, it was cold.

There were 13,471 medallions currently issued in New York, allowing the owners to run yellow cabs. Most cabs operated twenty-four-seven, two drivers each doing twelve-hour shifts. CCTV footage from a camera outside the Park Royale West Hotel had identified the cab that had picked up Judith Forshaw at 10.17 p.m., Wednesday 18 February. It took a private detective hired by Tooth's Russian paymaster less than two days to find it.

'Sorry, I'm off duty, sir,' the turbaned driver said, turning his head to see a wodge of ten-dollar bills being pushed through the small hole in the bullet-proof Perspex separating him from his passengers.

'Start driving.'

'I don't think you are understanding. I am off duty now, going home.'

'Drive!'

A car behind hooted, angrily.

'Please, I am going home—'

'Drive!'

There was another even longer blast of a horn behind them.

The cab lurched forward.

Tooth pressed his face up to the partition. 'You picked up a lady at Park Royale West on Wednesday night. Remember?'

'Wednesday?'

'You handed in a bag of cocaine later that night. You've already told the police everything you know, right?'

'I don't remember, sir.'

Another wodge of dollar bills – hundred-dollar bills this time – came through the hole. 'I'll give you enough cash you won't need to work for a week. She was my wife. I need to find her. Tell me something you didn't tell the police.'

As they pulled up at a stop light the driver said, 'I told them everything.'

Before he knew it, the front door opened and a moment later his passenger was sitting beside him, with a stiletto blade in his hand. Then the knife was digging into the base of his throat. 'No, you didn't tell them everything, did you?'

'Please, yes, yes, I did,' he said, terrified.

There was a bright Duane Reade sign visible through the window. Tooth clocked it out of the corner of his eye. 'What else did she say to you?'

'Nothing! She said nothing!'

'Can you feel how sharp this is?'

The driver gave a terrified nod.

Tooth pressed the blade in between the man's legs. 'You want me to cut your dick off?'

The driver shook his head. 'No, no, please.'

'What did you talk about? You and the bitch?'

'Nothing. Please, sir, nothing! I am swearing!'

'Want me to cut your testicles off and ram them down your throat? Or would you prefer a thousand-dollar tip?'

A van hooted loudly and swerved in front of them.

'Please, what do you want?'

'She gave you a big tip, yes? You told the police, when you handed in the cocaine, that she gave you a hundred-dollar tip. Right?'

'Yessir, yes, she did.'

'Where is that hundred-dollar bill now?'

'I – I—'

'Don't fuck with me. Where is it? This isn't your cab, right?'

'No, sir.'

'You're a journeyman. You drive this for someone else. What's your name?'

'Vishram, sir.'

'Vishram what?'

'Singh.'

'OK, Vishram, where is it? The banknote? The one-hundred-dollar bill? At home? You didn't hand it to the cab owner, did you?'

'No,' he stammered. 'No. I didn't.'

'You didn't bank it either, did you? You wouldn't want to have to pay tax on that. Did you spend it?'

'No – not yet.'

'So you still have it?'

'In my home, sir.'

'Where is that?'

'In Queens, sir.'

'Tell you what, Vishram. I'll do a deal with you. I'll give you a one-thousand-dollar tip if you drive to your home right now, give me that bill, then drop me off back in downtown Manhattan. Or would you prefer I tell the cab owner you ripped him off on this tip?'

'No, please. Please. This money I need. My wife is very sick. No insurance. I need the money for her medical bills.'

'Do we have a deal?'

'Yessir. Deal. Yes, please.'

Tooth suddenly wrinkled his nose in disgust at a vile stench filling the interior of the cab, and opened his window as the man drove on.

CHAPTER 18

Sunday 22 February

My darling Jodie,

I cannot believe we are going to meet on Tuesday! Just two more sleeps, isn't that what they say these days? I'm as excited as a teenager! You've said in our previous correspondence that you love fish and seafood, so I've booked a restaurant I've heard good things about, GB1 at the Grand Hotel. Meet for a drink in the bar first? How does 7.30 p.m. sound?

Your lover-in-waiting, Rowley. XX

Jodie, sitting in her den on the first floor of her house, blinds drawn against the darkness of the cold winter night – and just in case anyone might be lurking out there, watching her – typed her reply, then sent it. As she did so she heard scratching out in the corridor, behind her. 'Tyson!' she called out, sternly. 'Tyson, stop that!'

The room was functional, comfortably furnished in the modern style she liked, all in white and beige, with abstract prints of no value on the walls. There were just two photographs. No memorabilia. A flat would have been more convenient, but at this stage in her *career path* – as she liked to think of it – a flat would not have been practical – not for what she kept here.

After her bad experience with Walt Klein, she was being more careful with Rowley Carmichael. He'd checked out fine. A high-profile London art dealer specializing in Impressionists, he seemed genuinely to have amassed a fortune and sold out to a major auction house at the top of the market. Nowhere on any of the sites on which he was mentioned was there any hint of scandal.

My gorgeous handsome Lover-In-Waiting (love it!!!). 7.30 p.m. Tuesday, in the bar of the Grand, cannot come a moment too soon. Don't quite know how I will be able to wait until then . . .
J. XXXX

She heard more scratching. This time, exasperated, she stood up.

The cat, Tyson, whom Jodie had picked up from the cattery straight after returning home, scratched the wall at the end of the first-floor landing, repeatedly. He could smell something intriguing and possibly tantalizing on the other side. To his owner's annoyance, Tyson came up here and did this every day. He had scratched away the paint, and was now starting to wear away the plaster behind. That's how desperate he was to find what was on the other side.

Hearing her footsteps approaching, he turned and greeted her with a plaintive meow.

'Tyson!' she said with real fury – and some panic – in her voice. 'TYSON! I told you to stop scratching!'

She'd tried everything, from spraying the wall and the carpet in front of it with stuff she had bought from a pet shop, to putting up a child-gate on the stairs, to locking him out altogether. But he always got in, always found his way back up here, always scratched away at that very same place. Because there was something on the other side, something with a strong smell. Something that was clearly driving him insane with curiosity.

'You know what they say, don't you, about curiosity, Tyson? Eh? Is that how you nearly died before? Curiosity? Well, just stop bloody scratching, OK?'

She had found the grey and white moggie as she had arrived home one night, three years earlier, when the headlights of her car had picked out something lying by the kerb at the entrance to her driveway. It had been this cat, one she had never seen before, lying there barely conscious, making tiny little crying sounds. He'd had blood leaking from one ear, a broken leg and such a swollen area around his eye she thought he had lost it. He'd clearly been hit by a vehicle and just left there.

She'd scooped him up, brought him into the house, wrapped him in a blanket, then found a local twenty-four-hour emergency vet service and phoned them. When she'd told them the symptoms they'd said to come in right away but that it didn't sound good.

The vet scanned the cat for a microchip, to see if its owner could be traced. But there wasn't one. The unfortunate animal had a fractured skull, broken leg and ribs, bruised spleen, and a number of minor injuries as well. The vet was doubtful it would last the night. But it did, making a surprisingly rapid recovery. She'd never owned a cat before and had had no desire for one. But when the vet told her it would be put into a local animal rescue centre, she had softened and taken him home herself, regardless of the high veterinary bills yet to come for the creature's continued recovery.

She'd done a tour of the neighbourhood, heavily disguised so no one would subsequently be able to identify her, trying to find out if anyone had lost a cat or knew who he might be, but had drawn a blank. Then she gave him every chance to wander off to his home, but he just hung around, not interested in going anywhere.

She named him Tyson, after the boxer, because he was clearly a tough guy. He was sullen, too, never quite giving her the unconditional love and affection she thought that maybe, considering what she had done, she deserved. Instead, generally regarding her as little more than his personal can-opener, he spent much of his time outside in the garden, in all weathers, or else scratching away on that wall upstairs.

Just occasionally, if she left her door open, he would stroll into her room in the middle of the night, jump onto the bed and then, purring, nuzzle up against her face affectionately, licking her and waking her up.

'You know what, Tyson,' she said to him one time, wide awake in the middle of the night. 'I love you, but I just can't figure you out. But then again, I guess you can't figure me out either, can you? And the thing you really, really can't figure out is what's behind that wall, isn't it?'

CHAPTER 19

Sunday 22 February

Tooth, in a leather jacket, black T-shirt and chinos, sat on a sofa in a quiet corner at the rear of the Macanudo cigar bar on 63rd Street in New York, whiling away the Sunday evening by chain-smoking his Lucky Strikes and drinking Diet Cokes. A group of guys sat in front of the wall-mounted television screen at the far end of the room, watching a re-run of the Superbowl.

He didn't do football games.

He didn't do cold, either, and right now outside at 7 p.m. it was freezing cold, dark and sleeting. He shot a glance around the room, which was decorated like a gentleman's club and dimly lit. It was the way bars used to be in the years before the smoking ban had turned smokers like him into exiles in most places in the western world.

Apart from the waitress, who occasionally came over to check on his drink, no one took any notice of him.

He took from his wallet the one-hundred-dollar

bill that Vishram Singh had handed him, and looked at it. Looked again at the serial number printed on it. 76458348.

One phone call yesterday evening had established it came from a sequence of numbers from the new one-hundred-dollar bills, totalling $200,000, that had been in the suitcase apparently taken from the Park Royale West suite of a scumbag Romanian called Romeo Munteanu. He was a bagman for a bunch of Russian businessmen based in the enclave called Little Odessa, down in Brooklyn, near New York's Brighton Beach, who had become his main paymasters in the past year.

The first part of this job, for which he had been paid his requisite total fee of one million dollars in advance, into his Swiss bank account, had been accomplished. It had been to teach Romeo Munteanu a lesson that would send a signal to anyone else that his bosses were not to be messed with. That had been easy. The next part was more challenging.

Five thousand dollars, handed over in the back office of the night porter, had secured him a copy of the videotape of the woman who had checked in to the hotel under the name Judith Forshaw, and a copy of the registration form she had signed. But the porter reckoned he knew who she really was. Just as he was about to tell Tooth, a news bulletin came on the small television in the office. It featured further revelations of indicted financier Walt Klein's misconduct, stating that the scale of his fraud was even greater than at first thought. It referred to the arrival back in the USA, the previous week, of his body, accompanied by his distraught fiancée, Jodie Bentley. The images showed Jodie, looking bewildered in a storm of strobing flashlights in an airport arrivals hall, then subsequently entering the New York Four Seasons hotel.

'No question, buddy,' the porter had said. 'She was all nervous, had a British accent, I think that name was a cover or something. Guess maybe she's trying to escape the paparazzi, you know.'

The blade of his stiletto, which still had fresh blood on it from Romeo Munteanu, accompanied by his threat that the trembling porter would end up the same way as the man in Suite 5213 if he breathed a word to anyone, had also secured him the man's silence.

The address Judith Forshaw had put on the registration form was in Western Road, Brighton, England. A seaside city he had gotten to know. He'd been there twice before, once to kill an Estonian sea captain who'd attempted to run off with a cargo of drugs, in a harbour to the west of the city. And on a second occasion to avenge the death of the son of a New York mobster – which had nearly ended badly for him. If he needed to make a transatlantic trip to Brighton, at least he would be returning to a city he knew. Most of his assignments were to places totally alien to him.

With earphones plugged in, he played the video of her in the foyer of the Park Royale West Hotel.

Judith Forshaw. She had taken $200,000 that wasn't hers.

As well as something much more important to his paymaster. Something worth more than the million-dollar fee he had been paid. A USB memory stick that his paymaster needed back. Urgently.

Tooth studied her face for some moments. He would remember it now forever. He never forgot a face.

Judith Forshaw or Jodie Bentley. He would find her.

She might have gone to LaGuardia Airport, but he reckoned that was a false trail. Her fiancé, Walter Klein, was dead. Klein was a Jewish name. He knew the Jewish tradition was to bury their dead very quickly. He imagined the funeral would be taking place sometime this coming week, assuming his body was released by the Medical Examiner. As his grieving fiancée, Jodie Bentley would surely attend. Or would she?

Walt Klein was all over the news. His assets had been frozen. Clearly Jodie had been left high and dry – why else would she do a dumb thing like robbing a stranger? Desperation?

Was she going to risk hanging around Manhattan? To see an old crook, who'd left her penniless, being put in the ground?

Would he have hung around, in her situation?

He didn't think so. He'd have gotten the first plane out of this freezing hellhole.

CHAPTER 20

Monday 23 February

Shelby Stonor's mate, Dean Warren, had sat opposite him in the pub a few weeks ago.

'You know what you is, don't you? An effing dinosaur!' Dean said. 'No one burgles houses no more. Why you faffing around, being out late at night, taking all those risks? Anyone what's got anything worth stealing has burglar alarms, safety lights, dogs, CCTV cameras. There's much better stuff, and with less chance of getting caught – and lighter sentences. You could make several grand a week dealing drugs or doing internet scams, yeah? Or nicking high-end cars, like what I'm into right now. Range Rovers pay the best. A simple bit of technology that scoops up their keyless door and ignition codes lets you open and drive one off in minutes. They're paying ten grand for a top-end Rangie right now! Five grand for a convertible Merc SL! Within twelve hours of nicking 'em, they're into a container being shipped out of Newhaven to the Middle East or Cyprus!'

'All you have to do is nick it and deliver it somewhere?' Stonor asked him.

'Piece of piss,' Warren replied. 'You could learn to use the kit in a couple of hours. That and the garage-door opener – opens any door in seconds – I could teach you. It's quicker with two people – we could do a bunch of cars in a night – or better, in a day. Daytime is favourite. Less chance of being stopped in daytime. Really, you could learn to use the kit, easy mate.'

But Shelby Stonor wasn't into technology – he just didn't really understand it – beyond the basics of texting and the internet, and taking the occasional photo on his phone. 'Not my thing. I like my burgling, mate.'

'All right, but you could still help me, yeah? Well – we could help each other.'

'How?'

'I could give you commission on any cars you spot. Rangies, Bentleys, Beemers, Mercs, Porsches – anything high value that I nick. I get given orders, like a shopping list of cars, yeah? So if you see any on your travels – like in garages, on your burgling – text me their registration and address, and I'll give you five per cent of what I get. Fair?'

'I just have to text you?'

'Yeah.'

'When I see a car that might be on your list?'

'That's right.'

'Sounds like money for old rope.'

'It is. That and drugs. Money for old rope.'

Stonor didn't reply. They'd had this discussion before, arguing late into the night, increasingly less coherently as they got drunker and drunker. Dealing in drugs was immoral in a way that, in his mind, burgling wasn't.

Drugs destroyed people's lives. Whereas burgling was a game – always had been. You took stuff from rich people's homes and the insurance replaced it. What was the problem? Yeah, fair dues, occasionally you took a precious heirloom, some geezer's war medals – sentimental shit like that – and the old bloke got upset and had a whole page in Brighton's *Argus* newspaper showing him looking all sad and bewildered. But people had to remember all that biblical stuff about possessions. We all come into this world with nothing and we leave with nothing. Shelby hadn't had much in his life to be sentimental about. Taken into care by social workers at the age of seven from his alcoholic mother, after her divorce from his father, he had been shunted from foster home to foster home up until the time of his first incarceration. Shelby didn't have much understanding of sentiment. Nobody ever got a meal paid for by sentiment. But he'd had a lot of meals paid for from burgling.

He'd done his first house at the age of fifteen – a neighbour in the Whitehawk suburb of Brighton. Stupidly, he'd not worn any gloves, and he'd been nicked for that offence a few weeks later, after being arrested for joyriding. His fingerprints matched those on a video camera he'd flogged to a Brighton fence who in turn had flogged it, unwittingly, to an undercover CID officer.

By the time he came out of a young offender institution two years later, older and more street-wise, if not actually wiser, he had figured out that you faced pretty much the same length of prison sentence regardless of whether you did a poor house or a posh house. So he'd decided to specialize in Brighton's high-end homes, where there would always be rich pickings to be had.

For the next twenty years this had netted him a good living, despite being caught on almost too many occasions to count. But prison was fine. He enjoyed reading and being inside gave him time to indulge that passion. There was television in his cell, the food was all OK and he had plenty of recidivist mates.

Now he'd been out for nearly a year – one of the longest periods of freedom he could remember – and he had been doing a lot of taking stock of his life. A decade ago his wife, Trixie, had finally tired of his endless spells in prison while she was stuck at home with their three small kids. She'd met someone and moved abroad with the kids, Robert, George and Edie, whom she'd poisoned against him.

He'd never heard from her or the little bastards again. And when he stopped to think about it, he couldn't really blame the kids. Just how many days in all their years had he ever spent at home with them? He'd felt a stranger every time he'd walked in through the front door.

What he really wanted now, he realized, was what he had once had and lost. To be married, have kids, live in a nice house, drive a nice car. But above all to be a proper father. A parent. The father he'd never had.

But how?

Approaching forty, with 176 previous offences, that was not going to be so easy, he knew. Not many people would give him a job – and most of the limited options were menial and poorly paid. His best hope was to carry on with the lucrative trade he knew – and just hope to hell he could be smart enough not to get caught and arrested yet again.

He was seeing a new lady, Angi Bunsen. She was thirty, had her own house and a job as a book-keeper with a firm of accountants. She knew all about his past and didn't mind. She'd told him last night, in bed, that she loved him. She wanted to have his child. He'd proposed to her as he held her in his arms and she'd said yes, she would marry him. On one condition. No more burgling. She didn't want a husband she'd only get to see in a prison visiting room. She didn't want to have to fib to their children that Daddy was away on business or, worse, have to take them to see him in his prison clothes and with his prison complexion.

So he'd promised her previously. Told her a white lie that he had a job stacking pallets in a car spares warehouse, often working late and night shifts, and she believed him. He felt happier tonight than he could ever remember. He wanted to buy her a ring, a great big rock, put it on her finger and take her away to somewhere beautiful in the sun, somewhere that she deserved to be.

Angi!

He really did love her. Loved her name. Loved her tenderness. Her trusting eyes. If he could only get a bit of money together to give her all the things he wanted to, and that she deserved. There were a few ways for ex-cons to make big money legally. Telephone sales was one. He'd heard from a fellow cellmate a few years ago that some telesales companies didn't care about your background, so long as you could sell. But he wasn't sure he was much of a salesman. Driving a cab was another option which appealed more. An owner cabbie could gross fifty grand a year in Brighton. A journeyman driver got a lot less.

But to buy a taxi plate in the city was currently £48,000. And the gap at this moment between that and what he had in his bank account was precisely £47,816. He could probably get another few hundred quid towards it from flogging his shit heap of a car – his fifteen-year-old, clapped-out rust bucket of a Fiat Panda. But for a while longer, he needed it.

Forty-eight thousand quid wasn't an insurmountable gap. The *Argus* from time to time very obligingly printed a list of the top-twenty most expensive properties in the city.

It was as if they printed it just for him!

He'd wised-up in this past year out of prison. There was no point stealing cheap shit – just like the lesson he'd learned when he'd been caught burgling in Whitehawk. So he'd been doing his research on the internet, learning to identify expensive jewellery and high-value watches. He reckoned himself now to be a bit of an expert. And he'd identified a group of houses where he was likely to find these. Watched the movements of the owners over the past weeks.

He felt ready.

CHAPTER 21

The past

It was the last summer holiday that the four of them would spend together. As usual Jodie and her sister, Cassie, sat hunched and jammed-in in the back of their mother's ageing Saab convertible, surrounded by luggage for a three-week motoring holiday touring through France, Germany, Switzerland and Italy, being blasted by the wind. They'd have been more comfortable in their father's much bigger Jaguar, but he was adamant that a convertible was more fun for their holiday.

It was a cold, damp August day and their father insisted on keeping the roof down as they travelled along the French autoroute; the two girls, hair feeling like it was being torn from the roots, had a flapping tartan picnic rug over them for warmth. As their father drove, their mother attempted to keep their spirits up and boredom at bay by playing endless games. I-spy was their default game. Sometimes, instead, they would make up words from the letters on the number plate of the car in front of them. And the other game they played was spotting green Eddie Stobart and red Norbert Dentressangle lorries.

Cassie was five lorries ahead of Jodie. Cassie was always ahead of her in everything. Cassie had their mother's blonde hair and beautiful features. Jodie had her father's dark-brown wire-brush hair and hooked conk of a nose.

'I spy with my little eye something beginning with R!' their father said, glancing in the mirror. They were two hours south of Calais, in the Champagne region.

'Rheims!' Cassie shouted out as a sign for the city loomed ahead.

'No!' he replied.

'Road sign?' said their mother.

'No!'

A large, crimson limousine with GB plates glided past them. Jodie saw, in the back seat, a snotty-looking girl of about her age, wearing Walkman headphones, looking down at them disdainfully.

'Rolls-Royce!' Jodie said.

'Yep!' her father said, as the Rolls pulled away into the distance.

Jodie stared at it, enviously. Why weren't they in that car, instead of this crappy old Saab?

'Your turn, Jodie!' her mother said.

'I'm bored with this silly game,' she replied, sullenly, still watching the sleek car that was now barely a speck on the horizon. Where were those people going? To somewhere special with swimming pools and discos? They wouldn't be staying in the kind of crummy hotels they stayed in every night, she bet.

She should be travelling down through France in a beautiful Roller like that, too. One day, she vowed, she would. One day people would be staring up at her with envy, as she passed them in the fast lane.

It wasn't a dream, she knew. It was her destiny.

The following week they stayed three nights in Como. Not in the famous Villa d'Este on the waterfront of the glorious lake – the kind of place where the girl in the crimson Rolls-Royce would have stayed – but in a B&B in a narrow, dusty backstreet, where she was kept awake in the small bed she had to share with Cassie by the constant blatter of mopeds and scooters.

As a treat, their parents took them for a drink at the Villa d'Este the first night. At the table next to them, at the lake's edge, sat a beautiful family. The tanned father wore a silky white shirt, pink trousers and black loafers. The mother looked like a cont-essa, or maybe a movie star. They had a daughter, a few years older than herself, who was wearing a very cool dress, Manolo Blahnik shoes, and had an elegant Chanel handbag. Jodie wondered if they were famous, because a waiter in a smart red jacket fawned over them repeatedly, topping up their glasses from a bottle of champagne then replacing it in the shiny silver ice bucket. The three of them were talking, animatedly. The father puffed on a large cigar and the mother was smoking a slender filter-tip cigarette.

There were beautiful people at the other tables, too. Elegant women with silk scarves and jewellery; handsome, tanned men in white shirts and sleek trousers.

Her parents seemed so drab in comparison. Her father was wearing a yellow shirt with a fish pattern, boring grey chinos, socks and sandals. Her mother was looking a little smarter but the effect was ruined by a dreary white cardigan. Cassie wore an Oasis T-shirt and jeans. It took her father an age to attract the attention of a waiter, and when one finally came he seemed so aloof, as if he could tell they did not belong there.

God, Jodie wanted to slide under the table and vanish. *These are not my parents. This is not my family. I don't know these people. Really, I don't.*

At least the weather was better here. Sunny and hot. On the second day they went on a cruise on a tourist lake-boat. She sat with her parents and Cassie on the upper deck, listening to the running commentary from the boat's guide, as they sailed from Como to Bellagio, where they were due to stop for an hour for lunch.

Rising up behind the shoreline of the dark green water of the lake were steep, green hills, dense with olive, oleander and cypress trees. There were small towns and villages with yellow, pink and white houses, apartment blocks, church towers and factories, printing silk for the world scarf trade, the guide said. Then right on the waterfront, with their private docks and moored launches, were the grand villas of the rich and famous.

The guide pointed out each spectacular house in turn. The Versace villa, the Heinz holiday home. The Avon Cosmetics family's summer residence. A vast extravaganza under construction by a Russian oligarch. Another vast and slightly vulgar edifice being restored by a London hedge-fund gazillionaire.

While her father took endless photographs, and Cassie, bored, played Tetris on her Gameboy, Jodie stared in awe. She'd never, in her life, seen houses like this. Their home felt like a shack in comparison. She wanted one of these places. Felt a yearning, a pang of desire deep inside her. This was the kind of place she was born to live in. She could picture the chauffeur opening the rear door of her crimson Rolls-Royce as she stepped out onto the driveway, with a clutch of designer carrier bags from Gucci, Versace, Hermès and YSL.

As the guide talked about an island they were passing on their right, which had a famous restaurant with no menu, Jodie turned to her father.

'Daddy, how do you become rich?'

'What do you mean?'

'How do I get to afford a place like any of those villas we've just seen?'

She could see the same envy she had, reflected in her father's face. It was as if he was looking at all he had never achieved in his life, she thought. 'How do you get to afford one of those?'

'The way you do it, Jodie, is you marry a millionaire.'

'Yeah, but,' Cassie said, raising her head from her computer game. 'Only beautiful women marry rich men.' She turned to Jodie. 'Which kind of rules you out.'

Jodie glared at her sister. Cassie was almost seventeen, two years older than her. It was always Cassie who got the new bicycle, which would then be passed on to her three years later. The new music system, again handed down to her when Cassie was given a newer more modern one. Even her clothes were mostly hand-me-downs from Cassie.

They were cruising past a huge villa, set back a short distance from the lake with immaculate gardens in front of it. She saw a group of people sitting at a table beneath a huge cream parasol, having a lunch party. A large, beautiful wooden Riva powerboat was moored at the bottom of stone steps down to the dock.

She stared at it. At the group of people. At the boat. She was feeling deep envy, and even deeper resentment. Why wasn't this her?

Her father ran his fingers through Cassie's blonde hair. 'How are you doing, my angel?'

Cassie shrugged and nodded.

Her mother smiled at Cassie, then at her father, then took a photograph of the two of them together, as if Jodie did not exist.

'I'm going to live in a house like that one day!' she announced.

Her mother gave her a sweet smile. Humouring her.

CHAPTER 22

Tuesday 24 February

'Where the fuck did you get this, doll?'
Graham Parsons held up the memory
stick. They were seated at a corner table
in the Hove Deep Sea Anglers' club on the
seafront, with a blurry view through a salt-caked
window of upturned fishing boats on the pebble
beach. In front of him was a pint of beer. In front
of Jodie was a half-pint of lime and soda. A handful
of the other tables in the pub-like room were
occupied on this wet Tuesday lunchtime. There
was a quiet murmur of conversation in the room,
and a smell of fried food.

'Does it matter, Graham?' she asked.

He sat in his smart suit and tie, a silk handkerchief protruding flamboyantly from his breast
pocket. She was dressed in jeans, a roll-neck
sweater and a black suede bomber jacket.

'Yeah, it does. Quite a lot, doll.'

'Oh?'

He stood up. 'I need a fag. Be back in a minute.'

'I'll come with you. I could do with one, too.'

They stepped outside onto the terrace, with its empty tables and chairs. Head bowed against the icy wind and rain, Graham cupped his hand over his lighter and lit her cigarette, then his. 'Do you have any fucking idea who you're messing with?'

She stared out at the grey, roiling sea. 'No, that's why I gave it to you.'

He smoked his cigarette, holding it between his forefinger and thumb, as if it were a dart. 'What do you know about the Russian Mafia?'

'Not a lot.'

'Yeah, well, you've just bought yourself a front-row seat. Ever hear about blood eagles?'

'What?'

'I've met a few members of the American Mafia in my time. They're all right, in as much as you can say that. They get rid of their enemies by killing them quickly and efficiently – a double-tap – two bullets to the head. But the new generation of Russian and Eastern Bloc Mafia are different. They like to send out signals, yeah?'

'Signals?'

'*Screw us and you're not just going to die. You're going to go through living hell first.* Understand?'

'What kind of living hell?'

'You really want to know?'

'Yes.'

'Someone pisses them off, they'll go into their home. Torture and kill a child in front of the family. Just to teach them a lesson. Or they'll make the kids watch their parents being tortured to death, so they'll know never to mess with them.'

'I'm not scared, Graham.'

'Yeah? Well you should be.'

They finished their cigarettes and hurried back inside. Their plaice and chips was waiting for them.

As they sat down, he picked up the bottle of ketchup and shook it over his chips. 'I heard from my sources, there was a low-life Romanian found in a posh hotel room in New York a few days ago. He'd been *blood-eagled*.'

'What does that mean?'

'Believe me, you don't want that happening to you. It was what the Vikings used to do to their enemy leaders. Place them on their stomach and flay all the skin from their backs. Then they'd use their axes to chop all the ribs away from their victim's spine, while he was still alive. Next, they'd pull his ribs and lungs out with their bare hands and leave them sticking out, between his shoulders, so they looked like the folded wings of an eagle. If he suffered in silence, he'd be allowed into Valhalla. But if he screamed, he'd never enter.'

She shivered. 'That happened to . . .?'

'That's how the police found him in his suite at the Park Royale West. A bloke called Romeo Munteanu. Name ring a bell?'

She felt sick. A deep unease swirled through her. 'Ro-Romeo Mount-what?'

'Munteanu.'

She shook her head, vigorously. 'No. Never heard that name.'

'Good. Good to hear that.' He gave her a long, hard stare. Then he held the memory stick up in front of her again. 'If you don't want to wake up one morning with your innards all pulled out, you get rid of this pretty smartly. You don't want to mess about with these people.'

'What does it contain?'

'Names and addresses of the Premier League Eastern European and Russian organized-crime members in the US and their associates around the world, together with their phone numbers and email addresses – and their bank account numbers in several countries. There are police forces around the globe that would have all their Christmases come at once if they got hold of this.'

She reached forward and took the memory stick from him, slipping it into her handbag. 'Thanks for the warning. So you cracked the password?'

'I cracked the password.'

'Let me have it.'

'You want me to hand you your death warrant?'

'I said I'm not scared. Not of anyone, Graham.'

'You bleedin' well should be.'

'I'd much prefer to think they should be scared of me,' she said. 'If they've gone to those lengths to torture and kill, it tells me that someone wants this back rather badly. And might be willing to pay serious money for it.'

'That's not how these people do business,' he replied.

'Well, it's how I do.' She tipped some ketchup onto her plate, speared a chip and dunked it in the red sauce, then ate it, hungrily.

'You're playing with fire.'

'So what's new?'

CHAPTER 23

Tuesday 24 February

Roy Grace was seated behind his desk, with a sandwich beside him, scanning the weekly *Brighton & Hove Independent* newspaper. When he ate alone, he always liked to read – particularly about the city – and to get as balanced a view as possible from different sources. When he had finished the paper, he turned to the ream of paperwork from the Lyon police, via Interpol, on their processing of Dr Edward Crisp. It had come through, frustratingly, in French. A local firm he'd used before, Tongue Tied, did a fast-turnaround translation job for him.

Attached was the DNA and fingerprint confirmation that this was, without doubt, the Brighton serial killer. As Grace began to eat, a prawn fell out of the sandwich onto a sheet of the report, marking it. Cursing, he picked the prawn up and put it in his mouth. His phone rang.

'Detective Superintendent Grace,' he answered, chewing.

'Hey, pal, how you doing?'

Instantly he recognized the Brooklyn accent of his NYPD friend, Detective Investigator Pat Lanigan, who was on the New York Mafia-busting team. 'Doing good, thanks! How are you? How is Francene?' He dabbed the smear off the printout, as best he could, with a paper napkin.

'Yeah, she's good! Listen, hope you don't mind my calling you direct?'

'Of course not, always!'

'I kind of guessed I'd get a quicker answer from you than by going through the Interpol bureaucracy.'

'Tell me?'

'I'm dealing with a homicide here in New York. A pretty nasty one involving torture. It's looking organized-crime related – a courier for a Russian Mafia organization we've had under observation for some months. He was found dead in his hotel room, at the Park Royale West. Name's Romeo Munteanu – a Romanian national. But that's probably not going to mean anything to you. Word on the street is he lost a bag containing a large wad of cash he was carrying for a drug deal, and no one believed his story.'

'How much?'

'Two hundred thousand dollars. We're trying to trace an Englishwoman who was with him in the bar of the hotel, we believe under an assumed name, the last time he was seen alive. Probably a long shot, but I thought you might be the person to help us find her. We're not sure she's necessarily

132

connected – the bar staff we've interviewed say he appeared to have picked her up in the cocktail bar around seven in the evening on Wednesday last. They left the bar together around half eight. Then she checked out of the hotel just after ten that night. According to the staff she seemed pretty agitated.'

'Do you have her name?' Grace asked.

'The name she checked in under was Judith Forshaw. But we're pretty sure her real name is Jodie Bentley. It looks that way from the CCTV footage. Earlier in the day she had checked into the Four Seasons under her real name, and gave her address as her fiancé's apartment on Park Avenue. We think she was being hounded by the media and may have switched hotels and identities to get away, although we don't have all the details yet – the Four Seasons had a problem with their video, they're trying to recover it, but I can send you a copy of the Park Royale's CCTV footage if that would be useful?'

Grace jotted the names down on his pad. 'What do you have on this Jodie Bentley, Pat?'

'Her fiancé was a big-time financier, Walter Klein, who was under investigation by the Securities and Exchange Commission, and about to be charged. Rather conveniently for him, he died in a skiing accident two weeks ago. Possibly suicide. According to Klein's lawyer, she was a fortune hunter, but knew nothing about his true financial situation. The lawyer told us she's from Brighton

– which is why I'm calling, in case she's on your radar. The address the Park Royale has for her is in a street called Western Road, in Brighton.'

'Doesn't ring an immediate bell,' Grace said. 'But she sounds quite the grieving bride-to-be, picking someone up in a bar barely two weeks later, under a different name.'

'Oh, I hear she's a regular sweetheart. It gets even better. Her first husband died from a snake bite some years back.'

'She might be very unlucky – or perhaps there's more to it,' Grace said.

'Well, that's what I'm hoping to find out, Roy. There's two other things that may or may not be related to this. In the early hours of the morning, this character, Munteanu, looking a wreck, came down to reception at the Park Royale West, frantic to find this woman. He went bananas when they told him she'd checked out and left. He tried to bribe the desk clerk into giving him her address and any other contact details. He was offering a huge amount. The clerk had to get the night manager to try to calm Munteanu down – and it was only when the manager threatened to call the police that he finally went back to his room. He was subsequently found dead, and that's when we got involved. It was pretty nasty – a Russian ritual killing.'

Lanigan paused for a moment then continued. 'Around midnight, earlier that same night, a cab driver in the city brought a bag of cocaine – street value of around ten thousand dollars – into the 10th Precinct police station. Said he'd found it in the back of his cab – one of his passengers had sat on it and handed it to him. He gave a statement about all the passengers he could remember picking up that night. One was a woman, who he said seemed in a bit of a state. He'd picked her up from the Park Royale West Hotel, and she kind of fitted the description and time. Seems like she was undecided about which airport she wanted him to take her to – she eventually decided on LaGuardia.'

'How did she pay?'

'Cash. Gave him a big tip, he said.'

'Which airline terminal did he drop her off at?'

'American. The only flight at that time of night was a badly delayed one to Washington. Judith Forshaw was on it.'

'Judith Forshaw. Presumably she had ID?'

'Uh huh.'

'But she flew into the US under the name Jodie Bentley, presumably with a full ID for that, too?'

'Uh-huh. I've checked with Immigration.'

'Interesting. Why does she have multiple IDs – and even more to the point, how did she get them?'

'It's sounding like her dead fiancé is a very big fraudster, Roy. Word here is that it could be on the Bernie Madoff scale, a Ponzi scheme that's defrauded investors of billions of dollars. I wouldn't think coming up with alternative IDs would be much of a problem to a guy like him.'

'Two hundred thousand dollars is a lot for someone to lose,' Grace said.

'It is. We've run checks on Washington flights to the UK that she might have taken. There were fifteen to the UK the following day. We have CCTV footage of this same woman arriving at Dulles Airport in Washington around midnight – a match from the CCTV footage of her in the Park Royale West lobby. We have her crossing the departures concourse, but then she seems to have disappeared into thin air.'

'Did you check outward flight passenger manifests?' Roy Grace asked.

'Sure. Nothing. She vanished like a ghost.'

'I've been to that airport, it's massive,' Grace said. 'Wouldn't she at least stay in New York for her fiancé's funeral?'

'We've spoken to his lawyer. He told us that in his view she was just a gold-digger, and when he informed her about her late fiancé's financial situation, she stormed out of his office. Sure, we'll be looking out for her at the funeral – we don't have a date yet. The family weren't happy with the French police's opinion that he had committed suicide and his children want an independent medical examination of their father.'

'So either she went back into the city – by cab or bus or train – or she took a flight to England from another airport,' Grace said.

'Both are possible,' Lanigan replied. 'I'm waiting on a response from Homeland Security as to whether a Jodie Bentley has left the country – I'm hoping to hear later today.'

'I know someone who may be able to help if she changed her physical appearance, perhaps in a cloakroom,' Grace said. 'Do you have CCTV coverage on domestic terminals for that day?'

'I could get that for you.'

'We work with a pioneering forensic gait analyst here in the UK, Haydn Kelly, who's worked with a number of police forces here and abroad. Whatever her appearance, he could pick her out in a crowd.'

'You serious? *Forensic gait analyst?*'

'You don't use this technology?'

'I don't know about it, Roy.'

'If you could send me all the footage you have, I could get Haydn Kelly to check it over. However much she might have changed her appearance, he'd still be able to pick her out with his technology.'

'I'll get it to you in the next few hours. She may be innocent, but we'd like to talk to her as soon as possible.'

'Ping it to me as fast as you can.'

'You've got it.'

CHAPTER 24

Tuesday 24 February

The couple facing each other across a table in the restaurant of the Grand Hotel in Brighton had eyes only for each other. Through the window beyond them, beyond the lights of the promenade, stood the dark, rusting silhouette of the ruins of the West Pier, like some monster that had risen from the seabed, and the tall structure of the i360 tower under construction. But neither Jodie Bentley nor Rowley Carmichael looked at the view. For some moments they didn't even see the waiter hovering with their digestifs – vintage Armagnac for him, Drambuie for her. Their eyes were locked. His smitten eyes.

Her dangerous eyes.

He reminded her of someone but she couldn't think who.

Rowley Carmichael, a good three decades older, was elegant and suave, and smartly attired in a handmade suit and silk tie. His raffish hair was too long for any stranger to reckon him to be a banker or a lawyer, and certainly not an accountant – more

138

likely someone from the media, or perhaps the art world, which he was.

He leaned across the table towards her, raising his glass, gazing hard through his horn-rimmed lenses at her blue eyes. They had an intensity about them that made any man she stared at feel he was the entire focus of her universe. He was feeling that now, and it was deeply stirring. 'Cheers,' he said. 'It's such an amazing coincidence that we both have homes in Brighton!'

Mirroring him, as she had been doing all evening, copying his exact movements, Jodie leaned across the table towards him. 'Cheers,' she said. 'It is, an amazing coincidence. Sort of meant to be!'

'You know,' he said, 'I feel so incredibly comfortable with you. Although these past months we've only communicated by email, I feel as if I've known you for years.'

'That's exactly how I feel about you, too, Rowley,' she replied.

He leaned back a little.

She leaned back a little.

'Call me Rollo!' he said.

'OK!' She smiled seductively then added, 'Rollo!'

'Have you ever done this dating agency thing before?' he asked, slightly embarrassed.

'No, no, I've never dared. I'm really a very shy person.'

'Well, yes, that's me exactly. I'm immensely shy, too.'

She put her glass down, crossed her arms and

leaned forward. Without realizing why, he did exactly the same.

She was leading now and he was following. That was the intention of mirroring. If she bided her time and did it right for long enough, it always worked.

'I just got so lonely after my husband died,' she said.

'Me too, I've been very lonely since my wife passed away. We'd moved to Brighton for our retirement, but hardly knew anyone here, other than one close mate who sadly died unexpectedly. A friend of mine convinced me to give internet dating a go. But because of my shyness I couldn't pluck up the courage to contact any of the people I looked at on the website. Until I saw you. You just looked so warm and friendly in your photo, so I thought, hey, what's to lose by giving it a go, she can always say no!'

'That's exactly what happened with me! A friend convinced me to give it a go. I wasn't at all sure – and, actually, I didn't really like the look of anyone who contacted me – until your photo popped up. I thought exactly the same about you! You just looked like someone I could trust. In fact, more than that – I had the most strange feeling – when I looked at your picture I was thinking that you're a man who would make me feel safe.' Feigning nervousness, she twiddled with the chain of the silver heart-shaped locket she always wore round her neck.

'I'm flattered!'

She slipped her hand forward across the table and touched his, gently. 'I'm glad I plucked up the courage.'

'So am I,' he said. 'I'm so glad. But you know, you wrote in your profile "of a certain age". I think you're doing yourself a disservice. I would take *a certain age* to mean someone in their sixties. You look decades younger than that!'

She grinned. 'Maybe it's because I changed my hair! But, hey, I've always been attracted to older men,' she said, and squeezed his hand. 'So tell me, how did your wife pass away?'

'Alzheimer's. She had a particularly brutal strain of it that killed her within five years.'

'How dreadful.'

'It was. How about your husband – how did he die?'

'Cancer. I nursed him for two years. Then he had a bad fall.'

'A fall. That can be a big setback for elderly or ill people. It can be the thing that precipitates death.'

'That was exactly the case,' she replied.

'I'm so sorry to hear that.' He shrugged and then gave her a smile that was full of hope. 'Must have been hard for you. How old was he?'

'Fifty-two. Started with colon cancer and then it spread everywhere.'

'Fifty-two? That's no age.' He shook his head. 'You know I'm a lot older than that?'

She smiled. 'I don't feel any age difference. And – as I said – there's something about you, you make me feel secure.'

'It's so beautiful that connection I've felt through our emails, Jodie. It's as if I've been given a second chance. And now I've found you, I would die happy.'

'Don't die too soon, please! We've only just met.'

'I'm not planning to,' he said. 'I'm hoping to be around for a long time yet!'

She smiled again.

CHAPTER 25

Tuesday 24 February

Result! Oh yes, definitely!

Seated in his beat-up Fiat Panda, looking around at his surroundings, at all the flash metal parked in the driveways, Shelby Stonor was suffering serious car envy. He stared longingly at a gleaming Ferrari 488; at a BMW i8; at a white Bentley Continental. His dad, whom he had known only briefly before the bastard had pulped his mother's face and left home for good, when he was just four years old, had been a car nut. He had named Shelby after one of his idols, the American car designer and racing legend, Carroll Shelby.

Ironic, he thought, that he was now sitting in a vehicle his namesake would not have been seen dead in.

He was dressed in a black anorak and black trousers, over a skintight bodysuit and rubber balaclava – something he had learned from watching *CSI* – to avoid leaving any skin cells or hair that DNA could be obtained from – with black leather gloves and a black beanie. He was

143

parked in the darkness in the street that wound past the secluded mansions of Roedean Crescent with their fine views – in daylight – out across the cliffs to the English Channel.

One of the houses on the most recent *Argus* Top-20 list was just up to his left. He'd eyed that mansion for over a month, but dismissed it as too difficult. A huge place, lit up by floodlights and protected by electric wrought-iron gates and cameras. A black Range Rover Sport and a matching black Porsche 911 Targa sat ostentatiously on the driveway as if in a further statement of their owners' wealth. They shouted out, *Steal me if you dare!* In the hope of getting his five per cent commission, he dutifully texted his mate Dean Warren details of all the cars he had spotted on this prestigious road, including their registrations. Then he turned his focus back to his real reason for being here.

There were several other less swanky but seriously posh houses in this same street. And one in particular was his target for tonight. No. 191. It was set down, below the street, at the end of a short, steep driveway. Mock Tudor, like many of the houses in this city, with leaded-light windows.

He'd been watching its occupant's movements for some days. She appeared to be a single, rather attractive-looking lady in her mid-thirties, with a nice, almost new dark-blue Mercedes SL500 convertible. He'd texted the registration and address of that car to Dean, also.

The woman hadn't taken the Merc tonight. She'd left a while ago, looking smart, in a Brighton and Hove Streamline taxi. A nice Skoda Superb. One like he'd be driving soon, if all went to plan! He didn't know how long she would be gone – but a few hours at least, he presumed.

His years in prison hadn't all been wasted. He'd picked up a lot of tips and skills from fellow cons. One very valuable bit of information was about the budget cuts to the police service. A decade or so back, response times to burglar alarms could be just a matter of minutes. There was a Languard alarm box prominently on view on the front wall, just below the eaves. These days alarms no longer went through to the police, but instead to call centres which in turn rang keyholders or private security companies rather than the police. Unless you were very unlucky, you could have a good ten to twenty minutes before anyone turned up, and then it was unlikely to be the law – just a security guard. You just had to hold your nerve while the alarm beeped.

But the best tips he'd learned from a fellow con, an old hand at burglary, were to first see what you could learn by sniffing through the letter box, to find an exit route as soon as you were in, and to leave a rear window or door open.

He walked round to the rear of the house, noting the bin store, a side door, then the back garden where there was a patio door opening on to a terrace, with a hot tub beyond that. As he approached the porch at the front he was relieved that no lights came on. He pushed open the letter box in the oak door and peered into the hall, its lights left on. It had a modern, clinical feel, somewhat lifeless. He pressed his nose into the aperture. No scent of a dog, but there was a strong smell of perfume – presumably from the lady who had just gone off in the taxi. Dressed smart and all heavily perfumed; indicated she'd be gone for a while

'Woof!' he shouted, then 'Grrrrrr!' He had a piece of doped shin of beef in a plastic bag in his pocket. But there was no reaction. He waited some moments, glanced over his shoulder, then repeated the sounds, more loudly.

Silence.

You could gain extra time by choosing your entry point carefully. Usually not every room would be alarmed. Pick a small upstairs spare bedroom, and get access through that. Immediately plan the exit route. Then find the master bedroom where the jewellery and expensive watches were likely to be kept and you would have a good five minutes at least – more than enough time for a thorough search – then you'd be out and away long before anyone arrived on the scene.

Shelby had always been good at climbing. But tonight he was really lucky. There was now a builder's sign outside this lady's house and scaffolding had been erected on the right-hand side. Two of the windows on the upper floor had lights on. But the third was in darkness.

Keeping his head down in case there was a hidden camera, he began to climb the metal structure. The first window he could see in through looked like a spare room, but he noticed the telltale red light of an alarm monitor on the ceiling – though that was no proof the alarm had been set. He moved along and looked in the next window, which was lined with bookshelves and had a computer on a desk. Another red light glowing just above the door. He sidled further along and peered through the window into the room that was almost in darkness, with a faint green glow behind the blind. He stared hard but could see no red light.

Perfect!

He pulled a glass cutter from his pocket and made a small, square incision in one of the bottom panes of the leaded-light window. Then he pressed a suction cup against it, and pulled. But instead of coming neatly away, the glass splintered and he felt a stab in his right arm as it pierced his anorak sleeve.

'Shit!' he cried out in pain, then pressed his lips against his arm and tasted the metallic tang of blood. He stood still, holding the scaffold pole with his left arm, and sucked again, scared of leaving any drops, knowing the police had his DNA on record. He looked all around and behind him. But the street was silent, empty.

He remained still for a few minutes, waiting for the cut to clot. When he was satisfied his arm had stopped bleeding he reached inside through the slats of the blind, found the window latch, which had no lock on it, freed it and pulled the whole window open.

Immediately he smelled something rank and sour. He lifted up the blind, switched on his phone torch and shone the beam around the room. There was a glass door on the far side, with, rather strangely, a solid wall right behind it. The walls were lined with glass containers, illuminated with very weak green light, and there were two free-standing racks, tiered with rectangular glass showcases, each about three feet long by about two feet high. All of them contained creatures; snakes, spiders, frogs, and what looked like a scorpion in one.

He stared at them for some moments in revulsion. Then, as he jumped down into the room, his right foot caught the edge of the sill and he sprawled forward with a yelp of pain, straight into a rack of containers which tumbled over, taking the second tier over with them. One shattered, shards of glass glinting across the floor, and the lid came off. His mobile phone skittered across the floor.

'Shit, fuck,' he cursed, lunging for the phone and grabbing it. As he did so, the flash went off. Eyes all around seemed to be staring at him. He heard scuttling. Squeaking. A tiny pair of eyes gleamed at him in the torch beam. It was a small, strange-looking frog, gold with black eyes. It hopped straight towards him, jumping up onto his face.

'Yrrrrgrrroffff!' he yelled, grabbing it with his

gloved hand. It slipped free and hopped onto his arm. As he shook it away, hurling it across the room, he heard a sound like rustling paper. Then he saw a coiled snake, beige with brown and black markings, slithering across the floor towards him, propelling itself by coiling and uncoiling, its tongue forking out.

'No, shit, getttawwwaayyyy.' He pushed himself back with one hand, brandishing the phone in the other like a weapon, until he was right up against the wall beneath the window. The snake was still spinning across the floor towards him.

'Nooooooo!' he screamed, scrambling to his feet. He kicked out at it, saw its tongue leap out between its fangs and felt a sharp prick on his right ankle, like a nettle sting.

His heart pounding with terror, he propelled himself backwards through the window, ducked under the blind, hauled himself out and back on to the scaffolding, slamming the window shut to stop the creatures pursuing him, then clambered back down to the ground and ran, without looking behind him, to his car.

Shit, he thought. *Shit, shit, shit.*

He started the car and drove off, fast, his brain too jumbled to think clearly. He needed to stop somewhere and check the bite, which was tingling. He headed up Wilson Avenue, turned into the deserted Brighton Racecourse car park and pulled up as far from the road as he could get.

He reached down, rolled up his trouser leg,

pushed down his sock, then rolled up the bodysuit legging and shone his beam on the front of his ankle. Just two tiny red dots, no bigger than pinpricks.

Shelby didn't know anything about snakes. But his trouser leg and thick woollen sock and bodysuit must have protected him from a worse bite, he figured. There were three more houses on his list to target tonight, but he was too shaken up to think about another job. What if the thing that had bitten him was poisonous? He wondered if he ought to go to A&E and get the bite checked out. But what could he say? That he was bitten by something in a warehouse? Or while walking his dog across a park? There would be questions he couldn't answer.

He removed his glove and rubbed his finger over the bite marks. No blood smear. That was good, Angi would never notice them. He could tell her he'd gashed his arm on a strip of loose metal on a crate. That would work. He looked at the car clock. He couldn't go home now, because he'd told her he was working a late shift. And besides, he badly needed a drink to calm his nerves. He'd drive to the Royal Albion pub and maybe Dean would be there. Have a couple of pints with him, then, to explain the booze on his breath, tell Angi it was one of the lads' birthdays and he'd brought in a crate of beers to celebrate at the end of the shift.

Yeah. That was a plan.

He'd check the bite again in an hour or so and see if there was any swelling.

But, Jesus, who the hell kept all those horrible creatures in their home?

He started the car and headed over to Hove, and the enticing prospect of a couple of pints of Harveys, followed by the even more enticing prospect of a night in bed with Angi.

CHAPTER 26

Wednesday 25 February

It was a bright, sunny but chilly London morning, the kind when the city looked at its most beautiful. Forensic podiatrist Haydn Kelly had only recently arrived back from a long stint in humid Asia, and it looked even more beautiful than ever to him. He had always enjoyed the long walk along Harley Street with its sternly handsome red-brick Georgian properties, something he had done for many years before he went international; he was pleased to see Old Blighty again.

A sturdily built man in his forties, he had brown hair cropped short, and a tanned, amiable face. Conservatively but elegantly dressed in a fine black suit, light blue shirt and brushed silk black tie, he sat at his desk in his spacious consulting room with two floor-to-ceiling windows at one end, staring at the fifteen video files that had just arrived in his Dropbox folder from Detective Superintendent Roy Grace.

He had a clear diary for the morning. He had recently been elected as Dean of Podiatric

Surgery – his 'charity work' as he referred to it, as it was not a paid position but still took up a big chunk of his time and the committee's, too, in helping Podiatry advance. With over two decades in the profession which had been so good to him, he was pleased to give something back. He had kept the morning open in order to deal with the stack of emails that he knew would be waiting. He buzzed through to reception, asking them to hold his calls for the next couple of hours, then opened the first video, which was titled 'Park Royale West, NY, Lobby, 22.12 p.m., February 18th'.

He saw the woman that the detective superintendent had described after some moments. She was in her mid-thirties, dressed in a smart black coat and knee-high tan suede boots. She exited from a lift and strode over to the front desk, where she appeared to be checking out. After that she went out through the revolving door.

He ran the video through his Forensic Gait Analysis software, and opened the next video file. It showed an arrivals area at Washington Dulles Airport. He picked up within a few minutes the same woman he had seen in the Park Royale West, pushing a luggage trolley, and began to work his way through the rest of the files. Each covered the domestic departure gates.

After over an hour of working his software, the image froze on the gate for a 13.05 Delta flight to Atlanta. A woman walking towards the gate, wearing a grey felt trilby, dark glasses and a cream-coloured trouser suit.

Kelly perked up and took a big gulp of his black, piping-hot Colombian-blend coffee, put the footage into slow motion mode and clicked to enlarge her. Then clicked again. And again. Her image became fuzzy, and it was impossible to tell if it was the same face as the woman at the Park Royale West, and in the other photographs he'd been sent. There was very little hair visible below the hat – either she had crammed it up inside or had cropped it short.

He ran his eye down the various stats his software had thrown up. The different points of a gait match. Since he had first created Forensic Gait Analysis – the identification of a person by their gait or by features of their gait, involving assessment of whole body movements from head to toe – he had provided many expert opinions and forensic reports and had helped others do so, too. In the five years since he had developed his most recent advance of the technology, the reliability had been established beyond any possible doubt. His textbook, the first ever on the subject, had recently been published.

Every human being walked in a different way and some people were more distinctive than others. Everyone's gait was as unique as their DNA, but the quality of the footage was a factor in reducing the accuracy; or as Kelly described it when presented with very poor quality footage, quoting the old computer maxim, 'garbage in, garbage out'.

It was only a matter of time before he and his team successfully built more technology into the system to take account of the cheapskate companies that deployed low-grade CCTV, and never bothered updating it, and then expected law-enforcement agencies to work miracles with footage of such a lousy quality on occasion that it was impossible to decipher a tree from a lamp post, let alone one person from another. He sometimes wondered if they had ever even heard of digital. The added time and expense of companies not having up-to-date technology was costly in more ways than one.

Even from analysis of a single foot position, the software had the capacity to pick someone out in a crowd with reasonable accuracy. When good quality footage was provided of a person actually walking, certainty of identification could be very high. The technology could help determine whether a person was or was not present at a crime scene. It not only looked for similarity, it assessed for dissimilarity, too. It could be used to seek particular aspects of a person's gait, and the process of exclusion was a vital one.

Fortunately the quality of these images was good. The woman he was looking at was, without doubt, the same woman who had checked out of the Park Royale West.

With a very satisfied smile on his face, he picked up his phone, sat back in his leather swivel chair and called Roy Grace's mobile number.

CHAPTER 27

Thursday 26 February

Tooth didn't much like reading. He'd named Yossarian after a character in one of the few books he'd ever read all the way through. *Catch-22*. It held him because it captured pretty much what life in a war zone in the military had been like, in his personal experience. A lot of assholes, fighting an unwinnable war. Mostly he watched television.

Recently, back home, he had been curiously fascinated by an English TV series, *Downton Abbey*, and the place he entered now was pretty much what he imagined a stately home in England would be like. Except, as he stepped out of the elevator, walking between two suits of armour into an oak-panelled hall, the walls hung with stern, gloomy old masters, he was on the ninth floor of a New York Park Avenue East apartment block.

As the short, creepy-looking uniformed butler bowed unctuously, he could smell cigar smoke and fresh coffee.

Two large goons materialized, all in black, with

earpieces on coiled cables, and frisked him, removing the hunting knife strapped to his left ankle and the Heckler & Koch from his shoulder holster. Tooth stood, silent and sullen, until they had finished. He kept the weapons in a locker he rented in a storage depot in Brooklyn. He had weapons in storage lockers in several cities around the world.

'This way, please,' the butler said.

Tooth did not move. 'I want a receipt,' he said.

'You get them back when you leave,' one goon said.

'I'm leaving now.'

'I don't think so,' the other goon said, producing a large Sig Sauer with a silencer attached.

Tooth brought his left leg up hard between the goon's legs. As the man doubled up in pain, he grabbed the Sig, headbutted the second guard, then with his right foot delivered a roundhouse kick, swinging the instep through the man's knee, sending him crashing to the ground. As both guards lay on the floor in pain, Tooth covered them with the gun and said, 'Maybe you didn't hear me right. I said I'm leaving.'

He recovered his own gun and the knife, reholstering them.

'Please, Mr Tooth,' the butler said. 'Mr Egorov would really like to talk to you.'

'Yeah? Well I'm here.'

The two men stared at each other for some moments. Then the butler said, 'Mr Egorov is unable to walk.'

Tooth remembered. His client had been shot by someone he'd upset, paralysing him from the waist down. He tossed the Sig on the floor contemptuously, towards the two goons, then followed the butler.

Tooth didn't do art. But the long corridor he walked down was hung with oil paintings of landscapes, piles of dead game and portraits of stiff-looking men and women, all in ornate gold frames, that he figured hadn't come from a garage sale.

He was ushered through double doors into a grand room with curtains held back with tasselled ties, antique furniture and more paintings adorning the walls.

Four men sat at a long dining table which was laden with silver baskets full of croissants, decanters of orange juice, silver coffee pots, plates and tiny pots of jam. Three of them, who all looked faintly Neanderthal, though dressed in business suits, stared at him warily. The fourth, Sergey Egorov, was in a wheelchair. He had cropped fair hair, a massive gold medallion visible inside his white shirt which was unbuttoned to his navel, and a large cigar, with a white band, in his hand.

'Ah, Mr Tooth. Good to see you,' he said.

Unsmiling, and without acknowledging the greeting, Tooth strode across the floor towards him.

He sat down at one of the empty spaces at the table, looked at each of the three Neanderthals in turn, as if they were small piles of dog shit that he needed to step over, then turned to the man who had hired him, Sergey Egorov, staring him in the eyes as he reached for a coffee pot.

Instantly the butler was at his side, pouring it.

'What would you like to report to us?' Egorov said.

'It's fucking cold here.'

Egorov laughed loudly. He waved his arms expansively and each of his goons laughed, too. Then all around the table fell silent.

'Anything else?'

'Walt Klein's funeral is tomorrow. A service at Riverside Memorial Chapel, on 76th and Amsterdam, followed by a committal at Green-Wood Cemetery, Brooklyn.'

'And you will be there? You haven't found this woman yet?' Egorov asked. 'Why not?'

'I've been to every hotel in this city where she might be staying,' Tooth replied. 'So far no.'

'Why not?'

'Like I told you before, she's not here any more.'

'It's her fiancé's funeral. You don't think she'll be there for appearances?'

'That's what I thought at first. But now I don't think so. Why would she be?' Tooth replied. 'Klein's family despise her. She's not going to inherit a cent. I think she's back in England, as I've already told you.' Tooth pulled his cigarettes from his pocket and tapped one out. He put it in his mouth and lit it.

'It's a week now,' Egorov said. 'Are you trying hard enough?'

Tooth sipped the coffee the butler had poured. Then he looked back at his paymaster. 'Give me your bank account details.'

'My bank account details? Why?'

'I don't like you.' Tooth looked at the other three. 'You can always judge a man by the friends he keeps. You keep shit company.'

All three bodyguards stirred and it took a sharp hand in the air by Egorov to calm them.

'I'll repay you the million, no charge for expenses. You don't want to listen to me? Fine, I'm gone.'

'OK, OK,' Egorov said. 'I'm listening to you.'

Tooth eyed him for some moments. He was also weighing up just what this job meant to him. He needed the money, so he held his temper, as much as he could. 'What part of *she's not here any more* don't you understand?'

'Mr Tooth, we need back what this woman has. We need that memory stick. Don't bother about the cash, it's counterfeit. And we'd like you to teach that woman a lesson. You understand? One of your lessons. We'd like to see it, too.' He raised one hand in front of his eyes and with the other made a cranking motion, miming filming.

'If it's so important to you, who the hell entrusted that Romanian moron with it?'

'It is really important,' Egorov said, ignoring the question and puffing on his cigar. 'I want you to go to the funeral. If she's not there, fine, that's my bad call. Then you go to England. Get the memory stick. And kill the bitch. I'm told you are good at

160

filming the death of your targets. We'd really enjoy seeing that film. Understand what I'm saying?'

Tooth hesitated. He didn't like dealing with assholes who didn't listen to him. They were the people who got you caught.

But.

He needed the money. These assholes were good paymasters. If he upset them maybe they'd badmouth him. Maybe business would dry up totally.

He stared back at Egorov as if watching a poker opponent, then said, 'Your dollar, your call.'

CHAPTER 28

Thursday 26 February

It was 5.30 p.m., and pelting with rain outside his window. Roy Grace shuffled together a bunch of papers on the prosecution he was preparing for Dr Edward Crisp's eventual return to the UK, which he was going to take home and read later this evening. Then he stared at the screensaver on his phone, a picture of Noah and Cleo outside the front of their new home. He was looking forward to getting back in good time to play with Noah before bed, and then enjoy a drink and a meal with Cleo.

There was a knock on his office door.

'Come in!'

Following Haydn Kelly's report, he had, the day before, asked Jack Alexander to find out urgently from the US authorities what he could about Jodie Bentley's movements at Atlanta Airport. Had she or Judith Forshaw travelled anywhere else within the USA, or did their systems show Jodie Bentley leaving the country?

The DC came in, beaming, clutching a wodge

of papers on which were rows of names, as well as the blurry, blown-up image of the suspect woman's face from CCTV footage at Atlanta Airport, and a memory stick, which he put down on the Detective Superintendent's desk.

Grace indicated a chair in front of him.

'Sir,' Jack said, sitting down, 'I've found out that Jodie Bentley appears to have travelled from Washington Dulles to Hartsfield–Jackson Airport at Atlanta using the name Jemma Smith. She then flew out of Atlanta as Jodie Bentley, on a Virgin Airlines flight to Heathrow last Thursday, at 17.35, scheduled to arrive in London at 6.30 a.m. on Friday the 20th. I've obtained her address from her credit card details.'

'Where does she live?'

'Now we get to the interesting bit, sir,' Alexander said. 'I've checked it out. It's a rental mailbox address – the same as she used when she booked in to the Park Royale West in New York.'

'What did you find out about it?'

'I've been to see them and spoke to the manager, who wasn't too helpful, until I threatened her with a search warrant.'

Grace smiled; he liked this detective's attitude. He reminded him of himself at that age.

Alexander continued. 'She said they've never met the woman. It was all set up via email about a year ago. A Hotmail account, naturally. I've given it to the High Tech Crime Unit to see if they can find out any information – but they're dubious.

Donald Duck could set up an untraceable Hotmail account in a couple of minutes.'

'How did she pay for this mailing address?' Grace quizzed him.

'In cash, apparently. Delivered by a cab.'

'So she was planning in advance,' Grace commented, thinking hard. *Who the hell is this woman?* 'Who picks up her mail?'

'The manager says that the staff change all the time, and none of the current employees have any recollection of dealing with her.'

Jodie Bentley, Grace thought. 'Have you checked the electoral register?'

'Yes, I have. There's no one of that name.'

'Nice work, Jack.'

'Thank you, sir. Sounds to me like she doesn't want to be found.'

Grace smiled. 'You don't say!'

'I checked with the Border Control Agency at Heathrow. Her passport was scanned at 7.35 a.m. It would have been flagged if it had been recorded as lost or stolen, or if it had been a poor forgery – apparently forged passports often won't scan as forgers don't always get it absolutely right!'

'Do they retain information from these scans?'

'No, sir.'

'Great – why the hell not?'

'I don't know, sir.'

They both looked at the blurry photograph again for some moments. Then the DC continued, picking up the memory stick. 'I went up to the

CCTV Control Room at Heathrow to see if I could track Jodie Bentley's movements after passing through Passport Control. I've got her heading to the escalator down to Baggage Reclaim, but then she vanishes.'

'Vanishes?'

'Possibly she went into a toilet and changed her hair and put on a different hat. On this stick I've got the footage from the arrivals hall, but I couldn't see her on it. There's a dozen or so women of similar build emerging into it, but none of them that look like her, or are dressed like her. She had three large suitcases on a trolley at Atlanta Airport. She must either have got a porter or another trolley at the carousel.'

'What about the taxi companies and limousine services at the airport?' Grace asked. 'Any of those take a single woman to Brighton? Also, what CCTV footage is there of people outside the building?'

'I've put in a request for that footage and I'm working through the taxis and limousines, sir.'

Grace looked at the detective's eager face. 'Well done!'

'Thank you, sir.'

Next he called the Financial Investigations Unit at John Street police station. He spoke to Kelly Nicholls, and asked her to see if she could find anything on a woman, aged in her thirties, from the Brighton area who had recently been in the United States, going under the name of Jodie Bentley, Judith Forshaw or Jemma Smith.

Then he went home.

CHAPTER 29

Thursday 26 February

'Yes, yes, yes, yes! OH, YESSSSSS, YESSSSSS! Oh my God you are incredible! Yes, YES, YESSSSSSSSS! OHHHH, OHHHHHHHH, OHHHHHHHHHH!' Jodie screamed in ecstasy – or rather what she hoped sounded like ecstasy. She clawed her nails down Rollo Carmichael's naked back as, crushing her with his weight, he kept on thrusting as deep inside her as his not-very-well-endowed and slightly flaccid penis would go. She shot a discreet glance at her wristwatch. Only three minutes had elapsed. Too soon.

She'd been right in her original assessment of Carmichael. While he wasn't a lawyer or a banker, he had been a Mayfair art dealer in a very serious way. The Impressionists he'd dealt in ranged in value up to figures with ridiculous rows of noughts at the end. He had a house in Knightsbridge which he used just as an occasional pied-à-terre and which, from the address she had managed to get out of him, she had discovered on the internet to be worth a good ten million, and his main home was now here in the city, this beachfront house, valued at more than three million pounds. If she played her cards right, this could truly be the catch that set her up for life. And he had excitedly invited her to join him on an exotic cruise he'd booked – he was flying out on Saturday afternoon. He had no one to go with, could she possibly drop everything and join him – please?

He'd apologized earlier for not having any Viagra tablets. She'd whispered to him, very sensually, that she would consider herself quite a failure if she couldn't arouse him without them.

Now as he continued, as heavy as an elephant, grunting with grim determination, clammy with perspiration, his breath sweet with alcohol, she was reminded of a description by the former girl-friend of a grossly overweight MP, who had said that making love to him was like having a wardrobe fall on top of her with the key still in the door.

That was sort of what it felt like now.

To distract herself she thought about the different techniques of her past lovers – if that was the right word for her conquests. Walt Klein, fortunately, never lasted more than a few seconds before coming. Before him, Martin Granger, short and wiry, had used a curious rocking motion, as if drilling a bore hole. And before him, God, Ralph Portman was big on what he thought was erotic foreplay, repeatedly biting her nipples so hard she screamed in pain.

She glanced at her watch again. Coming up to four minutes. A respectable time. She needed him to feel a man, to believe that he was satisfying her because that would make him feel so good! Their first time. In this gorgeous house with huge bay windows overlooking the sea. Champagne in the ice bucket on the coffee table. Alcohol. Alcohol made these things bearable, doable and, just occasionally – although not right now – enjoyable.

It was their second date this week. She had a three-date rule, she'd told him cheekily when he'd made advances after their first dinner, just two days ago, on Tuesday. He would have come down to see her again last night, he told her, but he had to attend some tedious City Livery dinner, of which he was on the Court – whatever that meant.

She was still fretting about the break-in at her house. Although the house had an alarm, she never set it because the last thing she wanted was having to have keyholders, and the risk of the police going in and snooping around should it be set off. Hopefully this was nothing more than some low-life intruder taking advantage of the easy access via the scaffolding. Shit, the saw-scaled viper and the poison dart frog could have escaped out into the open – although in this cold air they wouldn't have survived for long. Luckily they were still there and she'd managed to put them safely into new vivariums. She had been so angry her first impulse had been to call the police – but she had worked hard to preserve her anonymity, and just had to swallow it. As well as the fact, of course, that keeping these creatures without a local licence was illegal. She had bought some of them at poisonous reptile shows in Houton, in Holland, and at Hamm, in Germany. Bringing them into England in their little cardboard boxes was always easy. She just walked straight through Immigration with them inside duty-free carrier bags.

She hoped the little bastard – or bastards – had been bitten. Serve them bloody right! It did occur to her this break-in might be connected to the memory stick and cash, but if that had been the case, the house would have been turned upside down. She doubted they'd have been put off by her reptiles.

She'd been fascinated by venomous reptiles ever since she was a small child and an uncle had given her a book on wild animals. The furry and fluffy ones hadn't interested her at all. But the snakes, spiders, crocodiles and frogs had. Other girls her age played with dolls. She kept snakes. Probably another reason, she had often reflected, why her father found her strange. Her snakes never minded that she had a big hooked nose and no tits.

One evening she put one of her grass snakes beneath the sheets at the bottom of Cassie's bed. Then she had lain in her own room and waited for the screams. They had sounded so sweet, so beautiful. Totally worth having the snakes confiscated the next day!

She'd met her first husband, Christopher Bentley,

in the reptile house of London Zoo when she was twenty-two; he was forty-eight and recently divorced. A few months before meeting him, she'd left home and used all her savings, together with a fake credit card – which she managed to use for a few weeks to draw out sums of cash – to have a Harley Street nose and chin job, followed by a boob job.

Having made a small fortune in property early on, and not needing to work again, Christopher's big interest was venomous reptiles. He had spent a considerable amount of his adult life travelling in India, Africa and South America, where he had developed a fascination for these creatures. He had written two books on venomous snakes and one on poison frogs, and had been the adviser on setting up reptile houses at several zoos in the UK.

She'd found him fascinating, too. And attractive. The first time she entered his own private reptile house, in the basement of his handsome Regent's Park home, a stone's throw from the zoo, she was captivated.

The walls were lined with glass showcases, housing a huge collection of deadly snakes, spiders and frogs. He knew so much about all of them, and delighted in sharing his knowledge. He had rattlesnakes, a death adder, a Gaboon viper, a saw-scaled viper, a tiger snake and a whole variety of black mambas, as well as a range of spiders, including redbacks and funnel-webs. He also had a fascination with scorpions, keeping Indian reds, deathstalkers and Arabian fat-tailed.

They excited her. She was awed by the power these small creatures had. The ability to kill a human being with a single bite or sting, or in the case of some frogs, just contact with their skin. Christopher told her, too, that a scorpion unhappy with its environment, or surrounded by a ring of fire, could commit suicide by stinging itself in the back of its neck.

She liked that. The thought that if she wasn't happy, she could just go, 'I'm outta here,' and end it all. She figured she would, one day. But not yet. Not, hopefully, for a long time. She was enjoying life and had plans. Big plans.

He had shown her the cabinet of meticulously labelled antidotes for the bites and stings of each of these creatures, and how to administer them – and in what time frame before paralysis or death. Most importantly of all, he taught her how to use the various implements he kept to handle his collection.

Mostly they were very basic, and the snakes he tended to handle with a metal stick, like a skewer with a curved end, and his bare hands.

On that first day, he took her to his reptile room to show her a new arrival, a small cardboard box sealed with gaffer tape containing a saw-scaled viper, which he cheerily told her had killed more people in the world than any other snake. It lived in Africa, the Middle East, Pakistan, India and Sri Lanka. It was extremely aggressive, he said, and moved fast, coiling and uncoiling in a sidewinder motion, making a sizzling sound as its scales moved together.

She was astonished to watch him pull away the gaffer tape with his bare, ungloved hands, and open up the box with his hooked metal stick. Then he upended it into a red plastic bin and slammed down a ventilated lid.

She'd noticed that even he had looked nervous during this last part of the operation.

'What's your fascination with these creatures?' she had asked him.

'Their power,' he had replied, simply. 'Here we are, us humans, with all our sophistication. Yet any of these creatures, some with brains the size of a pinhead, can kill us; some in hours, some in days.'

He had delighted in talking her through the biochemistry of their bites and stings. All the different ways that the venom acted on the human body without the antidote.

For some reason she found herself particularly drawn to the saw-scaled viper. The way its bite was fatal. And that there was only a two-hour window in which to administer the antidote.

Too bad, eight years after they were married, that Christopher had missed an antidote window. Well, not strictly true. She'd jolted his arm when he'd been holding a saw-scaled viper by the neck. And she had previously substituted the antidote with a placebo.

Hey ho, so much for the so-called *placebo* effect!

By the time he'd been admitted to the Toxicology

Unit at Guy's in London he was already bleeding through his eyes and every orifice.

He'd had to go. He was adamant he didn't want to have children, and that didn't fit with her plans. And he wasn't rich enough for all the things she wanted in life, including a child – she wanted this more and more badly as time went on, and her biological clock was ticking away.

But two good things had come from that marriage. A substantial chunk of his estate, after death duties, enabling her to buy property – a house and a bolthole flat in Brighton, and another bolthole flat in London – and not to have to worry about money in the short term. And she'd also learned the importance of having a glass door into the reptile room so you could see, before entering, if any of your pets were out of their containers.

Just like she had at home.

She glanced surreptitiously at her watch again. Enough time now. She began writhing, clawing wildly at him, and screamed out, 'OH, MY DARLING, YESSSS, YESSSSSS, YESSSSSSS, I'M – I'M – I'M—'

Suddenly, Rollo Carmichael shuddered, then stiffened in every part of his body except for the bit that actually mattered right now, which went limp and slipped out of her.

She felt his whole weight on top of her, crushing her.

'Darling?' she said.

There was no reply.

'Rollo? Did you . . .?'

He let out a faint gasp of air.

'Rollo?'

Gripping his head, she turned his face towards hers. He stared dead ahead. Unblinking. Nobody home.

'Rollo?' she said, gently. Then more loudly. 'Rollo? Rollo? No, don't do this to me. Rollo?'

There was no response.

CHAPTER 30

Friday 27 February

Jodie Bentley was a no-show. As Tooth had expected. As he had predicted. As he had told his paymaster, Sergey Egorov. If the Russian asshole had listened, Tooth wouldn't be standing in an icy wind, in falling sleet, freezing his nuts off. He'd be on a plane back to New York from Brighton, England, with the memory stick that Egorov had paid him one million dollars to recover. He always took his payment up front; he didn't need to do cash on delivery, because he always delivered.

He stood in a fleece coat, fur-lined boots and Astrakhan hat, a short distance up the hill at Brooklyn's Green-Wood Cemetery. At least, he figured, Walter Klein could take comfort in the fact that his casket was more luxurious than the jail cell he'd probably have spent at least the next fifteen years in. A plane, taking off from LaGuardia, thundered overhead. He heard the distant clatter of a helicopter and the even more distant, mournful *honk-honk* of a fire engine. Below, the funeral cortège was leaving. A long line of black limousines – a grand cortège, he thought, for a scumbag whose assets had all been frozen.

But Tooth wasn't here to judge the man.

A siren wailed. Another plane roared overhead. He put a cigarette in his mouth, cupped his hand over his lighter flame and lit it.

He waited, smoking it down to the butt, until the last vehicle had left the cemetery gates, then trampled it out in the grass. He walked back to his rental Ford, climbed in, started the engine and put the heater on full blast. Then he drove out of the cemetery, too. He headed to the storage depot where he deposited his gun and knife, then on to JFK Airport.

He dumped the car at the Sixt rental area in the parking lot, called his client from a payphone there and updated him.

'Go to England,' Egorov instructed him.

CHAPTER 31

Friday 27 February

It was Angi's birthday. Shelby told her he'd been given the night off from his warehouse job – by agreeing to work tomorrow, Saturday night, instead – so he could take her out to celebrate.

Angi had only recently moved to Brighton, from landlocked Coventry, having split up with her partner, and she was enthralled by the novelty of living in a seaside resort. So although he had no appetite today, he treated her to a fish and chip dinner with champagne at the Palm Court restaurant on the pier.

As she sat opposite him eating heartily, dousing her batter in salt and her chips in vinegar and ketchup, he sipped his glass of champagne and pushed his food around the plate, barely managing a couple of small mouthfuls.

'What's the matter, my sexy man – not hungry?'

'My appetite's for you,' he said with a forced smile. 'You're making me so crazy for you I can't eat!'

He felt her foot, minus shoe, pressing between his legs.

'I like you being crazy for me,' she said. 'I want you always to be crazy for me.'

He smiled again. He wasn't actually feeling that great, but he didn't want to spoil her big day. He finished his glass of champagne, called the waiter over and ordered a pint of lager, hoping that alcohol would make him feel better. Hell, he'd splashed out on a taxi here, so they could have a proper celebration, so might as well get his money's worth, he figured.

He'd woken that morning to find a small swelling on his ankle. But nothing that bothered him too much. It didn't seem to have grown any bigger during the day. But he definitely wasn't feeling right tonight, not one hundred per cent, not firing on all cylinders. He was a little giddy and a bit clammy, as if he had a touch of flu.

Of course, that was probably thanks to the horrible ride Angi had insisted he take her on, the Booster, before going to the restaurant. It had soared them up in the air, flipped them over and then over again. And then, when he thought he couldn't take any more, they'd gone over yet again. And again. His brain still felt as if it was revolving.

Angi looked at him and frowned. She took a tissue out of her handbag, leaned forward and dabbed his chin. 'It's still bleeding.'

Shelby touched his chin where he'd nicked himself shaving earlier. He'd put a styptic pencil on the cut, which normally did the trick. But as he removed his hand he saw fresh blood on his finger. He pressed the tissue to his chin, called a waitress over and asked if she could find a small plaster for him.

Then he downed the lager fast and ordered a second pint. Angi's plate was clean, he realized, as she picked up her last chip, mopped up the blob of ketchup on her plate and popped it in her mouth.

'Was it the ride?' she asked, chewing, looking at his huge, barely touched portion of cod.

He nodded, forlornly. ''Fraid so. Never been very good with them.'

'Feeling queasy, are you?'

'A little,' he admitted.

'I know a good cure for that!'

He felt her foot pressed into his crutch, stroking from side to side.

'Hmmmmn,' she said. 'I'm sensing some improvement.'

He gave her a weak grin. 'Yeah. Yeah, I'm sensing that too.'

'I think I need to take you home to bed,' she said.

'The night is young,' he said, evasively, unsure he could manage anything right now.

'My point exactly.'

She wiggled her foot.

He downed his second pint, hoping that might do the trick. It didn't. It sent him running to the toilets where he threw up violently.

CHAPTER 32

Friday 27 February

Tooth sat in the back of the limo taking him to JFK Airport. Whenever possible he took limousines in New York. He hated yellow cabs. He hated the often erratic nature of the drivers and the cramped rear quarters of many of the vehicles, sitting with his face pressed up against a scratched Perspex screen, having to endure an endless loop of advertising videos. He only took a yellow cab when he needed to.

Like last Saturday.

He wasn't looking forward to his shitty Continental night flight to London, in coach. He always flew coach, because no one took any notice of coach-class passengers. None of the cabin crew remembered them. And he had always survived by being a chameleon, by not being noticed or remembered. Just as he had in his days as a sniper in the military. He was good at being patient, waiting. He had nothing else to do with his time. No one to care for or worry about. Except Yossarian. And Yossarian was fine right now. Mama Missick would be spoiling the dumb mutt rotten. Just like himself, just like the dog, big old ugly Mama Missick didn't have anyone else in the world. They were three of a kind. Stuck together. Riding the carousel that was spinning at 1,040 mph. This meaningless Planet Earth. Riding and waiting for oblivion. Well, Mama Missick was different. She was waiting to go to Heaven.

Luckily for her, Tooth figured, one day oblivion would take care of her disappointment.

Tooth didn't do Heaven.

CHAPTER 33

The past

It happened eighteen years ago, but Jodie could remember it vividly. It *was* funny. Whatever her parents thought, Jodie found it funny. Almost hysterically funny. It still brought a big smile to her face. A smile of glee, a smile of satisfaction, a smile at the whole ridiculousness of it all.

But of course she hadn't dared to smile at that actual moment. She'd managed to look every bit as shocked as her parents.

It was the first anniversary of Cassie's death. Her sister was receding into the past in both her memory and in the photographs around the house. She was pleased to see that the really big portrait photograph of her, the one that sat in its frame on the windowsill in the lounge, the one in which she looked so truly beautiful, was starting to fade significantly.

There were so many photos of Cassie that the house had the feeling of a shrine. A shrine to Cassie. Beautiful Cassie. Daddy's pet, Mummy's pet, teacher's pet. Perfect Cassie. Jodie often wondered whether, if it had been her instead of her sister, would there have been this same outpouring of grief? This same kind of shrine?

She didn't think so.

Neither of her parents noticed that she had discreetly moved the big photo from its original shaded position into the bay window that got direct sunlight for hours. Already the colour was starting to leach out of her skin. *In a while*, Jodie thought, *she'll just look like a ghost. And that will be one less picture of her to haunt me!*

The family went to visit Cassie's grave that afternoon. Her father took the day off work. Her mother hadn't been back to work since Cassie died, she was still too distraught, still recovering after her breakdown from the shock.

Come on, woman, get over it! Jodie thought, silently. *You believe in God – you go to church every Sunday, so what's your problem? Cassie's in Heaven. She's probably the Angel Gabriel's pet. Jesus' pet. God's pet!*

Not that Jodie believed in any of that stuff. She didn't think her sister was any of those things. In her view, Cassie was just a bunch of rotting, desiccated skin, bone and hair in a fancy coffin that was rotting too, six feet under, in the huge cemetery off the Old Shoreham Road, where her grandparents were also buried.

Best place for her. *Good riddance*, she thought privately as she stood, sobbing and sniffing and pretending to be all sad that her sister was gone, cruelly snatched away – just as the wording said on her neat white headstone with the fancy carved script.

> *Cassie Jane Danforth*
> *Beloved daughter and sister*
> *Cruelly snatched away from us.*

'Cruelly snatched' – well that bit wasn't strictly accurate, she thought. *Fell to her death whilst walking along a coastal cliff path on a family holiday in Cornwall during the October half-term. Pushed actually.* But that was another story – best not to go there.

Later that evening, home in bed, Jodie wrote in her diary:

> We went for a pub supper after visiting the grave. Mum was too upset to want to go home right away and the poor thing was in no fit state to cook. So we drove out into the country to a gastro pub that mum and dad like, which serves the most horrid prawn cocktail I've ever eaten. Tiny little things, not much bigger than the maggots that are eating Cassie, and a lot of them still half frozen – and all smothered in a Marie Rose sauce that's had a flavour bypass. Mum has it every time and insists I should have it too. 'It's a very generous portion,' she always says.

184

A very generous portion of cold maggots in ketchup-flavoured mayo.

I can't believe I ordered it again tonight. It was even worse than before.

Even though he was driving, Dad drank two pints of Harveys and ate a steak pie and beans and ordered a glass of red wine with it – a large glass. Mum had a small sherry and they had an argument about who would drive. She insisted she would drive back. The food arrived but I had to run out of the room and into the toilet, to get away from the nauseating atmosphere.

It was just so ridiculous. The whole day and evening.

Mum's driving for a start. She drives like an old woman – well, she is an old woman, I suppose, forty-six is pretty ancient – but she drives like she's a hundred and forty-six – at a steady forty-six. She never goes over fifty, not even on the motorway. She never overtakes anything, not even bicycles unless she can see ten miles of clear road ahead. She just sits behind them. Irritating me. But not Dad.

He even told her to slow down tonight! We were doing fifteen miles per hour behind a bicycle and he actually said to her, 'Susan, slow down, you're too close.'

My family.

My embarrassing family.

The things they say.

But this really made me laugh. Mum suddenly said she wanted to light a candle for Cassie, have it burning on the table with us during our meal. So my dad went up to the bar and asked if they had a candle they could light for his daughter. Ten minutes later the chef and two other members of staff appeared with a small cake, with a candle burning in the centre of it, and walked towards us, all smiling at me and singing HAPPY BIRTHDAY TO YOU!

I'm still laughing about that, even though it's nearly midnight and I've got homework to do for tomorrow that I've not even started yet.

But, honestly, I have to say, I've not felt so great in a long time!

CHAPTER 34

Saturday 28 February

Six hours late. An hour out of JFK the flight had turned back because of a technical fault. They'd been deplaned and sat in the goddam terminal for over four hours before finally boarding again. They'd originally been scheduled to land at 7 a.m., now it was 1.30 p.m. Most of the day wasted.

Standing in the long, snaking queue for passport control at London's Heathrow Airport, Tooth yawned. He could stay awake for as long as he needed, and sometimes, concealed in enemy territory back in his days in the military, that meant staying awake for forty-eight hours or longer, waiting for a target to appear. But right now he was looking forward to a few hours' sleep in the room he had booked at the Waterfront Hotel on Brighton seafront. Maybe he was getting old.

He'd stayed awake in his cramped economy seat at the back of the plane for the entire flight, planning what he needed to do when he arrived.

Once the plane was taxiing at Heathrow and he

was able to get an internet connection, he'd pulled up a street map of Brighton and Hove on his phone, reminding himself of the layout of the city. Looking up the street Judith Forshaw had put down on the hotel registration form.

Western Road.

Was it a real or false address? Whatever. The news stories about Walt Klein said his fiancée was from Brighton. A city of just 275,000 people. New York was a city of eight and a half million people and he never had a problem finding anyone there.

It would be a slam-dunk to find her in Brighton.

He slipped his passport out of his pocket and checked the details he'd filled in on his immigration form. His name, for the purposes of this visit, was Mike Hinton. He didn't like travelling on false documents, they added a layer of risk that wasn't usually worth it. But with his recent history in Sussex, there would be a marker on his real name for sure. *Hinton. Mike Hinton. Accountant.*

Ten minutes later the immigration officer studied his passport, then asked him to remove his cap. Tooth lifted up the baseball cap, which he had pulled down low over his face, and gave the woman officer a pleasant smile, whilst trying to mask his concern that she had recognized him.

She looked at his passport again, back at his face, back at his passport, then closed it and handed it back to him. 'Have a nice stay in the UK, Mr Hinton,' she said and smiled back.

Tooth stepped forward without replying and took

the escalator down into the baggage reclaim hall, where he had his holdall to collect. He didn't like to let it out of his sight, but some of its contents would have been confiscated if he'd tried to take it as carry-on baggage.

When it arrived he picked it up off the carousel and strolled across to the green exit channel, his laptop bag and holdall both over his shoulder. He always travelled light. It was easier to buy clothes wherever he was, and bin them before leaving. In fifteen years of globetrotting, he'd never owned a suitcase. And for most of his jobs, he was in and out of a place without even needing to unpack what little he had with him. New York had been an exception; he'd been stuck there far too long, because he'd had to deal with assholes.

He was on his own here. Just himself and a woman who thought she was smart. But she clearly wasn't that smart. She'd been engaged to a crook with frozen assets, and now she'd stolen, clumsily, something she could never sell, and for which she was going to die.

Unpleasantly.

Tooth didn't do pleasant deaths.

CHAPTER 35

Sunday 1 March

'A friend of mine told me, many years ago, that the secret of life is to know when it's good,' Rowley Carmichael said, his arm tightly round Jodie's waist, wind whipping their hair about their faces. 'And right now it's really good. Incredibly good.'

She stared up into his eyes, her own sparkling brightly in the stern lights of the ship. As brightly as the stars above them, like gemstones in the velvety darkness of the warm night sky; like the diamond engagement ring on the black velvet pad of the ship's jewellery store that he had bought her just a few hours earlier, the price of which she had pretended not to notice. Although she was already thinking of a couple of shops in Brighton's Lanes where she would get a good price for it in a few weeks' time. 'I know it's corny, my darling, but I feel like that couple on the *Titanic* – remember that film?'

'Jack and Rose, weren't they called?' he said.

She nodded. 'Leonardo DiCaprio and Kate Winslet.'

'Weren't they on the prow of the ship?' he said.

'Want to go up to the prow?'

'Here's fine!' Smiling, he raised his flute of vintage Roederer Cristal and clinked it against hers. 'Cheers, my darling. To the future unsinkable Mrs Rowley Carmichael!'

'Cheers to my unsinkable husband-to-be!' she said, sipping her drink, then standing on tiptoe to kiss him. A long, long, lingering kiss as they both leaned against the stern rail, whilst she struggled not to let her revulsion show. His mouth was slimy, and his tongue felt like a foraging rodent running amok inside her own mouth. Fifty feet below them the wake of the ship glistened with phosphorescence before fading into the darkness of the Indian Ocean.

'I still can't believe you agreed to marry me,' he said. 'Incredible! We've only known each other properly for a few days.'

'I still can't believe you asked me,' she replied with a smile.

'I couldn't be happier, it wouldn't be possible,' he said.

Looking adoringly into his eyes, she was thinking that she could, she could be much happier. 'Wouldn't it be romantic to be married on this ship?' she said.

'On this ship – you mean – on board?'

She nodded enthusiastically. 'Yes! Wouldn't that be amazing? Just so romantic? I read somewhere that ship's captains can marry people!'

'I love your wildness,' he said. 'How spontaneous

191

you are! This is crazy! OK, let's do it, let's go and find the Purser and ask him the procedure!'

'God, I love you so much,' she said. 'I just love looking at you!' But as she continued staring at him she suddenly realized who it was he reminded her of. That faint flash of recognition she'd had on their first date.

Her father.

Below her feet she could feel the slight thrumming of the engines. She breathed in the scents, of varnish, fresh paint, the salty tang of the sea and the occasional whiff of diesel fumes. It was their first night at sea. The first port of call for the MS *Organza*, after departing her moorings in Dubai's Port Rashid cruise terminal earlier that morning, was Mumbai in three days' time. She was a handsome ship, resplendent in her gleaming white livery, barely one year old, carrying 350 passengers and from the sharp service, it felt there was double that number of crew. Rollo had already booked a four-week leg of a round-the-world cruise on the ship before they had met. It hadn't taken much persuading for her to join him.

She'd gone home in the early hours of Friday morning to pack her bags for the cruise, and then had taken her cat to board again at Coriecollies Kennels. Tyson hadn't been too happy about that, but then again, he was never too happy about anything. He'd get over it, and she'd make it up to him on her return. She'd also set up the timed feeds for the rest of her menagerie.

Their cabin was a glorious suite, with a balcony.

'Did you remember to take your insulin, my love?' she asked.

He patted the pocket of his white tuxedo, then pulled out the blue NovoRapid injector. 'Yep!' He put it carefully back in his pocket.

'You gave me such a scare the other night. I thought I had lost you – before I'd even properly got to know you. What do you remember about it?'

'Well, not much. It was a blur. That happens if my sugar levels get too low, I'm not able to think straight and then I pass out. It was my fault, I thought we were going to have some dinner, so I'd taken my jab and pill. Then somehow we never got as far as the door.'

She grinned. 'So it was my fault, really! I just couldn't keep my hands off you. I couldn't wait until after dinner, I had to have you, then and there. Right there! But, Jesus, I got so scared when you collapsed on me. The paramedics were really concerned when they arrived, you were delirious. Then I got really angry with you when you refused to let them take you to hospital.'

'I just needed sugar. I was fine. God, the thought of dying and losing you when we've only just met . . .'

She reached up and kissed him. 'Don't ever do that to me again, promise?'

'I think I learned my lesson.'

'Which is?'

'That when we're in the bedroom together it's impossible to keep my hands off you.'

'Don't ever let that change!'

'I won't.' He caressed her hair, running his fingers through her ringlets.

'Good!'

'You know, I still can't believe we met. I mean, we have so many things in common. Our love of art, opera, theatre, food, wine – and travel. Do you believe in soulmates, my darling?' he asked.

'I didn't, until I met you. But that's how you make me feel.'

'Me too! I think we met before, in a previous life, and now we've found each other again.'

'It's how I feel, exactly,' she lied, sweetly.

CHAPTER 36

Sunday 1 March

Shelby had stayed in bed all Saturday, vomiting regularly, and with an intermittent nosebleed. He'd vomited several times more during the night. He awoke, groggily, to see a concerned-looking Angi standing over him, dressed and holding a glass with a dark brown liquid in it.

'How are you feeling, my love?' she asked.

His head was swimming and he felt as if he was going to be sick again. His throat hurt from the acidic bile, which was all he had to puke up the last time, some hours earlier. 'What's the time?'

'Ten thirty. It's Mum's sixtieth birthday today, remember?'

'Urrr.'

'How do you feel? Do you want to come?'

Her parents lived in Watford. It was a good two to two and a half hours' drive away. No way could he face that. Nor her deadly dull mother who didn't like him anyway. He shook his head slowly from side to side, feeling the roundabouts.

'I have to leave in a minute. Try to drink some of this.' She handed him the glass.

'What is it?'

'Coca-Cola. I've been stirring it to get the fizz out. The sugar in it'll do you good. You've got to get something down you, you need electrolytes. You didn't eat anything last night. This will make you feel better.'

She helped him sit up and stared strangely at his face.

'What?' he asked.

'Where you cut yourself shaving – on Friday. It's bleeding again.'

'It can't be.'

'You must have knocked it and opened it up. I'll get a fresh plaster in a minute. First drink this.' She guided the glass into his hands and tilted it up towards his lips.

He sipped a little and screwed up his face. 'Yeccchhh.'

'Trust me,' she said. 'This will make you feel better. You've got a tummy bug – there's a lot of it going around at the moment.'

'I hope I haven't given it to you.'

'I feel fine,' she said. 'I've prepared two more glasses of this. Try to drink one every few hours, it really will make you feel better.'

'Coke?' he said.

'Trust me. Coke was originally created for stomach ailments.'

'You're kidding.'

She shook her head. 'It was a medicine originally, then people started to like the taste. I always drink it if I'm ill.'

He sipped some more, dubiously, unsure if he would be able to hold it down, and after a few moments, he realized it was actually making him feel a little less nauseous.

'Come on, get some more down – for me.'

He took a larger sip. Then another. 'Thank you, nurse.'

She kissed him on the forehead. 'Don't go to work tonight. If you give me their number, I'll phone them and tell them you're still ill.'

He shook his head. 'No – I – I'll see how I feel. I'll stay in bed and see how I feel later. I can't skip work again.'

'I'll speak to them, explain you're too ill.'

He sipped some more Coke. 'This is making me feel better. If I'm not right this afternoon, I'll ring the emergency doctor.'

'Phone me if you're not feeling better and I'll leave early and come back to you.'

'You're an angel.'

She grinned and kissed him again. 'I know.'

'Bitch!'

'You are feeling better, aren't you?'

'Come home as soon as you can. I've a feeling I might be really randy.'

'Keep the feeling!' She waved him goodbye and

slipped out of the bedroom. Moments later she rushed back in with a plaster and handed it to him. 'Sorry, nearly forgot!'

As soon as she was gone he pushed back the duvet. He'd kept a bandage round his ankle, intending to tell Angi he'd cut it tripping over some boxes at work, if she asked.

Gingerly he swung his legs over the side of the bed, leaned down and removed the bandage.

And stared in shock.

The skin around the bite was swollen, black and yellow and weeping blood.

Was it this that was making him feel so ill? A reaction to the snake bite? What had that thing been?

He dabbed the wound with a tissue, found some antiseptic cream in the bathroom cabinet, applied some and put on a fresh bandage. When he had finished he opened his laptop and started searching snakes. All he could remember was that the snake was brown and had a black marking on it. There were dozens and dozens of different species and types. He stared at the images without recognition. He'd only seen it fleetingly, in the beam of his phone torch.

If it was truly poisonous, surely he'd be dead by now, he reasoned. Didn't poisonous snakes kill you within hours? It was five days now. Maybe the bite was infected and he was suffering a reaction from that?

He'd see how he felt later.

CHAPTER 37

Fourteen years ago

The bandages had come off, and she looked like shit. Black eyes, her face blotched blue and red with bruises. But . . .

Her nose was brilliant! The kink had gone and now, instead, it was a perfect small, straight nose.

An exact copy of Cassie's.

The surgeon had done a brilliant job, working from the photograph of her sister that she'd brought in to the Harley Street clinic for her first consultation. On both her nose and her chin.

For the next two weeks she barely ventured out of her small flat, which was a short distance back from the sea in Brighton's Kemptown. And when she did, she was glad of the biting cold, because she could wrap part of her face in a scarf, mask her eyes with dark glasses and keep a cap pulled low.

Every day, checking in the mirror, the bruising was fading. The sculpting of her jaw the surgeon had performed was a masterpiece. Every day an increasingly beautiful woman was developing in the mirror, like a photograph in a darkroom tank, steadily coming to life.

Like the photographs of Cassie she studied daily, holding them beside her face in the mirror. As the scars faded, a more and more perfect image of Cassie appeared.

She had blown almost every penny of her childhood savings on this series of operations on her face and body, including money she had stolen over the years from her parents – as well as money she'd drawn out on the fake credit card she'd obtained – and it had been totally worth it!

And it was worth all the hard work waiting tables at a bistro in Hove in order to be free of her parents and independent.

They might have rejected her throughout her childhood as the ugly duckling, while they doted on Cassie. Poor long-dead Cassie.

But she hadn't finished with them.

A few weeks later, early on a Sunday evening, when she was certain her parents would be in, Jodie drove in her Mini to Burgess Hill. She hadn't seen them for months, ignoring the messages her mother left from time to time, and declining her request to spend Christmas with them.

Instead she'd spent the day alone in her bedsit, bingeing on movies she'd been storing up to watch, getting smashed on Prosecco and stuffing her face with a ridiculously large Chinese takeaway. She decided it was the best Christmas she'd ever had.

She parked outside the family house and walked past her mother's shiny new Audi, freshly washed and cleaned – no doubt by her father earlier today – and rang the front doorbell. The stupid triple *dingdong-dingdong-dingdong* chimed.

Inside, very faintly, she could hear the television.

Then the door opened and her mother stood there, in a baggy jumper, jeans and slippers. And just stared.

She heard her father's voice above the sound of the television in the living room. 'Who is it? Are we expecting anyone?'

Her mother continued staring straight at Jodie. As if she was staring at a ghost. Then she began shaking and called out, in tears, her voice quavering, 'Alastair! Alastair!'

Jodie stood and stared back. Her hair was dyed blonde and styled, from one of the photographs she had taken away, exactly the way Cassie's was on the day she died.

Her father came out into the hall, in loose-fitting brown cords and a blue V-neck over a pink shirt. He stopped in his tracks when he saw her, doing a double-take.

'Oh my God, what have you done, Jodie?' her mother said. 'Why – why've you done this?'

'Oh,' Jodie said, as if butter wouldn't melt in her mouth. 'You know, Sunday afternoon, hey! Just thought I'd swing by as I hadn't seen you guys in a while.'

Her father stepped forward into the doorway,

livid with rage. 'This is some kind of very sick joke, Jodie.'

Jodie shrugged. 'Oh, I see, you don't like my new look.'

'You nasty little bitch,' he spat back. 'You'll never change. Never. Just go away. Get away from our house, get out of our sight. Your mother and I never want to see you again.'

CHAPTER 38

Sunday 1 March

It had been after three in the afternoon by the time Tooth had finally got to his hotel, yesterday. He'd chosen this place because it was large and central, the kind of hotel he liked, where no one would take too much notice of him.

When he'd checked in, the lobby had been filled with men and women in business attire, each wearing a name badge sporting a company logo, all milling around, as if taking a break from whatever conference they were attending.

He was tired when he finally reached his room, and he knew it was dangerous to do too much when you were tired. That's when you made mistakes. So he just unpacked his few items, showered and changed into fresh clothes, went outside and smoked a cigarette, then returned to his room and crashed out.

He woke at 2 a.m., hungry, ate some chocolate from the minibar, then sat at the desk, flipped open the lid of his laptop, logged on to the hotel Wi-Fi and checked for emails. There weren't any. He wasn't expecting any. The email address he used, routed via five different Eastern European countries, was impossible for anyone to trace. And he changed the address every week. The only emails he got were replies to ones he sent.

He closed the lid and looked at the two photographs of the woman from the lobby of the Park Royale West Hotel. A good-looking woman, with some style.

Jodie Bentley or Judith Forshaw. Where was she?

This city wasn't on the scale of New York. If she was here, he would find her. All he had to do was recover the memory stick and teach her a lesson. Then he could head home.

It wasn't that long since he had last been here, and he could remember the geography of the city pretty well. And there was something that bothered him. The address he had for the woman, which she had given when registering in New York, was Western Road. From memory, it was a mix of shops and residential flats.

He googled the road and that confirmed it. A curious place for a woman like this to live – he imagined her, from her lifestyle, residing in a more ostentatious part of town. Perhaps this was a false address?

He wondered whether to put on his tracksuit and go out jogging and find it. His brain was wired, but his body felt leaden. He went back to bed and tried to sleep. A siren wailed outside. He heard drunken laughter in the corridor. He gave up after a while, got up and went for a run, in howling, salty wind and pelting rain, then returned to the hotel.

Eight hours later, wrapped in the padded anorak he'd bought in New York, and wearing a baseball cap, Tooth paid the Streamline taxi driver with a ten-pound note, telling him to keep the change.

Light rain was falling. It was freezing. He was tired. Jet lag. His body clock was all messed up. The route on his early-morning run had included where he was right now, 23A Western Road. The Brighton Barista.

Was there any shop in this goddam rain-sodden city that wasn't a coffee house?

He entered. Admittedly the place had an enticing smell. It was furnished with a number of tables, each with computer terminals. A single saddo sat at one, and a couple of men in bad jeans, bomber jackets and baseball caps sat at another, by the front window. Could they be plain-clothes cops, surveying the passers-by? He looked at them again and decided not.

He walked to the rear of the shop. There was a drinks menu on the wall and beneath it a display of cupcakes, a carrot cake and assorted panini under a glass counter. Behind the counter stood a bored-looking woman in her twenties, with a face that might have been prettier if it wasn't caked in make-up and her blonde hair hadn't been styled by Medusa, he thought.

'I'm looking for 23A Western Road,' he said.

'Uh-huh. You've found it.' She sounded like she'd rather be defrosting a fridge or watching paint dry than having to talk to him, or anyone. She had two black sticks in her hair. Tooth wondered for a moment how she would feel having them stabbed through each of her eyes.

'I've come to pick up mail for my girlfriend, Jodie Bentley. She also uses the name Judith Forshaw.'

'Uh-huh.' She tapped a keyboard beneath his line of sight. Then after a moment looked back at him with nobody-home eyes. 'Do you have her passport and password?'

Tooth gave her a smile. His best smile. 'I guess she forgot to tell me I needed them.'

'What's your accent?' she asked.

'American. Midwest. Wisconsin.'

She startled him by smiling. 'It's cute.'

'You think so?'

She nodded.

'Know what I think?'

She shook her head.

'You need someone to fuck your brains out.'

She smiled again. 'That's so cute. Know what I think?'

Tooth leaned forward, with the smile of a piranha. 'Tell me?'

'You're a nasty little perv and a lech. Go fuck yourself.'

She pointed up at the ceiling. He followed her

finger and saw the CCTV camera that was right on his face.

He cursed. Shit, shit, shit. Fucking jet lag. How the hell had he not looked for cameras when he'd come in? Instantly he turned and walked away, in confused fury. As he reached the door he heard her call out, in a big, loud, phoney Southern accent.

'Y'all have a nice day now!'

Without turning round, he raised a hand and gave her the bird with his middle finger.

'That the size of your dick?' she called after him.

Tooth stepped out into the drizzle. He was fuming. Tiredness had made him screw up and potentially be noticed.

He turned and stood for a moment, fighting his urge to storm back in. But that wasn't why he was here. It wasn't why he was paid to be here.

He strode angrily away.

CHAPTER 39

Sunday 1 March

While Rowley lay fast asleep, snoring beside her, Jodie was wide awake in bed, in their luxurious cabin, sitting up with her laptop balanced on a pillow, feeling the gentle motion of the ship rocking her in the light swell. Taking stock.

The daily ship's programme for tomorrow lay in front of her. The shore visit lecture; line dancing class; carpet bowls; craft class with Jill and Mike; bridge lessons; keep-fit classes – one in particular had made her grin, titled, 'Sit and Get Fit!' The evening highlight was the comedian Allan Stewart.

But she wasn't interested in any of the items. She was totally focusing on the plans she had made for her future, all those years back. The rich man Cassie had said she would marry only in her dreams. Well, there was one rich man who might be dreaming right now, judging from his rapid eye movements. And this time tomorrow she would be married to him. Sure, her right to inherit could be challenged by his family, but whatever the result she would be coming away with a handsome chunk of change after he died. All he had to do was make it through the night.

Then from tomorrow, with a ring on her finger and the marriage certificate signed, she could make her move. She looked at him. Mouth open, droning snore, drool running from the corner of his mouth, that same self-satisfied expression that so much reminded her of her father.

God, how I would love you dead!

She found a diary entry she had made way back in her teens – and, like all her old diaries, had scanned into a password-protected electronic document for safekeeping.

This entry, she remembered, must have been just before the time she'd put a nine-inch diameter Colombian Huntsman spider in Cassie's bed. The spider was totally harmless to humans, but both Cassie and her parents had a major sense of humour failure over it. And over the snakes and frogs – all harmless – that she liked to let roam free around her room.

All her arachnids and reptiles – even the ones her parents had actually *bought* her (at her request) for birthday and Christmas presents – had been confiscated, this time permanently. Afterwards she wrote:

There are a lot of myths about snakes – in particular about the venomous ones. Listen.

The saw-scaled viper is called the world's deadliest snake, because it kills more people than any other. In India alone it kills 58,000 people every year – 13,000 more than are killed in car crashes in the United States!

But it's not actually the world's most venomous snake – that title goes to the Belcher's sea snake – one bite has enough venom to kill one thousand people! But because it lives in the waters of South East Asia and Southern Australia, it rarely bites humans.

The black mamba is pretty cool. It's the world's fastest snake – it moves at twelve miles per hour and its bite can kill in thirty minutes. The king cobra can kill an elephant in an hour. The inland taipan can kill a human in fifty minutes.

I love that!

So many people are scared of them. Not me, though. No snake ever told me I had a hooked nose, no snake ever told me I had no tits. I don't judge them and they don't judge me. They need me to feed and water them. In return, they do me favours.

I feel they should be rewarded for services rendered. But how do you reward a snake? What do they appreciate? Food, shelter, water? Sometimes I think when I come back in the next life, I'd quite like to be a snake. Much less complicated. Did you ever see a snake look in a mirror and pull a face? Did you ever see a snake that had a complex about how it looked?

Me neither.

CHAPTER 40

Sunday 1 March

Tooth stood by the beach, in front of a row of shuttered Victorian arches, staring morosely through the rain out to sea. To his right was a large building site, with a central structure partially covered in scaffolding, out of which rose a construction like a huge spike soaring into the sky. A hoarding had a futuristic architect's drawing of something that looked to him like a spaceship and the wording *i360*. It reminded him of the Space Needle in Seattle.

A short distance out in the sea stood a rusting mass of girders, all that remained of what had once been the West Pier. Over to his left was the Brighton Pier and a short way along the shore, past the pier, what looked like a large wheel. He smelled rotting weed and boat varnish. He found seaside resorts in the rain depressing. This place reminded him in a way of Coney Island, where he'd once spent ten days in winter waiting for a man he'd been paid to torture and kill to show up. He didn't think there was a more depressing place on earth than Coney Island in the rain.

A new smell hit his nostrils, the aroma of a grilling burger or maybe French fries, that was making him feel hungry, despite the large room-service breakfast he'd eaten less than a couple of hours ago. He turned towards Brighton Pier, walking past a closed, gaily painted hut boasting the legend, in white letters on a turquoise strip, BRIGHTON SHELLFISH AND OYSTER BAR.

Head bowed against the wind, he was thinking hard about all the places a stylish woman like Jodie Bentley would visit, and where she would be known. He couldn't check the city records until tomorrow, so for now he decided to take her photograph around hotel bars, restaurants and cafés, and show it to cab drivers.

The one who had driven him to Western Road had shaken his head, blankly.

He walked up the steps onto the promenade and stared at the buildings across the road in front of him. A wide row of hotels and restaurants stretching for a mile or more in each direction. Right opposite him was the dark red facade of the Metropole Hotel. He crossed the road, entered, went up to the reception desk and approached one of the uniformed males behind it.

'I'm a private detective working for a US law firm,' he said. 'We're trying to trace this lady who has come into an inheritance that she's not aware of. We don't know her name, but we believe she

might be the deceased's only surviving relative.'
He showed photographs of Jodie Bentley.

Five minutes later, six different people had come to look at the photograph, and all of them had shaken their heads.

He left and walked the short distance along to the imposing white facade of the Grand Hotel, set behind its private parking crescent. Standing in front of the revolving door was a liveried doorman.

Tooth approached him with the same story. The doorman studied the photograph carefully, then said, 'Yes! I recognize her. She's been here a number of times, charming lady. She was here last week for dinner – let me think – was it Wednesday – no – I was off then. Tuesday. Yes, it must have been Tuesday!'

'Do you know her name?'

'No, but she had dinner here with a gentleman. Come with me!'

Tooth followed the doorman inside, past the reception desk, to the restaurant entrance, where there was a smartly dressed greeter.

'Michele, this gentleman's trying to find a lady who had dinner here last Tuesday.'

'Right, thank you, Colin.' She looked at the photograph Tooth proffered. 'Yes,' she said. 'Yes, she's been here a few times. Hold on a moment.' She opened a large, lined register filled with names and times, and flicked back a few pages. Then she ran a finger down it and stopped.

'I think this was her – the reservation was made

in the gentleman's name. Mr Rowley Carmichael. Is that right?'

'I wouldn't know,' Tooth said. 'What can you remember about them?'

She apologized for a moment as a group of four people turned up for lunch; she ticked them off her list and led them through into the restaurant. Then she returned. 'I'm trying to think. I'm afraid we have a large number of people every day. If you can wait a moment, I'll go and ask Erwan, the maître d', if he can recall anything. Can I borrow the photograph?'

Giving her his most charming smile, he handed it over, maintaining eye-contact flirtatiously.

She returned a few minutes later. 'Erwan remembers her!' she said. 'She was dining with a much older gentleman, and they asked him to call two taxis at about eleven o'clock.'

'Is there a particular cab company you use?' Tooth asked.

'A local firm, Streamline.'

Tooth thanked her. His charm offensive had got him what he wanted.

He left and walked along the seafront back to his hotel. He stopped outside to smoke a cigarette, then went up to his room and ordered a pot of coffee. As he waited for it to arrive, he worked on his story.

Then he picked up his phone and dialled the taxi company.

CHAPTER 41

Sunday 1 March

For the next few hours, Shelby slipped in and out of sleep. He tried several times to reach for the glass of Coke on the bedside table, but could not muster the energy. He listened to the continuous stream of cars and buses and lorries passing outside the window on the busy thoroughfare of Carden Avenue.

His phone rang.

It was Angi, calling to see how he was feeling and if he had been drinking the Coke she'd left him.

'Yes,' he said. 'Two glasses.'

'Well done!'

He put the phone back on the table and stared at the glass, untouched since she had left. It was now 1.30 p.m. His stomach felt as if it was on fire. Weakly, he hauled himself up in bed and managed to swallow some of the drink, then he checked his ankle again. It didn't look any worse than earlier; in fact, maybe a tiny bit better. Perhaps the antiseptic cream was helping. And maybe the way he was feeling was down to that damned bug. Dean hadn't made it to the pub on Thursday night because he'd got it. It was just a twenty-four-hour thing. So many people had been going down with it in Sussex – it had even made the local news. He'd start feeling better soon.

He had to.

It was Sunday. The one night of the week the couple in No. 27 Roedean Ridge went out. He'd tailed them for the past three Sunday nights, driving in their large BMW down to the Rendezvous Casino in the Marina Village, where they stayed and didn't return until well after midnight. Their regular pattern.

He'd found out from contacts that the secluded property belonged to a bent Brighton antiques jeweller. There had to be rich pickings in that house for sure. And if he went in early enough after they left, he would have sufficient time to find them. In another few weeks the clocks would go forward, which meant an hour less of darkness in the early evening.

He had planned to go there tonight to see if they went out again. He had to pull himself together and do it. He grabbed the glass and drank down the remaining contents, with difficulty.

Then he fell back into a sleep full of weird dreams in which hissing, crackling snakes spun across the floor like Catherine wheels that had fallen off their pins and were spitting sparks and flames.

He woke again, drenched in sweat, at 4.03 p.m.

217

with another nosebleed. He had to get up, somehow. He could not allow Angi to come home and take him to the emergency doctor. He didn't want the risk of having to lie to a doctor about where he worked and then have her phone them.

Up!

He hauled himself out of bed, placed his feet on the carpeted floor, then stood up. Instantly he sat back down again with a thump.

Shit.

He stood up once more, his stomach heaving, ran into the bathroom and sat on the toilet. He remembered something a cellmate had once said to him: 'When the bottom falls out of your world, come to Calcutta and let the world fall out of your bottom.'

He stood up and peered down. And a shiver ran through him.

The toilet was full of blood.

He flushed it, then stepped into the shower, feeling scared. What the hell was going on? Was this the bug or was it some kind of a reaction to the bite? And when was it going to stop? The powerful stream of hot water made him feel a little better.

He dried himself, then saw fresh blood was still coming out of his two-day-old shaving nick. He put more styptic pencil on it, then, to be sure, a larger strip of plaster, rolled deodorant under his arms and ran a hand across his damp stubble of hair.

Feeling slightly human again, he dressed in his dark clothes and trainers, and went downstairs. The two large tumblers of Coke that Angi had poured were on the kitchen table. He sat and sipped the first, slowly, thinking about the blood in the toilet. He must have burst a blood vessel in his backside, he decided.

Comforted by that explanation, he drained the glass and began to work, as Angi had instructed, on the second. After a couple of sips, he started to feel hungry. He stood up and walked, unsteadily, over to the fridge and opened the door. But everything he looked at – a wedge of Cheddar, a lettuce, a carton of tomatoes, a packet of ham, some eggs, sausages, bacon, a supermarket moussaka – all made him feel queasy again.

He closed the door, thinking. Maybe a joint might make him feel better. Kill or cure?

He stood up on a chair and reached for the tin marked BREAD, where Angi kept her stash. He lifted it down, put it on the table, removed the packet of cigarette papers, the plastic bag full of weed and a strip of cardboard, and rolled himself a fat joint.

Knowing she would not be happy, he replaced the stash in the tin and put it back on the shelf, then went out into the tiny back garden to smoke it.

Yes!

Wow, oh wow! That was powerful stuff. Wowwweeee!

When Angi arrived home, just after 6.30 p.m., he was standing in front of the television in the sitting room, with his fists balled, dancing to the sound of the Eagles, 'Peaceful Easy Feeling' blasting from the speakers.

'You're feeling better!' she greeted him, joyfully.

'Magic!' he said, still dancing. 'Magic that Coke!' He took her in his arms and nuzzled her neck. 'You know what, you're a genius! Magician! Will you marry me?'

'You already asked me that, and I said yes. Did you forget?'

'Just checking!' he said.

'Checking?'

'In case you'd gone off me during the night.'

'In sickness and in health,' she said. 'The marriage vows. OK? I'll be sick one day, too. Will that turn you off me?'

'Never!'

'What time are you off to work?'

He glanced at his watch. 'At 7.30. Just under an hour.'

'Have you eaten anything?'

'No, but I'm ravenous.'

'I've defrosted a moussaka. OK?'

'I'm so hungry I could eat the carton!'

'I'll save that in case you want to roll another joint,' she said, tartly.

Then he realized. Despite his elaborate precautions of replacing everything in the bread tin, and smoking it outside, he'd stubbed it out in the ashtray on the kitchen table.

CHAPTER 42

Sunday 1 March

The woman who answered the Streamline Taxi company phone could not have been more helpful after Tooth explained his predicament, in the very posh English accent he had practised for an hour before he made the call.

'Oh, hello, this is Andrew Mosley, General Manager of The Grand. We have a slightly delicate situation. Last Tuesday night we had a couple dining here who were – how should I say it – playing away. You sent two cabs, booked in the name of Carmichael, just after 11 p.m. One collected a gentleman, the other a lady. I'm afraid the lady's in a bit of a state. She's just rung to say that during the course of the dinner she lost the very expensive engagement ring her husband had given her. She thinks she took it off in the ladies' toilet when she washed her hands. He's due back tomorrow from a business trip and she's terrified he'll go berserk if she's not wearing it. Luckily one of our cleaners found it on the floor, but of course we've had no idea, until she just rang, who it belonged to. She's desperate to have it returned, but in her panic she forgot to give us her address or phone number! Could you possibly trace the booking and find out her address for me, and I'll get someone to run it over to her this afternoon?'

CHAPTER 43

Sunday 1 March

Shelby clipped on his seat belt then reversed his Fiat Panda out of the driveway and onto the street. Normally Angi would stand in the doorway to wave him off, but tonight, angry at him, she'd even turned her head sideways when he'd kissed her goodbye.

He struggled with the gear lever, crunching the gears loudly as he tried to engage first. Then the car bunny-hopped forward and stalled. He pressed the clutch in and twisted the key. The engine turned over and fired. As he started forward, the car bunny-hopping again, he heard the almost deafening blast of a horn as a van shot past him, nearly taking out a car coming in the opposite direction.

Shit. He checked his mirrors. Nothing behind him now. He accelerated and again the car jerked forward. Handbrake, he realized, and released it. Then he drove on, winding down past a pub called The Long Man of Wilmington, his vision blurry. He leaned forward in the darkness, peering through the windscreen, and switched on the wipers. But the screen was clear. Headlights came towards him. Two of them suddenly became four. He swerved slightly to the left and the car juddered over the kerb and on to the pavement.

Shit, shit, shit. He steered back onto the road, missing a tree by inches. He was clammy with perspiration. Ahead was a mini-roundabout, and suddenly he could not remember where he was supposed to be going.

Roedean. Kemptown. He halted at the round-about. There was nothing coming to his right. But he stayed there, eyes trying to focus. Checking then double-checking the road was clear. Then he heard an impatient toot behind him.

He wound down his window, pushed his arm out and gave the car behind two fingers. 'Fuck you!' he said.

Suddenly a shadow loomed towards him. A man, towering over him. Shelby smashed the gear lever into first and jerked forward, turning left into London Road, accelerating hard. He saw red tail lights ahead. Bright headlights coming towards him, one set after another. Each so bright they felt like they were burning his retinas, as he if was staring at the sun through binoculars. 'Dim your lights!' he shouted. 'Dim your lights, bastards! Dim your lights!'

Then red lights in front were growing brighter. Brighter. Brighter still. Shittttt! He stamped as hard as he could on the brake pedal. The little

Fiat slewed forward, its tyres squealing, and came to a halt just inches from the tail-gate of the lorry right in front of him.

He sat still, his whole body palpitating, his head swimming. After a minute or so the lorry moved forward again, over the green traffic light and on past Preston Park. He ought to turn round, he knew, he wasn't up to this – turn round, go back to Angi, go back to bed. But he drove on, fighting it, trying desperately to concentrate, to focus. 'Focus!' he shouted at himself.

His voice sounded strange. Sort of echoing around inside his skull.

He stared at the tail lights of the lorry, imagining it was towing him, that there was a long rope between them he needed to keep taut. No slack. He was safe all the time he stayed behind this vehicle. Just follow it. Follow it. He braked when it braked, accelerated when it accelerated. They crossed over more green traffic lights. Stopped at a red. Moved on. Keeping that rope taut.

But the lorry indicated right.

'Gooshbye,' Shelby slurred. He was going the other way. Left. East.

Then he frowned.

He was at a roundabout. Right in front of him were the dazzling lights of Brighton Pier. Shit. He'd come too far, totally missed the earlier turn-off he'd intended taking into Edward Street.

Bugger. Shit. But no matter. He could go along Marine Parade instead.

He continued to stare at the lights of the pier – and of the Brighton Wheel to the left. So many lights. Like a thousand torches all beaming straight into his eyes.

He heard the toot of a horn behind him. He put the car into gear and stalled it. He pushed in the clutch and the engine turned over without firing. There was another toot behind him, louder and longer. He twisted the key in the ignition and the engine again turned over without firing.

No, don't do this to me. Do not fucking do this to me.

Headlights flashed behind him now, flooding the interior of the car with a light so bright it was blinding him. Another blare of the horn. He tried again and the engine stuttered into life, backfired, then caught.

Drenched in perspiration, he crunched the car into gear and jerked forward, then stalled again. He was losing track of where he was and why he was here.

He'd engaged third instead of first. The lights behind him again flashed angrily. He started the car once more, got first, then shot forward, right in front of a taxi coming across the roundabout which also flashed its lights and hooted angrily at him. He accelerated hard onto Marine Parade, the front of the taxi filling his mirrors, still flashing its lights and hooting at him in fury.

He changed up a gear, holding the accelerator pedal to the floor, looking at the lights behind

226

him, in front of him, all around him. Mesmerized. Two big orange globes like setting suns loomed ahead.

Then, right in front of him, almost in silhouette, he saw a woman pushing a buggy.

Zebra crossing.

The orange globes.

The woman staring at him. Frozen.

He was closing on her.

His foot stamped on the brake pedal. But it wasn't the brake, it was the accelerator.

He swung the steering wheel wildly to the left. Almost instantly the car stopped dead, with a massive jolt, a metallic boom and, simultaneously, a loud bang, like a gunshot.

He smelled cordite.

Had he been shot?

He could see nothing through the windscreen except for the buckled bonnet pushed right up. Had he killed the woman and the child?

He stared, bewildered, around him, his ears popping. Then, in the moments before he passed out, he noticed what looked like a large spent condom hanging out of the steering wheel.

Or it could have been an octopus.

He heard someone shouting.

Then a massive bang above him sent his head crashing forward into the wheel.

CHAPTER 44

Sunday 1 March

The wind had died down and the rain had stopped, as Tooth climbed out of the taxi at the junction of Roedean Road and Roedean Crescent. He gave the driver a ten per cent tip, knowing he was more likely to remember the people who didn't tip than the ones who did, and strolled off into the darkness. He wore Lycra beneath his clothes and a hairnet beneath his baseball cap, to minimize any risk of dropping anything that could give an investigating team his DNA.

There were smart, detached houses all around. Mostly mock Tudor, reminding him of houses in Beverly Hills where he had once done a hit, and where he had met his dog. This was a much more likely place for Jodie Bentley to be residing than Western Road, he thought. He turned right into Roedean Crescent, and began to walk along it, looking at the house numbers and counting them down until he reached No. 191.

He stared at it. The house sat a short distance

below the street. There was an alarm box high up on the front wall. A light was on in an upstairs window, and another downstairs. A swanky place, architecturally in keeping with the neighbourhood, and with an integral double garage. There was a builder's sign by the entrance, and scaffolding had been erected along one side of the house. Behind the scaffolding, one first-floor window looked securely boarded up.

He stood still, watching the house for several minutes for any signs of movement inside. To his right he saw a bobbing light and the flash of a hi-viz jacket under a street lamp. An approaching cyclist. He took a few tentative steps down the tarmac driveway, keeping close to the bushes on the right. The cyclist passed. A few seconds later he heard a car. He held his breath, ready to step right into the bushes. But it carried on along the road above him.

He hurried down the drive and into the porch, rang the front-door bell and heard a faint, shrill ring. It was followed by silence. No frantic barking of a dog, which was good. He didn't like having to kill dogs; it wasn't their fault their owners were assholes. After some moments he rang again. A third time.

Then a fourth time, a real long ring.

He pushed open the letter box and peered through. The place had a feminine look about it. Parquet flooring. Contemporary furniture. Modern art on the walls.

No sign of life.

He'd figured that most likely she lived on her own. And was out right now. On a date? Gone to a movie? Away for the weekend? In another home she also owned, perhaps?

With gloved hands he pulled from his pocket a tool he had made himself, some years back. Its shell was the casing of a Swiss Army penknife. If any customs officer had searched his hold luggage, they would have dismissed this innocuous-looking piece of a traveller's kit. But he had removed all of its tools, apart from the large blade to which he had fitted a locking device, turning it into a flick knife, the marlin spike, which also could lock into place and was the perfect length to stab someone through the eye or ear and pierce their brain, the screwdriver and the scissors which always came in handy. The rest of the tools were replaced with his set of lock-picks.

If he needed further proof about the dubious nature of the occupant of this house, it was in the length of time it took him to work away at the three heavy-duty locks that secured the front door. It was a full five minutes before it finally swung open.

He stepped into the hall, the spike protruding between his fingers, and closed the door behind him, listening for any beeps of the alarm being triggered. Then he clocked the internal keypad on the wall, close to the door. A steady green light was glowing. It had not been set. Was someone in the house?

He called out, loudly, 'Hello?'

Silence.

The house had an empty feel and was cold. Scattered on the floor was a small amount of junk mail and one brown, official-looking envelope addressed 'To The Occupier'. Nothing else. Switching on his torch, he went through a door on the right, into a tidy living room. There were two modern white sofas, a curved-screen television on the wall, a coffee table on which sat a glass ashtray, and two framed photographs on the mantelpiece above a large fireplace with an empty grate. One photograph was of a grey and white cat, curled on a rug on the floor. The other was a woman in jeans and a black roll-neck, grinning at the photographer, with an enormous python coiled round her neck and part of her body.

He didn't need to check the photographs he had in his inside pocket to know this woman was his target. The woman using the names Jodie Bentley and Judith Forshaw.

He went back into the hall and down a short corridor on the far side, which led to a washroom. Then further along the hall he entered a large, high-tech kitchen, with an island unit in the centre. Lying on it was a notepad, with a blank top sheet of paper and several previous pages torn from it. In a corner, on a shelf next to a fancy oven range with an induction hob that looked like it had never been used, was a cordless handset sitting in an answering-machine cradle.

The display showed no messages. He picked up the handset and opened the calls list. It was empty. Maybe, like himself, she only used a cell phone, and kept this landline for emergencies, he speculated.

He noticed a strange, square stainless-steel machine that looked like it belonged in a laboratory rather than a kitchen. It had a raised section in the middle with several tube connectors, and a heavy-duty porthole on the front with a row of dials and switches beside it. The manufacturer's name on it was Lyophilizer, and the model number was LABGO MN4. It was a freeze dryer. Why did she have one of these? he wondered.

On a work surface there was a box of cat-food pouches. She had a cat. Where was it? Inside or out – or was it here at all? Had she gone away and taken the cat with her? Or put it in a cattery?

He went over to the fridge. It was one of those big American fridge-freezer affairs, all plumbed in with an ice and cold-water dispenser on the outside. He opened the door and peered in, interested to see what the sell-by dates of its contents were. He noticed a pack of smoked salmon, eggs, butter, an open carton of soya milk and a half-empty bottle of skimmed milk, with four more days of life according to the date stamp. Some apples, blueberries and grapes.

Opening the bottom freezer section, he recoiled in revulsion. It was full of packs of dead mice and rats. He loathed these creatures. He hated rodents.

Vermin. What were they doing here – treats for the cat? Was that the reason for the freeze dryer? He closed it, turned away and opened an internal door which led to a large garage, housing a dark-blue Mercedes 500SL convertible, shiny clean. He had a good look around the garage, then went back into the house, going upstairs and continuing his search.

There was a landing with a wall at the far end and five rooms leading off. He checked each of them in turn. A bedside light, plugged into a timer switch in a large bedroom, was on. It was as luxurious but as sterile as a hotel room. Three guest bedrooms equally could have belonged in a hotel. Then a small den, with a desk, bookshelves, wiring for a computer which wasn't there, and a router.

Something struck him as strange. There were barely any photographs anywhere in the house – only the two in the living room.

He went through all the drawers in the desk. In one he found two bunches of keys, both with a yellow tag marked 'Front Door'. He pocketed one set. Next he checked the bookshelves. There were companies that sold fake books, with hollow interiors where you could hide things like jewellery and keys. But all the books were real.

He went back out onto the landing and shone his torch up and down, noticing some scratches low down on the wall at the end of the landing.

Curious, he walked up to it and knelt. His training as a sniper in the US army had honed his eye to look for anything out of the usual in any environment he found himself in. Any signs that someone else might be there, maybe waiting to kill him.

Something had been scratching away at the paintwork, but only up to a height of about two feet. He thought about the pouches of cat food on the countertop. Had the cat been scratching? Why? Was there a mouse in the cavity beyond? He shone the beam of the torch over it. He'd learned to read tracks in the ground. Animal and human tracks. Fresh tracks and old tracks. Some of these scratches were recent, some much older. A family of mice or maybe rats breeding in the cavity? He rapped on the wall. It was hollow.

He thought about the layout of the house. The scaffolding outside. With the boarded-up window. But he'd not seen a boarded-up window in any of the rooms he'd been in.

He went downstairs and outside, and looked up at the scaffolding. The boarded-up window was, he realized, on the other side of that wall. What was behind it?

What was the cat so anxious to get at?

CHAPTER 45

Sunday 1 March

PCs Jenny Dunn and Craig Johnson, responding on blue lights and wailing siren to the Grade One call, saw several cars pulled up ahead, just past the roundabout in front of the brightly lit Brighton Pier. A knot of people stood around, several of them vulture-like, as was usual these days at an accident scene, taking photographs on their phones.

As they drew close, slowing down, they saw a small Fiat embedded in a lamp post a short distance from a zebra crossing, its rear sticking out into the road at a skewed angle. The top half of the lamp post had snapped off, crushing the roof of the car.

Both unclipped their seat belts before the patrol car had come to a full halt. Jenny Dunn pulled on the handbrake and Johnson switched the response car's lights to their stationary flashing mode. They jumped out, all their training for this kind of incident kicking in, and ran forward. It looked like a single vehicle RTC. Sunday night in central Brighton – possibly a drunk driver. Some of the onlookers, enjoying the last hours of the weekend, certainly looked like they'd had a drink or two. The ones standing out in the road were in danger themselves. A man in jeans and a bomber jacket was tugging frantically at the Fiat's jammed driver's door.

As quickly as possible, they needed to establish the status of anyone inside the car, clear the area around it, call the ambulance service – if no one had already called them – and, from the look of the impact, even from here, the Fire and Rescue would be needed too, with their cutting gear.

They pushed their way, urgently, through the growing crowd.

'I saw it 'appen!' a man shouted at them.

'Bastard nearly killed me and me kid!' shouted a woman with a pushchair.

They ran up to the car. It was an old model Fiat Panda, its bonnet embedded, in a V-shape, into the lamp post, the broken top half of which had partially flattened the roof. One person, unconscious, in the driver's seat, his head pinned at an unnatural angle, by buckled steel, against the steering wheel. PC Dunn shone her torch in and saw the limp white airbag. A chill ran through her.

'Oh, shite,' she said in her strong Northern Irish accent.

PC Johnson ran back to the car to grab a roll of police cordon tape. PC Dunn radioed for an ambulance and Fire and Rescue Service – and was told both were already on their way.

CHAPTER 46

Sunday 1 March

'Remember,' Johnny Spelt had said earlier that afternoon to the director of the Latest TV crew who had been shadowing them for the past week, making a documentary about the Kent, Surrey and Sussex Air Ambulance service, 'the pilot is always the best-looking person aboard the helicopter!'

In the rest room at the rear of the hangar at Redhill aerodrome, where the duty crew relaxed between call-outs, the pilots in green and the medics in red jumpsuits were seated around the table, ribbing Spelt for his remarks.

'Best-looking?' said Dee Springer, a short, ginger-headed Australian who was over in the UK on secondment, training for a career as a flying doctor back in her homeland. 'In yer dreams!'

'So in that case,' said Declan McArthur, a tall young doctor with a shaven head and easy smile, 'I guess we're going to have to switch roles, Johnny!'

'Haha!' He bit into his cheese and pickle

sandwich. It had been a long day and they were all tired. In an average twenty-four hours the Air Ambulance was called out five times. But today, in addition to interviews with the documentary film crew, they'd done five on their shift alone – the last to a motorcyclist suffering severe head injuries after a collision with a van in Eastbourne. They'd flown him to the best specialist unit for head trauma in the south-east of England, St George's in Tooting, and had only just returned. In thirty minutes they would be going off duty. Exhausted, they were all hoping there would not be another call.

The best chance patients have of recovering fully from severe head injuries is to be treated within four hours. Had the motorcyclist been transported by road, by the time the ambulance had reached and transferred him, it would have been a good four hours and probably longer. The helicopter crew had him on the operating table in just under ninety minutes.

'Declan,' the former military pilot said, good-humouredly. 'You want to take the controls? Be my guest. So long as I'm not on board when you do.'

'Wuss!'

'Live dangerously for once, Johnny,' Dee Springer said.

'Live dangerously?' the pilot retorted. 'I flew missions in Afghanistan. OK?'

'Respect!' Declan McArthur raised his hands.

'Yeah, I'll grant you that!' the Australian said.

'So don't you find this work a bit tame after a war zone?'

'You know what I like about this job?' Johnny replied.

'No, but I think you're about to tell us,' said Declan.

'It's very nice to land a helicopter without anyone shooting at you.'

Suddenly the purple phone in the room rang.

'Bollocks!' the doctor said, checking his watch as he walked over to answer it. 'Just a few more minutes and we'd be off shift! Typical!'

'Bad attitude!' chided the pilot.

CHAPTER 47

Sunday 1 March

Tooth, standing on the wooden platform on the first-floor level of the scaffolding, heard the distinct thrashing of an approaching helicopter. A short while earlier, listening to the howl of sirens, he had waited, concealed in the garden, holding the chisel and hammer he had found in the garden shed, in case they were coming to this house. But some distance away, the sirens had died down.

Emergency vehicles attending an incident – or accident – of some kind. He set to work on the window boarding. Someone had done a thorough job, and it was a full ten minutes before he'd removed enough of the wood to be able to see into the interior of the room.

He didn't like what he saw.

It was a very well-equipped reptile room, lined with glass vivariums, lamps, water pumps and timer-controlled feeders. That was the reason why she had all the dead rodents in her freezer.

He could see snakes, including a huge python, a

boa constrictor and some much smaller ones, spiders, frogs and several vivariums teeming with scorpions. Nasty-looking beige ones with tiny claws. For his last mission in the army, to Iraq, he'd been given a lecture on identifying these critters. The smaller the claws, the more deadly the sting. And the ones he could see, in a row of vivariums lined against one wall, had claws that were all but invisible.

Jodie Bentley had weird taste in pets, he thought. Not his thing at all. He hated all these fuckers. Not much scared him, but reptiles did.

The cat had been lucky not to scratch all the way through the wall. Didn't it know the saying 'curiosity killed the cat'?

He could see a glass door, but it looked like there was a solid wall behind it, and that made him very curious. How come she had a room that had no apparent door into it?

The helicopter was coming closer. He looked up and saw the lights only a short distance away. For a moment he wondered if it was a police helicopter looking for him, and flattened himself against the house.

CHAPTER 48

Sunday 1 March

The brightly lit skyline of Brighton was dead ahead of them in the clear night sky, as the twin-jet, black and white liveried MD 902 Explorer helicopter, flying on visual at 155 mph, tracked the A23 south. Johnny Spelt, the pilot, observed the familiar night landmarks of Shoreham power station to the west, the Palace Pier, as he still liked to call it, and the Brighton Wheel to the east of it. It was easy to see the entire shoreline – the long necklace of street lights, beyond which was the pitch dark of the English Channel.

He lived in Brighton and knew the geography of the city intimately. A short distance in front of the Wheel was a whole cluster of flashing lights of emergency vehicles. Liaising on the radio with the police inspector on the ground, he descended to 500 feet and hovered.

Below they could see a car embedded in a lamp post, part of which had fallen on the vehicle's roof, with a cordon round the scene. Inside the cordon was an ambulance, a fire engine and several police cars.

'Golf Kilo Sierra Sierra Alpha,' crackled the inspector's voice.

'Golf Kilo Sierra Sierra Alpha,' Spelt responded.

'Please land in East Brighton Park, there's a car waiting to transport you to the scene.'

As he spoke, Spelt could see below them to the left the wide, dark area of the park at the bottom of Wilson Avenue. He pulled on his night-vision goggles, wiggling the strap around his headset, and looked down, studying the area carefully. Apart from a figure some distance away exercising a dog with a ball-thrower, and the flashing blue lights of the waiting police car, the area was deserted. Plenty of room for them. He removed the goggles and switched on the helicopter's powerful search light, immediately able to see the greensward of the park.

Two minutes later they touched down. With the rotors still turning, Dee Springer and Declan McArthur unclipped their safety harnesses, removed their headsets and hung them up. Then, clutching their bags of medical kit, they jumped out onto the grass, clambered into the rear of the waiting police car and were driven the half-mile to the accident scene.

They were met at the cordon by a paramedic who briefed them quickly.

'His head and legs are trapped and the fire crew is cutting him free. He appears to have severe head and spinal injuries as well as what looks like internal haemorrhaging.'

The paramedic raised the blue and white police tape and they ducked under and ran across to the car, pulling on protective gloves and barely glancing at several police officers close by. The driver's door had been cut free and was lying on the road, and two Fire and Rescue officers were crouched down, cutting through the front of the roof with a huge hydraulic pincer. Inside the car was a thin man, all in black, wearing a black beanie and leather gloves, his neck twisted. Dee Springer shone her torch in. The man was barely conscious. His face was the pallid colour common in any trauma victim, but blood was leaking from his eyes, nose and mouth. He was breathing in short, clearly painful bursts.

'Fubar Bundy,' she said under her breath. The gallows humour of her profession. It stood for 'Fucked up beyond all recovery but unfortunately not dead yet'.

Declan kneeled and spoke to the driver. 'Hello,' he said. 'Can you hear me?'

'Lurrrrr,' the driver responded.

'I'm a doctor. What's your name?'

'Lurrrshhhh.'

'Can you move your arms?'

The driver raised them a fraction and half closed his hands.

Declan heard the crackle of a radio and a siren wailing in the distance, coming closer. 'We'll have you out in a few minutes and we're going to fly you to hospital.'

Normal practice with trauma victims was to inject them with a ketamine-based anaesthetic, to restrict the capillaries and reduce blood loss. Clearly some major internal bleeding was occurring.

He peeled off the man's left glove, to take his pulse. Then stared in shock for some moments, as he looked at the man's hand in the beam of his colleague's torch. Blood was leaking out under his fingernails. He curled his finger round the man's wrist and quickly found the median nerve. He'd been expecting him to have a weak pulse, but to his surprise it was hammering, dangerously. He counted, checking against his watch.

One hundred and eighty, he estimated broadly after counting for twenty seconds. Enough to kill someone with a heart condition or give them a stroke. He looked back at the man's bleeding eyes. His pupils were hugely dilated.

'Have you been taking any drugs?' he asked, gently.

'Lurrrrrrrshhh. Lurrrrshhh.' Without warning, he coughed up a large globule of bright blood which spattered on the white, sagging airbag.

The doctor's brain was racing. The man must have taken something – but what? Brighton was a party town. He'd attended people in a bad way here before, clubbers who'd swallowed a whole cocktail of stuff they'd bought from street dealers. But he'd never before seen symptoms quite like this.

'Can you tell me what you've taken tonight?' he asked, firmly but calmly.

'Shnufog,' the man murmured. His voice was almost drowned out by the grinding sound of the hydraulic cutter.

'Could you say that again?'

'Frog.'

'Frog?' Dee said, very gently, kneeling beside him. 'Did you see a frog?' she coaxed.

The whites of his eyes were veined with red and blood ran, like tears, from between his lids. 'Schfrog. Schnake.'

'You saw a frog and a snake? Have you taken any drugs tonight?'

The man's eyes were closing. Declan took his pulse again. The rate was lower this time. He wasn't sure whether this was a good or bad sign. He'd never encountered anything like this. He asked his colleague for the syringe and ketamine.

'Shankle,' the man said, suddenly. 'Shankle.'

'Stay with us!' Dee said. 'Please stay awake and tell us as much as you can remember. What have you taken?'

'I think he said *ankle*,' Declan said. He looked at the man's face. 'Is that it? Your ankle?'

But his eyes were shut now and he no longer responded.

The doctor leaned into the footwell, with his torch, pulled up the man's trouser legs and pushed his socks down. He could see swelling and bruising round the right ankle, and two tiny pinprick marks.

'Have you injected yourself?' he asked, but got no reply.

He then checked his pulse again. It was dropping at an alarming rate. Dee tapped him on the shoulder and signalled for him to move out of earshot of the patient.

As he stepped a couple of paces back from the car, Dee Springer said, 'Look, I think he's been poisoned – either taken some drug or eaten something. I heard of symptoms like this from someone who'd eaten a puffer fish that hadn't been prepared properly. Could it be something highly toxic like that?'

'Take a look at his ankle. I think he's injected something or possibly been bitten by something very small – and I don't know what to give him,' Declan said. Normally calm, able to cope with any victim however bad his or her condition, he seemed close to panic at this moment. The possibility was also going through his mind that this man might have some kind of tropical disease that could be contagious. If so, there was no way they could take him in the helicopter and risk contaminating it for future patients.

Dee leaned close to the victim. 'Sir, we're going to help you get better. But we need you to tell us what's happened. Did you eat something tonight? Have you taken any drugs? Has something bitten you? Have you been abroad recently?'

There was no response.

She stepped back and said to the doctor, 'We

247

need to get him to the poisons unit at Guy's in London – that's my view.'

Declan checked the man's pulse again. It had dropped to thirty-five. One hundred and eighty down to thirty-five in the space of minutes. Guy's was an hour's flying time away. It would be close to 10 p.m. by the time they got him there. They would radio the patient's symptoms ahead of their arrival, giving the hospital time to get a specialist team on standby. But if he had a tropical disease, which might be contagious, could they take the risk of him contaminating the helicopter?

They had to give it a go, he decided. They always gave it a go. And, more often than they sometimes dared to believe, they succeeded.

Those were the sweetest moments. The reason they all did this job.

CHAPTER 49

Sunday 1 March

Tooth found it after twenty minutes of meticulous searching. The remote control was at the back of a shelf above a row of dresses in dust protectors, hanging in a closet in a spare room. When he stood out on the landing and pressed it, the wall at the end began to move sideways, slowly, steadily, to reveal a glass door, the one he had seen through the window.

He stood, waiting until it was fully open, and stepped forward. Through the glass, to his disgust, he could see the containers of reptiles. He waited some moments, just in case something in there had gotten out, then armed himself with the locked blade of his knife and stepped in through the glass door, instantly screwing up his nose at the rank, sour smell of the creatures housed here.

He shone his beam around, all the time keeping a wary ear open in case the woman suddenly returned. But even more of a wary eye on the floor and up at the ceiling in case anything roamed free in here.

A large humidifier in the centre of the floor made a steady hum. The atmosphere was damp and warm, tropical. There were some broken vivariums on the floor, and on a shelf above them were several different-sized snake hooks; a pair of heavy-duty, long-sleeved gloves hung from a peg. Apart from this small area and the window area, the rest of the room was stacked to the ceiling and wall-to-wall with glass vivariums. Each was plumbed into a water system, with its own lighting, and most of the creatures inside appeared motionless.

Tooth's survival when he had been in the military, serving over-seas in desert and jungle environments, had partly depended on not being bitten by anything venomous, and he had a fairly good knowledge of dangerous reptiles and arachnids.

In one of the containers, with a habitat of small rocks, sand and plants, was a shiny black spider, about three inches across, with a leathery-looking black sac on its back shaped like a rugby ball. A funnel-web, he recognized. Capable of killing in fifteen minutes. In another miniature tropical forest he saw the ugly black carapace of a large scorpion. Without a swift antidote, its sting would be fatal to even a strong, fit human. Another section of vivariums, with misted sides, contained several small, ochre-coloured frogs with black eyes. Golden dart frogs, he knew. Reckoned to be one of the most deadly creatures in the world.

Next to them was a stack of vivariums containing small snakes. Saw-scaled vipers. Against the far wall was the biggest of the containers, a good six-foot square, with tropical plants in it, housing a huge sleeping python with a bulge in its midriff.

A rodent from the freezer?

In another container were brown cockroaches. It was filled with the disgusting creatures, each of them a good two inches long, all crawling over each other. *Yechhhhh.*

Not much made him shudder, but being in this room did. And his head was full of questions. Why was the window boarded up? To stop light getting in or to maintain the secrecy?

Why keep this room secret?

You only kept something a secret that you wanted to hide. What did Jodie Bentley want to hide – these creatures, or something else?

He went back out of the room, closed the doors and replaced the remote where he had found it. He spent the next three hours searching through each of the rooms in turn, careful to leave no trace. He found nothing.

Back in the hall he stood still, thinking. Was the memory stick, and maybe the cash, too, hidden in one of those glass containers, guarded by one of the host of venomous creatures in there? He wasn't about to go sticking his hand in any of them, gloves or no gloves. He'd wait until Jodie Bentley came home and get her to do that for him. Without gloves.

Or were the cash and the stick even here at all? Perhaps she'd stashed them in a safe deposit box somewhere.

He looked at his watch. It was ten past midnight. Late for someone to be out on a Sunday night. Particularly a grieving widow.

Where was she?

Where the hell was the stuff?

Where would he have put those items himself?

There were a million possibilities in a house this large. The reptile room was just one of them. It could be up in a roof space, or in the garden, buried someplace. He could search for a week and still find nothing. He needed Jodie. Within ten minutes of finding her, having her alone in a room, she'd tell him. She'd be begging to tell him. Screaming it out.

No one he'd ever gone to for information had remained silent.

Back in the kitchen he looked again at the notepad he'd seen earlier on the island unit. Looked at it closely. There were faint indentations.

He went over to the fridge and found in a drawer in the vegetable section what he had been hoping for. Lemons, inside a string net.

He removed one, cut it in half and began to squeeze, hard, letting the juice fall over the indentations on the sheet of paper at the top of the notepad.

When he was happy that it was saturated, he discarded both halves of the lemon in his pocket to avoid leaving any fibres from his gloves, went over to the oven, switched on the fan to 170 degrees and put the page inside.

Every few minutes he opened the oven door and peered in. Finally, he smiled and removed the page, putting it on the top of the hob.

He switched the oven off and stared down at the clear brown writing that had appeared, as if by magic. It was a conjuring trick he had learned as a child.

ORGANZA. EMIRATES 442 DUBAI.
11.35 LHR. PASSPORT!

Instantly he googled the name '*Organza*' on his phone.

Organza fabric . . .
Organza gift bags . . .
Organza cruise ship. Our flagship addition
   to our fleet!
Orient and Occident Cruise Lines.

Was that where the grieving widow had gone? Spending a chunk of her two hundred thousand stolen counterfeit dollars? To help her through her grief?

How sweet.

How long was she going to be away? Certainly long enough for him to take this house apart. He didn't know how long you could leave a collection of reptiles for, even with timers fitted. A few days, probably. A week? But not much more. Either she had someone who would come in to look after them, who could almost certainly provide him with useful information, or she was planning to be back in a week – or perhaps two at the most.

He'd look up the *Organza*'s schedule on his computer back in his hotel room and check out the ports of call. Tomorrow, he decided, he'd come and have a chat with the builders. See what he could find out from them. He looked forward to her return. To see what choice cuts he could take from her back home to Yossarian. He liked to reward his associate for his patience in waiting for him with body parts from his victims. And thanks to her well-equipped kitchen, he might be able to take something really tasty. Freeze dried.

CHAPTER 50

Monday 2 March

Tooth arrived back in his hotel room shortly after 1 a.m., tired now and getting increasingly angry. Angry with the rain, angry with the goddam cold, angry that he had totally failed to find what he was looking for. And angry he had got a splinter in his finger putting the window boarding back.

He ordered steak and fries, coffee and a bottle of Maker's Mark bourbon from room service and stood by the window, looking down at the lights of Brighton seafront and the black water of the English Channel beyond.

While he waited for his meal and drink to arrive, he was planning to return to Jodie Bentley's house and make a search of every inch of the property. The memory stick could be anywhere. The bitch might have it with her, of course, that was a possibility. He'd searched plenty of residences and offices in his time. He knew all the places where people hid stuff, thinking they were being clever, like fake books, bathroom cabinets, sock drawers, on top of kitchen cupboards, in empty containers, under floorboards. Mostly when people hid stuff, there were indications.

You'd see the tiny indent in a floorboard where a screwdriver had been inserted. The books not entirely flush. Clothes stacked a little bit too neatly at the back of the drawer.

But tonight, nothing. Nada. Goose eggs.

After the room-service guy had delivered his tray and departed, Tooth hung the 'Do Not Disturb' sign on the door then, standing on a table, taped over the smoke detector.

He sat down at the table and poured himself a large whisky, then using the coffee cup saucer as an ashtray, lit a Lucky Strike, flipped open the lid of his laptop and googled '*Organza*', adding, 'cruise ship'.

Moments later an image appeared of a sleek white liner with a single, rectangular funnel.

He typed the words 'Itinerary, March'.

The ship had sailed from Dubai yesterday, bound for Mumbai, India, due to arrive in three days' time. The itinerary carried on for months, the ship steadily making its way to Cape Town, then up the west coast of Africa, then across to Ascension Island and on to Rio de Janeiro. It was a round-the-world cruise.

But there was no way Jodie Bentley would be staying on it for all that time.

He looked at the different legs and journey times. If she disembarked in Mumbai, she could be home in four days. If it was Goa, that would be six days at least before she'd be back. It looked like he had a minimum of four days to occupy himself in this freezing, wet hellhole. Four days to search her place again, if there was any point.

He stared at his meal, the room filled with the smell of it, and wished he was back home in the sunshine, on his boat with Yossarian, the trawl lines stretched out behind him, catching healthy food for them both.

He drained his glass, refilled it and lit another Lucky Strike. A printed sign warned him there was a £250 fine for smoking in this room.

As he dragged on his cigarette, he began to form a plan.

He turned back to his laptop.

CHAPTER 51

Monday 2 March

At lunchtime that day, at a private ceremony in the intimate Polaris bar, Rollo and Jodie were married by the *Organza*'s captain. The service was attended by an elderly American couple as witnesses, with whom they had shared a dinner table last night – Irv and Mitzi Kravitz.

Rollo slipped a wedding band in platinum, purchased from the ship's jewellery shop, onto Jodie's finger, and she had placed a ring onto his, too. Throughout the entire ceremony he had looked utterly gooey-eyed.

Sweet.

For the next few days of what he called their *honeymoon*, and she viewed more as an endurance test of feigning adoration and horniness, they would be to the outside world the besotted newlyweds. Most of their fellow passengers were either elderly couples or elderly widows, and she had noticed, since embarking on the cruise, the frequent glances thrown in her direction – some of disapproval, some of envy, at the considerable age gap between herself and her new husband.

Irv had quietly asked Rollo if he was concerned about the age gap, and in reply, Rollo had quoted Joan Collins. 'If she dies, she dies,' he'd said.

But it didn't bother her. She was focused, and full of excitement, about their first port of call, Mumbai, India.

And especially about one choice of shore excursion listed in the ship's daily newspaper.

The Mumbai Crocodile Farm
Walk through Mumbai bush to a crocodile swamp.
See these prehistoric reptiles in their natural environment. And don't worry, we feed them daily on chickens – not tourists!

It was one of four shore excursions on offer. Rollo was keen to take the one that offered a visit to a gallery displaying the work of local artists, followed by a crafts market. But he deferred to his new bride and her fascination with reptiles, and they signed up at the Purser's office to the crocodile farm tour.

She gave him a big kiss. Followed by another. She told him he was the most wonderful man in the world.

He replied that he still could not believe his luck. That such a gorgeous, smart, caring woman, so much younger, could have fallen in love with an old git like himself.

She'd replied that she'd always loved the wisdom of older men, right from her late teens. That older men made her feel safe, and that she found them – and Rollo in particular – extremely sexy.

Not as sexy, she excluded from the conversation, as what she had learned about his personal wealth from her assiduous trawls through the internet. He had sold his gallery in Cork Street plus goodwill, according to one website, for a figure in excess of ten million pounds. He had a personal art collection, housed partly in his Knightsbridge townhouse and partly in his Brighton seafront mansion, estimated to be worth over eighty million pounds.

For that amount of loot she was prepared to put up with pretty much anything. But thanks to his neglect of his diabetic condition, his libido was at a fairly low level. So far on this trip she'd only had to endure sex with him once.

She had a plan in place. India was home to a number of venomous creatures.

And one in particular.

CHAPTER 52

Monday 2 March

It was part of Roy Grace's nature that he started to worry whenever things were going well in his life. There was always a balance, a yin and yang. One quote that often came into his mind at such times was from Anthon St Maarten: 'If we never experience the chill of a dark winter, it is very unlikely that we will ever cherish the warmth of a bright summer's day.'

He was thinking about this as he let himself out of the back door of their cottage into the darkness of the morning, in his tracksuit and trainers. It was shortly after 5.00 a.m. Breathing in the fresh, chilly country air, he switched on his headlamp torch and stretched, then set off.

Humphrey barked happily and jumped up exuberantly, trying to snatch the red tennis ball out of the plastic thrower his master was holding high up above him.

'Wait, boy, OK?'

Humphrey responded with another bark.

'Sssshhh! Don't wake up Noah, he'll never go

back to sleep, and your mum will be mad with me! They're going to take you for another walk later, OK?'

He strode in the breaking morning light across the frosty wet grass of the unkempt lawn, passing the hen coop – and in the beam of his torch saw all five of their hens huddled together on the roof of their house, where they seemed to spend every night.

'Why don't you sleep inside in the warmth?' he chided them, wondering how many eggs he'd find when he checked later.

God, he was loving country life, wondering as he had done so often these past couple of months why he hadn't made the move sooner. They'd bought the cottage shortly before Christmas and, thanks to his leg injury, he'd been able to spend almost all of January here on sick leave, helping Cleo to get the house straight. She had started back at work last week and they now had a part-time nanny helping to take care of Noah, Kaitlynn Defelice, a personable and competent young Californian who they had found after hours of research.

Grace hadn't yet got used to having a nanny around and needed to remember, constantly, that he could no longer walk about naked or just in his boxers. Cleo was really happy to be working again, back at the mortuary; much though she loved their son, she had been getting restless, starting to find being stuck in an isolated house, with just the relentless baby routine, not fulfilling enough. She missed adult company and the stimulus of work. In addition, things that would take minutes at home, pre-Noah, now took hours.

As Grace opened the back gate and flicked the ball, watching Humphrey bound forward across the huge, barren field that the local farmer had given them permission to walk in, he thought how blissful it was to be able to take the dog out without having to bring a plastic bag to pick up his mess. He set the timer on his watch and began a brisk walk.

He broke into a trot for a few steps, testing his right leg as he crossed the eight-acre field, stopping several times to retrieve the ball from Humphrey's mouth and flick it again, until he reached the stile on the far side. The dog ran beneath it as he climbed over it, then carried on striding across the next, equally barren, field. When he reached the ten-minute limit set by his physiotherapist he dutifully slowed into a normal walk.

It was growing lighter now and he switched off the head torch. He turned and looked back at the house, which was little more than a speck in the distance. A small, rectangular farm cottage, sitting up on a slight ridge. It was very secluded, almost half a mile down a rutted driveway from the lane, and ten minutes' drive from the centre of the village of Henfield.

In many ways the house was an ugly duckling,

with tiny windows, each a different shape and size, looking as if it had been designed by an infant playing with bricks. Much of it was clad in unruly ivy and – at this time of year – skeletal wisteria. But he loved it, and Cleo loved it, too. This was their first proper home together. He felt that his family was safe here, away from the city, and that it would be a paradise for their son – and for any future children who came along. Cleo said she would be happy to have two more and hoped at least one would be a girl, not that she really minded. He didn't care whether it was one, two or three more. He was pretty happy with his lot, right now.

But with it came the feeling that this couldn't last. There were dark clouds on the horizon. One of these was his boss, his old adversary Cassian Pewe, ACC with responsibility for Major Crime. During his month at home with his family, Grace had had the chance to rethink his values. He wasn't going to let Pewe stress him. He did his job to the best of his ability – and always had. He cared about the victims of all the crimes he had to investigate and did everything he could for the families.

Another dark cloud was Dr Edward Crisp. The knowledge that he'd had him in his grasp, and then the serial killer had escaped, had been eating him up. But at least Crisp was now once again behind bars, albeit in France. And as soon as the French police had completed their enquiries, he would be brought home to face justice. That reminded Grace he needed to contact the police in Lyon for an update.

With the stack of evidence they had against the creepy doctor, the man would spend the rest of his life rotting in jail, with no chance – not even with today's absurdly lenient legal system – of ever being released.

But the darkest cloud of all was his missing first wife, Sandy. Something that he'd kept to himself since early January, which was when he'd flown to Munich at the request of a German police officer friend of his, Marcel Kullen. Kullen believed a woman lying in a coma in a hospital ward there after being run over by a taxi might just be Sandy.

Looking down at her damaged and intubated body in the private room at the Klinikum Schwabing, her face covered in scars, scabs and bandages, it had been hard to tell for sure one way or the other. However, he believed in his heart of hearts that it was her. But the major issue was her ten-year-old son. He had no idea who the father was, and he didn't want to think about the possibility of it being him, and of having responsibility for the boy.

Sandy had made her choice, ten years ago, to walk out on him and disappear. At some point, he had learned many years later, she had become a drug addict, although she had apparently managed to come through that. There was too much history, too much baggage.

So he had walked away, denying it was her.

A few days after his visit to Munich, Marcel Kullen had phoned him, asking if he could send some item from Sandy – if he still had anything – that they might get DNA from, to make one hundred per cent sure she could be eliminated.

It had placed Grace in a dilemma. He had promised to see if he could find anything, but told Kullen a small lie, that he didn't think he had anything left of hers. The truth was he had kept some of their things. A week later, aware he would never have closure unless he knew the truth for sure, he mailed Kullen one of Sandy's old hairbrushes. But he already knew what the outcome would be. And that he would have to tell Cleo.

Now he waited on tenterhooks for another communication from Kullen, one that would change his life dramatically and not in a good way.

Next weekend, on Saturday, he and Cleo were going on a date night. Dinner at the Cat Inn at West Hoathly, one of their favourite country restaurants. They'd booked the romantic Grand Suite for the night and arranged for the nanny to stay over in the house with Noah. They were both really looking forward to having an evening together away from everything.

He looked at his watch. At 6 a.m., he would be handing over to a new duty Senior Investigating Officer. Sussex and Surrey normally had around twenty-four homicides a year between them. So far this year, Sussex was enjoying a below-average rate. The odds had been badly stacked against him for this weekend, and although homicides were his meat and drink – there was nothing he loved better than to investigate a murder – he was glad to have had a quiet period.

Just as he thought this, bending down to tug the red tennis ball free from Humphrey's jaws, his phone rang.

'Roy Grace,' he answered, and was immediately dismayed to hear the somewhat neurotic voice of Andy Anakin – known to his colleagues as 'Panicking Anakin' – one of the city's duty inspectors. Anakin was known colloquially within the police as a shit magnet. Incidents happened whenever he was on duty. A nervous man, he frequently spoke in short, staccato sentences.

'Oh, sir, good morning. Just wanted to give you a heads-up, sir. In case. You know?'

'Heads-up on what? In case of what?' Grace replied.

'Well, the thing is, a major Brighton target died last night in suspicious circumstances.'

'You're talking in riddles, Andy. Who died?'

'You didn't hear? Shelby Stonor.'

'Shelby Stonor?' Grace quizzed him. 'That scrote?'

'Yep, the very one. DI Warner was called out and has looked at the circumstances and has asked that you be informed.'

Like any city, Brighton had its share of persistent offenders who were well known to the police.

Shelby Stonor was up there on the A-list of the worst of them. Grace had first encountered him in his early days in the force, as a beat copper. Back then Stonor had been a frequent joyrider and a petty thief. He had graduated to becoming a house breaker – and a fairly rubbish one at that. During the past twenty years Stonor had spent more time in prison than out. And one of the crimes Grace hated, almost more than any other, was domestic burglary. In his view – and a view shared by both Sussex Police and all other forces – violating the sanctuary of people's homes was up there amongst the vilest of offences. Currently, Grace knew, Stonor was a major target for Brighton Police who also believed he was connected to a gang stealing high-value cars.

'That's what you're calling me at this hour to tell me? That Shelby Stonor's dead?' He added, cynically, 'Are we going to have a whip-round for flowers or something?'

'It's how he's died, Roy. That's why I'm calling you.'

Does anyone care? That little bastard, he was tempted to reply. He took a deep breath. 'Tell me.'

CHAPTER 53

Monday 2 March

Rollo had gone to play a rubber of bridge with the couple who had been witnesses at their marriage, earlier. Kind of a strange way to spend the start of their honeymoon, she'd thought, and he'd offered to cancel, but she had insisted. He couldn't let them down and ruin their game, not after they'd been so sweet.

He promised to be back by six for champagne, then a romantic wedding-night dinner *à deux*. She'd told him not to hurry, she was happy for him.

And she had work to do.

Luck was really going with her. Ever since she had changed her appearance all those years ago, luck had gone with her. It seemed she just had to think lucky to be lucky. Klein had been a hiccup along the way. She was now back on a roll. Even before setting foot on the ship she had been planning Rollo's demise. The discovery that the ship's captain was licensed to carry out marriages recognized in English law, and her plan to seduce

Rowley into marrying her, had worked so brilliantly. No one would suspect a loved-up bride of just a few days of killing her husband. And the location was perfect, given to her on a plate, with plenty of dangerous creatures in addition to crocodiles.

She was thirty-six and her body clock was ticking ever faster. She had very few years left to achieve her dream of a lifestyle to match that of her old school friend, Emira. Enough money to buy one of those villas on Lake Como, to have all the other luxuries she could ever want, to have a man she really loved and to bring up her own family. This opportunity with such a deadly combination of elements might take years to occur again. It was too good to miss – she had to grasp the moment.

Carpe diem!

The ship was rolling a little in a heavy swell. The captain had warned them in his 9 a.m. address that it would be a little rough for a few hours, and to make sure everyone held the handrails on the stairs. She walked unsteadily across to the door, opened it and peered out into the corridor. Rollo was forgetful and had a habit of returning to the cabin minutes after he had left, for his glasses, his phone, his wallet or his insulin pen. But all she could see was a liveried butler delivering drinks on a silver tray to another cabin.

She closed the door and locked it. Then she went to the fridge where she kept the freezer pack that, she had told Rollo, contained the drops she needed for her dry eyes, and where his insulin pens were stored. Inside was a tiny rubber-stoppered vial of amber-coloured crystals she had brought with her, from a small stash she kept in her freezer at home. It lay among the sachets of eye drops that she did not need. She removed it and one of his grey Lantus twenty-four-hour pens, and placed both items on the dressing table.

Next, from a compartment inside her handbag, she took out the hypodermic syringe, a small bottle of sterile water and surgical gloves from the kit she always travelled with. She liked to be prepared, never knowing when an opportunity might present itself, although she'd had a feeling from the start, with Rollo, that the cruise might provide too good an opportunity to miss. And with his rocky health, she wanted to do it sooner rather than later – which might be too late. Happily, events were panning out much faster than she had expected. With luck, this would more than make up for all those precious months she had wasted with Walt Klein.

For protection she snapped on the gloves and firstly rehydrated the vial of freeze-dried crystals with the sterile water. She had studied the way Rollo took his insulin, by screwing a fresh needle into the base of his throwaway insulin pen. Whilst the crystals were dissolving, she took the empty syringe and pressed the needle against the base of the pen, pushing it firmly and carefully up inside. Then, glancing nervously at the door, she withdrew the plunger, drawing out the clear insulin until the pen was empty. She went over to the washbasin and, pressing the plunger firmly, squirted the insulin down the plughole, breathing in its distinct, clinical reek.

Her hands were trembling, she realized. Again she looked at the door. *Don't come back, please don't come back.*

Then there was a knock.

Shit!

She looked down in panic, wondering where to hide everything. 'Hello?' she called out.

'Canapés!' a sing-song voice replied. Their regular afternoon delivery of caviar, smoked salmon and prawns, with a glass of champagne, that Rollo had ordered for them.

Relief surged through her. 'Can you come back later, please. Half an hour?'

'No problem! Sorry to disturb you!'

Shaking, she returned to her task. She picked up the vial and the syringe and carefully drew up the rehydrated venom, watching carefully, hoping to hell she had not miscalculated. Then she smiled. Perfect! The pen's clear-plastic barrel was full and the faint yellow tinge was barely discernible!

She marked the pen, to be sure she could identify it, with three careful scratches from her nail scissors, then placed it with her eye drops back in the opaque freezer pack and put it back in the fridge. Picking up the syringe and the empty vial, she stepped out onto their secluded balcony, in the warm late-afternoon sunshine, leaned over the rail and carefully looked around for anyone who might notice her, but there was no one about. Then she tossed the syringe and vial overboard into the deep blue ocean.

Returning to the cabin, she checked carefully that she hadn't left any evidence. Then she unlocked the door, showered, washed her hair, put on her make-up and perfume, and slipped into the black lace underwear and camisole she'd bought especially for this trip. She picked up the novel that she was reading, and lay back on the bed to wait for her husband of just a few hours to return.

CHAPTER 54

Monday 2 March

Thirty minutes later and Shelby Stonor might have been someone else's case in the Surrey and Sussex Major Crime Team. But after a long period, first of convalescence, then of quiet, Roy Grace was suddenly fired up. The first possible murder of the year on his watch might just have fallen into his lap. Albeit this was the kind of murder enquiry he and all his colleagues liked least – that of a known low-life scumbag. There was no specific evidence at this stage that it *was* murder, but the death was definitely suspicious.

Given the choice, like all other detectives, he would have preferred a more classy homicide investigation. But he wasn't about to let this opportunity pass him by and, with an offender like Stonor, there was every likelihood of a quick resolution. It appeared that Stonor had been killed by a snake, but how and where did that happen? One possibility was his links to crime in Brighton – burglary, drug dealing and, more recently, car theft. But, equally, Grace knew from his long experience never to prejudge any situation.

ABC.

ASSUME NOTHING, BELIEVE NO ONE, CHECK EVERYTHING was the mantra drummed into every detective in the country when they started. The first place to look, in a suspicious death, was the victim's home. Eighty per cent of victims were killed by a loved one or by someone they knew. His first task was to establish where Stonor lived and who, if anyone, he lived with. Perhaps they had killed him. Or, alternatively, he could easily have been killed by a competitor or through some other crime connection.

Cutting short his early-morning walk with Humphrey, he started to notify the on-call enquiry team, and already information was starting to come in.

Kaitlynn arrived to take care of Noah, and Cleo left shortly after. The working day at the mortuary began early, with Cleo and her team starting at 7 a.m. to prepare the bodies that required post-mortems.

An average of three bodies a day were processed through the city's mortuary. The good thing about the early start, from Cleo's perspective as the mother of a young baby, was that on most days she would be home by 4 p.m. After the brutal intrusion of a post-mortem, her next duty, with the help of her assistants, was to make the body look present-able for viewing and formal identification if it was required. That meant replacing all the internal organs, stitching the body up, washing it, doing the hair and applying make-up. Then receiving and treating the loved ones with sympathy and respect in the non-denominational chapel.

The moment any human being died, their body became, in law, the property of the Coroner. If someone, already ill, had died of natural causes and their doctor was happy to sign off the death, the body could go straight to the funeral director.

In most circumstances where the cause of death was not suspicious, such as when someone in poor health had died more than twenty-eight days since they last saw a doctor or as the result of an accident, one of the team of three local pathologists would perform the post-mortem. But on deaths where the Coroner had reason to believe there were suspicious circumstances, then a highly trained Home Office pathologist – of which there were just thirty-two covering the whole of the UK – would be called in. A standard post-mortem took less than an hour. A Home Office one could sometimes take all day – or even longer.

Roy always found it hard to see Cleo when she was at work, with the constantly grim duties she carried out every day, in contrast to her home life. And he admired her all the more for it. She'd often told him her greatest satisfaction came from helping bereaved loved ones through one of the most difficult tasks they ever had to face in their lives.

He knew all too well from some of the narrow

escapes he'd had in his own career – and the dangers which all police officers faced – that there was the constant possibility that one day he could end up on one of those post-mortem tables himself.

It was something Cleo knew only too well, also. The elephant in the room that they rarely talked about. Regardless of the size of its shadow. He respected her enormously for her work, and her attitude.

He hurredly showered and shaved, and went down to the kitchen. He put some porridge into the microwave, then went over to Marlon's tank and dropped in some food flakes. 'Morning, old chap, had a good night? What you been up to?'

The goldfish's response was the same as ever. It opened and shut its mouth a few times, then swam to the surface and gulped down some of the food. Strange to think, Grace considered, but this was probably the highlight of Marlon's day.

He carried his porridge over to the breakfast table, sat down and began to eat, flipping through the pages of *Sussex Life* magazine. But after only a few moments, his mobile phone rang.

'Roy Grace,' he answered.

'Good morning, Roy.'

He recognized instantly the voice of the Coroner of Brighton and Hove. 'Good morning,' he replied. 'Inspector Anakin said you would be calling.' All their conversations were straight down to business; she was not one, normally, for pleasantries or small talk.

'Roy, I've been informed about a Brighton resident, Mr Shelby Stonor, who died following a road traffic accident in Marine Parade in Brighton. There are serious concerns about the nature of his death.'

'Yes, I have questions about his death, too.'

'As you know, those who treated him don't believe the injuries he sustained in the accident were sufficient to be fatal. They think he might have been poisoned – possibly bitten by a venomous snake – or he had a tropical disease. One of the paramedics worked in Africa some years back – she says that Stonor had puncture marks on his right ankle that could have been a snake bite. We need to bring in a Home Office pathologist who has experience in this field. There's one, Dr Nick Best. I've contacted him and he could be available later today or tomorrow. They're going to carry out toxicology tests – I will have more information later, but I just wanted to give you a heads-up.'

'Thank you,' Grace said. 'My thoughts exactly.'

'I'm off on holiday later today,' she said. 'I'm short-staffed at the moment, so West Sussex Coroner, Penny Schofield, has seconded one of her officers to me, Michelle Websdale. She'll liaise with you.'

'I'll wait to hear from her. In the meantime, I'm contacting London Zoo, as soon as they're open, to see if they could send down an expert in snakes to accompany a search team to Stonor's home, as a precaution. I've just established he lived with his girlfriend, a woman called Angi Bunsen, who has no criminal record.'

Roy ended the call and returned to his now lukewarm porridge. Too often with murder enquiries he felt deep empathy for the victims. But it would be harder to feel much for such a vile shitbag as Shelby Stonor, as many of his past victims had been old and vulnerable.

So often, people like Stonor, who blighted the lives of decent folk, got away with it for decades, thanks to the injustices of the legal system. Equally, he recognized that he was a human being who, regardless of his criminal past, deserved the same in-depth enquiry he would give anyone. Undoubtedly, as was the case with most villains, Stonor's past would turn out to be a tragic one: a broken home, or alcoholic or abusive parents, who had never given him much of a chance in life, never set any kind of example or moral boundary for him. A sad victim of life and robbed of any future by an early death. Grace knew now that Stonor had had a girlfriend and probably a family, and they, too, deserved his best efforts.

CHAPTER 55

Monday 2 March

Tooth arrived back in his hotel room soon after 11 a.m., having walked the few miles there and back to Roedean Crescent. He'd talked to two builders who were Polish and they had trouble understanding him. He explained he was a private detective working for a car insurance company, and that the occupant of the house, Jodie Bentley, whom he was trying to find, had given her name as a witness at an accident. But he got very little from them.

They worked for a London property management company engaged by the house's owner, and were currently fitting new guttering. There had been a break-in last week, which was why they'd boarded up that particular window – it was the one where the intruder had entered. They seemed pretty glad the window was boarded up, because of the reptiles in the room, which neither of them had liked the look of. They'd seen the woman – she'd asked them to board up the window, but they were not able to tell him anything about her, or when she was due back.

At this moment there seemed only one way to find out. And that was to keep watch on her house until she returned. However long that took. Which was fine.

Back in his days as a sniper, he'd once sat for three weeks in the shell of a building, in blistering heat, permanently thirsty and hungry, with scorpions, spiders and the occasional curious snake as his only visitors, waiting for his target to appear in the cross-hairs of his sight. The spray of crimson from the exploding enemy head, when he'd finally pulled the trigger, had made it all worthwhile.

Sitting in a rental car, for however long it took for Jodie Bentley to return home, would be relative luxury.

CHAPTER 56

Tuesday 3 March

'What are you reading, my angel?'

Luxuriating on a blue-cushioned lounger on the open-air pool deck of the *Organza*, with her third Mimosa of the afternoon in a champagne glass beside her, Jodie Carmichael tilted up her straw hat and turned, with a smile, to her husband of just twenty-six hours, who had an art magazine folded across his plump, reddening stomach.

They were protected from the wind by tall windows all around, and there was a round Jacuzzi at the far end. A row of wheelchairs, mobility scooters and Zimmer frames were lined up beyond it.

'I've just finished the Simon Toyne. I'm now reading a book on Mumbai I got from the ship's library. I'm so excited – I've never been to India.'

'Crazy place, Mumbai,' he said. 'I went to a cricket match there a few years ago. It's their national game – almost their unifying religion. Ever watched a game?'

She shook her head. 'Never really understood it. Have you played much, yourself?'

'I was quite a useful spin bowler in my youth,' he said, digging his fingers into a bowl of nuts beside him. Then he snapped his fingers at a passing steward and barked an order for a pink gin for himself and another Mimosa for his bride. Jodie cringed at his rude treatment of the sweet, young Filipino.

She continued reading. It was the four pages on the crocodile farm that she was focused on and studying intently. Sizing up the opportunities. There was plenty of wild terrain that visitors had to walk through, and that was good. That was exactly what she'd hoped.

Wild terrain.

The perfect home for the kind of cold-blooded creatures she was fond of, and understood.

'Actually,' he said, 'there's cricket on in Mumbai when we arrive there – they have a magnificent stadium. I think you'd find it quite something! But, of course, if you'd still prefer the crocodile farm . . .?' His voice was full of hope and she didn't want to dash that.

'My darling, of course, if you'd rather we do that?'

'Wouldn't dream of it, my angel,' he said. 'If my beautiful bride has set her heart on the crocodile farm, that's what we'll do. Hell, I can see cricket any time.'

'Are you really sure?'

He took her hand and held it. His palm felt sweaty, repulsing her. 'Being with you is all that matters. I couldn't possibly concentrate on a cricket match – my mind would be on far more naughty thoughts!'

'I love your naughtiness!'

'And I love yours. Fancy going back to the cabin – you know – get out of the sun for a bit?'

'Haven't you just ordered more drinks, my love?'

'Ah – yes – ah – good point.'

She slipped her free hand across and down the front of his orange trunks, which had dollar signs all over them, and gently stroked him. 'Now this is what I call a *good point*,' she said, feeling him stiffen in her hand.

He let out a gasp of pleasure.

Then, as the steward arrived with their drinks, she hastily removed her hand and returned to her book. To the photographs of the crocodile farm.

How lucky she was, she thought, to have such a sweet, understanding husband.

How sad that it would only be for a short while longer, if all went to plan.

So sad she almost shed a crocodile tear.

CHAPTER 57

Tuesday 3 March

Haydn Kelly had positively identified the woman from the footage DC Alexander had obtained, entering the arrivals hall at Heathrow Terminal Three on Friday 20 February, and heading towards the exit.

But, so far, none of the taxi drivers or limousine companies had come up with anyone remotely matching her description.

Shortly before 9 a.m. Roy Grace drove past the black and gold sign which read BRIGHTON AND HOVE CITY MORTUARY. As he pulled into a parking space at the rear, Glenn Branson drew up alongside him. There was no sign of the Home Office pathologist, who was due to start the examination of Shelby Stonor's body at 10 a.m. after travelling down from Birmingham.

'Morning,' Branson greeted him, then, as his self-appointed style guru, eyed him up and down as usual, to Grace's annoyance. Grace was dressed for work in a dark suit, white shirt, plain tie and polished black shoes. 'Expected to see you in tweeds and muddy wellies, chewing straw – you know – with your move to the country and all.'

'Haha. How's Siobhan?'

'Yeah, all right. We took the kids to a farm shop place at the weekend to see the animals – they have chickens, rabbits, guinea pigs roaming around. Noah would love it. If you need any chickens, they sell them.'

Grace grinned. 'I usually get mine from the butcher in Henfield.'

'Very funny. Listen, we came back along the coast and the kids had brilliant burgers in a place in Peacehaven. Big Mouths – know it?'

Grace shook his head. 'How were the kids with Siobhan?'

'Yeah.' Branson smiled, and Grace caught a glimpse of something wistful in his expression. 'It's hard for them, you know. But Siobhan's finding ways to their hearts – mostly by spoiling them! And they're really taking to her, which is a good thing cos there's going to be times when she's going to have to look after them without me there. At least she understands about working round the clock, you know, with her own job. She's not like Ari, she gets what we do and the crazy hours we have to work. But she's finding being a journalist much more demanding than she'd expected whilst she was a student.'

'Where did she study?'

'Here in the city at a place called Brighton Journalist Works.'

'What's that?'

'A specialist college. They train journalists – they work closely with the *Argus*.'

'Let's hope they trained her better than her predecessor – bloody Spinella,' Grace retorted.

Part of the reason Glenn Branson's marriage had broken up was the long and frequently unsociable hours that he worked. Ari had taken up with a new man who had started to act as a father to their son, Sammy, and their daughter, Remi. Branson had taken back that role as soon as Ari had died. Grace was relieved he was now with someone who understood his world.

To be a homicide detective meant putting work above your family. You could be called out at a moment's notice, any time of the day or night and any day of the year. If the phone rang during Christmas lunch or in the middle of your daughter's birthday party or while you were out at dinner celebrating your wedding anniversary, that was it. You just grabbed your go-bag, that was always packed with essentials as you might need to sleep in the office, working very long hours for days on end.

'Does she want kids of her own?'

Branson nodded, then shrugged. 'That could be a problem.'

'You don't want any more?'

He shrugged again. 'This job – you know? When I was a nightclub bouncer at least I worked regular hours, even if I was out most nights. Everyone knew when I'd be home and when I wouldn't be.

I was able to be a decent father to them then. Even when I first joined the police it was OK. All that changed when I moved to Major Crime – and no longer had a proper home life.'

Grace put his arm round his friend's massive, powerful shoulders and squeezed. 'It's what it is.'

'Yeah. I know. And it's always going to be.'

'Unless you apply for a transfer to another department or transfer back to division.'

Branson shook his head. 'No way, I love this work. You said to me once that you never wanted to do anything different. I get that, I'm the same.'

'Make sure you make it up to her when you get home late. Offer to cook dinner or buy her a nice, thoughtful present.'

'Good advice.'

They reached the mortuary's front door.

A large, opaque window to their right provided light for the main post-mortem room. Grace rang the bell.

Moments later, Cleo, in green scrubs, gloves and white rubber boots, opened the door. Her face brightened when she saw them. 'Hi, guys – great you've arrived before the pathologist – I need you to help me with a bit of a dilemma.' She gave Branson a peck on the cheek and Grace a kiss on the lips, and ushered them into the changing room.

They gowned up and put on rubber boots also, then Cleo led them through into the large, open-plan post-mortem room. The place had a neat and tidy post-weekend feel about it. All except one of the steel post-mortem tables were empty and spotless. In the alcove to the left lay a motionless figure encased head to toe in black rubber, with two tiny eye-slits in a gimp mask.

Cleo stood over it and peeled back the mask to reveal the face of an elderly man. His eyes were wide open and, despite being dead, they seemed to have a twinkle in them.

Branson giggled, irreverently. 'A proper little bouncing boy you've got here!'

Grace smiled. The poor man looked ridiculous. 'Seems like he died having a nice time,' he said.

'He was,' Cleo confirmed, also smiling. They were joined by Darren, Cleo's Assistant Mortuary Technician, a sharp, good-looking and pleasant-natured young man in his twenties, with spiky black hair, similarly clad to the rest of them.

'They called him Rubber Johnny,' Darren said, his mouth twisted into a grin.

'Who did?' Grace asked.

'All the girls who worked there, apparently.'

'Didn't Rubber Johnny use to be slang for a condom?' Branson asked. 'I saw that in a movie – was it *Quadrophenia*?'

'The problem I have,' Cleo said, 'is that this sweet little old man, Ian Rolf, has been visiting a dominatrix dungeon in Saltdean every Monday morning for the past ten years. Apparently he would tell his wife he was off to play golf, put his clubs in the car and then go to this dominatrix place. Yesterday, he suddenly stopped breathing.

They panicked, tried to resuscitate him, then called an ambulance.'

'Either a heart attack or a stroke?' Grace asked.

'Seems likely,' Cleo said.

'Lucky sod,' Glenn Branson said. 'That's the way to go. Out with a bang and a hard-on. Beats being wheeled around an old folks' home, playing tiddly-winks and pissing in your pants any day.'

All of them laughed.

'Maybe,' Cleo said. 'But what the hell am I supposed to tell his widow?'

'The truth,' Grace said.

'I can't, Roy! That would just be so cruel. Can you imagine finding that out about the man you loved? That he'd been deceiving you for so long?'

They heard the doorbell and Cleo went off to answer it.

'Does his widow need to know, Roy?' Branson asked.

Grace stared down at the dead man's face. He really did look happy. Most dead bodies he'd attended had their faces frozen in shock or pain. 'I'm sure it would be better for her and her family if she didn't. But she has to know the truth – it'll come out.'

'You implying I'll tell Siobhan so she can write it in the *Argus*? Never!'

'That's not what I'm saying. But it's going to come out at the inquest. Better to let his widow find it out sensitively.'

Grace reflected for a moment on his own massive issue, and when he was going to tell Cleo.

'Morning all!'

They turned to see a tall, reedy man in his mid-thirties, with lank, floppy hair, dressed in a jacket over a black T-shirt, blue jeans and fancy, knobbly, black and white trainers. He strode into the room in light, bouncy steps, followed by the Coroner's Officer, Michelle Websdale, a slim, fair-haired former Border Agencies officer, whose attractive model looks belied her tough character. She even managed to make her baggy green scrubs look like they were designer chic, Grace thought. Behind her was the youthful Crime Scenes Investigator, Chris Gee, also gowned up and holding a camera. Grace always thought Gee, much like Cleo, looked too gentle a person for such a grim job, yet Gee was unfazed by almost anything – except children. Children were the one thing that most affected all those in the emergency services, without exception.

Grace held out his hand to the stranger he presumed must be the Home Office pathologist, Nick Best. 'I'm Detective Superintendent Grace – and this is my colleague, Detective Inspector Branson.' He introduced Websdale and Gee also.

Best had a warm smile but a rather brusque nature. 'Good to meet you all. So, my information is we have a suspected death from poisoning?'

'That's correct,' the Coroner's Officer said.

'I'll go and get my kit on.'

'I'll show you the changing room.' Cleo smiled at him. 'This way.' She led the way back out into the corridor.

The pathologist looked at Cleo in a way, suddenly, that Grace did not like. It was a really lechy stare.

Nor did he much like the smile Cleo gave the man back.

Shit, he was jealous! And he felt almost ridiculously relieved when Cleo came straight back in. It was the first time, ever, that he had felt such an emotion. He didn't like it. And he didn't like himself for feeling it.

'So, guys,' Cleo said. 'What am I going to do with – er – *Rubber Johnny*?'

'Remove his kit for the viewing,' Grace said. 'The widow's going to have to formally identify him. It'll be easier for her if he's not in a latex shroud.'

'Yep, you're right,' she said. 'Thanks.' Then she led them all through towards the Isolation Room.

As they crowded round the door, peering in through the glass panel at the body on the solitary table, Cleo instructed them all to put on their face masks.

'Righty ho!' said Nick Best, joining them. He was gowned-up in white, head to toe, with a full head mask and visor, as if ready to enter a nuclear waste site, and holding a small bag. 'Let's go and check out *le plat du jour*!'

He entered the Isolation Room, followed by the others. Last in, Grace closed the door behind them. As he did, Glenn Branson took a shocked step back and said, his voice muffled, 'Oh Jesus!'

CHAPTER 58

Tuesday 3 March

After Rollo had left the cabin to play bridge again, at 4 p.m., Jodie waited a few minutes to ensure he didn't come back for something he had forgotten, then she changed. She slipped on a push-up bra, slinky top, a short skirt and high-heeled sandals, then admired herself in the full-length mirror, mouthing, with a grin, 'You are so sexy!'

She made her way along to the ship's doctor, on a lower deck down in the bowels of the ship, placing her hands in the wall-mounted disinfection unit before entering. She explained her reasons for her visit to the nurse, who asked her to take a seat and fill in a form. Then she was ushered into the consulting room, which contained an examination couch, eye-test chart, towel dispenser and a desk with a computer screen and keyboard.

Dr Gordon Ryerson was a charming grey-haired man, in a smart white outfit, and of a similar vintage to Rollo, she estimated. And with a roving eye, she guessed, too, from the way he looked her

up and down appreciatively. As she was a generation younger, at least, than most of the rest of
her fellow female passengers, she guessed he didn't
get to flirt with young women that often on this
voyage. So she flirted coyly with him now, meeting
his gaze. She loved it, always. Loved seeing in
men's eyes just how damned attractive she was.
And sometimes she would think back to her
younger days as an ugly duckling and count
her blessings. Life now was very much more fun.

'Nice to meet you, Mrs Carmichael,' he said, as
if suddenly ending the game and going into
professional mode, pointing to a chair in front of
his desk. 'Have a seat. What can I do for you?'

She crossed her legs, then uncrossed them slowly,
smiling to herself as his eyes followed them. 'I've
been feeling queasy ever since we sailed from
Dubai, doctor,' she lied. 'I was wondering if you
could suggest anything? I've seen people wearing
motion sickness bracelets, but before buying one
I thought I'd ask your views.'

'Oh dear,' he said. 'Poor you. I'm afraid it does
take some people a few days to get their sea legs.
Are you on any medication of any kind?'

She shook her head.

He studied the form for some moments that
she had filled out for his nurse a few minutes
earlier. Then he asked, 'You're not pregnant or
anything?'

'God, I hope not! My husband's had a
vasectomy.'

'They're not always foolproof, of course. I've had patients in the past who've fallen pregnant when they thought they were safe.'

'I'm not pregnant, believe me!' Changing the subject, she said breezily, 'This must be a nice job. Do you work on this ship permanently?'

'No, I'm retired, really. I used to be a general practitioner in Chipping Norton in Oxfordshire. I do a bit of locum work to keep my hand in, and a couple of times a year I do this – my wife and I enjoy a free cruise in return for my working a few hours a day. It's very pleasant.'

'How nice!'

'Well, you know, it's nice to work with happy people. People come on a cruise to have a good time. Are you and your husband enjoying yourselves?'

'Very much. So you're an expert in everything medical?'

'I began life as an army surgeon, so I wouldn't call myself an expert in everything, but I can cope with most emergencies that are likely to happen on board ship.'

'You do operations?'

'I can whip out an appendix, if needed. But for anything more serious we'd put a patient ashore or have them airlifted off.' He smiled.

She smiled back. Good. Very good.

He pulled open a drawer behind his desk and produced a blister pack of pills. 'I'm sure we can clear up this motion sickness very quickly, then you can focus on enjoying yourself!'

'Thank you,' she said, as he handed her the pills and gave her instructions on taking them.

She'd already got all she needed from this brief meeting.

The knowledge that he was limited in his experience. He could deal with all the basics. Fine.

She doubted he'd ever had to deal with what she had in mind.

CHAPTER 59

Tuesday 3 March

Throughout his career, Roy Grace had been known as an innovative thinker, with a highly organized mind. He was also sentimental and he was sad this would be one of his last investigations to take place in Major Incident Room One – or MIR-1 for short – the place where all the homicide enquiries he had run or worked on for over a decade had been based. It was a large open space, with three huge workstations, and capable of housing three different major crime enquiries at any time. But for now he put all his issues about the changes out of his mind, to concentrate on the task confronting him.

Operation Spider was the name the Sussex Police computer had randomly generated for this operation. Already, since the completion of Stonor's post-mortem, as was the tradition, one of the team had stuck up on the door to MIR-1 a cartoon parodying the operation name. Today's was a depiction of Spiderman climbing up the side of a high-rise building.

Grace had assembled just a small team of his trusted regulars, including DI Glenn Branson, DS Norman Potting, DS Guy Batchelor, who he had appointed as Office Manager, DS Cale, DCs Emma-Jane Boutwood, Alec Davies and Jack Alexander, indexer Annalise Vineer, as well as a researcher and a HOLMES analyst.

They were all seated around one of the curved workstations in the room. The others were empty, which Grace was pleased about. It meant that if he needed to step up this enquiry, as instincts told him he might, there would be space to expand right here.

Four whiteboards were on the wall behind them. On one there were photographs of Stonor taken during the post-mortem, some in wide angle and some in close-up. On the second was an association chart for Stonor, with several photographs of him, including standard prison mugshots, both face-on and side profile, and a strange flash-lit, blurry image of him that looked to be accidental, blown up to an eight by ten. On the third was a photograph pulled off the internet, of a snake with beige, brown and black markings. On the fourth was a map of the east side of Brighton, with an area of about a square mile crudely ringed by red marker pen.

In front of Grace lay his notes typed by his new Command Secretarial Assistant, Lesley Hildrew, his policy book and a tepid cup of coffee, which he'd had to stir with a knife because as usual all the spoons in the kitchenette had vanished. Reading from his notes he said, routinely, 'The time is 6.30 p.m., Tuesday March 3rd, this is the evening briefing of Operation Spider, the investigation into the suspicious death of Shelby James Stonor.'

He went on to outline the circumstances, especially the concerns of the helicopter's alert on-board paramedic that, although he had died at the scene, the injuries Stonor had sustained in the accident were not severe enough to have killed him – although he might have ended up as a paraplegic. The paramedic arranged to have blood samples biked up to Guy's Hospital where there was a specialist department in tropical diseases and poisons.

It was found that Stonor had toxins in his body from a saw-scaled viper snake, as well as complications from septicaemia. What had at first been mistaken for needle puncture marks had been established as a snake bite. The septicaemia was probably due to the bite causing contaminated clothing fibres to be injected into his leg, enabling bacteria to enter the bloodstream.

Norman Potting raised his hand.

'Yes, Norman?'

'In case it's of interest, chief, I read that tens of thousands of people die annually in India from snake bites. Quite a high percentage from this particular creature.' He pointed at the whiteboard.

'Thanks for sharing that, Norman,' Grace said.

'Shows how deadly the thing is,' Potting grumbled.

'Perhaps you'd like to find out if Stonor had been to India recently,' Grace suggested.

'The little shit,' Potting said. 'I imagine the nearest he got to India was a takeaway that he didn't pay for.'

There was muted laughter from the assembled team.

Potting's fiancée had died tragically some months ago, and Grace was still treating him gently whilst he was going through the grieving process. 'Quite,' he said, and looked back down at his notes. 'The initial purpose of this enquiry is to ascertain how and where Stonor came into contact with this reptile. Was it accidental or did someone use it to kill him? We've established there were no snakes kept at the home of his girlfriend, Angi Bunsen, where he'd been living. According to her, Stonor had been working a late shift stacking pallets at the Sussex Autospares warehouse on the Davigdor Industrial Estate. We've checked with them and they have no record of any such employee. Stonor's mobile phone and laptop computer have been sent to the High Tech Crime Unit for fast-track analysis, and we'll see what they reveal. There is one photograph on his phone that could be of immediate interest to us.'

Grace pointed at the whiteboard containing the photographs of Stonor and the association chart. 'That weird blurry one. I'll come back to its relevance shortly. Hopefully we'll get a plot of Stonor's recent movements from triangulation of his phone. Shame he didn't have a more sophisticated one, we could have got the exact address from geo-mapping. Let's not forget Stonor was a key target in a Brighton operation relating to the thefts of high-value motor vehicles. We need to establish whether his death has more suspicious connotations and is connected to that; has he fallen out with anyone from that team? Do we know if any of them keep snakes? In the meantime we need the following intelligence.'

He sipped his coffee and went on, giving actions to members of his team in turn. 'We need a search of the police data systems to update all Stonor's associates. Who he's linked to. Who has been in cars with him when he's been stopped. What speeding tickets and parking fines he's had recently. We need a full ANPR on his car, to see where he had been in the days before his death.'

ANPR – automatic numberplate recognition cameras – covered many of the roads throughout Sussex, and the UK. During the past few years it had become increasingly possible to plot the movements, sometimes on a minute-by-minute basis, of all vehicles in many parts of the country.

Grace continued. 'We have searched the property he shares with his girlfriend, Angi Bunsen.'

'She sounds hot,' Potting said.

'Hot?' Grace quizzed him.

'*Bunsen* burner!' Potting chortled at his joke,

then looked around, but was greeted only with silent stares and, on Guy Batchelor's face, a hint of a smile.

'Thank you, Norman,' Grace said. 'I'm tasking you with obtaining a list of all poisonous reptile dealers in Sussex, Surrey, Kent and Hampshire. Also check out all internet trading sources. I'm informed you have to have a Department of the Environment licence to keep venomous creatures in this country. See if Stonor kept any poisonous creatures.'

'Other than being one himself?' Potting could not resist.

'And find out, urgently, who in this city keeps venomous snakes, Norman. If one has escaped, we need to find out fast.' Grace turned to DC Alexander. 'Jack, I'd like you to obtain a list of all licences for dangerous animals held in these same counties. Also see if there are any reptile associations or clubs in the area – they might be a useful source of information.'

'Yes, sir.'

Then he turned to DS Cale. 'Tanja, I'm giving you the action of talking to the source handlers, see what you can find out about Shelby Stonor's movements in the past couple of months, particularly the last two weeks.'

'Yes, sir.'

All of the team kept glancing, in a mixture of horror and curiosity, at the first whiteboard. Graphic photographs from the post-mortem which

Grace and Branson had attended, earlier that day, were pinned to it. In the central one was a close-up of Stonor's face, coagulated blood rimming his horrifically bulging eyes. In another close up, of his hands, there was more coagulated blood that had leaked beneath each of his fingernails.

Grace turned the page of his CSA's notes, then looked up, briefly. 'For those of you interested in the toxicology of a saw-scaled viper bite, this is the pathologist's report.'

He studied the page in front of him briefly, before reading slowly, stumbling over some of the words. 'Haematological abnormalities are the most common effects of snake envenoming globally. Venom-induced consumption coagulopathy (VICC) is the commonest and most important. Other haemato-logical abnormalities are an anti-coagulant coagulopathy and thrombotic microangiopathy. Venom-induced consumption coagulopathy is an activation of the clotting pathway by procoagulant toxins, resulting in clotting factor consumption and coagulopathy. The type of procoagulant toxin differs between snakes and can activate prothrombin, factor X and factor V or consume fibrinogen. The major complication of VICC is haemorrhage, including intracranial haemorrhage which is often fatal. With *Echis carinatus* – the saw-scaled viper – the duration of abnormal clotting can be reduced from more than a week to twenty-four to forty-eight hours.' He looked up and smiled. 'Everyone still with me?'

Guy Batchelor shook his head. 'You lost me in the first sentence.'

Potting piped up again. 'If I understand it correctly, from these toxins, under some circumstances Stonor might have been slightly dead – but now he's actually very seriously dead?'

'Couldn't have put it better myself, Norman,' Grace replied. 'To cut through all the complex medical jargon, the saw-scaled viper kills its victims by turning them into haemophiliacs. Its venom causes the blood's coagulation system, which is our defence against bleeding to death when we have a cut, to go into overdrive. Once all the coagulant has been used up, the body starts to haemorrhage. If you cut yourself shaving you're likely to just bleed out.'

'Sounds to me like he's been bitten by one of his friends,' Guy Batchelor said.

There were several nods around the table.

'But why would any snake want to be friends with Shelby Stonor?' Jack Alexander asked.

'All right!' Grace said. 'Enough of that!' Then, studying his policy book for a moment, he said, 'This is my hypothesis. It would appear that Stonor has died from snake venom poisoning, and that could have occurred accidentally, but could also be linked to his current criminal activity. It may be that someone wanted to get rid of him. That's why we're looking into the death, we need to try to establish the facts. It is also possible he may have been attempting to steal these creatures – either for himself or perhaps to order for someone. My reason for thinking this is that photograph.'

He stood up, walked over to the whiteboard and pointed at the flash-lit blurry image. 'Take a close look and I'd like any of you to tell me what you see.'

'A bloody ugly-looking git,' Potting said.

'Anything else, Norman?' Grace said.

'Yes, looks like a photograph of a ceiling. The ceiling's in sharper focus than Stonor,' Potting said.

'Quite ornate cornicing – the sort you'd get in a Victorian house,' DS Batchelor said. 'But that window to the right, the top part of it just visible, with leaded lights, looks like mock Tudor. I know that because Lena and I used to live in a mock Tudor house.'

'What are those glass cupboards?' DC Davies asked. 'They look a bit like the kind you can get from Ikea.'

'I think they're storage boxes.' Glenn Branson stood up and peered closer. 'Or aquariums?'

'Vivariums, Glenn?' DS Batchelor said. 'I think that's the proper term for them.'

'It is, Guy. Containers that reptiles are kept in, providing them with a microcosm of their natural environment,' Grace said. 'Some of them look free-standing but others seem to be fitted.'

'Ah, so Stonor lived in one of them, did he?' Potting asked. 'A very suitable home for him.'

Ignoring him, as most of the team did when he

became irritating, Branson asked, 'What's the significance of this photograph?'

'It looks like it was taken accidentally,' Grace said. 'There are no other photographs for several days before this one and none after. Even though it's hard to see Stonor's expression too clearly, he's not posed for it, and he's not actually looking into the camera. The date's interesting – it was taken last Tuesday evening, February 24th. The toxin from a saw-scaled viper takes from around forty-eight hours to several days to kill its victim. It was about 8 p.m., Sunday 1st March that Stonor crashed his car.'

Grace looked down at his notes. 'The High Tech Crime Unit obtained that information. They've also given me the approximate location, from triangulation – it was taken in presumably a house, in the Roedean area of the city. Significantly, there have been a spate of reported burglaries in this area over the past two months, all bearing Stonor's MO.' He stood up and walked over to the whiteboard with the map of east Brighton, and ran his finger around the red-inked perimeter.

'So you think he might have broken into a house to steal some poisonous reptiles to order, it went wrong and he was bitten, sir?' DC Boutwood asked.

'That's one line I'm considering at the moment, EJ,' Grace said. 'The accidental photograph. The small cut on his right arm the pathologist noticed. Maybe he fell over and the creatures got out. We need to re-interview Stonor's girlfriend, Angi

Bunsen, urgently. We also need to find out where those vivariums came from, and who fitted them. There can't be many houses that have these.' He looked at DS Cale.

'Tanja, it's going to be a big task – can you get some staff – borrow some from John Street, if you have to – checking building firms and individual carpenters who might have fitted these vivariums in a house in the Roedean area within the past few years?'

'Yes, sir,' she said.

Grace liked her. The redhead had joined his team after the tragic death of Bella Moy last year and she had a warm personality and a willing nature.

'Did anyone report a break-in that night in that area, sir?' DC Davies asked.

'No,' Grace replied. 'But it could be because they were keeping these creatures illegally.'

'Or maybe one of these reptiles bit them too,' Potting said. 'And killed them?'

'Why would anyone want to keep a thing like that as a pet?' EJ asked. 'Wouldn't you have to be a bit weird?'

'Yep, well I think I'd rather have something a bit more cuddly,' Grace retorted. 'I can't imagine you can just walk into the average pet shop and come out with a snake that can kill someone.'

He was interrupted by his phone ringing. Glancing at the display, he just saw the word *international*. Raising an apologetic finger, he answered it, in case it was to do with Dr Crisp.

Instantly, he recognized the German detective's voice. 'Marcel!' he said, quietly. 'I'm in a meeting. Is it urgent, or can I call you back in half an hour?'

Kullen was sounding more sombre than usual. Strangely sombre. In a few words he told him the reason for his call.

Grace froze.

CHAPTER 60

Tuesday 3 March

As Jodie lay back on the bed in their cabin, sipping the glass of champagne the butler had brought her, she reflected on how it was all going with Rowley. So far so good. She knew enough about marriage laws to fend off a challenge from any of Rowley's family, but she did not know the full size of his estate nor his inheritance planning. She'd walk away from this with a decent sum, a few million at the very least, she hoped. But not enough to buy a £50-million villa on Lake Como.

More than anything in the world, she longed to fly her parents to Italy, take them out on a boat on Lake Como, past all the fuck-off villas, past George Clooney's, Richard Branson's and all the others. Then they would see the most stunning villa of all, and she would tell the driver of the boat to go to the dock and tie up.

And she'd look at the strange expression on her parents' faces.

And she'd say, 'Welcome to my little holiday home!'

And Cassie, finally, would have said, 'Wow!'

All thanks to a snake.

Well, some of it, for sure. Beautiful, beautiful snakes.

On her laptop she typed into her password-protected diary:

So just how different are we humans from snakes? Like, here's an intriguing mathematical puzzle: Cows share twenty-five per cent of their genes with snakes. Humans share eighty per cent of their genes with cows. So we share about twenty per cent of ours with snakes.

I reckon that percentage is a lot higher in some people. There are some seriously reptilian people out there.

Snake charmers use a musical instrument called a Pungi. It's a wind instrument made from a gourd with reed pipes. But snake charmers have removed either the fangs or the venom glands, and some sew the mouth shut. The charmer sits out of biting range because the snakes actually consider the charmer and the Pungi a threat.

It's all a con.

You just have to turn to the Bible. Psalm 58, verses 3–5: 'The wicked turn aside from birth; liars go astray as soon as they are born. Their venom is like that of a snake, like a deaf serpent that does not hear, that does not respond to the magicians, or to a skilled snake charmer.'

I can tell you another thing that snakes don't like – I learned it from my late husband, Christopher Bentley, keeper of snakes and expert on poisonous creatures in general. And that is having their venom extracted.

It's an incredible sensation! You hold the snake – in my case a saw-scaled viper – with your fingers, right behind its head, and press it down on a hard surface. I can tell you, it really does not like this. But if you keep the pressure up, in the right place, at the top of its neck, on the edge of a glass beaker, it spits its venom out. This is not a great way to make friends with a snake – but the reality is, none of us, ever, will become buddies with a creature that will only ever view you as one thing – lunch!

Kill or be killed. It's the story of the animal kingdom. And of the human race. If you want to be a survivor you must, like me, follow in the path of Ka, who said, 'Life is not a matter of chance . . . it's a matter of choice.'

I made my choice. It's all working out pretty well.

One important thing Jodie knew about snake venom was that it begins to break down soon after being extracted and loses its potency. The only way to preserve that potency is to freeze-dry it immediately.

Freeze-dried venom when rehydrated is almost as potent as a freshly delivered bite.

And she already had some in the minibar fridge.

CHAPTER 61

Wednesday 4 March

Morning broke to a milky-white vista of the bay of Mumbai. Jodie leaned on the deck rail, yawning. She'd risen early, kept awake most of the night by her husband snoring like a warthog. But she hadn't wanted to wake him. Hey, he might as well enjoy his last few days, she thought. But not out of any kind of altruism.

She didn't want to do anything that might arouse his suspicions.

Dressed in a long-sleeved T-shirt, lightweight jeans and plimsolls, holding a mug of coffee, she savoured the warm, humid morning air, and the glorious sight of the Gateway of India monument on the waterfront looming ever closer. The mass of skyscrapers. The long, curved bridge with what looked like a sail in the middle. Men in small fishing boats waving at them.

She waved back.

Three hours later the minibus moved in short, stop-start jerks through the almost solid wedge of

Mumbai morning traffic, and the constant blare of horns. Pulling a shawl round her against the freezing air-conditioning, she dozily watched a man pulling a trailer loaded with canisters worm past them, then leaning against Rollo, who was photographing everything in sight – which was mostly just buses, lorries, mopeds and bicycles – she fell asleep. When she woke up, the minibus was still crawling through the same din of horns in the same heavy traffic. Tall, shabby, white colonial-looking buildings were all around them.

'Amazing city, isn't it, my angel?' he asked.

'Amazing.'

She dozed on and off again and finally felt their speed picking up. She was next woken by the sensation of the minibus slowing. Through the window she saw a sign.

SANJAY GANDHI NATIONAL PARK BORIVALI

Moments later they entered a lush forest.

The smartly dressed cruise-ship shore guide, Deepak, speaking loudly, told them that if they were lucky they would see an array of birds, including the Blue Flycatcher and the Maribar Whistling Thrush. He went on to list all the other birds they might see then added that if they were *really* lucky they might spot a tiger.

She didn't give a fuck about any of the birds. That was not why she had wanted to come here.

314

The reason was in the right-hand pocket of her trousers.

Finally the bus stopped and their cruise guide told them they could leave any of their belongings in the vehicle, they would be quite safe. Jodie put on her sunglasses and straw hat, and as she stepped down they were surrounded by a shouting horde of people, many of them kids, holding up plastic crocodiles, photographs of Mumbai, models of the Taj Mahal and a plethora of other tourist tat.

Ignoring them, holding Rollo's hand to help him down, she was already starting to perspire in the steamy late-morning heat, beneath a fierce sun. Wearing a floppy white hat of the kind favoured by cricket umpires, a linen shirt, bright blue slacks and sandals, a paparazzi-sized camera slung round his neck, and blinking at the light and the surrounding mob, Rollo looked every inch the tourist – and, in this debilitating heat, as if he had aged ten years since leaving the sanctuary of the ship.

Deepak shepherded them past a long queue filing towards a ticket gate that looked like a miniature temple, to a separate entrance where he introduced them to another guide, a smiling Indian in a white kurta, and a set of teeth that looked like they had been borrowed from his grandfather. He held up a bunch of tickets in one hand and a paddle in the other on which was written the words 'Organza VIPS' and shouted a greeting at them all.

'Hello, I am Prakash, your crocodile farm guide!

We are going to visit the crocodiles. Everyone OK with crocodiles?'

The group of ten *Organza* passengers – all elderly apart from Jodie – gave half-hearted smiles.

'You do not need to worry. These are man-eaters, but we feed them on plenty of chickens, so they are not very hungry. I am guide here for fifteen years – and in all my time, we have not had one visitor eaten – yet! This is my guarantee to you – if you are eaten, then you get full refund of your ticket! Yes, fair?'

'Very fair!' an old lady shouted back.

Several of them laughed. Nervously.

'OK, so now follow me – in crocodile formation, yes! Please be keeping close together. Safety in numbers!'

Jodie stopped to fiddle with the laces of her trainers, as the rest of the group filed off, obediently, in crocodile formation. Rollo waited patiently, then they followed on a short distance behind.

'Maybe we should catch them up, my love,' he said, sounding a little uneasy.

'I hate organized groups,' she said.

They maintained a steady pace, some thirty or so yards behind the rest of the pack. After ten minutes they reached the start of a forest, bordered, on one side, by a wide, swamp-like lake. A small crocodile lay basking in the sun just a few yards from the path. In the water she could see a pair of eyes above a ripple.

'They give me the heebie-jeebies, these things,' Rollo said.

'I think they're beautiful, darling! Take a photo of me beside this one.' She stopped and stepped back until she was just inches from the basking reptile.

'My love,' he said. 'I don't like it. Do you know how they kill their prey? They pull them into the water and drown them, and then keep them underwater, in what is their larder, to tenderize the meat for a few days before eating them.'

'These are all fed – Prakash told us!'

Looking dubious, he removed the camera from round his neck, focused it on her and snapped away, quickly. 'OK, let's move on!'

The rest of the group had almost disappeared from sight. They continued along a narrowing mud-baked path, with forest and murky swamp to their left and the open water, filled as far as they could see with more and more crocodiles, to their right.

'Don't you think there's something magical about them, darling?' she asked, slipping her hand into her trouser pocket. She had practised the movements several times, to make sure she had it absolutely right.

'No, I don't. I think they're hideous and scary. And they can outrun humans.'

They walked on a few paces, the forest thickening to their left. Then suddenly she stumbled and fell over, crying out in pain, and lay, face down in the undergrowth. 'Owwww!' she cried out. 'I've bashed my bloody knee.'

'Jodie!' he said. 'My poor angel!' He knelt beside her. 'Here, give me your hand.'

She reached up towards him, then as he began to pull her up, she used a manoeuvre she had learned in a judo lesson some years ago, to pull him, sprawling forward, without him even realizing it was deliberate. As he landed flat on his face she pulled the fang from her pocket and jabbed him in the right ankle with it, then returned it to her pocket.

'Owww! Shit!' he cried out. 'I've been stung or bitten by something!'

'What, my love, what is it?'

'My ankle! Shit!'

'Which ankle?' She helped him to his feet. 'Which ankle?'

'My right one.'

She knelt and pulled up his trouser leg. There was one tiny spot of blood showing. 'I can't see anything, my love,' she said.

'I felt something! I definitely felt something.'

'Where?' She ran her finger across his ankle, wiping away the blood spot. 'Here?'

'Yes.'

'I can't see anything.'

'Hello! Hello! Mr and Mrs White Hat and Straw Hat! Is everything all right?' the guide called out, anxiously running up to them.

'Fine!' she said.

'Absolutely fine,' her husband confirmed. 'I just tripped over.'

'But was it a nice trip?' Prakash asked, with a winning smile.

'Very nice,' Jodie said.

'I am always obliged to be at your very best service. Nowhere will you find better trips! Are you in need of any help?'

'I'm fine, thank you, Prakash,' Rollo said.

'If you are happy then I am happy!'

'We're very happy,' Jodie said. 'Couldn't be happier.'

CHAPTER 62

Wednesday 4 March

The package Tooth had ordered on the internet arrived at his hotel at 11 a.m. on Wednesday. He tipped the young man who brought the large box up to his room, then hung the 'Do Not Disturb' sign on his door.

It was all there, just as he had requested. He took each item out and tested it. They were all working fine. He went out and bought a rucksack, then placed them all carefully inside it. Tonight, when it was dark, he planned to return to the empty house. It would take a while to complete the task, but there was no rush. He would have all night.

And after that, peace of mind.

Tooth didn't smile often. But he smiled now.

CHAPTER 63

Thursday 5 March

'Roy? Roy? Roy?'

'Urrr?'

'Are you OK? You're so restless.'

'Wassertime?'

'Two fifteen. You keep tossing and turning and shouting out. What is it? Is your leg hurting?'

Grace rolled over in bed and touched Cleo's face with his nose. 'I'm sorry.'

'Were you having a bad dream?'

'Yeah. Sorry I woke you.'

They lay still for a moment.

'Want to tell me?'

He did want to tell her, so badly. They'd always promised each other they would have no secrets. Yet how could he tell her? The taboo subject. Sandy.

So often over the time that they'd been together, Cleo had tried to get him to move on from his first wife. She'd been understanding, yet in bad moments had told him that at times she felt she wasn't married only to him, but to him and a ghost.

Sandy.

Back in January Roy had looked at the woman lying in her hospital bed. Sandy. He had denied to himself that it was her, but he knew the truth and had been suppressing it. At some point it was going to have to come out, and how on earth was he ever going to start that conversation? And deal with the fallout that would follow? It was something that would take many hours, maybe days, to work through with Cleo – if she would accept the situation at all – and with all the authorities.

The information he had, to date, was that for a time she had been a heroin addict – and had then gone clean. And she had a son.

Whatever.

He and Sandy had tried repeatedly for a child, with no success. So now this woman had a child.

And there was too much at stake with his new life. The past was the past. So the woman in the bed at the Klinikum was Sandy. But she was no longer *his* Sandy. She had made the decision, whatever had been going on in her mind at the time, to walk out on him and fabricate her disappearance – and cause him ten years of hell. He wasn't about to disrupt his life now, however unfortunate her circumstances were.

But for the last two nights he had been unable to sleep properly.

Ever since that phone call from Kullen. Grace had met him for the first time a few years ago. Since then Kullen had helped him through a possible reported sighting of Sandy in the past, when he had gone to Munich on what turned out to be a wild goose chase.

'Roy,' he had said this time. 'All is good?' His voice had sounded strangely hesitant.

'Very good. You? Still driving crazily, like Lewis Hamilton?'

'Yah! I have a new car, a Scirocco Storm. It is fast! I take you for a drive sometime!'

Grace remembered his friend's driving on his first visit to Germany. He loved fast cars himself, but at 160 mph on the autobahn, with Kullen constantly taking his eyes off the road to talk to him, he had been somewhat nervous. 'Look forward to it!' he had replied, with bravado.

'So, this woman you came to see in January, in the Klinikum Schwabing? To make sure she was not your former wife, Sandy?'

'Yes? How is she doing?'

'Not good, Roy. Her condition is unstable. The prognosis is bad. But there is something you need to know.'

'Tell me.'

'I sent the hairbrush you mailed me to the DNA laboratory. I just got the results back this morning. The match is conclusive. This woman is Sandy.'

CHAPTER 64

Friday 6 March

Tooth watched a man, in his sixties, warmly wrapped up, who appeared at the same time every day, so regularly he could set his watch by him. He was walking along the street towards him now, reading a novel, holding it so high he had to tilt his head upwards to read it.

Some days Tooth walked the round trip of several miles here and back to the hotel for exercise, and being on foot gave him a good opportunity to look carefully around. Also, and importantly, there were Neighbourhood Watch signs displayed in the windows of several of the houses. Someone vigilant would be likely to report seeing a car in the area, for several days running, with a lone occupant. He was less noticeable on foot.

As he strolled around the vicinity of Jodie's house, he noticed some of the other regulars, too. The sad-looking man who pushed his wife along in a wheelchair, their fat dog waddling along beside it. The mad-haired woman in a white SUV who drove to the end of her drive and then spent a good sixty seconds checking in both directions before pulling out into the deserted street. The school-run mums. The newsagent in his little Mazda stopping outside houses and running in, then out again. The postman, in his red van, at 9.30, doing his delivery round.

The postman had only delivered three items to Jodie's house all week. Tooth entered after it was dark to check them. All of them were circulars addressed 'To the Occupier'.

He kept an eye on the house each day from eight in the morning until it grew dark, around 6 p.m. The weather had been good to him all week until this morning, when it had rained hard. That was fine, it meant fewer people were out walking around. But now it was dry again and there were patches of blue sky. He wondered how she was enjoying her cruise on the *Organza*, paid for out of the counterfeit $200,000 she had stolen, perhaps?

At 10 a.m., a grimy white van turned in through the gates of No. 191 Roedean Crescent and went down the steep drive.

Tooth strolled along the street. As he drew level with the entrance to No. 191 he glanced down and saw that the rear doors of the van were open, and a rugged-looking man in his forties, in work clothes and gum boots, was busily pulling some gardening tools out of the interior. On the van's side panel was written 'Stepney Garden Maintenance Services'.

He sauntered casually down the drive, and up to the man. With his fake English accent he said, 'Hi, we've just moved in and are looking for a gardener.' He jerked his thumb vaguely over his shoulder.

'I'll give you a card,' the man said. 'You'll need to go through the office. Hang on a sec.'

Tooth waited while the gardener went to the front of the vehicle. A moment later the man handed him a card with green writing on it.

'The people who live here, they'd be able to give a reference for you?' Tooth asked.

'It's a lady on her own,' the man said. 'Hardly ever see her.'

'Right. What's her name?'

The gardener shrugged. 'I dunno. I work for the company and just do the addresses they give me. I've probably not spoken ten words to the lady in two years.'

'Does she rent the house or is it hers?' Tooth asked.

'Couldn't even tell you that, sir, sorry.'

Tooth left him and walked back up the drive, then headed down towards the sea, thinking about the mysterious woman. Very few photos in the house. No contact with her household staff. No messages on her landline answering machine. It seemed she liked to keep herself invisible. That suited him very well indeed.

It could mean that it would be a long while before anyone started to miss her. Time for him to be long gone. With the memory stick. Wherever she had hidden it, he would find it. She would tell him.

Not wanting to draw attention to himself, and starting to feel hungry, he walked back towards the centre of Brighton, deciding to resume his vigil later. As he strode along, he remembered a burger place called Grubbs, where he had eaten last time he was here, that made what he called proper burgers. He navigated his way along St James's Street to it.

After his meal, he headed towards the sea, took the steps down to Madeira Drive and crossed over the road. Then, heading west, with the tracks of the Volks Railway to his left and the deserted pebble beach beyond that, he was thinking hard as he walked, but was distracted every few minutes by the clatter of a bicycle or ping of a bell on the cycle lane at the edge of the pavement. A cold, blustery, sou'westerly wind was blowing against him.

Where would he have hidden the memory stick? He'd searched every inch of the house, the loft, the garden shed. He wasn't comfortable being in Brighton. Although he had travelled here under one of the aliases he used, he knew he was still a wanted man in this city. After his escape at Shoreham Harbour last year, he'd checked out the local news online from back home. That detective, Roy Grace, and his team had stated that he was missing, presumed drowned. But from his dockside wrestle with the black cop, he knew they were likely to have his DNA on file. The sooner he got out of here, the better.

He was feeling frustrated and aimless. How long was he going to have to wait for this bitch to return? He wanted to be back home, out on his boat in the warmth, with his associate.

He missed his associate.

Missed him more than he'd ever missed any human.

As he walked by the pier with its stalls out front – *Moo Moos, the best Shakes in town, Donuts & Churros, Delicious Donuts, Crepes, The Hot Dog Hut* – the clock tower over the entrance, with a pyramid sign in front of it advertising *The Best Fish & Chips in Brighton* – he was suddenly reminded of his childhood vacations in Atlantic City with one of his foster mothers. Hot summer days ambling alone, aimlessly, along the boardwalk, avoiding tourists in push carts, while she played the slots.

She played them all day long, coins stacked up beside her, plastic beaker of beer in one hand, yanking the handle or pushing the buttons, peering at the revolving fruits through curling smoke from the cigarette dangling permanently from her lips. When she was winning, she'd bribe him with a handful of coins, and he'd immediately go and spend them at one of the shooting galleries.

He always tried for, and normally succeeded, in getting the maximum score. When he didn't he got angry, and on more than one occasion cracked the glass or wrenched the grip of the gun so hard that it broke.

There was an aquarium to his right and, across a busy intersection, a cream and red building advertising *Harry Ramsden Fish & Chips*.

Ahead, across the far side of the intersection, was the yellow and white Royal Albion Hotel. A stack of beer barrels was piled on the sidewalk. He ambled on, passing a café to his left and a flint-walled groyne. How long before the bitch came back from her cruise?

He crossed the cycle lane and waited for a green light at the pedestrian crossing, heading back to the modern slab of his hotel, unsure what the rest of the day held for him. Waiting. He was OK with waiting. He was fine with waiting. Letting time slide by. Maybe he'd catch a movie in town or on his hotel television.

The light changed to green. He was about to cross the road when he had a thought. He'd check the pier out, why not? See if it had any shooting galleries. It was something to do.

He turned back, totally forgetting the cycle lane. As he stepped forward he heard the ping of a bell, a clank and a shout then a loud squeal of rubber on metal. An instant later a shadow descended on him. He felt a crashing blow that hurled him off his feet. He saw the sidewalk coming up to meet his face.

Then a firework show inside his head.

Then silence.

CHAPTER 65

Friday 6 March

Shortly after midday Roy Grace, still distracted by the news he'd had about Sandy, sat in Cassian Pewe's large office, drinking coffee from a china cup. He absently noted the spoon in the saucer – and doubted that spoons ever vanished here, in this hallowed Police HQ building. He updated the ACC on the processing by the French authorities of their extradition request for Edward Crisp, and the progress on Operation Spider, the investigation into the suspicious death of Shelby Stonor.

Or to be more accurate, and to his old adversary's clear irritation, the lack of progress on both. With luck there would be an update from the French police, so he had been assured, within a few days. But there was little progress from the actions on Operation Spider that he had given his team at their briefing three days ago. A check of Stonor's movements since his last release from prison had revealed some relevant information, but not much.

Plotting from the ANPR cameras and footage from the city's network of 350 CCTV cameras, showed Stonor had recently made numerous visits to the expensive and exclusive Roedean area of the city. These visits coincided with a spate of reported house burglaries in the area. But thanks to the budget constraints, housebreaking, except where life was in imminent danger had, to Grace's fury, become a lower priority. He could quite seriously envisage a time, in the near future, when someone would wake to find an intruder in their home, dial 999 and be told to send an email.

Angi Bunsen, Stonor's girlfriend, had been questioned extensively, but had not provided anything useful. It appeared that Stonor had lied to her about having a job in a warehouse – presumably to cover for his burglary activities. She had said nothing of significance in any of her interviews. Stonor had given her every indication that he planned to go straight and save up to buy a Brighton taxi plate. She couldn't understand why he might have any connection to venomous snakes.

DC Jack Alexander's action of checking all holders of licences, under the Dangerous Wild Animals Act of 1976 in the city of Brighton and Hove, had revealed just a handful, including a police inspector they knew who kept a pet python. They were all legitimate.

Suppliers of vivariums had been contacted, the addresses of all customers they held on record visited, to reveal nothing more lethal than a tank of gerbils who had ganged up on one of their own and bitten a toe off. There was a reptile owners' association but none of its members knew of Shelby Stonor.

Information from source handlers about Stonor and his associates, since he had last been freed, so far had provided nothing new. Nor had the High Tech Crime Unit's interrogation of his pay-as-you-go mobile phone and computer revealed any unexpected contacts, or anything else of significance other than the blurry photograph. The main person he saw regularly was a small-time drug dealer and car thief called Dean Warren, who also appeared to be part of the gang conspiring to steal high-value cars. Like Warren, Stonor had connections to the Sussex towns of Crawley and Hastings through a number of small-time criminal associates, all of whom were being interviewed, but so far nothing had come from any of them.

To Grace's surprise, rather than being angry at him for failing to bring the case to a swift conclusion, Pewe took a pragmatic view. 'I think we have to accept that whatever happened, Stonor is not someone worth throwing unlimited expensive resources at, Roy. Yes?'

'In the current climate, I'd have to agree, sir.'

'Good man.' Pewe, in his white shirt with epaulettes, shiny blond hair and angelic blue eyes, gave Grace a condescending smile. 'Now I have a nice bit of news, which I'm sure you will like. I've just heard from our new Chief Constable, Lesley

Manning, that Bella Moy has been posthumously awarded the Queen's Gallantry Medal. I understand that she and Norman Potting had become an item?'

'More than an item, sir. They were engaged to be married.'

Pewe nodded. 'It sounds as if DS Potting will be accompanying Bella's mother to the ceremony, then. A member of the Royal Family will be presenting the medal later in the year. But to recognize the award in Sussex we are having a small local event with the Chief.'

'Very appropriate.'

Pewe nodded. 'I'll see to it. Now, back to business. I want you to stay on the Stonor enquiry, but don't bust your balls on it. I'd like you to focus your energies on Crisp. Once he has been released back to us there's going to need to be a lot of work preparing for his prosecution, and it has to be watertight, belt and braces. It's going to be one of the highest profile trials we'll ever have been involved with and I need it to be in a safe pair of hands. Understood?'

'Yes, sir.'

As ever with ACC Pewe, Grace waited for the sting. It came rapidly and subtly from the man who had once secretly ordered a team to scan and excavate the garden of the home Grace had shared with Sandy, on the suspicion that he had murdered her.

'Such a shame the glory for his capture goes to

the French police rather than to us, don't you think, Roy?'

Actually, no, he felt like replying, defensively. But that would have been an argument he could not win. The truth was that Operation Haywain, which he had run, had successfully identified and found Sussex's first serial killer in many decades. Through his efforts and those of his team, Edward Crisp had been trapped in an underground tunnel which had collapsed, nearly killing Grace and several of his colleagues. It had seemed certain that Crisp must be dead. Yet, somehow, he had escaped.

The buck stopped with Grace as the Senior Investigating Officer. However improbable the odds on Crisp having survived, somehow he had. Which meant that in the eyes of Pewe, justifiably, Grace had screwed up. He'd had the offender in his grasp and the man had slipped the net. It didn't matter that Grace had been in hospital, his leg filled with shotgun pellets, when Crisp had escaped. He was the SIO and ultimately to blame. And to make it worse, the recapture was down to pure luck. Although swift circulation of Crisp's details had meant the French police were able to act decisively.

'Yes,' Grace said. 'I think Crisp makes Harry Houdini look like an amateur.'

In his sarcastic tone, Pewe said, 'I would have thought – given all you had found out about the man during your operation – you would have been aware of that.' He stared sternly at Grace for some moments, then went on. 'Quite frankly, most people in my position would have taken you off the case after such a fiasco. But I want you to understand, despite our past differences, I'm not a vindictive person. I appreciate with your injuries there were extenuating circumstances, and I've not forgotten that last year you risked your life to save mine. So I'm going to give you a reprieve. Just make sure there are no more screw-ups from the moment Crisp is released to us. Bringing a successful prosecution is going to be on your head. Do I make myself clear?'

Grace said, stiffly, 'Very clear, sir.'

'I'll give you some words of wisdom, Roy. We don't learn from our successes – we only learn from our mistakes. You'd do well to remember that.'

'I'll remember that.'

CHAPTER 66

Friday 6 March

'How are you feeling, Mr Carmichael?' Dr Ryerson asked, entering the cabin. It was just after 6 p.m. and Jodie's husband had stayed in bed for the past two days, throwing up constantly, sustained only by sugary drinks. He had resisted the doctor, telling Jodie that, from his experience on cruise ships, if the doctor believed you might have a contagious bug they would confine you and your partner to your cabin for days. But finally he had given in and told her to ask him to come.

'Terrible,' he said, holding a handkerchief to his nose to staunch his latest nosebleed.

'Your wife tells me you had oysters for dinner the night before last. Afterwards Martinis, then champagne and white wine?'

Jodie, holding her husband's hand, said, 'You did rather go for it, didn't you, my darling?'

He nodded.

'It's possible they haven't agreed with you. Oysters and spirits can be a dangerous mix. But is there anything else you can think of?'

'Yesterday,' he said listlessly. 'Sorry – day before yesterday – at the crocodile farm. Mumbai. I got bitten.'

'Bitten?'

'Something bit me.'

'Where were you bitten?'

'On my leg – ankle – my right ankle.'

'He fell over in the crocodile farm and thought he had been bitten by something,' Jodie confirmed. 'I had a look but I couldn't see anything.'

The doctor lifted away the sheet and examined his ankle carefully, frowning. 'There is a faint mark but I can't see any swelling,' he said. 'It might be an insect bite. If you'd been bitten by something venomous, a snake or a spider, there would almost certainly be swelling.'

He took Rollo's temperature then studied the thermometer. 'Hmmn,' he said. 'You have quite a high temperature. It might be something you've eaten, a bug, or a reaction to some sort of insect bite.' He looked at Jodie. 'Do you feel all right?'

'Absolutely fine.' She gave him a smile.

The doctor quizzed Rollo about his medical history, then delved into his medical bag, which he had placed on the floor, and removed a syringe and a vial. 'I'm going to give you a shot of anti-biotic, and then I'll come back and see you in a few hours.' He turned to Jodie. 'I think you should stay with your husband and keep an eye on him. I suggest you have room service tonight.'

'Yes,' she said. 'Yes, of course. I wouldn't want

to leave him on his own. Can you explain his nosebleed?'

'His blood pressure is up quite a bit, which I'd expect in his condition at the moment. That's probably causing it.'

'Thank you.'

'Good,' the doctor said, preparing the injection. Then he smiled. 'I'm sure you'll be feeling right as rain very soon, Mr Carmichael!' he said. 'Best if you don't eat anything, but I'd like you to drink as much water as you can.'

'Don't care for water,' Rollo Carmichael said, looking at him balefully. 'You know what W. C. Fields said about water?'

'W. C. Fields, the actor?'

He nodded. 'Never drink water,' he said. 'Cos fish screw in it.'

The doctor laughed. 'Well, he had a point, I suppose!'

Then suddenly, and without warning, Carmichael vomited a jet of bile and blood.

CHAPTER 67

Sunday 8 March

The unconscious American in bed 14 had been brought in to the Intensive Care Unit of the Royal Sussex County Hospital on Friday afternoon. He was in a bad way, with an MRI scan showing a brain contusion from a small, hairline skull fracture, as well as two broken ribs and severe bruising to his right leg. The two cyclists, who had been racing each other along the cycle lane, were both taken to the hospital as well; one with a broken arm and dislocated shoulder, the other with a shattered knee.

The American had been identified from his driving licence as John Daniels, with an address in New York City. He had a bar receipt in his wallet for the Waterfront Hotel in Brighton. The hospital had checked with the hotel, but they said they had no record of any John Daniels, though they did have a large group of Americans staying for a conference in the city. A request had been sent by Brighton Police to the New York Police Department for the contact details of the man's next of kin, but so far nothing had come back.

Now, this afternoon, the duty nurse in charge of him had called the registrar, excitedly, to say that he was showing signs of coming round.

'Welcome back, Mr Daniels!'

Tooth blinked. The man was a fuzzy outline. As his focus slowly returned he saw a man in his early thirties, with close-cropped fair hair, dressed in blue surgical scrubs and holding a clipboard. Beside him stood an Arabic woman, similarly attired, and another man in dark trousers and a white short-sleeved shirt, who looked authoritative.

Tooth stared at them blankly. Was he in Iraq? 'Back?' he asked. 'Back?'

'I'm Dr Martin, this is Mr Buxton, our consultant neurosurgeon, and our registrar – you're at the Royal Sussex County Hospital.'

'Hospital?'

All Tooth could think was that he was in hospital in Iraq. Had he been shot? He remembered a shadow looming over him. That was all. 'Hospital?' he repeated blankly. 'Doc Marten. Boots?'

The man in the white shirt, with the faintest trace of a smile, said, 'Very good.'

Tooth squinted at him. *Was the man CIA?*

'Wolverine,' Tooth rambled. 'One Thousand Mile Boots.'

The man in the white shirt smiled again. 'Very good!'

'How are you feeling, Mr Daniels?' the one with the short hair, in scrubs, asked.

340

He'd been trained to keep silent if ever captured. So, staring at the blue curtains all around him and the monitor showing his vital signs, he said nothing.

He was in some kind of military hospital. American, he hoped.

He closed his eyes and drifted off.

The medical team remained around him for some moments, then stepped away and out through the curtains, safely out of earshot.

'He'll be confused for a while yet,' the neuro-surgeon said. 'There are no abnormalities showing on his brain scan. There are a number of contusions consistent with this kind of accident, which will take a while to subside. I'll come back and see him in a couple of days. If there's any dramatic change in his condition either way please let me know immediately. The biggest danger is a cerebral haemorrhage from damaged blood vessels, and that's something we cannot see from the current scans.'

As they walked away across the ward, Tooth grappled with his mind. It felt like he was trying to grip a wriggling fish with a greasy hand.

It slipped free.

Everything went blank again.

CHAPTER 68

Monday 9 March

The wet weekend had only worsened Roy Grace's sense of gloom and confusion. On Saturday, he'd tried hard to put his troubled thoughts away and focus on spending time with Noah who was now, at eight months, able to crawl at some speed. He'd also busied himself stripping the wallpaper off the spare room in their cottage, and exploring a new area of the surrounding countryside with Humphrey – and trying to train him – unsuccessfully so far – to ignore sheep in the neighbouring field. They'd also had a site meeting with a man from Sussex Oak Framers, who was going to quote for an extension they wanted to add to enlarge the kitchen – provided they could get planning permission.

Planning permission was a dirty expression in the village at the moment, due to proposals, which everyone in the area thought were absurd, for an entire new town to be built nearby. It was being actively fought by a protest group, LAMBS, who had invited him to be their spokesperson. He'd had to decline, reluctantly, because of his position as a police officer, but he privately supported their aims.

On Saturday night, leaving Noah in the care of Kaitlynn, Cleo and he had packed an overnight bag and gone to dinner at the Cat Inn at West Hoathly. Both of them had ended up drinking far too much, in an effort to relax, and had returned yesterday morning, with bad hangovers, to Noah screaming. He felt guilty that for much of yesterday Noah had been propped in front of the TV for his entertainment, whilst they had recovered.

All he could really think about was Sandy. Lying right now in the Munich hospital. With her life slipping away?

He had to see her again one more time before she was gone for good, either into a grave or a crematorium incinerator.

Had to have closure for both himself and Cleo.

Cleo had asked him, repeatedly, over the weekend what was wrong, and each time he'd fobbed her off by telling her he was fretting about Crisp.

But the reality was he'd barely thought about the serial killer. And he'd hardly slept a wink over the weekend.

Sandy.

He'd simply not been able to pluck up the courage to talk to Cleo, unrealistically hoping it would all go away.

But it wouldn't. It would never go away. Not until they had closure. There was only one way to do that.

He had to go to Munich and see her again.

That scared the hell out of him. He remembered the saying, 'And the truth shall set you free.'

But would it?

What if it was quite the reverse?

He had a bad feeling, a really bad feeling.

As he stood in the shower after his early-morning run, feeling as if he'd had no weekend at all, he knew what he had to do.

But he really wasn't sure how to do it.

CHAPTER 69

Monday 9 March

An hour later, in his office, Roy Grace began the week as he always did, by glancing through the serials of the past few days. He saw several dwelling burglaries, two Range Rover thefts and a missing vulnerable teenager who had last been seen heading towards Dukes Mound, a popular gay cruising area. A nasty bicycle accident on Friday, close to the pier, where an American visitor and two cyclists had been hospitalized, and a reported robbery at 5 a.m. on Sunday morning by two youths and a woman who had taken a mobile phone and wallet from a man in the city centre.

Soon after making a start on the papers relating to Crisp, his phone pinged with a text from his sister asking when she could next come over to see her 'favourite and only' nephew – and spend some time with them all.

He texted back with a photograph of a giggling Noah with a thumb raised in the air, looking like he was in agreement, and gave her some dates that worked for him and Cleo.

At 10 a.m. he had a meeting in his office with financial investigators DS Peter Billin and Kelly Nicholls, who had been piecing together the complex paperwork relating to ownership of the house next door to Crisp's home, where several of his murders appeared to have been carried out, and which clearly linked Crisp to the property.

Then an unexpected call came from an Interpol detective in London, Tom Haynes, shortly after 11 a.m.

'Sir,' he said, 'formal arrangements have been made for two of your officers to travel to Lyon to liaise with French police over Edward Crisp.'

As soon as he had finished speaking to the man, he informed ACC Cassian Pewe; then he called Glenn Branson and asked him to come to his office. Whilst waiting, he leaned back in his chair, closed his eyes and lapsed back into his troubled thoughts.

'Can't take the pace at your age?'

Grace looked up with a start to see the tall detective towering over him. 'Ever heard of that basic courtesy, knocking?'

'Yeah – didn't want to wake you. Old people can die from sudden shocks.'

Grace gave him a smile. 'Haha.' Then he looked him up and down. 'Have you got a part-time job as a lighthouse?'

'What?'

Branson was attired at this moment in a slim-fit, shiny, chocolate-coloured suit and a yellow tie that looked luminous. Grace pointed at it. 'Could be useful at night in a power cut.'

'Is that why you wanted to see me – to be rude about my rig?' Branson sat down on the chair in front of the desk, swinging it round, as was his custom, and sitting astride it, folding his arms over the back and staring quizzically at his boss.

'Looks like your jolly to Lyon is happening,' Grace told him.

'That means I have to eat one of those stinky Andouillette sausage things? And frog's legs and snails?'

'If the French police offer you their hospitality and take you to a Lyon restaurant, it would be rude to refuse. Don't want you messing up our *entente cordiale*!'

Branson wrinkled his face. 'Yech.'

'Don't screw up this one, mate!'

Glenn Branson stared back at him. 'I'm not planning to screw up, yeah?'

'Crisp is a twister. Don't let him start sweet-talking you.'

'I'm not planning to have sex with him.'

Grace grinned. 'You're not his type, so I wouldn't worry. And just to ensure you're not there for any romance, I'm sending Norman Potting with you.'

'Norman? He's my date for this trip?'

'I want two of you there. Norman's still hurting badly from Bella's death. I think it would do him good to have a break for twenty-four hours. Not that I'd wish your company on my worst enemy.'

'You're a bundle of laughs this morning. Remember that night we watched *The Last Detail* at your place, when Ari had thrown me out?'

Grace frowned. 'Rings a bell.'

'Jack Nicholson and Otis Young had to escort a young sailor – Randy Quaid – to jail. Yeah?'

Grace nodded. 'Yes, I seem to remember you said it was one of your favourite films. So what's your point?'

'It was about bringing a prisoner back.'

'Nicholson and Young took Quaid to a brothel, didn't they?'

'See! Your memory's still good. Not bad at all for an old man.'

'Sod off! And don't come back telling me you took Crisp to a brothel because you felt sorry for him.'

Branson raised his hands in the air. 'Joking!'

'I don't find anything funny about a man who killed five, and probably a lot more, women. Just so you know.'

'Me neither.'

'OK, speak to Tony Case and get him to sort out the travel arrangements. I'm told you can take a Eurostar train to Lille and then a train from there to Lyon.'

His phone rang again. It was Marcel Kullen. It was the second of the calls he had been awaiting this morning.

348

Asking him to hang on for a moment, then covering the receiver with his hand, he said to Branson, 'OK? *Alles ist klar?*'

The DI got the message and stepped out of the room, closing the door behind him.

'I'm sorry to disturb you,' Kullen said. 'But I thought you must know that Sandy's condition is improved a very little. Perhaps you would like to come over and talk to her?'

Grace thought for some moments. 'Yes, yes, I would like to. I – the next few days are difficult as I have to deal with something – but I'll see how quickly I can do it.'

'*Jah.* You let me know. She's not in such a hurry to make her last journey.'

Grace smiled at the German's gallows humour. 'I'll call you as soon as I know.'

'Good.' Kullen paused for a moment and the silence was palpable. Roy Grace could sense his hesitation. Then he added, 'Roy, I just want to say, I think you are making a good decision to come. It is the honourable thing to do.'

'I hope so, Marcel.'

He hung up, and called Glenn Branson again. 'Glenn, I need to ask your advice on something – could you come back in?'

As Glenn sat back down opposite him, Grace told him the news from Germany. 'What the hell do you think I should do?'

'Shit, mate! Oh, shit!' He was silent for a few seconds. 'Bloody hell. God. What does Cleo think?'

'She doesn't know.'

'What?' Branson was silent again, thinking. 'You've always known in your heart, haven't you? That she's still alive?'

'Have I?'

The detective inspector stood up, walked around the desk and gave him a hug. As Grace breathed in his pungent aftershave, Glenn said, 'Yes. You know you have. You've got to tell Cleo.'

'What the hell do I tell her?'

Branson went back round, sat down in front of him and leaned forward so they were eyeball to eyeball. 'How about the truth?'

Grace stared back at him. 'I'm scared of losing everything.'

'Cleo's a smart lady. I'm sure she also believes in her heart that Sandy is still alive, out there somewhere. Look, you can see how much she loves you, everyone can. But I can also see fear in her eyes sometimes. The fear that it might not last. The fear of what would happen if Sandy suddenly walked back into your life.'

'I've told her many times that it wouldn't make any difference. That I love her more than I now realize I ever loved Sandy.'

'And she believes you?'

'I think so.'

'OK, so now's your chance to show her.'

'What do you mean?'

Glenn Branson raised his hands in the air. 'Look, shit, what do I really know? I loused up big time with my marriage. I'm not really a good person to give advice. But I'm going to give you some anyway.'

Grace smiled at him. 'OK?'

'You go home today and you tell Cleo. You need to tell her immediately. And, mate, you offer to take her with you to Germany, to meet Sandy.'

An email pinged on Grace's screen, but he ignored it. 'Are you off your rocker? Take Cleo to *meet* Sandy?'

'It's like so many things, mate. What you have in your imagination is worse than the reality, nothing we see can ever be as scary as what we imagine. Like that scene in *Psycho* with Janet Leigh being slashed to death behind the shower curtain. Hitchcock was clever. You don't actually see very much at all. You see the dagger striking again and again. You see blood. But you don't see her naked body being slashed to ribbons – that's all in your mind.'

Grace looked at him quizzically.

'Ever since Cleo and you became an item, from her point of view there were three of you – you, her and the ghost of Sandy. She's probably lain in bed with you every night since you fell in love imagining what would happen if Sandy returned. Show her the truth. Take her to meet the monster.'

'What if it backfires on me?'

'There's only one way it could backfire on you. And that's if you stood over Sandy's hospital bed and realized you were with the wrong person. Is that going to happen?'

'No,' Grace said, emphatically. 'Not in a million years.'

'So you have a golden opportunity. If you truly love Cleo, as I know you do, this is the only chance you might ever have. Slay your demon.'

'What if Cleo—?'

'Trust me. She won't. She won't say no.'

As Branson departed again, closing Grace's office door, leaving him in turmoil, his phone rang.

'Roy Grace,' he answered.

It was the Coroner's Officer, Michelle Websdale. 'Ah, Detective Superintendent?'

'Yes, hi, Michelle. I was told you'd be calling.'

'Well – ah – yes, sir – but actually I'm not calling about Shelby Stonor, it's another matter. It's regarding an elderly Brighton resident, a Mr Rowley Burnett Carmichael, who has died after being taken ill on a cruise ship. The circumstances of his death are regarded as suspicious.'

'Oh? Do you have the cause of death?'

'Well, yes, this is why I thought you might be interested. He became ill, apparently, after a shore visit to a nature reserve near Mumbai in India. The doctor on board suspected initially he'd either caught a bug that had been going round the ship or possibly had food poisoning, but then became very concerned when Carmichael developed further symptoms, and wondered if they could be related to what in his opinion looked like a puncture mark on his leg from a bite – although there was none of the localized swelling that would normally have been present. As soon as they docked in Goa, he was transferred to a local hospital but he died en route. The subsequent post-mortem examination indicated that he died from a venomous snake bite, the symptoms of which are consistent with that of a saw-scaled viper, but they are awaiting confirmation from toxicology tests.'

'A saw-scaled viper?' Grace said.

'Yes.'

'The same venom that we believe killed Shelby Stonor?'

'Precisely.'

Grace considered this carefully. Today was Monday 9 March. Shelby Stonor had died a week ago from the venom of a saw-scaled viper. 'That's a bit of a coincidence. Two Brighton residents dying from the same thing in one week – and – about what – four thousand miles apart – don't you think?'

'You're the detective, sir,' Michelle Websdale said, breezily. 'What do you think?'

Remembering Potting's nugget of information, he said, 'I understand that saw-scaled vipers kill thousands of people a year in India alone.'

'And how many in Sussex?'

'Rather fewer, I would imagine,' Grace replied, drily.

'I've checked deaths in Sussex by poisonous bites as far back as records go,' the Coroner's Officer

353

said. 'There have been none. Now two Sussex residents in one week. Let's hope it is, as you say, just coincidence. Do you have any possible reason to believe it's not coincidence?'

Grace hesitated, thinking hard, wary of falling into the trap he so often warned about, of making assumptions. But he didn't like what he had just heard. 'I think we need to know more about the circumstances. Do we need a second post-mortem here, Michelle?'

'Our laws require a repatriated body to be embalmed first.'

Grace cursed under his breath. Although being embalmed didn't make a second post-mortem impossible, it would be less likely they would find anything of evidential value.

'Did the pathologist in Goa give an exact cause of death?'

'Yes, he confirmed cause of death as being a snake bite, almost certainly from an *Echis carinatus* – that's the Latin name, sir, for the saw-scaled viper.'

'Thanks for the biology lesson! What information do you have on the victim?'

'Well, only scant information so far, supplied by the ship's Purser. Rowley Carmichael's a retired art dealer. I googled him and looked him up on Wikipedia. He was a very prominent figure in the art world. The tragedy is that he got married on board a week ago – last Monday – to a very beautiful and apparently much younger lady. She's understandably distraught.'

'So they were on their honeymoon?'

'It seems so. She's also a Brighton resident.'

'Has she been interviewed?'

'She accompanied her husband ashore, and gave a statement to the police in Goa. I'm having a scan of it sent to me – I'll email it to you as soon as I receive it.'

'When will Carmichael's body be repatriated to England?'

'I'm liaising with the Goan police on this now, Detective Superintendent. Within the next few days. I believe his widow intends to accompany it home.'

'What information do you have on her?' he asked.

'So far only what she put on the form: her name, Jodie Carmichael, née Danforth, and an address in Brighton, in Alexandra Villas.'

Grace made a mental note to get one of his team to place a marker at the relevant UK airports for her return. Then he asked Websdale if she could arrange for photographs of the couple to be emailed over to him, as well as the cruise ship's itinerary and passenger and crew manifests.

In addition to his unfolding personal nightmare, something about this case was starting to trouble Grace, though he wasn't yet sure exactly what.

CHAPTER 70

Monday 9 March

As soon as he had ended the call, Grace sat thinking, Sandy temporarily put to one side. Two Brighton residents dead from snake bites within one week of each other. And the same kind of snake. His naturally suspicious mind was telling him this might not be a coincidence, however much it seemed to be.

He started jotting down thoughts. Then he picked up the phone and asked DS Guy Batchelor to come to his office.

A few minutes later, with the burly detective, reeking of tobacco smoke, seated in front of him, he said, 'Guy, I may have to be absent for a couple of days. I'd like you to give these actions to the Operation Spider team.'

'Of course, boss. What do you need?'

'Firstly, I want you to find out everything you can about a Jodie Carmichael, previously Danforth, with an address in Alexandra Villas, in the Seven Dials area of Brighton – I'll be getting the details imminently. Find out who she is, and what her background is.' Then looking down at his notes, he continued, 'Have someone speak to that expert from London Zoo. I want more specific information about venomous snake bites.'

Batchelor pulled out his notepad and began to write.

'I want to know everything about this snake – where it lives, what countries you can find it in, how venomous it is, what the antidotes are, if it's ever kept as a pet, what does it look like, how big it is, would you need a licence to keep it, how could you import it into the UK, what conditions would it need to be kept in if you did have such a snake in England.'

Batchelor nodded, writing furiously.

Grace went on. 'What would the bite symptoms be, how quickly would you need treatment if bitten, and is it always fatal?'

'Got all that, sir.'

'Good man.'

'Leave it with me.'

'Good news regarding your promotion, Guy. Hopefully you'll stay with the team. It would be useful for you to spend the next few days as an Acting DI, whilst Glenn and I are both away.'

Batchelor looked delighted. 'Thank you, sir, I won't let you down.'

CHAPTER 71

Tuesday 10 March

For the second time in a month, a grieving woman accompanied her loved one's body on a flight home after his sudden, tragic death in a foreign country.

And for the second time in that month she consoled herself on the flight, whilst composing and rehearsing her story, with the very acceptable bubbly served in British Airways First Class.

As her glass was topped up by a smiling, sympathetic steward, she dug her fingers into the bowl of warm, roasted nuts. Chewing on a sweet cashew, she switched her thoughts to the book she planned to write one day from her villa on the shore of Lake Como. The villas had gone up in value since that holiday, all those years back with her family. It would take somewhere upwards of fifty million pounds to buy a place impressive enough to be pointed out by a tour boat. Enough to impress her father. And her mother.

'How do you get to afford one of those? The way you do it, Jodie, is you marry a millionaire.'

Meaning, *No way on earth will you, little ugly girl.*
She would show them. She longed for the day
– the day that would happen – when he ate his
words.

On her iPad she entered her password and
opened her diary. Then she typed:

OK, so anyone want to tell me how long is
a respectable time to spend with a partner?
Husband? Whatever?

It's a bit of a tired cliché these days, that
old saying: 'Live every day as if it's your last
because one day you'll be right.'

But honestly?

People talk about managing your expectations. Everyone has different expectations
from life.

They say money cannot buy happiness.
So I'll tell you what I've learned in my thirty-
six years, to date. First, here is a list of things
I hate:
1. Marmite
2. Gooey-eyed mummies
3. Holy Joes
4. People who tell you money doesn't buy
   happiness.

Here's a list of things I love:
1. My cat
2. Looking at my bank balances
3. Good quality Chablis

4. Oysters Rockefeller
5. Lobster
6. Jimmy Choo shoes
7. Mercedes-Benz sports cars

Here's a list of things I want:
1. An apartment in New York. A villa on Lake Como.
2. Private jets, so I never have to take my fucking shoes off again in an airport.
3. Enough money never to have to work again.
4. To marry a man I truly love.
5. To start a family.

Is that so unreasonable? I'd like to think of myself as a woman of simple tastes. I want the best of everything. I want it now, all the time I'm alive. And I'm fully aware that one day will be my last.

When that day comes, I want to die with a big smile on my face. Not, as too many people do, in a hospital corridor with a hung-over medical student jumping up and down on my chest, or withering away from old age or disease in an old people's home.

Is that really so unreasonable?

Life's a game.

So sad most of us never realize that.

I feel so lucky I worked that out while I was still young enough to make it happen.

Can you imagine what it must feel like to be on your deathbed thinking of all the things you wish you'd done? We're not just a long time dead, we are dead forever.

Don't let anyone tell you any different.

The formalities at London's Heathrow Airport were less arduous than Jodie had been expecting. She signed over care of her late husband's body to the Brighton and Hove Coroner, and was on her way down to Sussex, in the back of a BMW limousine, in just over an hour and a half after touchdown.

She had been very fortunate, she knew. It was something of an urban myth that all of ships' captains could perform legal marriages. To do this they needed to be an officially recognized wedding celebrant, and few were. Very conveniently for her, Rowley Carmichael had chosen to go cruising with a line that recognized, with its romantic destinations, there could be a call for such services, and a lucrative one, so all their captains were legally recognized celebrants.

And what kept that smile on her face broadening by the minute was the knowledge that the moment someone was married, any existing will they had made became instantly invalid.

The only thing bothering her was that Rowley had four children, and would probably have made trust provisions for them. But she had no doubt that at the end of the day she would end up with a decent chunk of change. As any wife would be entitled to. And it would be a substantial addition to her declining savings. But perhaps not the golden egg she craved.

As the black BMW turned off the M25, onto the M23 south towards Brighton, she was only too aware that the real jackpot she sought still lay, at this moment, elusively ahead of her. And she was already busy on her laptop, googling hard, searching for Mr Right across the websites where she had registered.

He was out there, somewhere. And she would find him.

Someone who would be grateful to meet her. Someone rich enough to make all her dreams come true.

Someone rich enough to make Cassie turn in her grave.

CHAPTER 72

Tuesday 10 March

Always an anxious flyer, at 7 a.m. the following morning Roy Grace buckled himself into his seat next to Cleo, who was by the window, near the back of the packed British Airways flight to Munich. He felt even more nervous than usual. A swarm of butterflies was going berserk in his stomach. He had taken a day's leave – which was fine, he was well in credit.

He reached out his left hand and gripped Cleo's. The aisle seat to his right was, so far, empty.

Breaking the news to Cleo had been far from easy. She was furious that he hadn't trusted her to be all right with it, and instead had lied to her. She initially questioned what this meant for them long term – what else had he lied to her about in the past, and would he lie to her again in the future? They'd talked it over and over, late into the night, and he admitted he'd made the wrong call, because he'd been scared of losing her.

The fact that he asked her to come with him to see Sandy helped eventually to bring them to an understanding. Cleo could see that Roy really wanted them to confront this whole issue together.

They didn't talk much during the flight, each immersed in their own thoughts.

Normally Cleo did not wear much make-up, and Roy liked that, she didn't need to. But today she had more on than normal. As if she might have been trying to compete with Sandy, he wondered. Not that she needed to have any fears.

As the plane touched down on the runway at Munich Airport, they held each other's hands tightly.

'I'm really nervous,' she said.

'Listen, I love you. There's nothing Sandy might say that could change anything between us. I wanted you to come with me to show her – let her see for herself – that we're a unit. You're my wife, and nothing's ever going to change that. You're Cleo Grace. Right?'

She smiled, thinly.

Grace tried to consider all that was happening at work, but he couldn't. He just kept coming back to just what was going to happen when he entered the Klinikum Schwabing with Cleo, and saw Sandy.

There could be no pretence that it was not her any more.

How the hell was he going to feel?

He again tried to switch his thoughts back to

Crisp, and to the victims of the snake venom, but it was impossible. Just one thing occupied his mind right now.

Sandy.

Less than an hour later they were hurtling down the autobahn in Marcel Kullen's white Volkswagen Scirocco sports car, Cleo, knees against her chin in the rear, Roy, his seat forward as far as it would go, inches from the glove compartment.

Kullen was good-looking, with wavy black hair and a voice perpetually filled with humour. Much of the journey into Munich was taken up with Cleo quizzing Kullen on how he knew Roy, and about his life, his wife and kids, and what had made him become a policeman.

Roy sat in silence, grateful for Cleo's wonderfully inquisitive mind, listening to the conversation that was going on between them in the background. Meanwhile, his nerves were tightening the nearer they got.

Was he making a massive mistake?

The car slowed and halted. He looked out of his window and saw the building he recognized. It looked like a cross between a hospital and a monastery. A beige brick facade with a crimson-tiled roof punctuated with gabled windows and a portico of three arches.

Klinikum Schwabing, München.

Panic momentarily gripped him. He took several deep breaths. Was he making the worst mistake of his life? Should he tell Marcel to turn the car round and head back to the airport?

But instead, silent as an automaton, he unbuckled his seat belt, climbed out, helped Cleo to tilt the rear seat forward and took her hand as she wormed her way out.

Kullen told them he would wait for them here.

A few minutes later, after signing the visitors' register, Roy and Cleo were met by a very business-like woman with iron-grey hair, who introduced herself as the ward manager. She led them along a network of corridors that were vaguely familiar to him from his previous visit here, in January, then up in a lift.

His nerves began to jangle again. Cleo gripped his hand, hard.

'Are you sure about this, my darling?' he asked her for about the tenth time.

'Yes.'

He could smell disinfectant as the doors opened. A man, his shrivelled face the colour of chalk, was wheeled past them on a trolley as they stepped out into the orange-painted corridor. There was a row of hard chairs on either side, a snacks vending machine and several picture frames on the wall with staff portraits of doctors and nurses with their names beneath.

His heart was thudding. Here again. It all felt so familiar. A man hurried past them in blue scrubs and yellow Crocs and went into the alcove where there was a drinks vending machine.

Shit.

This was *Groundhog Day.*

The woman with the iron-grey hair had told him that the patient, Sandy, had been conscious intermittently during the past few days, with moments of lucidity.

He glanced at Cleo. She was conservatively dressed, in a plain navy coat over a black sweater, blue jeans and knee-high suede boots, with the large, dark blue Mulberry handbag he had bought her – for an insane price last Christmas – over her shoulder.

She looked back at him. An expression he could not read.

They followed the woman through double doors into the Intensive Care Unit, breathing in the sterile smells as they passed rows of beds, each with a patient surrounded by a bank of monitors, and screened off on either side by pale green curtains. Turning a corner, they entered a small, private room.

Inside lay a woman with short brown hair, in a blue and white spotted gown, connected to a forest of drip lines, in a bed with its sides up like the bars of a cage.

Sandy.

He looked at Cleo again. Her face had paled.

He stepped forward. 'Sandy?' he said.

There was no reaction.

'It's Roy,' he said, more calmly than he felt. He waited some moments, but still there was no reaction. 'I'm so sorry – about your accident.' His voice choked, as he became increasingly emotional. 'I'm so sorry. I – I don't know – I don't really know what to say. I've moved on. I have my new wife, Cleo, with me. She wanted to meet you.'

He turned away, clutched Cleo in his arms, holding her tight.

Behind him, unseen by either of them, Sandy's eyes opened briefly, flickered, then closed.

He composed himself, then leaned down and touched Sandy on her forehead. 'I – I can't believe it's you. It's really you. After all this time.'

Then, holding hands tightly, Cleo and Roy stood, watching her.

Sandy remained silent. Breathing rhythmically.

'Sandy?' he said. 'Can you hear me? It's Roy.'

There was no reaction from her for some moments, then suddenly she opened her eyes wide, startling them. She looked at Roy then stared hard at Cleo.

'So you're Cleo?' she said. 'You're the woman he's married?'

Cleo smiled awkwardly. There was a nervous pitch to her voice as she answered. 'Yes. Yes, I am.'

Sandy's eyes narrowed into a glare. 'Good luck,' she said, acidly. Then her eyes closed.

A nurse came in, saying she had to change some of the patient's dressings and administer her medication, and would they mind stepping outside for a few minutes. They could get themselves water or coffee, if they liked, just down the corridor outside the ward.

CHAPTER 73

Tuesday 10 March

Standing in the small bay with the vending machines, Roy squinted at the choices then pressed the button for a large espresso.

'Christ,' Cleo said, 'she looks awful. What did she mean by *good luck*?'

'I don't know – I've no idea.'

'Listen,' Cleo said, sipping her scalding tea, looking a little numb and shaken. 'You have a lot of questions you need answers for. I think you should go back in and spend a few minutes with her alone. I don't need to be there.'

He hesitated, then nodded.

'I'll go downstairs for some fresh air, wait for you out the front. Get some answers, she owes you that at least.'

He headed back to the ward and entered Sandy's room again, closing the door behind him. She appeared to be asleep. His heart was hammering as he looked down at her silent figure, her eyes still closed, then perched on the end of the bed.

'Hi, Sandy,' he said. 'I – I can't believe it's really you. After all this time. Nearly eleven years.'

He stared intently at her, at the woman he had loved so much, once. Despite much of her face being covered in scar tissue and bandages he could see how much she had aged in the intervening years. She wasn't the Sandy who had walked out on him any more. All kinds of memories flashed through his mind, and he tried to link them to this woman lying here. But she remained a stranger. 'What happened? Tell me. Why didn't you contact me?'

She did not respond.

He took her hand, and lapsed back for some moments into his thoughts. Thinking how different things might have been. Wondering what he would do if she suddenly opened her eyes and threw her arms round him. 'I've got a son,' he said. 'Noah. He's eight months old. Maybe one day when you're better we can meet and be friends. I'd like to think that's possible. But before any of that can happen I need some answers. I need a lot of answers. Why did you leave? Why didn't you make contact? Do you have any idea of the hell you put me through? Do you not care at all? I think I deserve to know.'

Her face showed no sign of any reaction.

Her hand felt strange, alien. 'You were always so ambitious for me, wanting me to get to a higher rank than my dad. Well, I've been lucky. I reached Detective Superintendent. Did you ever think I'd do that?'

He waited, then said, 'Me neither. I'm head of Major Crime for Sussex – although our branch has merged with Surrey. Lots of politics now that we didn't have eleven years ago. I love my job, but there are days when I have doubts. Policing has become so damned politically correct. There's good things about that and bad. All of us walk on eggshells, scared of offending almost anyone.' He paused and looked down at her. 'God, I wish we could just talk, tell each other all the stuff that's happened in each of our lives in this past decade.'

He looked up at the bank of monitors and dials. They were all meaningless to him. 'There's a million things I want to ask you. One day, yes? Maybe?'

He glanced at his watch. Then as he looked back at her, he suddenly had a flash of déjà vu. He remembered sitting beside his father's body, laid out in the funeral parlour in his pyjamas. His stone-cold hand. That was no longer his father, Jack Grace, the man he had loved so much. It was just a husk. An empty shell. His father had long departed it. And that was how he felt now. This was a husk, too. Breathing, perhaps, but a husk all the same. It wasn't the Sandy he had known and loved. It was just a shell. The Sandy he had known and loved no longer occupied it.

Letting go of her hand, he stood up, abruptly. Her eyes opened, and she said, 'Going already, Roy?'

He felt a catch in his throat. He sat back down, on the edge of the bed.

'I'm pleased you've done well at work, that

371

you've got to where you always wanted to be. Head of Major Crime. Detective Superintendent. I like that, it sounds good, sort of suits you.'

He smiled. 'Thanks.'

'And you've got the son you always wanted. Noah's a nice name. Very biblical.'

'Yes, I suppose it is. We both just liked it. So you've heard my download; now tell me what's been happening in your life. I've heard bits and pieces.'

She gave him an almost guilty smile. 'I expect you've heard the bad bits, the drugs and depression and failed relationships. I've got some good bits too – I'm independently wealthy and I've got a son who's ten.'

'OK, so what I have to know is why you left me? What happened, where did you go? Did I do something wrong?'

'It's a long story, Roy, but not for today. I will explain, I promise.'

'OK, tell me about your son. Bruno, is that his name?'

She nodded.

'Who's the father?'

'That's also for another day, Roy.'

'OK, let's focus on the future then. How's your recovery going, what are your plans when you get out?'

'I haven't been doing that well. They told me a while ago that I was lucky to be alive – that when they brought me in they didn't expect me to survive. I've had a serious head injury, I've got a spinal injury and I don't know yet if I'll ever be able to walk properly – without a limp or a stick. They've removed my spleen. My face is a mess, I'll be permanently scarred – who's going to want me? And I worry about Bruno.'

'Where is he now?'

'Friends are looking after him for the moment. It's not been easy bringing up a child as a single mum, even with the money.'

'Have you spoken to your parents?'

'No.'

'Do you want me to call them?'

'No, I'll speak to them when I'm – when I'm ready.'

'Are there any other people you'd like me to contact?'

'No, certainly not. How did you find me anyway? I didn't want you here, I really don't want to be doing this. I don't need this right now, it's too much, Roy.'

'You know there are all kinds of legal ramifications. I'm going to have to report this to both the German and Sussex Police.'

'You had me declared dead.'

He started to raise his voice. 'What the hell did you expect me to do?'

She closed her eyes for some moments and appeared to have fallen asleep again. Suddenly, she said, 'I'm due to see the consultant this week, he's going to talk about my treatment in the future and my prognosis. Now I'm starting to get stronger, slowly, they'll be wanting to move me out of this hospital. But I'm quite worried about that, I don't know how I'm going to cope on my own. I feel so alone, Roy. So alone in the world. Now you're bringing me all this, I can't face it.' She began to cry.

He took her hand again and held it tightly. 'You'll be fine. I'll do what I can to help. It wasn't my intention to upset you, but I have to know the truth – you turned my life upside down, and now you're doing it again.' He paused for a moment. 'There's something that might make you smile. Remember Marlon? The goldfish I won at that fairground on the Level in Brighton by target shooting – I guess about eleven years ago? We brought it home in a plastic bag, and we didn't know if it was a him or her. You named him Marlon, after Marlon Brando, because you thought he was such a moody creature. You said that fairground goldfish never live for long and it would be dead in a few months. Well, you know what, he's still alive! Still going strong. Still miserable as hell! I've bought him several companions over the years, and each time the sod has eaten them! I love that fish because – it may sound daft – because he's been the one connection I still have to you. Every day when I wake up and go downstairs, I hope he's still alive and that I'm not going to find him floating on the top of his tank. And when I see him, I smile. You probably think that's daft, don't you?'

'I think you should leave now, Roy, I didn't ask you to come. I'm getting tired,' was all she said in reply.

He let go of her hand. 'Well, I still need answers. I'll come back and see you again soon.'

He turned and walked out of the room, looking back at her one last time.

Sandy lay there, tears streaming down her face.

CHAPTER 74

Tuesday 10 March

The plane touched down at Heathrow Airport, shortly after 4 p.m., slowed and then began taxiing. A cabin crew member's voice crackled through the intercom that passengers were now welcome to use their mobile phones.

Roy Grace had already jumped the gun and switched his back on. As soon as he got a signal, his phone beeped with a series of text and voice-mail messages.

The first was from Kelly Nicholls, the financial investigator he had tasked to find anything she could on the names he had given her. Nicholls asked him to call, saying she had some information for him.

He rang her back and it went to voicemail. He left a message.

The next was a text from the Coroner's Officer, Michelle Websdale, saying that Jodie had cleared Heathrow immigration that morning at about 7.15 a.m.

The next was a text from Branson.

Arrived in Lyon. Tell me your news?

He rang him. Glenn answered after two rings.

'How did it go, mate?' Branson asked him.

'Didn't get many answers, she looked bloody terrible. But she is awake and getting stronger, so we'll see her again soon – and hopefully find out just why on earth she left. And she's got a kid. There are all kinds of legal questions I'm going to have to sort out – God knows how she's going to start explaining it to everyone. Especially her parents. It's a complete mess.' He looked at his wife. They'd spent the entire short flight from Munich talking about Sandy.

'Jeez,' Branson replied.

'How about you, what's your news, mate?'

'I have a significant development to report regarding Crisp. The French police are dropping charges.'

'What?'

'Seems he wasn't the killer of the sex worker. Her boyfriend has confessed. According to the police here he was her pimp, high on crack cocaine, and had a row with her about money after seeing her get out of Crisp's car. He thought she was pocketing some of her clients' money. Apparently he's made a full confession.'

'So our dear, sweet, Dr Crisp is an innocent little baby?'

'So far as the French police are concerned, yes.'

'Great. So now we can move forward with the extradition process?'

'As I understand it, they're very happy to get him off their hands. Formalities for his extradition are being fast-tracked and the paperwork authorizing his release to the Extradition Unit should be signed later today by a French Presiding Magistrate. The Extradition Unit are arranging to bring him back to the UK tomorrow.'

'So where are you now and what are your plans?'

'We're checking into a hotel at the moment. Norman's been trying to chat up the receptionist. We're going to liaise with the Extradition Unit and see Crisp tomorrow morning.'

'Good man.'

'Doesn't seem the French police are over the moon to see us. No one's invited us to any gourmet dinner. Looks like it's going to be me and Norman – and the receptionist if he pulls.'

'Good to know he's getting back to his old form.'

'Yeah? That stingy sod Tony Case has booked us into a double room. I'm going to have to share with Norman and put up with him snoring. Just hope he doesn't get anywhere with the receptionist. Don't fancy the idea of having to listen to him shagging his arse off all night.'

Grace grinned, then winced. 'I'm with you on that one! Bell me tomorrow, when you're on your way.'

'You're right about one thing, though, Roy.'

'What?'

'Lyon – it's a nice city.'

'Enjoy!'

'Huh.'

As Roy Grace drove out of the short-term car park he felt drained.

'Thank you,' Cleo said.

'For what?'

'For taking me with you. I know it was hard.'

'Listen, it was hard for both of us. Not something we thought was going to be coming into our lives.'

She shrugged. 'From what you said on the plane, that conversation must have been really hard for you both. It really shook you seeing her, didn't it?'

'It did. Even more than I'd expected. The irony is that I still don't really know anything. For all this time I'd hoped one day to have answers. Now finally I find her and get to talk to her and she's told me little I didn't already know, and still no explanation as to why she left.'

'She'll tell you one day, Roy. The important thing is you've had contact finally, she's alive. She sounds really stressed. You'll get a chance to ask again.'

'I hope so. I really do need to know. I have to know. So many questions.'

'At least she's not been found dead somewhere, abducted and murdered.'

Grace fell silent, looking at the satnav screen, then at the road signs. Rain was falling. The wipers clunked, the sky above them was dark and gloomy.

'Thank you for coming,' he said. 'You were brave.'

She shook her head. 'No. That wasn't about being brave. I needed to know.'

'To know what?'

'About you. I lost the last man I loved, to God.'

Grace nodded. He knew the whole story, she'd told him before. Richard, the barrister she'd dated for three years, who'd joined a charismatic church.

'I needed to know I wasn't losing you too, to a ghost.'

He stared at her bleakly. 'Sandy put me through ten years of hell. I didn't believe it would ever be possible to be happy again. You've made me happier than ever, and you know I love you more than I knew was possible. Nothing could change that.'

She leaned over and kissed him. 'I believe you.'

He shot a glance at her. 'For years I wondered how I would feel if she turned up on my doorstep. I would have taken her back, I guess. But not now. Not any more.' He sniffed, blinking away tears. 'You won't lose me. Not to a ghost. Not to anything.'

As he focused on the road ahead, out of the corner of his eye he saw Cleo looking at him, And he felt deep in his heart the intensity of her love.

One thing he knew now for sure was where his future lay.

Even if Sandy did make a full recovery, it would change nothing.

CHAPTER 75

Tuesday 10 March

Jodie had been flat out since arriving home. Her first priority had been the creatures in her reptile room. Checking their automated water and food supplies and cleaning their vivariums. And checking the excretions.

She checked one snake in particular, her nine-foot boa constrictor. So far, nothing. It could be days yet.

Then she turned her focus to coping with the formalities of her deceased husband, about whom she knew so very little, other than the important stuff, to her, such as where he lived and how to get in. She'd visited his beachfront house, but she could find hardly any documentation there, other than a few banking details in his study, but she did locate his address book and took that home with her. She'd also made a very thorough inspection of his antiques and paintings, photographing some to see if she could find them on the internet to see what they were worth. Back home she also checked on Zoopla for the current value of the property.

Whilst in India she had informed Rowley's eldest daughter of his unfortunate demise, explaining, to his daughter's shock and dismay, about their marriage a few days earlier, and asked her to inform the rest of the family.

She found the name of Rowley's family solicitor in the address book, and called him. He told her that he had already been informed, and had been asked by the *Daily Telegraph* to write his obituary. The man had sounded genuinely sad, as if he had lost not just a client but a dear and treasured friend. He'd told Jodie they should arrange to meet, and asked if in the meantime she could send him a copy of the death certificate. He added that their marriage had revoked the previous will and that her husband had actually died intestate. He explained what that meant to her and told her he would get back to her with more information. Then, in finishing, he told Jodie that whilst Rowley Carmichael was a very wealthy man, he had a decade ago made over a substantial part of his assets to his children and grandchildren, to mitigate inheritance tax and death duties.

She was still confident she would inherit a reasonable amount from Rowley, but it was unlikely to be anywhere near enough to fulfil her dreams. As she was still contemplating this, a lady, who introduced herself as Michelle Websdale, the Coroner's Officer, had called her on the mobile number she had given the Goan police, to ask a series of questions.

So far, she felt, she had acquitted herself well as the suddenly bereaved newly-wed. In the past twenty-four hours she'd shed more tears than she could remember.

She had engaged a firm of funeral directors, whom she was going to meet later today to discuss the details of Rowley Carmichael's funeral. His eldest daughter, a very frosty and haughty woman, said that her father had a fear of crematoriums, and wanted to be buried. Jodie had decided to ignore that. She'd read enough around the subject to know that buried bodies could be exhumed, sometimes years after burial. Cremation would be a much safer option. So, without informing any of the family in advance, she told the funeral directors that her husband's express wish was to be cremated.

Screw his last wishes. She was going to have enough of a fight on her hands as it was. And hey, dead men didn't complain, did they?

CHAPTER 76

Tuesday 10 March

Grace dropped Cleo home, played with Noah for a few minutes, then headed into Brighton. He was glad of the time alone in his car to reflect on the past twenty-four hours.

Sandy had looked so fragile and vulnerable. When they were together she had always been strong and positive. She'd made the decision to walk out on him. Now, finally, his life was back together, and he was at a crucial point in his career, with a boss who would seize on any weakness he showed. He owed it to Cleo, to Noah and to himself to put the past behind him and focus on the present and the future.

But he was determined to get answers to all his questions out of Sandy.

Ten minutes later he pulled into the parking bay marked HEAD OF MAJOR CRIME in front of Sussex House, and hurried in, just in time for the 6.30 p.m. briefing of Operation Spider. He dashed into his office, grabbed his policy book and notes, prepared by his assistant Lesley, along with a copy of the *Argus*, which she had placed there with a Post-it note beside a photograph on page five of a woman in an evening dress and a man in a dinner jacket, then headed through into the Major Crime suite.

As he walked along the corridor towards the conference room, his phone rang and he answered without stopping. It was a very apologetic Kelly Nicholls, the financial investigator.

'So sorry, sir, I've been in court all day. You asked me if I could find anything on a Jodie Bentley, also using other names.'

'Yes, Kelly. What do you have?' He leaned his notebook against a wall and pulled out his pen.

'Well, it's taken a while, and as you can understand it's a huge process. DS Billin and I wanted to be sure, and we are now. We've found credit cards in three names: Jodie Bentley, Jemma Smith and Judith Forshaw. We've obtained copies of all the original credit card application forms and there are a number of similarities, which we are now investigating further. She is currently using cards in all three names, with the balance paid off in full, monthly, via direct debit.'

'Good work, Kelly,' Grace said.

'Thank you, sir. There's more. The credit card companies all use sophisticated software now that can sift through not just the original applications for similarities but also the subsequent spending patterns.'

'On these spending patterns, did you find the

same shops being used repeatedly, Kelly?' he asked.

'Yes, sir, there was recent expenditure in France and New York and in and around Brighton, Sussex. The same shops and the same merchandise on the cards that were used. The same brands of hair and beauty products, as well as tampons. Similar wine and food items. Cat food. And rather curiously, perhaps, repeat purchases from a reptile food specialist supplier.'

'Reptile?' He felt a beat of excitement. 'Can you email me over the details of that, urgently?'

'Right away, sir. And it might be interesting for you to know that one place where her credit cards have been used regularly is at the Asda superstore in Brighton Marina. Also on one card there is expenditure in France for a coffin and a number of transatlantic and internal American flight tickets.'

'Bloody hell!' Grace said. 'That's very interesting. Brilliant work!'

'Thank you, sir.'

'What address has this woman put for these applications, Kelly?'

'Well,' she said, sounding doubtful, 'that's where the trail runs cold. The mail for each application address seems to have been forwarded to PO boxes at mailbox companies. The direct debit to pay them comes from a company with nominee directors based in Port Victoria, Mahé, Seychelles.'

'How cooperative is the Seychelles, Kelly?'

'Unfortunately she's chosen well, sir. At the moment, all the financial links end up in the Seychelles. It's a notoriously secretive country and any request for information would have to go via NCA – the National Crime Agency – which could take some considerable time.'

'Good work. Have you any more information that might lead us to her?'

'Not yet, sir.'

He thanked her again and was about to hang up when the financial investigator said, 'The second thing, sir, may be a more tenuous link, but I have a feeling it could be significant. There's a connection between these three cards and a fourth card being used in the name of Jodie Danforth in the Brighton area.'

'Jodie Danforth? Shit! Can you spell it?'

She replied, 'D-A-N-F-O-R-T-H.'

He was thinking hard. Jodie Danforth. The name that Michelle Websdale had given him of the Brighton widow whose husband had died on a cruise from a snake bite.

'OK, Kelly, as a priority action find out all you can about Jodie Danforth and come back to me as soon as possible!'

He ended the call and immediately rang the Coroner's Officer's mobile.

'Michelle,' he said when she answered. 'It's Roy Grace. Listen, what's the process from now with Rowley Carmichael's body?'

'It's at Brighton and Hove City Mortuary until the Coroner agrees to release it for the funeral.'

'I've got some significant new information. Can you ask the Coroner not to release it until I give you the OK?'

'Sure, I'll inform her.'

'Thanks. It might be really important.'

CHAPTER 77

Tuesday 10 March

After finishing his call to Michelle Websdale, Grace, feeling parched, debated whether to make himself a quick coffee. But he was already late, so he hurried on. Entering the conference room he saw the whiteboards set up, and all his team members, minus Glenn Branson and Norman Potting, seated around the oval table.

Pinned to one whiteboard was a blow-up of the photograph Lesley had flagged in the *Argus*. An elderly man, handsome and distinguished-looking, if a little portly, in a white tuxedo with a black bow tie, the woman in a long evening dress, her hair in ringlets, with mesmerizing blue eyes. He immediately recognized her from the CCTV images Lanigan had sent.

She sported an enormous, sparkling rock of an engagement ring. But although they were standing together, the man's arm affectionately round the shoulders of his bride of just a day or two, her body language told Grace everything. She was angled very slightly away from him, and there was too much of a gap between them. Whilst he had a proud, happy smile on his face, her smile looked more like it was put on for the camera – her eyes were very definitely not smiling.

Grace sat down at his place, laying the newspaper, his policy book and his briefing notes in front of him, then began by bringing his team up to speed on the information he now had on the death of Brighton resident Rowley Burnett Carmichael.

Next he reported on the information he had just received from Kelly Nicholls. 'What may be highly relevant is the Asda in the Marina. So far as I'm aware it's the closest superstore to the Roedean area of the city. The location where the geo-mapping puts the blurred photograph on the whiteboard, the one taken almost certainly accidentally by Shelby Stonor. The post-mortem confirms Stonor died from a saw-scaled viper bite. Jodie's new husband has just died from a saw-scaled viper bite. And she has been buying products from a reptile food supplier. Since there is no reported death from a snake bite of a Brighton resident since records began over sixty years ago, I'm viewing this as significant. One question still unanswered is how Shelby Stonor got bitten. Is it possible the house where the photograph was taken was a burglary? Had he broken into Jodie's house – somewhere in this city – and been bitten in the process?'

He glanced at his notes for a moment. 'This is

391

an important line of enquiry but we do need to keep an open mind. The newly-wed Carmichaels were in a part of India where I'm told these snakes are commonplace and kill many thousands annually.'

DS Cale raised her hand. 'Boss,' she said. 'I have something that may be significant here. Two hours ago I received a phone call from a Mr Harvey Dexter, a retired consultant radiologist, who lives in Eastbourne. He said he'd just been reading the newspaper – the one you have a copy of in front of you – and he believes he recognizes the woman in the photograph.' She pointed at the whiteboard. 'He is convinced he stood opposite that lady in a cable car in the French resort of Courchevel a month ago – he was wearing a GoPro camera on his helmet.'

'Nice life,' Guy Batchelor commented. 'Skiing one month, cruising the next.'

Ignoring him, Grace said, 'And his point is what, Tanja?'

'Well – he said his career helped him become extremely analytical of photographs. He said that even though she and the man she was with both had ski helmets on, he's convinced she was the same lady as in this photograph in the *Argus*. But his GoPro video is of a man who's not Rowley Carmichael, but Walt Klein – the disgraced American financier who fell to his death over a precipice in Courchevel.'

'So this is eye-witness evidence that the woman

on the slopes with Klein is the same person as Jodie Carmichael,' Grace said.

It was more confirmation of what he already knew.

'Look on the bright side, Walt Klein did better than the next bloke she had her claws into,' Guy Batchelor commented. 'He only lasted four days!'

Some of the team laughed.

'Two dead lovers in a month?' Grace questioned.

'To lose one may be regarded as a misfortune. To lose two looks like carelessness,' DS Exton said. 'In the words of Oscar Wilde!'

'I think Wilde was referring to *husbands*, Jon,' Tanja Cale said.

Grace remembered an Oscar Wilde play he and Sandy went to see in the city's Theatre Royal. 'I think the line was about *parents*, actually, Jon and Tanja. But I get your drift.' He turned to Tanja Cale. 'How certain is this Harvey Dexter character?'

'Absolutely adamant, sir.'

'Does he still have the footage?'

'Yes, sir.'

'We need to get him interviewed, and get a copy of the video.'

'I'm seeing him straight after this briefing, sir. I'm going to his house.'

'Nice work.' He turned to DS Batchelor. 'Any progress on what I gave you, Guy?'

'Not much I'm afraid, boss. I've looked up everyone in the local area who might have a licence to keep a saw-scaled viper and there's no one. But that doesn't mean much, I'm afraid. I've also spoken to one of the country's leading experts on venomous snakes – a herpetologist called Mark O'Shea. He's the Consultant Curator of Reptiles at the West Midland Safari Park, and a well-known broadcaster. He told me that although we have strict rules about keeping venomous snakes in the UK, under the Dangerous Animals Act, anyone can buy them over the counter at the regular snake days at reptile fairs in Hamm, Germany, and in Houton, Holland, where no licence is needed and no questions asked. Saw-scaled vipers cost around one hundred and fifty euros, and you can take them away in a plastic container the size of a sandwich box. You can also walk through UK Immigration with a bunch of these in a bag completely legally – although you are supposed to register them within forty-eight hours.'

'Seriously? *Supposed* to?'

'Hardly anyone does.'

'This is incredible!' Grace said. 'You can't bring a harmless poodle into the country without a whole raft of veterinary certificates, but you can walk straight in with any number of creatures that can kill within hours?'

The detective sergeant raised his arms in a gesture of despair. 'Yep. Unless a particular creature falls under CITES – the Convention on International Trade in Endangered Species – where they require what's called either an Appendix 1 or

Appendix 2 permit, no one is breaking any law by bringing creatures like this into the country. You could bring in cobras, black mambas, trapdoor spiders, scorpions, anything.'

'Great,' Roy Grace said grimly. 'So we've no idea how many of our citizens have venomous reptiles in their homes?'

'Nope,' Batchelor said. 'I've found a helpful Met officer who keeps poisonous frogs as pets – his name's Andy Gibbs. He said most collectors keep their venomous snakes in secure vivariums – these are essentially glass cages with heaters and flora replicating the inhabitants' natural environments. But as he said, there are some nutters who keep them under the bed in cardboard boxes secured with elastic bands.'

'Why would anyone want to keep any poisonous reptile?' EJ asked.

'All kinds of reasons,' Tanja Cale said. 'I read up on it. Some people are just plain fascinated by them. A few get a power kick out of it. It's like those gun freaks in other countries who get off on owning an arsenal of weapons.'

'Or people who like bumping off their loved ones?' said Alec Davies.

DS Batchelor went on. 'I've checked Jodie Bentley's mailing address – or at least one of them – at a specialist company called Brighton Poste Restante, which is also an internet café, at 23A Western Road, and no one there has ever seen her. But there is something that may be of interest.

I was told by the manager there that a strange guy turned up on the morning of Sunday March 1st, around eleven o'clock, enquiring about Jodie – an American, who was quite bolshy. He was rude to her, then went away.'

'Did she give you a description?' Grace asked.

'Not much of one. Said he was short and weaselly, wearing a padded anorak, a baseball cap and aviator sunglasses.'

'Might have been someone on Walt Klein's trail,' Grace said. 'An official or unofficial investigator from the States. But if it was official, we should have been notified and asked for assistance. Have you got any CCTV?'

'I've requested it, but it'll be touch and go whether there's any that hasn't already been recorded over.'

'Anything else, Guy?'

'Yes, boss. We've checked the address that Jodie Carmichael gave to the Goan police, according to the Coroner's Officer. It's a flat in Alexandra Villas, near the Seven Dials. There was no answer and the neighbours our outside enquiry team officers spoke to say they've not seen anyone there for many months. They believe it's owned by a single woman who lives overseas.'

'Did anyone give a description of her?'

'Yes. It sounds like our dear Jodie.'

'Interesting,' Grace said.

Batchelor smiled. 'Something the guys here might want to know – I read it on the internet

– some venomous snake bites have a very un-pleasant side effect for survivors.'

'Which is?' Grace quizzed.

'It shrinks the male victim's dick.'

'Don't let one near Norman Potting!' Jon Exton said, lifting his head from his laptop. 'Rumour is that it's a bit small anyway.'

'Thank you, Jon!' Grace said. 'Too much information.'

Grace made some notes in his policy book, then he looked up at the photo on the whiteboard obtained from Shelby Stonor's mobile. 'We urgently need to find the house where that was taken. Guy, you said you recognized the style of window as mock Tudor, but unfortunately that's one of the most common architectural styles in the city. It's definitely not the style of the Alexandra Villas area. I'll give you the action of finding an architect and going with them to The Keep, where all the city's architectural records are, to see if you both can find the house from any of the plans they have there. An architect may be able to work out the room dimensions from what's on that photograph, and see if there is anything corresponding to the plans. I know it's a big ask but it's vital we find it.'

'Yes, boss.'

Grace turned to Emma-Jane Boutwood. 'EJ, I want you to take charge of viewing all the CCTV footage that Jack has asked for from 23A Western Road around eleven a.m., Sunday March 1st.'

'Yes, sir.'

'I don't imagine all snakes eat the same thing. Tanja, can you work with Guy to find out the diet of a saw-scaled viper and establish what that reptile food company was supplying.'

'Scrotes?' someone proffered.

'Endless supply of them in this city,' Dave Green, who had been brought in as the Crime Scene Manager, retorted.

'A bit indigestible most of them, even for a snake,' Jon Exton added.

Grace turned to Alec Davies and Jack Alexander. 'I want you two to arrange the organization of a house-to-house supervisor and a team to cover the Roedean area.' He pointed at the photograph of Rowley Carmichael and Jodie Bentley on the cruise ship. 'See if anyone recognizes her, or knows of a neighbour who keeps reptiles. I don't care how invisible she's tried to make herself, you can't live in a city without someone noticing you eventually. There's got to be a plumber, or electrician, or a builder who's been to her home, for God's sake! She'll be paying council tax; check the electoral register with all those different names. And the driving licence records. Has she ever had a parking ticket?'

He looked down at his notes. 'The next task we have is to set up a family tree for our mystery lady. Jodie Danforth; Jodie Bentley; Jodie Carmichael; and where do Jemma Smith and Judith Forshaw fit in? She has detailed knowledge of venomous reptiles. And it's likely she has a house in the

Roedean area of this city in addition to this Alexandra Villas flat. Jack and Alec, I'm giving you the action of finding her. See where the flat in Brighton leads us. Is there a connection with Roedean?'

He paused, then went on. 'Let's see if we can trace her through her mobile phone – hopefully she'll still have the one that we have the number for with her. Perhaps we can flush her out using Michelle Websdale – see if she can arrange a meeting with Jodie, which might make finding her a lot quicker. At the same time we have to find this woman's hunting ground. One place to look is internet dating sites – particularly those for people seeking wealthy partners. I'm told there are a number of sites where rich partners can be targeted. OK? We also need to find out where she met her previous conquests.'

Then he turned to Tanja Cale. 'Keep me updated on any addresses within the Brighton area which have been supplied with saw-scaled viper delicacies. You might find something for your supper tonight.'

'Thanks, boss, I'll stick to Waitrose for that.'

After the briefing ended, Roy Grace, feeling drained, went back to his office. He closed the door, sat in his chair and stared through the darkness at the glow of lights from the Asda superstore car park and the city beyond. Chilly air blew through the window onto his face. From time to time throughout criminal history, 'black widow' female characters cropped up. He'd dealt with one earlier in his career, who'd knowingly left her husband-to-be to die trapped in a coffin.

Did he now have another?

His phone rang. It was Kelly Nicholls again. 'Sir,' she said. 'There's some new information come to light which might be significant.'

Grace listened. 'Bloody hell, Kelly! Well done!'

CHAPTER 78

Wednesday 11 March

F ew police officers liked entering a prison on any kind of business. There was always the lurking fear that if you were unlucky enough to be inside the locked compound when a riot kicked off, you would rate even higher than the nonces and the prison officers as the biggest object of hatred and the No. 1 target.

Both Glenn Branson and Norman Potting, in the back of the French police car, were thinking this as they were driven through the tall gates into the wire-mesh enclosed outer perimeter of the Centre Pénitentiaire de Saint-Quentin-Fallavier some kilometres from the city, shortly after 7 a.m. on a damp, chilly morning. To the two Englishmen, the utilitarian modern building looked more like a factory on an industrial estate than a prison. Their driver, who had picked them up from the hotel earlier, was friendly enough, attempting to converse in his very limited English, and they had tried to respond in their even more limited French. But neither Potting nor Branson was in a chatty mood; they were both suffering badly from the previous evening.

Knowing they had to be up at sparrows, they should have been sensible and had an early night. Instead, at a restaurant close to their hotel which their French hosts had suggested, they had downed beers, followed by a bottle of cheap red wine, then a second, as Potting had poured his heart out over the recent loss of his fiancée, and Branson, in turn, had reminisced on his failed marriage and the subsequent death of Ari. Then when they'd returned to their hotel they'd stayed up well past midnight downing cognacs, while Potting confided his fears to Branson about his recent prostate cancer diagnosis, and of having surgery.

Branson had at least eaten fairly sensibly last night: fish soup then steak and chips. Potting had gone for escargots in garlic butter and then what he had thought was akin to an English banger, after looking it up on Google Translate, forgetting Grace's warning to Branson about Andouillette. He had nearly gagged from the stench that had risen from the plate when it had been presented to him. But, hungry, and numbed by the alcohol, he had dutifully consumed it. Now it was all repeating on him, and his stomach felt like it had turned into a tumble dryer.

The plan, in as much as they had been able to understand from their driver, was to witness the collection, by three officers from the UK Extradition Unit, of Edward Crisp from his cell in the hospital wing, accompanied by the prison doctor because of Crisp's broken arm from his skiing accident. The doctor would accompany Crisp in the prison van, which was waiting in front of them, to the nearby Lyon-Saint-Exupéry Airport, where they would escort him back to England aboard a British Airways flight at 10 a.m.

Both British detectives were chewing gum to mask the reek of alcohol on their breath. They followed the Extradition Unit members and a prison officer in a black uniform and sturdy boots, clutching a bunch of keys, through a series of double doors, each being locked behind them as they entered the prison's interior.

Glenn Branson's main experience of prisons had been the grim Victorian one just outside Brighton, in Lewes. This one, despite being more modern, had the same claustrophobic feel, with bars, grilles and bare walls, the same slightly rank smell. Potting, who had mumbled about badly needing a toilet, ambled a few steps behind him along a corridor lined on both sides with cell doors. There was a smell of cigarette smoke. A male voice shouted out something in French, which was ignored.

They stopped outside a door. The prison officer slid back an inspection hatch and peered in, then indicated to Branson and Potting to take a look too.

Despite his pounding head, Glenn Branson felt a beat of excitement as he peered at the motionless, slumbering man inside, facing the wall, his head obscured with a blanket.

Two other prison officers materialized from the far end of the corridor. The one they had followed in turned to them and said, '*Attendez!*'

He unlocked the door and went in, accompanied by the other two officers and the doctor, and approached the bed.

'Got to find a toilet,' Potting whispered to Branson. 'Bloomin' stomach's on fire.'

'We'll stop on the way out, Norman.'

Then they heard a shout from inside the cell. '*Non! Non! Ce n'est pas possible!*'

Branson stepped in and saw the first officer pull the blanket back. Then he stood stock-still, staring in disbelief. 'Shit,' he said. 'Shit, shit, shit.'

CHAPTER 79

Wednesday 11 March

Roy Grace was not sleeping properly. His mind was still working overtime and, in addition, Noah was teething and cried almost continuously, despite his and Cleo's efforts to soothe him.

Each time Noah was quiet and asleep again, Grace had gone back to bed and closed his eyes, listening to the sounds of his son's breathing. Terrible memories of several cot deaths which he had attended when he'd been a uniformed officer still haunted him. He knew that now Noah could turn himself over in bed, there was less danger of him overheating. But there was still a risk, nonetheless.

As he lay awake, an endless succession of names presented themselves to him in sequence, like newsflash footage. *Jodie Danforth*; *Jodie Bentley*; *Jodie Carmichael*; *Jemma Smith*; *Judith Forshaw*. And now from his late phone call with Kelly Nicholls he had added another name, *Cassie Danforth*. Jodie's sister who had died in a cliff fall when Jodie had been out for a walk with her on a family holiday.

Her sister dead in a cliff fall. Her fiancé dead in a fall from a precipice. Her first husband dead from a snake bite. Her second husband dead from a snake bite. A string of names, some real, some fake.

He'd googled Christopher Bentley and learned he was an eminent herpetologist, and the author of books on venomous and poisonous creatures. His wife, Jodie, was mentioned but there was no photograph. Bentley also had an elaborate website, but it was basically an information-sharing forum for other herpetologists, and there had been no posts on it, other than a few condolence messages, for several years.

His search also revealed a wide range of obituaries, including *The Times*, *Telegraph*, *Guardian* and *Independent*, as well as a humorous and slightly cynical article in the *Spectator*, talking about the irony of a man who had met many of the world's most dangerous snakes, scorpions and spiders in their natural habitat, yet had died from a bite at his own home. The article went on to warn people of the danger of *experts*. It quoted the late Peter Ustinov as saying that if the world was to explode, the last words anyone would hear would be an expert explaining why it couldn't happen.

Despite all the coverage on her first husband, Grace could find nothing at all, other than a few brief mentions, about the earlier life of Jodie

Bentley. But in the past few weeks there was plenty on her in relation to the tragic death of Walt Klein and the financial shenanigans surrounding him.

Through the night that was both long and far too short at the same time, a course of action steadily began to take shape in his mind.

Finally, he'd lapsed into deep sleep. It seemed almost moments later that his alarm was buzzing beside his face. It was 5.00 a.m. He tapped the off button, instantly awake. Had to be awake. Snoozing wasn't an option. And he was feeling strangely energized.

He rolled over in the darkness and kissed Cleo's cheek. She did not stir. Then, very gently and slowly, trying not to wake her, he slid out of bed into the chilly air. He gulped down the glass of water on the table beside him, then went through into the bathroom, closed the door behind him, switched on the light and peered blearily into the mirror. He looked ragged, he thought. He looked like shit. Yet he felt positive.

His master plan was a gamble; Cassian Pewe might reject it out of hand. But he was fired with excitement. He squeezed toothpaste onto his electric toothbrush and worked around his mouth for the next two minutes, feeling even more sure of what he needed to do.

He went through to Noah's room in his dressing gown and slippers and gently placed his hand on his son's back, checking that his breathing felt fine;

then, careful not to wake him, went downstairs. Humphrey came bounding up to him.

Grace knelt and stroked him. 'I'll take you out, Humph, but I'm afraid no run today. Make it up to you tomorrow, OK?'

He opened the back door and walked out into the streaky dawn light with a torch. The smell of wet grass and the silence of the countryside gave him an intense feeling of calm. He loved it here. This little piece of paradise. The moon was low in the sky. He felt just how insignificant he was in the universe. A tiny speck. Here for a fleeting moment in time.

Humphrey squatted and did a dump, then ran towards him, looking pleased as punch.

'Good boy!' He knelt and patted him. He walked over to the hen coop and, in the beam of his torch, saw all five sitting on the roof, not yet ready to start their day.

'Hi, girls! What are your plans today? Maybe lay a few eggs? Rob a bank? Get up to some internet fraud? Help me lock up some villains?'

He went back inside and microwaved a bowl of porridge. While the machine was whirring he took six red grapes from the fridge. Cleo had read somewhere that six red grapes a day warded off ageing and all kinds of disease. He loved how she took such a keen interest in health matters.

Then he made the first of several phone calls, apologizing for the early hour, brimming inside with excitement. It was a gamble. A massive gamble. But he was convinced it was the right thing to try.

When he had finished, he ate his porridge, which was now tepid, but in his eagerness to get to the office, he barely noticed. He hurried upstairs. Cleo was sitting up in bed, checking messages on her iPhone.

'Lots on at work today?' he asked.

'Five post-mortems,' she said. 'You?'

He told her quickly about his plan.

'I like it!' she replied. 'But could you really do that?'

He shrugged. 'I'm going to give it a go!'

He showered and shaved, and dressed quickly, then left the house shortly after 6 a.m. As he pulled into his parking slot outside Sussex House at 6.20 a.m., his phone rang.

It was Glenn Branson. Grace did a quick calculation – he would be an hour ahead of UK time in France.

'*Bonjour!*' he said. '*Ça va?*'

'*Merde!*' Branson replied, grimly. 'I think that's the right word for it.'

'Tell me.'

Grace listened for some moments in almost stunned silence. 'Disappeared? Escaped?'

'Looks like he used that old Ted Bundy trick of faking a broken arm. Lured a prison officer into his cell in the hospital wing to help him remove his T-shirt for bed, overpowered him, whacked him unconscious, tied and gagged him and put him on his bunk, facing the wall, with a blanket over his head. Left the two halves of the plaster cast in the bed with him.'

'Didn't anyone check his bloody arm when he was booked into custody?'

'Clearly not. He was taken straight to the prison hospital.'

'Even so, how did he get out of there – surely it was secure?'

'Nobody knows at this stage. Perhaps through the sewers or drains.'

'Shit!' Grace responded when he had finished. 'Shit!' he repeated. 'That seems to be his MO. He's a cunning bastard – I've heard of wanted people using a prop to steer attention away from their faces when they travel through airports. That's what he must have done. But how the hell did the French authorities let this happen? He's got away twice, he must be having a right bloody laugh on us.' God, even though it wasn't his fault, how on earth was he going to explain this to Pewe? he wondered.

'Let's hope he had to wade through plenty of *merde*,' Branson replied.

'Yeah. So what's the French for the stuff we're in now – *deep doo-doo*?'

CHAPTER 80

Wednesday 11 March

Having woken full of excitement, Grace now felt totally deflated. Edward Crisp, the big prize he had been expecting Glenn and Norman to escort home, had vanished. Now they were flying home alone. He was increasingly fretting about the reaction he would get from his ACC.

He phoned the mobile number of their Interpol case officer in London and got his voicemail. He left a message, informing him of the disastrous developments in Lyon, and asking the officer to call him back urgently.

Five minutes later, mug of coffee in his hand, he sat down at his desk deep in troubled thought. He called Cassian Pewe's mobile but it went to voicemail. Was nobody bloody answering their phones this morning? He left a message.

He briefly checked what had happened overnight on his computer but there was nothing of significance to him – just the usual muggings, robberies, fights, vehicle thefts – a Mercedes and a BMW – mispers, break-ins and RTCs.

Next he checked his emails and saw one from his NYPD detective friend, Pat Lanigan.

> Call me, pal, I've something of interest for you.

The email had been sent at 10 p.m. last night, Eastern time.

Grace did a quick mental calculation. New York was five hours behind the UK. 6.30 a.m. here; 1.30 a.m. in New York. He'd wait a few hours before ringing him back. Instead he made a phone call to someone for whom he had great respect.

It was answered by the eager-sounding voice of Ray Packham, who had recently retired, on health grounds, from the High Tech Crime Unit.

'Ray, it's Roy Grace. I'm sorry it's so early, but I have something I need to run by you. Are you OK to talk?'

'Roy! Good to hear from you. I've been up for ages, bored out of my mind, if you want to know the truth. How can I help you?'

Grace told him. When he had finished the conversation, feeling very upbeat about his plan, he sat still, reflecting. Crisp had escaped from his cell somewhere between lock-up at 9 p.m., French time, last night and 7 a.m. their time this morning. All his possessions would have been taken from him, surely, when he had been booked into custody there? He would only have had the prison officer's uniform and gun. Enough to have enabled him to hijack a car and flee the country. He could be in Switzerland or Italy or Germany by now. Or Austria, he thought, looking at the map of Europe on his wall.

God, they'd had the evil bastard. How the hell had he done it? How the hell had he pulled off his escape again? No doubt with the same cunning and planning he'd used to escape from his underground hideout in Brighton back in December. Now he was playing international hide and seek. One certainty, he knew, was that Sussex Police did not have the resources, however heinous Crisp's crimes, to embark on an international manhunt. They would have to rely on Europol and Interpol for that.

Right now he had to focus on Operation Spider. If there really was a 'black widow' operating in the city, and the evidence pointed to it, he needed to stop her before another victim died. But the plan he had concocted during the night seemed fraught with problems. In a different era he could just have gone ahead with it on his own initiative. Now he had to seek permission, and jump through a whole bunch of potentially hostile hoops.

Which might have fatal consequences.

He needed to strengthen his evidence in every way that he could, and one thought had been going through his mind during the night on how he might possibly do that.

He googled 'saw-scaled viper', then leaned forward, peering closely at his screen as he scrolled through a wide range of information and links about the snake and its genus, *Echis*. He was looking for one very specific thing. Something that Jodie might have slipped up on. It was just a hunch, a long shot, but worth a few minutes of his time.

As he read what came up, he felt a beat of excitement. 'Yes!' he said, punching the air. He read it carefully again, then phoned Guy Batchelor, who was acting as the office manager for Operation Spider. 'Guy, the venomous reptile expert from London Zoo who came down to accompany the team that searched Shelby Stonor's home, Dr Rearden right?'

'Yes, boss, he said if someone was needed to advise on the snake bite, we should contact the Liverpool School of Tropical Medicine, who are world-renowned experts.'

'Liverpool, bugger, that's quite a distance. Can you contact them as soon as you can and see if there's anyone who could get down here today?'

As he ended the call, his phone rang. It was ACC Pewe. Grace took a deep breath.

Pewe was not as angry as he had expected, but he guessed the reason why. This was something Pewe would be able to bank and hold against him at a later date, however much it had not been his fault.

'What a bloody mess, Roy,' he whined down the phone.

'Crisp? Yes, sir, I agree with you. But not Operation Spider. I have a strategy – I'd like to come and talk it through with you. Do you have any time free today?'

'I'm free now,' his boss replied. 'I've one hour.'

CHAPTER 81

Wednesday 11 March

At a few minutes before 7 a.m., the security guard at the barrier of Malling House, the sprawling Sussex Police Headquarters where Major Crimes was soon going to be housed, waved to Roy Grace as he passed through.

He drove his unmarked Mondeo up the steep hill, passing the car park to his right for the Road Policing Unit and the Call Centre, and pulled up at the entrance to the visitor car park. He held his access pass up against the electronic reader and the barrier rose.

He reversed into a bay in the almost empty car park, then went into the reception area of the prefab building and exchanged pleasantries with the duty receptionist, whom he had known for years.

He sent a text to Guy Batchelor telling him to delay the morning briefing until 9 a.m., then made his way through the back entrance into the grand Queen Anne building that housed the senior staff of Sussex Police. He greeted his old friend, Acting Superintendent Steve Curry, then switching his phone to silent, went up the stairs and into Cassian Pewe's majestic office, with its view across the trim lawn below and one of the modern housing estates of the county town of Lewes beyond.

The ACC rose from behind his large desk to greet him. Dressed in immaculate uniform, he extended a delicate hand.

'Good to see you, Roy,' he said. He indicated a leather chair in front of the desk.

As Grace sat down, Pewe asked, 'Tea or coffee?'

'Black coffee would be good, sir, thank you.'

'I see, a heavy night?'

'No, sir,' he said, always aware of Pewe's hidden agenda in every question he asked. 'An early night, actually, but that's hard with a young baby.'

'Yes, of course.' Pewe spoke into his phone, ordering the coffee, then looked across the desk at Grace. 'How is little Noah?'

'Getting feistier by the day – and night.'

Pewe gave him a patronizing smile. 'And do I understand you went to Munich for a couple of days?'

'No, sir, just the one day. Sandy has surfaced, after ten bloody years. She'd been involved in a traffic accident out there – hit by a taxi.'

Pewe avoided eye contact. 'She's alive?'

'Badly injured.'

He was dying to say to Pewe, *So she wasn't buried in my back garden after all, was she?* Perhaps that was why the ACC wouldn't meet his eye.

'Oh? I'm sorry to hear that. And where does that leave you, Roy?'

'I've moved on, sir. But I had to go and see her.'

'Of course you had to.'

'There'll be a lot of legalities to resolve, but that's for another day.'

There was an awkward silence for some moments. Pewe finally broke it. 'So, Roy – you mentioned a strategy?'

The assistant brought in the coffee and a plate of shortbread biscuits.

'Yes.' He sipped the scalding coffee, waited until she had left the room, closing the door behind her, then talked the ACC through it.

When he had finished, Cassian Pewe stared at him in total silence, his expression impossible to read. Then he said, 'This is insane, Roy.'

'It's a risk, sir, I agree with that.'

'Have you thought about all the different ways it could backfire on us?'

'Yes, I have. But in my view we are dealing with a monster potentially every bit as evil as Edward Crisp. It's looking like she might have murdered three men, and we have no way of telling, at this moment, if there are any others before Bentley she may have killed. We're currently searching the UK and internationally for potential matches. This might be a way to flush her out.'

'Or to get one of our officers killed?'

'Not if we risk assess it properly, sir.'

'You mean the way Crisp's confinement in the Lyon jail was risk assessed?'

'That was out of our jurisdiction.'

'Luckily for your career, Roy. What you're proposing now isn't. Before you even start to go there you need the Crown Prosecution Service on board. You're putting an awful lot on a rather shaky assumption, don't you think?'

'Shaky? I have a suspect who appears to be using different identities, and targets rich older men. There are three that we know of and there could be more. Her first husband died after being bitten by a venomous snake – and I accept that he was an expert who worked with these creatures, so was at a higher risk than anyone else. Her most recent fiancé skied over a cliff in France.'

'Yes, Roy,' Pewe interrupted him. 'Walter Klein, a fraudster who knew the game was up. All the evidence points to suicide.'

'With respect, sir, there is no evidence.'

'Leaving that aside, you're trying to link the death of a small-time burglar in Brighton with the death of her second husband in India?'

'Second husband that we know about – I'm trying to get more on that, sir. I've already briefed and prepared a plan with the Force Authorizing Officer, Detective Superintendent Nick Sloan, whose job it will be to manage and supervise the operation. I've also made contact with Wayne Gumbrell at the Crown Prosecution Service, who's on board. We all agree that this is the only option available at the moment to prevent this woman targeting and killing another victim. I'll have the paperwork drawn up for you to sign as it needs your written authority.'

'OK, Roy, but screw this one up and I'll have you writing out parking tickets for the rest of your career. Do I make myself clear?'

Clear as merde, Grace said, under his breath.

CHAPTER 82

Wednesday 11 March

As he went back down to his car, Roy Grace played a voicemail from Guy Batchelor on his phone. He was in luck – an expert from the Liverpool School of Tropical Medicine was attending a conference in London and could be with them by midday.

He phoned Guy and told him to delay the briefing further, to 2 p.m., then he phoned Wayne Gumbrell, left a message on his voicemail updating him on his conversation with Pewe, and returned to Sussex House. He wanted to spend a quiet hour alone, reviewing everything, checking for anything he might have overlooked, and writing up his policy book.

Stopping by the tiny kitchenette, he switched on the kettle, then spooned some coffee into a mug with the only available implement, the handle of a bent fork, then carried the coffee through into his office. A while later, Pat Lanigan rang. Grace glanced at his watch. 9.25 a.m. It was 4.25 a.m. in New York. During the past couple of weeks he'd been in regular communication with the New York detective, sharing information.

'Hey, pal, how you doooin'?' Lanigan said in his nasally Brooklyn accent.

'Yep, good. I was going to call you in a bit. You're up early!'

'Always! Look, I've got something maybe of interest. Remember a while back you had a character name of Tooth visiting your city?'

'Only too well,' Grace said, putting his phone on loudspeaker on his desk, along with the mug, then peeling off his jacket. 'We thought he was dead, but then again, we thought Crisp was dead, too.' He remembered how Tooth, a professional hitman, had disappeared from Sussex Police's clutches, presumed drowned in Shoreham Harbour, after a fight with Glenn Branson at the edge of a dock.

'Yep, so you told me,' said Lanigan. 'We got some intel on him from undercover operations. One of his aliases, John Daniels, just got flagged up on our radar. Seems he's very much alive and might be headed back your way. There's a link with our friend Jodie.'

'Tooth still alive, a connection with Jodie, heading back to Brighton? Bloody hell. That's a bit of a bombshell, Pat. This has suddenly got very, very interesting. Tell me more.'

'We believe he travelled to the UK, using the name Mike Hinton, to recover a memory stick from Jodie.'

Grace remembered DS Batchelor's report from Tuesday about the poste-restante and internet café at 23A Western Road, Brighton.

I was told by the manager there that a strange guy turned up on the morning of Sunday March 1st, around eleven o'clock, enquiring about Jodie – an American, who was quite bolshy. He was rude to her, then went away.

'What more do you have, Pat?'

'Hinton flew to England the weekend before last. I don't have any more information at this stage, but I can get you the flight number. I thought you'd want to do some checking.'

'Right away, Pat. Thank you.'

'Don't mention it, pal. We gonna see you and your bride over here anytime soon? Francene and I'll take you to dinner.'

'Cleo's keen to see New York at Christmas.'

'My favourite time of year in this city! Come over, we'll go to the Christmas show at Radio City Music Hall. Then we'll take you to dinner at the best Italian in the world. OK, buddy?'

'If we can, it's a date!'

Grace hung up then sat, thinking, for some moments. Tooth. So he had survived? And was back here? Under the name of Mike Hinton?

Tooth was suspected of the revenge killing of a lorry driver who had been in a fatal road accident. He was also suspected of murdering the van driver involved. And he had come close to murdering the young son of another person also in that same

423

accident. Shoreham Harbour had been searched by trained divers who knew the waters, the tides and the currents. Nothing had been found. It was concluded at the time that it was possible, however unlikely, that Tooth might have survived. And now he was back?

Grace phoned Guy Batchelor and asked him to come and see him, urgently.

Five minutes later, DS Batchelor eased into the chair in front of Roy Grace's desk with an amiable smile. 'Yes, boss?'

'Guy, top priority, use whatever resources you need to see if an American national, under the name of John Daniels or Mike Hinton, has checked into any hotel or boarding house in the city of Brighton and Hove, or surrounding area. Start with the city and work outwards to as far as Gatwick Airport for starters. And have all car rental companies checked, too.'

'Do we have a current description of him?'

Grace nodded. 'The one the woman in the internet café at 23A Western Road gave. A small, bolshy weasel with an American accent. There's also a very poor quality CCTV image of him that Jack got. We think that man is the professional killer, Tooth, from Operation Violin, and may be armed. Call me instantly if you find anything, and we'll decide on a course of action. I've intelligence that he could lead us to our target lady – and I want to get to her before he does, because I'd like to have her alive. And I'd quite like to keep you alive, too.'

'I remember him, boss, I'll look after myself.'

Grace shook his head. 'Don't underestimate him, Guy. He's not your average Brighton villain. He's smart and seriously dangerous. I mean it. Find him and keep your distance. I don't want to have to go knocking on Lena's door telling her you've died a hero, OK?'

'Understood.'

'Good man.'

CHAPTER 83

Wednesday 11 March

The expert from Liverpool, Dr James West, was already seated in the tiny reception room at the Brighton and Hove City Mortuary, gowned up and with a mug of tea, when Cleo showed Grace through at a few minutes past midday.

A tall, thin man in his late forties, with a gaunt, rugged face framed with a shock of curly ginger hair and the kind of beard someone who had been several weeks in the jungle might sport, West rose and greeted him with a strong, bony handshake.

'Apologies for keeping you waiting,' Grace said.

'Not at all, I was early.' His voice had a trace of a South African accent. 'It's an honour to meet the famous detective.'

'Famous?' Grace grinned. 'I don't know about that!'

'I googled you. You seem to have solved most major crimes in your county over the past decade or so.'

'Very flattering of you. Let's see if we can solve this one.'

'Cup of tea or coffee, Detective Superintendent?' Cleo, also gowned up, asked him, cheekily.

'I'm good, thank you. I'll go and get dressed.'

Cleo led him through into the changing room, put her arms round his neck and kissed him, before pointing to a set of scrubs and a pair of white rubber boots. 'I'll go and get Mr Carmichael out for you – I'm afraid we've had a hectic morning.'

'But not Rowley Carmichael – he's just chilling, right?'

'Naughty!' She wagged a finger at him and disappeared.

A couple of minutes later Roy led Dr West through into the suite of two post-mortem rooms separated by a wide archway. To their right, three naked cadavers were laid out in the main room, two elderly men and an elderly woman, over whom Mark Howard, the youngest of the city's team of pathologists, was bent, taking stomach fluid samples, attended by Cleo's senior assistant, Darren Wallace, and his colleague, Julie Bartlett. All three greeted Roy.

Over to the left, Cleo had opened a door in the wall of fridges and was sliding out a tray on which lay a body encased in white plastic sheeting. 'Do you need him on a PM table, Roy?' she asked.

He shook his head. 'The tray's fine, thanks.'

As she began to unwrap Rowley Carmichael, Grace lifted his face mask up to cover his nose and mouth, and the professor did the same, as a normal precaution.

'You do know he's been embalmed?' Cleo said.

'Yes,' Grace replied. 'Unfortunately.'

The process of embalming involved replacing all blood in the body with a number of preservative chemicals, as well as dyes, to slow down the decomposition process and make the body look more lifelike.

Grace had already been through the detailed Goan toxicology report, and the cause of death, from the venom of a saw-scaled viper, was not in question. But from his earlier trawl of the internet, he had a couple of big questions that could help very substantially with this investigation – depending on what Dr West had to say.

Both of them looked down at the elderly naked man. The embalming had done its stuff and his flabby flesh had a pink hue, more that of someone sleeping than the usual alabaster colour of a person recently deceased.

'So, OK?' West said, turning to Grace. 'You want my views on the bite?'

Cleo pointed to the man's right ankle. There was a small blue oval, drawn with a chinagraph pencil. Inside it was one barely visible mark, the size of a pinprick.

As if he had stepped straight out of an Indiana Jones movie, West produced a fold-out magnifying glass and peered at the mark for some moments in silence. 'Hmmmnnn,' he said. Then he said, 'Hmmmnnn,' again, sounding more dubious. 'Interesting.'

'Is that a bite?' Grace asked.

'Hmmmnnn,' the expert said for the third time, looking deeply pensive. 'You know, detective, you are quite right to query this. Yes, it is a snake bite, just a single fang, uncommon but it does happen.' He continued studying the mark, putting the magnifying glass even closer. 'You see, what is bothering me is the lack of any sign of ecchymosis.'

'What's that?'

'Well, in layman's terms, local discolouration of tissue. Your toxicology report identifies all the symptoms of death by *Echis* venom. But post-mortem, I would expect to see signs of inflammation, swelling and ecchymosis around the bite mark from the fang. The puncture here is in character with a snake bite. But without the ecchymosis I'd expect.' He turned and looked up at Grace. 'To be honest, in my opinion, I doubt strongly that the venom entered the body through this bite mark. Where exactly was this unfortunate chap when he was bitten?'

'That's the second thing I wanted to ask you,' Roy Grace said. 'He was in the swampy area of the crocodile park in Borivali East, outside Mumbai.'

'Are you sure?'

'Yes.'

West shook his head, his beard moving like the tendrils of an underwater sea anemone. 'Not possible,' he said. 'I've been there, I know that place well. The *Echis* lives in open, dry, sandy and rocky terrain. Under rocks, in the base of thorny plants. This snake would not go near that swamp area.'

'You're sure?'

'Detective Grace, I've studied these creatures for much of my life. I could stand up in court and testify under oath that you would not find a saw-scaled viper in that particular area of that crocodile park.'

'Thank you.'

'Anything else you need to know?'

Grace smiled. 'Not at this stage, no, that's more than enough.'

'Then I'll head up to London, I ought to get back as quickly as possible,' James West said.

'Sure, I'll drop you at the station.'

CHAPTER 84

Wednesday 11 March

Reflexes in the animal kingdom are the key to survival. An instant decision has to be made. Friend, foe or food. Every creature develops the senses it needs for survival through natural selection. Saw-scaled vipers, like most snakes, have poor eyesight, and their hearing is pretty rubbish too. In common with all snakes they have forked tongues which are chemosensory, picking up minute scents on wet surfaces and taking them back into the roof of their mouths, the olfactory Jacobson's organ. It is smell and taste combined; in effect that's the survival armoury of this genus of reptile. The more anxious a saw-scaled viper becomes, the more its tongue flicks, and it makes its defensive sawing sound by coiling and uncoiling, rubbing its scales together. It can see only movement, in shades of grey, and cannot discern shape, unlike raptors, such as eagles, hawks and falcons, which can see eight times more clearly than the sharpest human eye. A golden eagle can identify a hare from a mile away and a peregrine falcon can dive on its prey at 200 mph.

Villains depend on heightened senses for their survival, too. Just the same way that the best cops develop a sixth sense for spotting them.

Out on the streets, one of the first things villains see is a police car. It's like a magnetic force, drawing their eyes to it, and then to the cops inside. A good crim can spot an unmarked car from a distance just as easily as one in full Battenburg livery, decked out in blue lights. Cops sit in a certain way, look around in a certain way.

Roy Grace remembered, eighteen years ago, as a young detective constable, soon after his move from uniform to CID, travelling across lush Sussex countryside on a fine August day to a murder scene, turning to the highly experienced detective inspector who was driving, and asking him if he viewed the world differently from most people.

The DI replied, 'Roy, you're looking through the windscreen at a beautiful summer's day. I'm looking at a man who's standing in the wrong place.'

Grace had never forgotten that. As he drove away from Brighton Station having dropped off Dr West, he pulled up at the junction with New England Road, waiting for the lights to turn green. A Streamline taxi passed in front of him heading up the hill. And as if drawn by a magnet his eyes locked with those of the passenger slouched in the rear of it, wearing a baseball cap.

For just one fleeting instant.

Then an articulated lorry halted in front of him, straddling the junction and blocking his view of the taxi's licence plate.

Shit! Shit! Shit!

He had a near photographic memory for faces, and he was sure the one he had seen in the rear of the taxi was the American hitman Tooth, although he was aware his mind might be playing tricks, as he'd spent most of the morning talking about him.

He pulled back the plastic cover on the dash that concealed the buttons for the lights and sirens, and hit the one for the pursuit blue lights, but not the siren, not wanting to alert his quarry. The lorry was still stuck in front of him, completely blocking his path.

'Get out the bloody way!' Grace yelled in frustration. But still the lorry didn't move.

His brain raced. He knew every road in this city. The taxi heading up the hill could either go straight on or fork right in a few hundred yards. At the top of the hill was the Seven Dials roundabout, giving six different options – as well as a left turn-off shortly before.

The lorry moved on up the hill and a van behind it stopped to let him through. Grace pulled out to try to overtake the lorry, but there was a bus in the oncoming lane and he pulled back in to let it pass, then pulled out again. The lorry indicated it was pulling over, and he shot past, squeezing into a narrow gap left by an oncoming car that had halted. But the road ahead was blocked by another lorry, waiting to turn right under the viaduct.

He radioed an urgent request for the Ops-1 Inspector, gave him the information and asked for any units in the area to look for a Streamline Skoda taxi heading up New England Road, with a passenger in the rear wearing a baseball cap. He told them to follow if they spotted it and inform him immediately, but not to stop it. He also asked his colleague to contact Streamline to see if they could get a carefully worded message to the driver. As soon as the lights changed, and the lorry moved on, turning right, he saw a whole line of buses coming down the hill, completely blocking the opposite lane.

He followed the lorry, then pulled out to overtake, thinking he would try to get ahead of the taxi this way and cut it off at the Seven Dials. He screamed past the lorry, crested the hill and eased left through a red light at the junction with Dyke Road, then driving on the wrong side of the road, hitting the alternate wail and honk sirens, bullied his way through the oncoming traffic all the way to the roundabout.

But there was no sign of the taxi.

It could have gone in any damned direction.

He did a full circle of the roundabout, thinking hard. The taxi was heading up New England Road. That was a route people took coming into the city.

Was it then going to head down to the seafront? Or the town centre? Those were the most likely options.

He made a left turn off the roundabout into Montpelier Road, again driving as fast as he dared, weaving through the oncoming traffic and peering left and right down each side turning. Then he saw a Skoda taxi in Streamline livery heading west. He raced past it, pulled in front, switched on the red flashing STOP lights, and braked sharply to a halt. In his mirror he saw the taxi pull up behind him. As he was debating what to do next, the rear door opened and a young woman got out, reached in and lifted out a small child.

Shit!

Grace climbed out, removed his warrant card and walked up to the cab, raising an apologetic hand to the woman and the driver, who wound down his window, peering out nervously.

'It's fine,' Grace said. 'You can continue.'

He returned to his car, wondering. Had it actually been Tooth he had seen? Or just wishful thinking?

Twenty minutes later, as he arrived back at Sussex House, the Ops-1 Inspector called him back to report no success. Grace thanked him and went in through the front door of the building. Climbing the stairs to the Major Crime suite, he reflected on just what he had seen in the back of that taxi. Had he imagined it? He didn't think so. Offenders had a way of looking at coppers that was different from all other people. But maybe he was just a regular Brighton villain who had picked up on him. Maybe it was just his imagination working overtime.

Back in his office, he phoned Pewe to update him on his meeting with West at the mortuary, and the expert's opinion. When he had finished, he said, 'Do you need anything else, sir?'

'No,' Pewe said, grudgingly. 'I don't.'

As he ended the call, Grace's phone instantly rang. It was Guy Batchelor and he sounded excited.

CHAPTER 85

Wednesday 11 March

'Boss, something of significance to report!' Batchelor said. 'I think we may have found Tooth.'

'Yes?'

'Last Friday, there was a report of a man in collision with two cyclists close to Brighton Pier. He was taken unconscious to the Royal Sussex County Hospital. His US driving licence identified him as *John Daniels*, with an address in New York City. And there was a bar receipt from the Waterfront Hotel in his wallet.'

'Jesus!'

'I sent two officers to the hospital but he's gone – seems to have discharged himself, sometime during this morning. But the hospital says he has severe bruising to both his legs and would be limping significantly. Someone's going to have noticed him.'

'Is this a genuine injury or a phoney one like Crisp's, Guy?'

'I haven't checked that, boss, but I assume that

the hospital wouldn't have said so if it wasn't the case.'

'Yep, well you know my views on assumptions,' Grace retorted.

'I'll get someone to double-check.'

'Good. Have you contacted the hotel?'

'Yes, they don't have any guest by the name of Daniels registered. Nor Hinton.'

'Bizarrely, I think I may have seen Tooth heading up New England Road in a Streamline taxi, twenty minutes ago,' Grace said.

'Seems an odd route from the Sussex County Hospital, wherever he was going,' Batchelor said.

'I could have been mistaken. Can you get on to Streamline and ask them for details of all pick-ups from the hospital this morning? All of them have CCTV in their cars now. Also can you see if there's an update on possible sightings from our message to Streamline earlier?'

'Right away, sir.'

'OK, good work, Guy. And can you arrange an accommodation check in the city for Daniels, Hinton, or any single American males – but keep it low-key for now.'

As soon as he ended the call, Grace phoned Lanigan. He got his voicemail and left a message. 'Pat, it's Roy in Brighton. You said John Daniels was one of the aliases of our pal, Mr Tooth, and there's Mike Hinton also. Can you let me have any others? I need to know very urgently.'

He hung up and then sat and thought. Had it

been Tooth in hospital? Had it been him in the back of the taxi? If he had just left the Royal Sussex County Hospital, what was he doing at the north end of the city? New England Road was a route many people who came south into the city on London Road took to get to the beaches, or the western side of the city. Why would Tooth have gone north only to head south again? That route didn't make any sense. Unless he was trying to shake someone off his tail.

Or be deliberately confusing.

CHAPTER 86

Wednesday 11 March

Jodie Carmichael, returning home in light drizzle from a trip to the Asda superstore at Brighton Marina, turned into her driveway and clicked the remote button to open her double-garage door. She reversed her blue convertible Mercedes in, clicked the remote to close the door behind her, then climbed out of the car. She removed her bags from the boot and let herself into the house through the internal door.

As she laid out the bags on the kitchen table, her mobile phone rang. She saw the name of the funeral directors, P & S Gallagher, appear.

She hesitated for a moment, then putting on her grief-stricken voice, she answered. 'Hello?'

It was the very charming boss of the firm. 'Mrs Carmichael, it's Mr Gallagher, how are you?'

'Oh, you know, bearing up, I guess.'

'Good,' he said. 'I'm pleased to hear it. I'm afraid I've got some rather frustrating news – the Coroner still hasn't released the body. And I've also had a call from Mr Carmichael's son who wants to engage the services of another pathologist to conduct a second post-mortem.'

'Bloody hell!' she said, furious. 'My darling husband died at the start of our honeymoon. Doesn't he think I've suffered enough? And he's been embalmed – what the hell does he think another post-mortem's going to achieve? I'm his wife! Don't my wishes count?'

'Well, there is another complication,' he continued. 'The police have also informed us that further enquiries are taking place, so I'm afraid our hands are tied.'

'My poor Rollo has to suffer the indignity of a mortuary fridge while everyone squabbles over his body, is that what you're saying, Mr Gallagher?'

'Not at all, Mrs Carmichael. They just need to establish beyond any doubt the cause of your husband's tragic death.'

'He was killed by a fucking snake bite, right? By a saw-scaled viper. The Coroner in Goa certified that. What else do they bloody need?'

'I'm sure it will all be sorted very quickly,' he said in a soothing voice. 'I'll do my best to get all of this resolved, and your husband's body released to us, just as soon as possible.'

When she hung up, Jodie sat, wondering what Gallagher had meant by 'enquiries'. What were the police sniffing around for? She made herself a coffee and switched on her computer. One thing was becoming certain, she would have a fight with Rowley's family on her hands. At the end of the day she would get some of the inheritance. But from the way Rowley's family already seemed to be heading for a legal battle, it could be a long way down the line. It certainly wasn't likely to be the jackpot that she'd hoped for, which still seemed to be eluding her.

That was out there somewhere.

She needed to be more selective, she decided, as she started to trawl through the various replies to the advertisements she had placed on dating sites for the rich.

www.sugardaddies.com
www.seekingmillionaire.com
www.millionairematch.com
www.daterichmen.com

And a whole ton more. But she dismissed all the replies she saw waiting for her. She'd learned, through experience of dating dozens of them, how to spot the ones that were only out for affairs. And she didn't just want someone wealthy. She wanted someone who was super-rich. Would she find him on a website, or in one of the playgrounds of the rich?

She remembered something her beautiful childhood friend, Emira, had once said to her, that had been at the same time disparaging and consoling. 'Don't worry, one day you'll find Mr Right. There's someone out there for everyone.'

Maybe she'd been too hasty recently. She just needed to bide her time.

She went upstairs, pressed the remote to open

the sliding wall then peered through the glass door, into her reptile room, checking as she always did that nothing had escaped. She went in and over to the vivarium containing the nine-foot boa constrictor she called Silas.

A smile broke out on her face as she saw what lay on the floor of the toughened glass container.

CHAPTER 87

Wednesday 11 March

Tooth hobbled on the walking stick he'd stolen from the hospital corridor, clutching his huge package of shopping and a smaller carrier bag as he crossed the foyer of the hotel to the bank of lifts. It took him a good minute – a journey he could normally have made in seconds – to get from the elevator to his room on the fourth floor. Every step was uncomfortable, but for anyone else would have been agony. Tooth had been born with an abnormality – his tolerance levels to pain were far higher than those of most human beings.

Finally, in the sanctuary of his room, after looking around carefully, he sat at his desk and flipped open the lid of his laptop. Nothing seemed to have been touched here. But he couldn't rely on that for much longer.

He'd always had a rule. He never stayed in one place for too long. Staying in one place was how people could catch up with you, whether it was picking up your scent or picking up your financial trail. He'd had to leave the hospital this morning, because the hotel was only paid up to today; but more than that, ten days was already too long in one place, and he couldn't risk any longer. Earlier today he'd taken advantage of the shortage of hospital staff to slip away.

But had that cop recognized him in the taxi?

He wasn't certain, but he sure as hell wasn't going to take the risk that he had. And that cop sure as hell would not recognize him the next time he saw him.

He began to scan the videos from the sixteen cameras he had concealed in Jodie's house and the four he had put in her flat in Alexandra Villas. He started with the two he had placed in her reptile room, and it didn't take him long before his hunch paid off.

He watched her pull on rubber gloves – the time recording gave it as just two hours ago. She removed the lid of a vivarium containing a huge boa constrictor, then took out what looked like a white clay sausage. She placed it on the table, then pulled it open with her hands and removed a memory stick from inside it.

'Clever girl!' he said aloud. 'Oh yes, you are one very clever girl!'

He watched her place the memory stick back in the vivarium, dropping it out of sight into the foliage, then deposit the sausage – the boa's excrement – into a bin.

'So clever!' he thought. 'You really are very

445

clever.' *And very sexy too*, he thought. *I'm sure it would be nice to fuck you. Too bad I'll never find out.*

He opened his packages.

CHAPTER 88

Wednesday 11 March

'Mice, lizards, frogs, scorpions and insects,' Tanja Cale said, as she joined Roy Grace heading along the Major Crime suite corridor towards the conference room for the 2 p.m. briefing.

'That what you had for breakfast, Tanja?' he said. 'No wonder you look so healthy!'

'No,' she grinned. 'It's what Jason cooks me for dinner every evening!'

He raised a finger to his lips. 'Sssh, don't share your secret, everyone will be wanting some!'

'Guess it depends on the recipe.'

'And yours is?'

'Raw and preferably alive,' she said. 'You asked me to find out what a saw-scaled viper likes to snack on.'

'And that's its diet?'

'Yep!'

'In which case, on the whole, I'm glad I'm not a saw-scaled viper.'

'And Jason's glad I'm not a black widow

447

spider. They eat their husbands after they've made love.'

'I think if I was a male black widow, I'd be pretty happy if my wife told me she had a headache!' Grace retorted, as they entered the packed conference room.

'Well, in case you fancy a change of diet, sir, I've found several companies who tie in with the credit card statements who can supply all these creatures, and more.'

'And get me points on my Tesco clubcard?'

'Well, unfortunately not that many, sir. I spoke to a gentleman called Danny Yeoman from a large Sussex store, Pets Corner. One of the saw-scaled viper's favourite foods is cockroaches. But if you buy a box of them, that's all you need. From then on you can culture them yourself. So long as you have the right bedding and substrate and you give the creature access to water and a warm environment, you really don't need anything else.'

'I'll remember that next time I'm thinking of buying Cleo a saw-scaled viper for Christmas,' Grace said.

Taking their seats, he brought his team up to speed on the overnight developments regarding Edward Crisp, informing them that Branson and Potting were flying back, and then went on to describe his conversation with Kelly Nicholls last night, his meeting with Pewe earlier this morning and his subsequent meeting with Dr West at the mortuary.

'I updated the ACC on the latest developments with Operation Spider and our belief that we may well have a black widow operating in this city, who is targeting, marrying then killing elderly rich men. And with West's opinion that Rowley Carmichael's death from the venom of a saw-scaled viper might well be suspicious, in that he was apparently bitten in an area of the crocodile farm that is not this creature's natural habitat, and that there was none of the *ecchymosis* – skin discolouration – around the bite mark that he would have expected to see.'

'When you say *suspicious*, boss,' Jon Exton asked, 'what do you – or Dr West – actually mean?'

'In Dr West's view,' Grace replied, 'the venom might have been delivered to Rowley Carmichael by some other means than a bite.'

'What kind of other means?'

'Well, according to West there is only one other way to deliver it in a lethal form and that's by injection. Carmichael was an insulin-dependent diabetic, who injected himself four times daily. Could his darling new bride have *accidentally* substituted his insulin with snake venom? It's a possibility we can't rule out, given her past form, which is pretty interesting. There are all the identities of Jodie Bentley, who would have become Jodie Klein by marriage, but whose prospective husband fell over a cliff in Courchevel, France. She then married Rowley Carmichael, who died a few days after their marriage. Interestingly, Jodie Bentley's first husband, Christopher, also died from a saw-scale viper bite some years ago.' He paused to sip his coffee.

'She seems very adept at creating false identities. I informed ACC Pewe that at the present time, whilst we are putting a lot of resources into finding her, we do not know the whereabouts of this extremely clever and dangerous lady. We are aware of one poste-restante address she is known to use, and we have asked them to notify us when she next turns up, but not surprisingly they are reluctant to cooperate. And we don't have the resources to place surveillance on her known addresses to see if she appears. What we are doing is keeping an eye on the CCTV camera footage in the streets outside them, but it's a huge task. We've had nothing back on her phone, and therefore Michelle Websdale has not been able to set up a meeting with her.

'We have two problems right now. The first is locking this woman up before she finds her next husband – and possible victim. The second is that so far all evidence against her is largely circumstantial and we need something more solid to arrest her.'

He brought the briefing to an end, and asked Tanja Cale and Glenn Branson, who was just back from Lyon, to come to his office.

A few minutes later, sat around the table, Roy began the meeting by saying, 'If we are correct in our assumption that Jodie Carmichael is targeting wealthy older men, I suggest we put someone in place, with a carefully created background, who fits this mould. A retired, secretive multimillionaire, whose wife died some time ago, who is perhaps terminally ill and has returned to Brighton to spend his last days here. We use social media to seed his fake background as a rich philanthropist. I'm thinking we work with some of the local papers, the *Argus* in particular, but also the *Brighton and Hove Independent*, the *Mid Sussex Times* and the *Sussex Express*, to run features on him, and consider the local media, too – such as Radio Sussex, Latest TV, perhaps get an interview with him on the Albion Roar – about how much he's missed attending his home football team's games; and how honoured the city is that he's chosen Brighton to spend his last days, that sort of thing.'

'Isn't there a problem, sir?' Tanja said. 'That anyone checking would see there is no historic social media trail?'

Grace nodded. 'You are quite right, Tanja. I discussed this with the Chief Superintendent of the Financial Crimes Unit at the City of London Police and with the Commander of the Scotland Yard Fraud Squad.' He smiled. 'They're well ahead of the curve and they anticipated these kinds of problems very early on. Almost from the get-go of so-called "social media", they've been on it. Seeding and creating false identities first on MySpace, then Facebook, Twitter, and more recently on Instagram, Pinterest, Snapchat and all the others. Name an identity and they have it. In our case, a reclusive multimillionaire, who's a widower and has made the decision to leave the bulk of his estate to charity.

'Bloody hell, that's smart!' Glenn said.

'I thought so, too!' Roy Grace replied. 'Mostly in the police we're constantly playing a game of catch-up with villains. Nice to think we have some visionaries who occasionally put us ahead of the game. The Financial Crimes Unit of the City of London Police are sending one of their detectives down to advise us today.'

'Do you have someone in mind for this undercover officer, sir?' Tanja asked.

'I don't yet,' he replied. 'The Surrey and Sussex Major Crime Team can approach the Covert Policing Unit to identify a suitable officer who has been trained in this field. It's actually been so well managed, historically, that no one knows who any of these people are. The normal procedure would be to use a detective from out of area, but that's not always possible.'

'What about risk to the officer concerned?' Tanja Cale asked.

'That's what we have to manage in the full risk assessment,' Grace said. 'But that's what we all do, every day, isn't it? We try to make our city a safer place. To do that, all of us at some time have to take risks. I've never met a good police officer who, at some point, didn't have their life on the line. The day we aren't willing to do that is the day to quit.'

Cale and Branson nodded.

CHAPTER 89

Wednesday 11 March

After the meeting ended, Roy Grace called DC Maggie Bridgeman, who was the liaison officer at the Covert Policing Unit. He gave her the specifics. He needed a male officer immediately available, who could pass as someone terminally ill in their sixties, and someone who had local knowledge.

Unfazed, as if she dealt with requests like this all day long, Bridgeman said she would check with Resourcing and get back to him.

A few minutes after ending the call, Pat Lanigan rang him back from New York.

'Hey, pal! I got some of the other aliases you wanted. Try James Beam and George Dickel.'

'Aren't they American whisky distilleries?' Grace asked.

'You got it. Amazing to us all, seems like our mutual buddy, Tooth, has a sense of humour.'

There seemed to be so many false names involved that Grace was starting to wonder if this operation's name should be changed from Operation Spider to

Operation Alias. As soon as he ended the call, he passed the information to one of his team.

Ten minutes later a Detective Constable Ballantine called him back from the Waterfront Hotel's front desk. They had a guest named George Dickel in room 407.

Grace sometimes let excitement rule his head. That had led to Glenn Branson being shot. Had the bullet gone an inch to the right his mate would have either been dead or paralysed from the waist down. He remembered that and other lessons. Yet at the same time adrenalin surged through him. Tooth would be a major prize – a massive prize. He had to be certain the man did not slip through his fingers this time.

First he asked the reception desk to check that Mr Dickel was in his room, suggesting they phone up on a housekeeping pretext of checking he was happy with the way his room had been cleaned. Then he phoned the Ops-1 Inspector, and was glad to hear the voice of the one he trusted the most, Don Mark, on the line.

Grace spoke with the Silver Commander who, within ten minutes, had an Armed Response Unit, two dog handlers and members of the Tactical Firearms Unit heading towards the Waterfront Hotel. And as an extra precaution, Silver had the helicopter NPAS 15 on standby – hoping it wasn't called away to another police or medical emergency, as Sussex Police no longer had an exclusive helicopter of their own.

It wasn't often, in his current role as Head of Major Crime, that Grace was present at operations, but this one was different. It was personal. He'd led the last manhunt for this monster from the front, when after a ferocious struggle with Glenn Branson, Tooth had dived recklessly into a dock at Shoreham Harbour and vanished. If this really was him, and he was still alive, Grace was determined to be the officer who finally read the evil bastard his rights, although he knew that the TFU – Tactical Firearms Unit – officers would have to secure him first.

So for the first time in some while he grabbed his Kevlar vest off the hook on the back of his door, pulled it on and headed downstairs.

CHAPTER 90

Wednesday 11 March

As Roy Grace raced down to the seafront in his unmarked Ford Mondeo, blue lights flashing, talking to Ops-1, he saw to his dismay that the traffic was gridlocked ahead with roadworks.

He eventually parked up and approached the side entrance of the hotel. Guy Batchelor, also wearing a bulletproof vest under his coat, was waiting with Roy Apps, the Duty Inspector, and a tall TFU sergeant, who quickly outlined the plan that had been agreed between him and the Silver Commander.

'Tooth is in room 407. We're ready to rock and roll, sir,' Batchelor said.

'Are we certain he's there?'

'There's a "Do Not Disturb" sign on the door and the television's on very loudly, which may have meant he didn't hear the housekeeper's call. He's due to check out tomorrow, so it would seem he must be here.'

'OK, good.'

'We've got TFU officers up on his floor, covering his door, the lifts and the fourth-floor fire-escape stairs, sir,' the TFU sergeant said. 'Up on the sixth floor, there are more waiting. They're ready to go in.'

That made Grace feel better. His biggest nightmare was to have another officer injured by a gunshot wound. The TFU knew what they were doing – and the risks.

'OK,' Grace said.

He heard from Ops-1 that the Silver Commander was satisfied everything was in place.

'I want to be up there when they get the bastard, Guy,' Grace said.

'Be careful, boss,' the DS cautioned.

'I will. Which way are the stairs?'

Batchelor pointed.

Adrenalin surging, Grace ran up the stone staircases, his heart pounding harder with each floor. Two armed officers turned warily as he reached the fourth floor, then smiled at him.

'All OK?' he said, breathless and perspiring.

'All good, guv,' said one.

He went through into the corridor and saw the Firearms Team ready to enter the room. Two held semi-automatic rifles and two of them handguns. Another, a solidly built woman, wielded the heavy red battering ram, affectionately known as the bosher. An instant later they all broke into a run, lumbering down the corridor and halting outside a door. Grace, standing behind them, had his view of the room number blocked.

They paused for a moment, the two officers with rifles braced in front of the door, the two with handguns at their sides. Then their leader, a female sergeant, gave the signal. Grace had agreed with the Silver and Firearms Commander that once the team had entered the room and secured the target, he would be called in to make the arrest.

As one officer put an electronic pass key against the door lock, the officer with the bosher standing ready, there was a click and a green light on the door lock. She kicked it open and in unison they yelled out, 'POLICE! POLICE! POLICE!'

The two holding the automatic rifles went through the door, yelling, 'FREEZE! POLICE!'

At an empty room.

The television was on, with an afternoon game show playing. The bed was made, the room spotless.

Followed by the rest of the team, but with Roy Grace holding back outside for the moment, as he had been instructed, the armed officers raced across the floor and opened each of the doors for the bathroom, the toilet and the cupboards.

But the room was bare, pristine, fully cleaned by the housekeepers as if awaiting a new guest to arrive.

Grace was given the all-clear to enter.

'Shit!' he said, looking around. 'Shit, shit, shit, shit!' There was no sign that anyone had been in this room all day.

'Do we have the right room?' he asked the equally frustrated-looking sergeant.

'George Dickel. Four zero seven, guv.'

Grace radioed down to Guy Batchelor and told him what they had found.

Two minutes later Batchelor radioed back. 'That's his room, chief. He checked in the Saturday before last.'

'So where the hell is he?'

CHAPTER 91

Wednesday 11 March

From behind the curtains in the sanctuary of his fifth-floor, sea-view room at the Royal Albion Hotel, Tooth watched the commotion on the seafront below him, concentrated around the Waterfront Hotel a short distance to the west, with a wry smile.

Did that dickhead Detective Superintendent Roy Grace and his team of morons really think he would make it that easy for them?

He had news for them. He was here to do a job; they could raid every hotel room in the city but they weren't going to find him, because they weren't going to catch up with him.

He had paid in advance for a week. But ten minutes later, unnoticed, he slipped out with his bags, then headed for the Russell Square car park to recover his rental Ford.

CHAPTER 92

Wednesday 11 March

Roy Grace arrived back at Sussex House shortly after 5 p.m. in a despondent mood. Where the hell in this city, and under what name, was Tooth?

He went straight to MIR-1 and was pleased to see Glenn was there, as he wanted an update on Lyon. The DI apologized for Norman Potting's absence – he'd told him he had to attend a medical appointment – then gave Grace a short debrief on Crisp's disappearance from custody in Lyon. It seemed the security in the hospital wing was severely lacking, but as yet no one could explain how the man had escaped.

Disappointed as he was that the suspected serial killer had yet again evaded justice – for now – Grace was at least relieved this was not something he or any of his fellow Sussex officers could be blamed for. He told his team the next briefing would be at 8.30 a.m. tomorrow and headed back to his office. He was badly in need of some time alone to think. But as he entered his room, his phone was ringing.

It was Maggie Bridgeman from the Covert Policing Unit, sounding excited. 'Roy,' she said, 'I think I have the perfect undercover operative for you. UC 2431. Can you give me until tomorrow morning?'

'Brilliant, thanks, tomorrow morning is fine!' Then he asked, 'Do you have a name for him?'

'Yes – you'll know him as J. Paul Cornel.' She gave him some details.

Instantly, while he continued talking to her, Grace googled the name. A long list of Cornels appeared. A Paul J. Cornel on LinkedIn. One who was an attorney. One who ran a driving school. One who had a web page on 'Knowledge Management For Development', whatever that was. One who was involved in the wine business. One who was an academic at Brighton University.

It was a smart choice for a name, he thought. Plenty of diversity. Then he googled images for J. Paul Cornel. A dozen different faces appeared, including a black electric guitar player, and several other characters of differing ages and appearances.

He narrowed the search to 'J. Paul Cornel, millionaire philanthropist'.

Over a hundred different faces and identities appeared, from John Paul Getty and a bloated John Paul Getty Junior, to people of every age and race, as well as cartoon drawings.

He tried 'J. Paul Cornel, Brighton'.

A whole raft of hits appeared related to Brighton University.

Then, drilling down to the third page, he found what he was pretty sure was the target. An obscure photograph of a thick-set man in sunglasses, seemingly deliberately in semi-darkness, looking as if the camera had caught him unawares and in hiding. The caption read: 'One of the rare public appearances of reclusive Brighton-born technology billionaire J. Paul Cornel.'

It was followed by another hit, dated six years earlier. 'English tech tycoon who made his fortune buying emerging companies in California's Silicon Valley, stalks US baseball team as his next trophy.'

And another: 'Charles Johnson, 25 per cent owner of the San Francisco Giants baseball team, and Larry Baer, Chief Executive Officer, have successfully seen off a bid by reclusive ex-pat Brit dot-com billionaire J. Paul Cornel for control of the team.'

Then a further related hit from five years ago. 'US-domiciled billionaire and baseball fanatic Brit recluse J. Paul Cornel sets sights on Boston Red Sox after failing in bid to acquire control of the San Francisco Giants.'

Grace smiled. Brilliant stuff! He'd believe J. Paul Cornel was real. Hey, he'd even try to tempt him into sponsoring the rugby team!

He checked his emails; glancing down them he clicked on one he did not recognize, from someone called Kate Tate of the City of London Police Financial Crimes Unit, about the undercover operation.

Tate said she would be with him mid-morning tomorrow.

Grace glanced at his watch. 5.30 p.m. He'd told Cleo he would try to be home early tonight. She'd sent him a picture of the inflatable baby play ring they'd ordered from Amazon and it looked like Noah was loving it! He really looked forward to getting home and seeing it for himself.

His phone rang. It was Cassian Pewe returning the call Grace had put in half an hour ago to update him on the latest developments.

'Maybe you should retrain as a magician, Roy,' Pewe said. 'I saw a very good one called Matt Wainwright. He works as a Fire and Rescue Officer and is a close magician in his spare time. You ought to have a word with him.'

'Beg your pardon, sir?'

'All these disappearing acts, Roy,' Pewe said, his voice sounding more whiney and snide than ever. 'Jodie Bentley, Dr Crisp and now Mr Tooth. Perhaps you need the help of a magician to un-disappear them all?'

'It's beginning to feel that way, sir,' Grace said, holding his temper with difficulty.

'I have to warn you that our new Chief Constable is not impressed. Perhaps you're becoming too distracted by the latest developments with your missing wife, Sandy? Would you like some compassionate leave?'

Grace took a moment to gather his thoughts before replying. 'Sir, with respect, if it hadn't been for my relationship with Detective Investigator Lanigan of the NYPD we wouldn't even know that Tooth was in this country. Crisp was out of our jurisdiction when he absconded from custody. And I believe we are closing the net on Jodie Bentley.'

'I'm happy for your sanity that you're having that fantasy, Roy, but I'm less happy for the citizens of this county we're here to serve and protect. Because at this moment you're not serving or protecting them.'

Before Grace could reply he heard a click. The ACC had ended the call.

Roy sat, smarting with anger and said, aloud, 'You tosser.'

He left his office and walked back through into MIR-1, and stared at the whiteboards, which had been returned from the Conference Room after the 2 p.m. briefing. He looked at the photographs of Christopher Bentley, Walt Klein, Rollo Carmichael.

Three dead lovers.

Three, at least, that they knew about.

Would she take the bait of number four?

Would he get to her before Tooth did?

What – if anything – was he overlooking? One thing he had not informed Pewe of was the danger to any undercover operative from Tooth. Should he pull the operation on the grounds of it being too risky?

It was at times like this that he felt lonely. All major crime investigations were teamwork. But the one at the head of the team shouldered the ulti-mate responsibility. Decisions made by the Senior Investigating Officer could make the difference between life and death. As so many times before, the buck stopped with him. This dangerous bitch was out there, undoubtedly planning, scheming. And, if Pat Lanigan was right, so was Tooth. He didn't allow himself the luxury of thinking how simple it would be to just let Tooth carry right on and take her out. In his job, moral judgements too often needed to be put to one side. His job was to enforce the law. And however unsavoury the target of a professional hitman in Brighton might be, he could not let that hit happen.

An email appeared in his inbox that was a salutary reminder of the potential dangers all police officers faced every day, throughout their careers, whether they were front line or off-duty and acting out of civic responsibility. It was from the Chief Constable's staff officer.

Roy, there will be a small ceremony here at Malling House at 3.30 p.m. next Thursday, 19 March, to recognize the posthumous Queen's Gallantry Award to Detective Sergeant Bella Moy. We would like you to attend with Norman Potting and a couple of other members of your team. We are picking Bella's mother up and bringing her to Headquarters.

He checked his diary, knowing it had been pretty much cleared by his assistant for the first crucial weeks of the Operation Spider investigation. Then he typed a reply saying that he would be honoured to attend, copying in Lesley so she could log it in his diary.

He arrived home shortly after 6 p.m., to be greeted by Humphrey holding a squeaky, furry, toy rodent in his mouth. Cleo was spark-out asleep on the sofa, her Open University coursework spread out around her, and the nanny was on the floor playing with Noah. Marlon was on his eternal, eager quest around his new tank, in search of what? Grace wondered often. An escape route? A female mate?

He took the dog for a walk around the neighbourhood, thinking hard, refreshed by the cold evening air. If Tooth really was in town – and he trusted Pat Lanigan's information, plus his own possible sighting – where the hell was he? If they could find him, would he lead them to this woman?

He arrived back at the house to the appetizing smell of hot food. Kaitlynn, who had been asked to stay on this evening, was cooking a lasagne that Cleo had left out. He sat on the sofa, eating it in front of the television, with a glass of red wine, while Cleo continued to sleep beside him. There was a cop drama playing, but he didn't engage with it. Too often when such shows were on he found himself shouting at the screen about all the inaccuracies. And this one looked even worse than most. A crime-scene tent had been erected over the body of a dead boy on a beach, who had seemingly fallen from a cliff. Quite correctly, several SOCOs emerged in their protective clothing. Then the SIO walked out in mackintosh and brogue shoes. Hadn't anyone on this production done their basic research? He would never have been allowed inside this crime scene without wearing protective clothing to prevent him from contaminating it.

'What?' Grace hissed furiously. 'You arsehole!'

'Uh?' Cleo stirred.

Grace kissed her forehead. 'Sorry, darling.'

CHAPTER 93

Thursday 12 March

Grace travelled to Worthing to meet the undercover officer and his handler. They had chosen a small discreet café, the Old Bakehouse in Tarring village, well away from police premises. A stocky, shaven-headed man with grey, neatly trimmed stubble, in an expensive-looking suit and dark glasses, was seated at a table, absorbed in his iPhone. Sitting alongside him was a slim woman with short, chestnut hair. There were cups and a steaming teapot on the table in front of them.

'Roy! Good to meet you! I'm DI Kate Tate from the City of London Financial Crimes Unit, and I'll be acting as the Cover Officer on this operation.'

He shook her hand warmly.

'And this is UC 2431, Roy,' Tate continued. 'Julius Cornel – better known as J. Paul Cornel!'

'Good to meet you!' Grace leaned forward and shook his hand.

'Well, you know, it's very good to meet you too, Detective Superintendent!'

The man's accent was deep BBC English, tinged with a mid-Atlantic drawl. Perfect for an Englishman who had spent the past forty years in California. But not quite perfect enough. Grace stared hard at him in disbelief. Stared at the elegant suit, the tailored white shirt, the silk tie, the shiny black Gucci loafers, the shaven head, the designer stubble. Oh yes, he looked the part all right. And no doubt he could fool a lot of people.

But he wasn't fooling him.

Did he blow his cover now or go along with it? He decided, to test him, to go along with it for the moment. 'Congratulations, Mr Cornel. Great to see a Brit do so well overseas! I've read of your success on the internet, with great admiration.'

'Well, that's pretty generous of you, Detective Superintendent. Guess I've been lucky, you know. Someone up there likes me! Well, until recently, anyhows.'

'I was sorry to read about the death of your wife.'

Cornel shrugged. Then, keeping up the accent perfectly, he replied, 'Jackie and I had thirty-two happy years together. How many couples can say that?'

'Not many,' Grace said. He shook his head and grinned and Cornel grinned, too. Both men knew it was game over.

'Bloody hell!' Grace said. 'You're good, Norman!'

Potting removed his dark glasses, beaming. 'You think so?'

'I never knew you were a trained UC.'

'Have been for years, chief. It's part of our brief that no one else in the force must ever know. We're sort of like those sleeper spies in the John le Carré stories. Never knowing if or when we might be called into service. Tell you the truth, I thought I was past it, entering the sad old gits' club, and I'd never be called on. Then this opportunity came along – had to volunteer for it!'

'Norman's perfect, you see, Roy,' Tate said. Then, with exquisite lack of tact, she continued, 'And of course we can't allow any UC to have sex with their target, so Norman will be able to tell her, with only a little white lie, that he has prostate cancer, leaving him impotent.'

'How does DS Potting feel about that?' Grace quizzed her. 'Have you asked?'

'Let's hold it here for a moment, Roy, and let Norman speak,' Tate said, holding up her hand.

'I'm good, Roy,' Norman Potting assured him. 'I'm OK playing along with that. I was the one who actually raised it with Kate.'

'Norman, I don't know how well you've been briefed, but there's a couple of things I need to warn you about,' Grace said. 'The first is that Jodie Carmichael is an extremely cunning and manipulative lady. If the information we have so far is correct, she has been responsible for the death of at least three men – and possibly more. The second is that I have good evidence there may be a contract on her life from a New York-based Russian

471

organized-crime gang. They've sent the man we previously knew only as Tooth, who is currently travelling under different names including John Daniels and Mike Hinton. As you're well aware, this man is very clever and dangerous. What you are doing may put your life in extreme jeopardy.'

Potting – and it was hard to accept it was Norman Potting and not the billionaire persona he now had – peered up at him. 'Roy, you need to understand that the day Bella died, some part of me died too. I've got cancer. If I can do some good things with the rest of my life, then I'll go out with a smile on my face, whenever that might be. OK?'

Grace smiled at him. Potting was ever the rugged old bugger. 'OK, Norman. But take care. We're putting every possible protection in place to look after you.'

'Won't need 'em, Roy. I can take care of myself. I'm a survivor!'

'You'd bloody better be! I want you surviving this bitch and your cancer, OK?'

Potting grinned and then, in the accent he had pitch-perfect, replied, 'You got it, buddy!'

CHAPTER 94

Thursday 12 March

As Roy Grace sat back down in his office, he was in a quandary. Was he exposing Norman to too much danger?

But if he pulled him from the operation, without doubt someone else would be in danger. The black widow's next victim. If they got it right, Potting would lead them to this woman, and they could keep a visual on him and protect him. But he needed that protection.

Grace phoned his ACC and updated him on the latest information, and his concerns.

'Roy,' Pewe replied after some moments, 'you're the SIO on this case, and you have to make the decisions here, including the cost implications – so long as you continue to be the SIO.'

As he ended the call, Grace was fuming again. *So long as you continue to be the SIO. Great*, he thought. *Yeah, right.* If it all worked out well, ACC Pewe would take the credit. And if it all went tits up, Pewe would be dumping the blame squarely at his feet and using it as the excuse he dearly sought to ease him out.

And he knew exactly what Pewe would be thinking at this moment.

Please, God, have Roy Grace screw up.

What was crucial now was connecting Norman Potting with Jodie. That needed very careful handling of the local media. Any inkling that J. Paul Cornel was a set-up and it was game over for that plan.

But he had to admit to himself, with a wry smile, good old Norman, with a makeover including teeth whitening, made a very convincing elderly billionaire.

Would she take the bait? That was something he would be discussing in detail with Detective Superintendent Nick Sloan, the Force Authorizing Officer, who was managing the operation.

But, more importantly, how did he protect Potting?

CHAPTER 95

Thursday 12 March

The mildly eccentric-looking lady, her face heavily made-up, dressed in a calf-length coat, woollen hat and old-fashioned glasses, looked every inch the elderly bohemian artist. She hobbled slowly through the door in the white facade of the corner store premises of Lawrence Art Supplies in Hove's Portland Road, supported by her silver-topped walking stick.

She made her way to the counter and politely requested a large tub of aluminium powder and a hot-glue gun. She paid for them with an American Express card in the name of Mrs Thelma Darby. Five minutes later she emerged with her purchases in a carrier bag and approached the waiting taxi. The driver helped her in, passing her the stick and carrier bag after she was seated.

Then, as instructed, he took her to a nearby aquarium store. Thelma again asked him to wait, then entered the store. She came out a short while later with two carrier bags, containing four boxes of oxygenating tablets and a frozen white mouse.

Climbing back into the taxi, she asked the driver to take her to the plumbing supplies store on a nearby industrial estate, where she bought an eighteen-inch length of malleable steel pipe with screw-ends. Then, as a precaution, she changed taxis and ordered the next one to take her to an electrical store on London Road.

There she bought a mini Arduino relay that was just half an inch across, a mercury tilt switch and an assortment of USB memory sticks. The assistant behind the counter gave her an odd look, as if wondering how on earth a batty-looking old lady like this even knew what these things were, let alone what to do with them.

Carrying her purchases, she stepped out and turned right, walking along London Road, stopping at a chemist to buy a cold gel-pack, then at a hardware store where she purchased a short length of heavy-duty insulated wire, a roll of insulating tape and a pair of pliers. She hailed another taxi and instructed the driver to take her to a kitchenware shop in Western Road, where she made her final purchases of a small set of digital kitchen scales and a coffee grinder.

She then asked the driver to take her to the Jurys Inn Hotel, opposite Brighton Station.

As she made her way across the hotel foyer towards the lifts, leaning on her stick with grim determination, she was looking forward to getting down to work. Her shopping trip was complete and one hundred per cent satisfactory, no problems at all.

She didn't do problems.

CHAPTER 96

Thursday 12 March

At 12.30 p.m. Roy Grace did the Asda run to get his lunch and something to drink. He'd eaten nothing since a few mouthfuls of porridge at 6 a.m., and a muffin in the café, and he was hungry again.

His eyes ran along the superstore's sandwich shelves, and he was tempted to get an all-day breakfast bacon and egg feast. But guilt held him back. Cleo had repeatedly warned him of the dangers of the rubbish diet that so many police officers survived on. He looked at several cakes and doughnuts, too. Often in the past he had ignored her – and Sandy's – entreaties for him to eat healthily. But Noah and Cleo had added a new dimension and purpose to his life. He felt an extra strong need to take care of himself, for his family. So in the end he bought a tuna and sweetcorn on brown bread and an apple, and allowed himself just two naughty treats, a Diet Coke and a KitKat.

As he walked across to the '10 Items or Less'

till he saw a rack of *Argus* newspapers. The headline read:

BRIGHTON'S FAVOURITE SON SAYS: I'VE COME HOME TO DIE!

Good! The seed had been sown. He bought a copy.

Back in his office, Grace laid the paper in front of him. The front-page splash was accompanied by a photograph of the stocky, tanned billionaire barely recognizable, even to himself, as Norman Potting. The accompanying story, written by a reporter he didn't know, told of one of the city's favourite sons, born on the Whitehawk Estate, who had truly gone west to make his fortune in California's Silicon Valley. He was now terminally ill with prostate cancer, and had decided to return home to his roots for the last months of his life.

Instead of buying a home in the city, because the doctors had told him he had so little time left, J. Paul Cornel had moved into a suite at an undisclosed hotel for a few days, before returning to California to tie up his business affairs there. With no dependants, he was intending to look at worthy local charities to leave the bulk of his estate to, and something by which the city would remember him. He said he hoped, if his health permitted, to return to Brighton to spend his remaining days here.

When I asked Mr Cornel if it was true he had been thwarted in his attempts to buy a US baseball team, he replied that it had once been a dream but now his love affair with the US was over. Did he have his sights set on anything closer to home? Perhaps Brighton and Hove Albion?

'Well, you know,' he replied in his American drawl, 'I've got this damned cancer but I'm not done yet. Watch this space, eh?'

As he peeled open the wrapping round his sandwich, Roy Grace read on. J. Paul Cornel's journey from Dorothy Stringer School – winning a scholarship to Boston's MIT, the leading technology university in the USA – was documented in detail as were the visionaries he'd met and helped finance on the way, including acolytes of Danny Hillis, the founder of Thinking Machines Corporation and pioneer of the parallel processor, and of Nicholas Negroponte, head of the MIT Media Lab, plus half a dozen former employees of Apple and Microsoft.

Due to smart tax planning, the article continued, just as the *Sunday Times* Rich List team had found, Cornel's true wealth was impossible to estimate. But many financial analysts put it as not far short of the $17.4 billion of Paul Allen, the co-founder of Microsoft.

Since arriving back in our city earlier this week, Cornel has, understandably, gone to ground in a suite at a rather grand Brighton hotel which he has asked me not to disclose.

One thing I spoke to this delightful gentleman about, before our time was up, was romance. I asked him if he felt he still had the time and the energy for love in his life. He replied with a smile, 'What else matters in life, at the end of the day? And you know what, this is going to sound strange. I know I don't have much time left, but I would like to find love again – and I'm gonna keep looking!'

Yes, Grace thought. *Brilliant stuff! Yes, yes, yes!*

CHAPTER 97

Thursday 12 March

Jodie Carmichael walked through the busy concourse of Victoria Station to the Brighton line platforms. She was in a foul mood after a distinctly unsatisfactory meeting with her lawyers. She used a top London firm of solicitors as she felt more anonymous there than with a local Brighton firm.

She reflected, as she walked, on the costly hour and a half of advice she had received from one of the firm's senior matrimonial law partners, Drendia Ann Edwards. Jodie had been correct, Edwards had told her, the captain of the ship was a certified registrant and the marriage was indeed legal and binding. But, with almost unprecedented speed, a marker had already been put down by the law firm acting for Rowley Carmichael's children. Alarmed at the haste of their late father's marriage – and subsequent death – she confirmed they were not accepting the Goan Coroner's report and, despite the fact that their father's body was embalmed, were demanding a second post-mortem.

They were prepared to take their fight to any level – and they had pockets deep enough to do so, Edwards had warned.

Which meant she would almost certainly be in for a massive fight over Rowley's estate, too. Something that could easily drag on for a couple of years, maybe longer, with costs that could run into tens, if not hundreds, of thousands, which she would have to fund. At the end of the day she should certainly inherit some of his fortune – but that could easily be some while into the future.

Most of her inheritance from her first husband, Christopher Bentley, had gone on buying the house in Roedean, and on living and travel costs. She had the $200,000 windfall from the Romanian in New York, which would see her through for a bit, and she had a small emergency fund stashed away, but bloody Walt Klein had caused her to eat into that. She'd had to pay for everything out in Courchevel on her own card, because both Walt's card and the one he had given her had been declined at checkout; on top of that, she was out of pocket for that ridiculously expensive coffin she'd bought him.

If she didn't find another source of funding quickly, she might need to sell one of her properties. The Roedean house had soared in value in the years since she had bought it, but having to sell and downsize would be a worst-case scenario. An admission of defeat, and an end – even if only temporarily – to her plan, to the goals she had set herself.

Perching on her Standard Class seat – the first time in years she'd not travelled First – she was feeling a slight sense of panic that she was going to have to start making economies. She decided the first thing she would do when she got back home was sift through all the replies from the internet dating agencies that would be in her inbox, and contact a few of the most promising ones.

She slumped back and picked up an abandoned copy of the paper on the seat next to her, which had been left open part way through. She liked to keep updated on local Brighton and Sussex news – and especially anything that might refer or relate directly or indirectly to her.

The page seven headline of the *Argus* read:

POLICE WARN OF BRIGHTON CITY CAR-THEFT EPIDEMIC

She scanned it. A gang was operating in Brighton and Hove, breaking into houses not to burgle their contents but to get the keys to high-end cars, particularly Range Rovers and top of the range sports cars.

She thought back to the break-in at her home. Was that what the thief had been after? Her Mercedes?

She turned a few pages and saw another, smaller headline.

SUSSEX POLICE MORNING-AFTER CAMPAIGN TO REDUCE ROAD DEATH TOLL

She speed-read the article, which said that the police were mounting a series of spot checks in the city to catch people still over the drink-drive limit the following morning. She flipped through a few more pages then closed the paper, and immediately the front page splash caught her eye.

BRIGHTON'S FAVOURITE SON SAYS: I'VE COME HOME TO DIE!

She looked at the photograph of the man, read the article, then looked back at his photograph again; not that she really cared what he looked like. She was thinking to herself, *OK, I could shag you for seventeen billion dollars. Not a problem. I could definitely be the love of your life. For the short amount you have left of it!*

She actually found him quite sexy. And, she noted, the *Argus* said Cornel would be in Brighton for just a few days before returning to California to tie up his affairs there. Shit, she was going to have to strike fast to catch him while he was here. She read on, avidly.

Cornel has, understandably, gone to ground in a suite at a rather grand Brighton hotel which he has asked me not to disclose.

So how many hotels in this city would I go to ground in? she wondered. The Hotel du Vin? The Hilton Metropole? The Grand? One of the other smaller boutique hotels?

A rather *grand* hotel.

Oh, you wonderfully clever bitch of a reporter!

CHAPTER 98

Thursday 12 March

Tooth removed his hat and coat, and the really uncomfortable flat ladies' shoes, which he had bought, with the rest of the outfit, from a vintage clothing shop. He discarded the walking stick he'd picked up earlier in a charity shop, propping it against a wall, and hobbled, unaided, through to the bathroom, where he leaned on the side of the washbasin and stared at his face in the mirror.

A hideous old lady, with Pan-Cake make-up, stared back.

She reminded him of his mother.

Taking out a face wipe, he rigorously cleaned his face of all the gunk.

Changed back into the clothes he felt comfortable in – navy chinos and a grey T-shirt – Tooth set to work. His first task, as always in a hotel room, was to cover the smoke alarm.

Next, he lifted a corner of the bed's mattress and saw the coil springs that held the base in place. Removing one of the springs, he took it over to his temporary workbench, the desk. He unwound a few inches of the coiled wire, then cut it off with the pliers. Next, he folded the wire into a U-shape, and pushed it into the end of the heavy-duty insulated wire he had bought earlier.

He programmed the mini relay for thirty seconds and connected it, via the wire, to the mercury tilt switch. Then he angled the switch downward. The mercury inside slid down to complete the circuit to the motion sensor, which in turn would set the timer going. After exactly thirty seconds there was the flash of a spark, and a smell of burned electrics reached his nostrils.

Excellent! It worked fine.

Good, very good. He disconnected the timer.

He plugged in the coffee grinder, filled it with potassium chlorate oxygenating tablets from the aquarium supplies store, and switched the machine on. When they were ground into a small mound of powder, he tipped it out onto the scales, and then into a tumbler from the bathroom. He repeated the process with further tablets until he had the exact amount he required.

Next, he measured out and carefully weighed some of the aluminium powder from the art shop, and tipped it into another tumbler from the bathroom. Then, very carefully, he mixed the two compounds together.

When he was satisfied, he unscrewed one end of the steel tube and poured in the concoction.

Then he pushed in the end of the insulated wire with the bent metal of the coil spring, working it through the mixture until it was completely embedded, and secured it in place with the hot-glue stick. As an extra safety precaution, he carefully wound insulating tape round the two exposed wires at the other end of the cable, then pushed them into the tube, followed by the mercury tilt sensor and the Arduino relay, which fitted snugly. He replaced the screw-cap. It had been some years since he'd last made one of these, but the good thing today, he thought, was if you were unsure about anything you could always look it up on the internet.

He searched around for a suitable hiding place for his bomb and the timer that would detonate it. One secure place presented itself: the air-conditioning grille above the door. He removed his Swiss Army penknife from his suitcase, stood on a chair and undid the four screws holding it in place.

Five minutes later, the grille securely back in place, he climbed down off the chair, and then began to do some exercises on his legs. He had to get everything working again. He was on the mend, but he needed to be in a lot better shape before he attempted to complete his mission. And he knew what he had to do. He checked the temperature of the gel-pack, which he had placed in an ice bucket, wrapped it in a towel then pressed it against the worst bruise on his right leg.

To occupy himself for the ten minutes that he was going to hold it there, he opened his laptop and took a look at what was going on in Jodie Carmichael's house.

CHAPTER 99

Thursday 12 March

J. Paul Cornel, installed in his vast fourth-floor suite at the Grand Hotel shortly after 4 p.m., walked around exploring his plush new surroundings. He could fit his little flat about five times in here.

The suite, overlooking the English Channel, had a master bedroom with a huge ensuite bathroom, a second bedroom and a living room, which was decorated in Regency style with two large sofas beneath an ornate chandelier. The four large suitcases that had accompanied him, as part of his cover, lay unopened, two of them on the trestles which the porter had helpfully placed there for him. They were filled with clothes that had been purchased for him from an array of clothing stores around the city, as well as a classy washbag crammed with toiletries.

He put the iPhone he had been given on charge. It was loaded with hidden software, which relayed his position, down to six feet, to a round-the-clock monitored screen in an Intelligence Team office at police HQ, as well as a voice-activated sound recorder. He popped each of the cases open and unpacked, hanging up the jackets and trousers and putting the shirts and underwear away in the drawers. Many of the clothes bore American designer labels. An hour later he had truly moved in. The next step was to find this dangerous lady, Jodie Carmichael. Or, if his colleagues had laid the bait according to plan, to let her find him.

Shortly after 6 p.m., dressed in a dark blue suit, white, open-neck shirt and black suede Gucci loafers, he took the lift downstairs, then strode across to the bar, taking in all the people in the room. There were a few groups of what looked like businessmen and a couple drinking champagne. But no single women. Easing himself onto a seat, positioning himself so he could see anyone entering the room or walking past, Potting wondered what J. Paul Cornel would order in a cocktail bar.

A Martini, perhaps? Or a Manhattan?

He looked at the cocktail menu the barman gave him. Two businessmen in suits, with conference tags on their lapels, sat next to him, drinking pints of beer. A beer might be more sensible, he thought. He didn't know how long he might have to wait. Another man in a suit, further along, was drinking what looked like a gin and tonic from a highball glass.

There was an assortment of cocktails he had never heard of. The barman placed a fresh bowl of peanuts in front of him, and Potting began to munch his way through them, spilling some. Would she show up? There was no telling. Whatever, he had a feeling it might be a long evening.

In his well-rehearsed Californian twang, he ordered a Perrier with a slice of lemon in a long glass. If she did show up, at least it would look like the gin and tonic he was craving at this moment.

The next hour passed slowly. He whiled away some of it by checking his iPhone. All the time he kept an eye on the door, ready to act if Jodie did appear. Then his thoughts went back, as they always did whenever he had time to think, to Bella.

His heart heaved and he felt sad.

She had been a genuinely good person. They had had such a wonderful future in front of them. After so much shit, he had finally found the love of his life. Then she had gone and done what any police officer would have done in those circumstances, whether on duty or off – and she had lost her life.

The barman interrupted his thoughts, asking if he needed another drink.

He did, badly. Instead he dutifully asked for the same again, consoling himself with the knowledge that he was having a better time this evening than the two poor Surveillance Team guys, in their car out in the darkness somewhere close by, doing their tedious twelve-hour shift guarding him. He supposed it was comforting to know that for the duration of his time undercover, there would always be two officers never more than seconds away if he needed them. All he had to do was push one button on his phone.

His drink arrived and he stared at it bleakly. Then he asked the barman to bring him a gin and tonic, and make the gin a double.

When it came he downed it in two gulps.

CHAPTER 100

Thursday 12 March

Determined not to fall foul of another Walter Klein, Jodie Carmichael had spent the past two hours rigorously checking out J. Paul Cornel on the internet.

His Wikipedia tallied with what she had read in the paper. His humble origins growing up on the Whitehawk Estate. His education, first at Brighton's Dorothy Stringer School, then winning a scholarship to study computer sciences at MIT – Massachusetts Institute of Technology. Followed by a five-year spell working under Dr Josef Kates, in Toronto, one the world's first pioneers in computer time-sharing, and later in traffic systems. Then his move to Microsoft in California, before making his first fortune in his own Silicon Valley-based technology company developing facial-recognition systems for the US military, before funding a succession of highly successful tech start-ups. With his passion for classic cars, he had built up a highly valuable collection.

One thing that particularly excited her about

him was his lack of heirs. In his only marriage he had produced two children, a son born with cystic fibrosis who had died at nineteen, and a daughter who had died in a TWA air disaster out of New York. His wife had died from cancer.

He had twice been thwarted in attempts to buy major US baseball teams, and during the past decade had given many millions to charities, including those for cystic fibrosis and genetic engineering research.

She actually found herself feeling sorry for Cornel.

And thanks to the newspaper interview, she had a strong clue where she might find him right now, here in Brighton.

She began to google images of Cornel's wife. And as she did so, Jodie smiled. The wife had been slim and attractive, brunette and glamorous. With her new hairstyle, she would fit very nicely into that template.

Shortly after 6 p.m., she began to get ready.

Tooth sat at the desk in his hotel room, smoking a cigarette and drinking whisky, watching Jodie on the cameras he had concealed around her house. She was sitting in front of the dressing-table mirror in her bedroom, applying her make-up carefully. Her computer screen was not visible to any of his cameras. What had she been looking at on the internet? he wondered.

What was she dolling herself up for tonight?

When did this woman stop? Her husband had only just died and she had brought him home to bury him. He had to admit to a sneaking admiration for her. She was a predator like himself.

He stood up and hobbled around the room. The discomfort in his ribs was lessening. The bruising in his right leg looked a little better now. In a few days he should be fit enough.

Shortly after half past six he watched – and heard – Jodie Carmichael order a taxi to take her to the Grand Hotel. She booked it in her alias, Judith Forshaw.

'Have a nice evening, Judith,' he said, quietly. 'Stay out late. The later the better.'

The opportunity had come sooner than he had expected. But as he had been trained in sniper school, you always had to be ready for when a shot presented itself; you might not get a second opportunity.

He stood up and removed his clothes, and began to reapply his make-up. Afterwards, going over to the closet, he pulled out his dress, shoes, coat and wig.

Fifteen minutes later, Thelma Darby, with the aid of her walking stick, limped along the corridor, clutching her large handbag, took the lift down to the lobby, then headed out across the road to her rental car.

CHAPTER 101

Thursday 12 March

The buzz of the gin had worn off and Norman Potting – or as he had to keep reminding himself, J. Paul Cornel – was contemplating ordering another. He was also wondering just how long he would have to stay here before declaring Jodie Carmichael a no-show.

The bar had filled up and although he had done his best to defend the seat next to him he'd finally had to concede it, and was now sandwiched between a large man, who sounded Scandinavian, engaged in loud conversation with a Brit beside him, about nuclear power, and a couple of gay guys talking affectionately to each other. He'd had the liberal policies of Sussex Police drummed into his head by Roy Grace, under pain of being kicked off the Major Crime Team, so he was doing his best to be more broad-minded. But he was in a world that had changed so much since he had first joined the police, and he found it increasingly hard to understand.

A stunning woman entered the bar. He'd been

a copper long enough to tell the difference between someone casually glancing around and someone casing a joint.

She was casing the joint.

And her eyes alighted, fleetingly, on him.

She was in her mid-thirties, in a silky grey dress that clung to every contour of her slender body, and stopped short of her knees. Her legs were long and slender, and she wore glittering high heels. Her hair was long and dark, elegantly styled, and her neck and wrists were adorned with tasteful jewellery and a classy watch.

She gave him a second glance, and possibly a smile, before sitting a few places away, at the end of the bar.

Was that her?

And if it was, how did he make the next move? He had a dinner reservation for 8.00 p.m. An hour's time. He was peckish and looking forward to a good meal, courtesy of Sussex Police.

Maybe, if he played it right, he could get her to join him. *If* it was Jodie Carmichael.

Whilst pretending to be texting on his iPhone, he leaned forward to catch her order to the barman. A glass of Chardonnay. Then, continuing his pretence of texting, he looked at the photographs he had been given of the woman.

It was her!

He drank another Perrier. The irritating Scandinavian and his pal, to his left, climbed down off their stools and walked away. Ten minutes later the two other couples between him and his target had also left.

Potting looked across and caught her eye again. He gave her a friendly smile, which was returned. He turned to the barman and in his best J. Paul Cornel accent asked him to offer the young lady at the end of the bar a glass of champagne, on him.

It had the desired effect. Minutes later, glass in hand, the young woman slid off her bar stool and sat down next to him. 'Thank you! Drinking alone?' she asked.

'Drowning my sorrows.' He smiled.

'You know,' she said, 'that people who drink to drown their sorrows should be told that sorrow learns to swim.'

'That right?' Cornel said.

'In my experience, uh-huh!' She grinned.

'I've buried two children and a wife,' he said. 'And I've never learned to swim.'

'It's never too late to learn anything.'

They clinked glasses. 'Let's hope not. So, to paraphrase one of my favourite movies, out of all the gin joints, in all the towns, in all the world, what brings a beautiful lady like you into mine?'

She smiled. 'I could ask you that same question!'

'Be my guest!'

'So?'

He shook his head. 'I'd like to give you a smart answer, but I don't have one. I grew up in this city – well, it was a town back in my youth – and I've lived away for many years. Now I'm near the end of my life, and I decided to come back to my roots. You?'

She plucked an olive from a bowl in front of them. Then she sipped her champagne and ate another olive, giving him a seductive look. 'I'm trying to get over the train crash that I call my life. This is the first night I've been out in a long while. I was meant to be meeting an old friend here, but he's just stood me up – gave me a lame excuse about having a flat tyre.' She shrugged. 'Guess he had a better offer.' Looking deliberately vulnerable, she twiddled with the chain of her locket.

'A better offer than *you*?'

'He's an old flame. We're just good mates now. But you know, men . . .'

He smiled. 'Tell me about the train wreck.'

She shrugged. 'You know, it's very weird being here in this hotel.'

'Why's that?'

'Well, the thing is, I met my husband here. He died just after we were married – he was bitten by a snake, in India.'

'That's terrible,' he said.

'We were so in love.'

'I'm so sorry.'

'That's very sweet of you.' Her eyes locked on his. They were mesmerizing eyes. He was aroused by her stare, and had to focus hard through the alcohol he had consumed.

He held out his hand. 'Paul Cornel.'

Shaking it, she replied, 'Jodie Carmichael.'

'Good to meet you,' he said.

She stared back into his eyes. 'It's good to meet you, too,' she replied. 'So tell me the real reason you're in town?'

'I've come home to die.'

'I'd rather you didn't die too soon – we've only just met. I think that would be rather impolite.'

He laughed. 'OK – I'll try to last out the evening – but on one condition.'

She held out her glass. 'And that is?'

He clinked his glass against hers. 'That you join me for dinner here – if you're free, that is?'

She gave him a faraway look. 'Well, that puts me in a difficult position. I've got a lasagne-for-one defrosting in my fridge right now. So it's a choice of that or dinner with you here. Hmmmn. Any other inducements?'

'All the champagne you can drink.'

She spiralled her index finger, flirtatiously signalling, *More?*

'The restaurant here, GB1, is meant to be one of the best in the city. Oysters, lobster, Dover sole.'

Again she spiralled her finger.

'And they have a great wine list, I'm told.'

She spun her finger again.

'A few hours of my scintillating company?'

She grinned and nodded. 'OK, now you're starting to convince me.' She looked mischievously into his eyes.

'I don't like dining alone. You'd be doing an old man a big favour by joining me.'

Another spin of her finger.

'I think you're incredibly beautiful.'

'You are too kind.'

'No, really, you are!' he said. 'And I think your evening would be significantly improved by spending it with me.'

'Oh, yeah? Well, I'd be lying if I said I wasn't drawn in by your charm.'

'Now you're talking bullshit!'

'No, I always tell the truth. And I'm seriously in need of cheerful company. I'd be delighted to have dinner with you. But I do warn you, I have expensive tastes.'

Very fortunate Sussex Police have given me an almost unlimited budget, Potting thought. 'Well, that makes two of us,' he replied.

She dipped her finger into her glass and held it out to Cornel, touching his lips with it. He licked the champagne off the tip.

Christ, he thought. *I can see why men fall for her.*

And he was uncomfortably aware that the two officers, outside in their car, were listening to every word.

CHAPTER 102

Thursday 12 March

A fine drizzle was falling and a haze of mist shrouded each street light. Tooth, again dressed as Thelma Darby, drove his small rental Ford along Jodie Carmichael's road as the wipers clomped away in front of him, pleased with the weather conditions. Poor visibility. Perfect. In this affluent neighbourhood, where every home had its own private driveway and off-road parking, there were only a few vehicles out on the street which, he was aware, made him conspicuous. He passed her driveway and pulled over behind a Range Rover one hundred yards or so further along.

With every movement sending twinges through his chest and ribcage, he wormed his way out of his dress. Beneath he wore black jeans and a black roll-neck sweater. He pulled on sneakers, struggled into his anorak and slid the steel pipe down inside the front of his sweater. Then he put the dead mouse, which he had bought from the aquarium store, into one of the pockets and zipped the anorak tight.

He removed a pair of black leather gloves from another pocket, put them on, and glanced at his watch. 7.05 p.m. He didn't know how long he had, but for sure a good hour at the very least. She'd only left at 6.45 p.m. Dressed to kill. He probably had plenty of time, but he wouldn't need long. He intended to be in and out in minutes. Pulling on a baseball cap, he left the car and made his way through the rain towards No. 191.

A man in a raincoat appeared out of the darkness walking towards him, tugging a toy poodle on a lead. 'Cicero!' the man called out to it, petulantly. 'Cicero, come!'

Tooth crossed the road to avoid him, then strode quickly and stealthily back to Jodie Carmichael's front gate and down the steep driveway to the house, checking over his shoulder every few steps.

As he stood in the front porch he used the set of keys he had taken on his last visit to enter the property. Closing the door behind him, he switched on his torch and shone it on the alarm box. A single green light glowed.

As before, she had not set it. *Don't like to attract attention to yourself, do you, lady? Very wise. Nor would I, if I were you.*

He stepped across the hall, glancing up at the light fitting where he had placed one of the cameras, vaguely amused that when he returned to his hotel he would be able to watch himself on video. He found the Mercedes keys easily, in the first place he looked – the central drawer in the hall table – then unlocked the door to the garage.

All garages had a familiar smell, of oil, metal, leather and rubber compound, and this was no different. The dark blue Mercedes sat there in front of him, in the beam of his torch. There was not much else in here apart from a trickle charger, a tyre pump, a mountain bike with flat tyres, a stack of suitcases and some gardening tools.

He pressed the unlock button on the Merc's key fob. The indicators flashed, along with a satisfying clunk from the door locks, and the interior lights came on. He opened the driver's door and inhaled the sweet, rich smell of the cream hide leather. Then he pulled the metal pipe out and set to work.

He unscrewed one end and carefully pulled out the Arduino relay, the mercury tilt switch and the end of the rubber-coated wire. He removed the insulating tape from the wire, then set the relay timer to thirty seconds. Too many bombers were killed by their own devices with faulty timers, but he'd always found Arduinos to be reliable. Thirty seconds gave him a safety margin to get away in case he activated it accidentally. Using the insulating tape, he connected it to the tilt switch. When she drove it up the steep ramp of the driveway, the mercury would slide down and activate the timer. Thirty seconds later the device would detonate.

He inserted the tilt switch and timer back into the tube, being very careful to hold it parallel to the ground, then slid it under the driver's seat until it was out of sight.

He then closed the car door, locked it and went back into the house. He replaced the car key, climbed the stairs and walked along the corridor towards the secret door. Entering the room before it, he opened the closet door, took out the remote and pressed the button to slide the false wall open. Then he checked through the glass door to ensure there were no escaped creatures and entered the warm reptile room, wrinkling his nose against the sour smell.

Lamps glowed behind the glass of each of the stacked vivariums in there. Trying not to look at the ones containing large, hairy spiders and small, sleeping snakes, or another containing dozens of small, live white mice, and another teeming with cockroaches, he took the heavy-duty gloves hanging on a wall hook and pulled them on, with difficulty, his hands a lot bigger than Jodie's.

He fumbled nervously with the catches on the lid of the vivarium containing the huge coiled boa constrictor, its long narrow head bigger than his fist, with a jagged black stripe running diagonally up to its right eye; slowly, warily, he lifted the lid away.

He waited for some moments. The snake did not move.

He removed the plastic bag from his pocket and shook out the dead, thawed-out white mouse, ensuring it dropped close to the snake's head.

The snake fixed its eyes on him.

'Eat the fucking mouse!' he said.

The snake looked like it would rather eat him.

He stared down into the dimly lit environment. Rocks, ferns, branches and dense, miniature undergrowth. He could see the memory stick lying deep inside the undergrowth. Very tentatively he reached forward.

The snake, still looking at him, did not move.

He reached further, slowly, cautiously. He was never normally afraid, but this creature was scaring the shit out of him.

'Eat the goddam mouse!' he said.

There was no reaction.

He lunged his hand in, grabbed the memory stick and withdrew it, then immediately slammed down the lid. He tugged off the heavy-duty gloves, put the stick down on the table, then pulled out the handful of assorted memory sticks he had bought earlier today. None was an exact match, but one was close enough. If Jodie lived long enough to find it, she would never spot the difference. Until she tried to load it into a computer.

And discovered it was blank.

Once more eyeballing the monster snake, he lifted the lid and dropped the blank stick in. To his relief it tumbled to the bottom of the foliage, in pretty much the same place as the one he had taken out.

He replaced the lid and closed both of the locking clips. Then he carefully zipped his prize, the USB memory stick that his paymaster so badly wanted back, into the top pocket of his anorak, glanced around, checking he had left nothing behind, and left the room, closing the glass door behind him. Then he shut the electric wall, too.

Not that he particularly cared but it would be nice, he thought, if Jodie discovered her memory stick was blank before she died.

He liked it when people got what they deserved. And there was no pain greater than mental anguish.

When he was a small boy, one of the series of foster mothers who had taken him in had dragged him along to a strict Baptist chapel every Sunday. People there talked constantly about forgiveness of transgressions. But they also often quoted from Romans 9:18: 'God will have mercy on whom He will have mercy, and whom He will He hardeneth.'

On the wall there had been a sign.

IT IS A FEARFUL THING TO FALL INTO THE HANDS OF THE LIVING GOD.

He liked that sign. He believed that if there was such a thing as God, He was like himself, with a heart full of hatred. He took all the darkest passages to heart, constructing in his twisted mind a God who was a monster, who hated His creation:

'Vengeance is mine; I will repay, saith the Lord.'

'At His wrath the earth shall tremble, and the nations shall not be able to abide His indignation.'

'And I will execute vengeance in anger and fury upon the heathen, such as they have not heard.'

That was the closest Tooth ever came to a connection with God. His belief was that God wasn't that big on forgiveness. That came later with His son, Jesus.

Tooth identified with that interpretation of the Old Testament God. Like Him, he didn't do forgiveness.

CHAPTER 103

Thursday 12 March

Norman was aware he had drunk too much and was feeling a little pissed. Warning flags were going up. But so was the confidence the alcohol was giving him. And he liked Jodie.

He was having to focus, really focus.

To remember his mission.

But this beautiful woman was making that hard. He was feeling all kinds of emotions right now, including guilt. Guilt that the woman he loved was dead and that he was here, being chatted up by a gorgeous woman who was turning him on. A deadly, dangerous woman. As well as guilt that he had drunk alcohol whilst on duty, albeit as part of his cover. Or so he assured himself.

Their meal was over and now Jodie was drinking a Zombie whilst he was on his second vintage Armagnac. Thirty quid a glass. What the hell, Sussex Police would pay. It was on their credit card – or rather Paul Cornel's credit card. Hey, a few drinks either way weren't going to make a hill of beans of difference.

'You know, Paul,' she said suddenly. 'It's weird, but I feel an extraordinary connection. Do you believe in soulmates?'

'I lost my soulmate in a house fire,' he replied after some moments.

'I'm so sorry to hear that,' she said.

He froze for an instant, realizing he had revealed something about himself.

'When did that happen?'

'Oh, a long time ago, before I was married.'

Her hypnotic eyes were fixed on him. 'But you're still suffering, aren't you, you poor darling?'

He smiled. 'You know something, you're the first person I've met in years who . . .' His voice tailed off.

'Who *what*, you lovely man?' She slipped her hand across the table and touched his.

He shrugged, entwining his fingers with hers. Her back was to the window. Behind her through the darkness and the misty rain he could see the street lights of King's Road, the beams of the passing cars and the inky blackness of the English Channel beyond. He was enjoying himself, he really was. And only partly acting.

'I suppose what I'm trying to say, Jodie, is just how good you make me feel. That just when I thought my life was over, you've come into it. I know it probably sounds – you know – crazy. We've only just met and all that, and hell – I'm old enough to be your *father*!'

She smiled. 'I need a cigarette. Do you smoke?'

Yes, I smoke a pipe, he nearly said but just contained himself in time. An American computer tycoon wouldn't smoke a pipe. *Shit,* he thought, *that was close. Need to sharpen up my act. No more alcohol.* 'Cigars,' he said. 'I enjoy the occasional cigar, although my doctors advised me to give them up. I'll come outside with you if you'd like a smoke.'

'Would you like one?'

'Sure, why not?'

A few minutes later they stood outside the front of the hotel, huddled together against the elements, his arm awkwardly round her waist as she lit their cigarettes. He wondered where out there the surveillance car was parked.

'I really like you, Paul,' she said.

'I really like you, too, Jodie. But I can't offer you any kind of a future. I'm terminally ill – I've inoperable prostate cancer that's spread elsewhere.'

'Come on, let's talk about something more fun! What other famous people like you come from Brighton?'

She drew on her cigarette, then exhaled. As he breathed in the sweet smell he said, 'Do you remember the actress Vivien Leigh, in *Gone with the Wind*?'

She nodded.

'I remember when I was a child, she was once married to Laurence Olivier – and they lived a short distance from here, in Royal Crescent, in Kemptown.'

'Vivien Leigh's the person who once said something that's been a kind of maxim to me all my life. "The best thing to do with the past and the future is to ignore them, otherwise there's never an enjoyable present."' She gave him a knowing look.

He nodded. 'Wise words.'

'Aren't they?' She took another drag on her cigarette. Both of them were shivering in the cold. 'You might be old enough to be my father, and I could be hit by a bus tomorrow. So?'

'Hopefully not by one that's got my name on the front!'

'I thought you had to be dead to get your name on a Brighton bus?' she said. Then she added, hastily, 'Sorry – I didn't mean it that way.'

He grinned. 'Hey, you know, the Ancients needed pyramids or grand tombs in the Valley of the Kings to achieve immortality. I guess it's a lot simpler to be on a Brighton bus.'

She crushed out her cigarette in the ashtray on the wall and shivered again. 'Shall we go inside?' He did the same with his and nodded.

Seated back at their table, Norman raised his glass and clinked it against hers. 'To both of us keeping away from buses.'

'I love your sense of humour.'

'Yours, too.'

'So what are your plans now you're back here?'

'You know, for the first time in decades I've freed

myself from the tyranny of plans. I've worked my butt off for fifty years, trying to make something of my life and distance myself from my roots. It's cost me dear. I never spent the time I should have done having fun with my wife and family. A couple of months ago I woke up the morning after the doctors had given me the diagnosis that I had less than a year to live, and I thought to myself, you know, what the hell has your life been all about? Building up empires and trying to acquire more – for what? To become the richest man in the graveyard?'

'And have your name on the front of a bus?'

He grinned. 'Well, I guess that would mean more to me than most achievements. A humble Whitehawk Estate lad. Immortalized on a bus. Seriously.' He drained his Armagnac and, though aware he had had more than enough already, he summoned the waiter for another one and a refill, despite her protests, of Jodie's glass. Then he continued. 'Guess I had my epiphany that morning. I thought, you know what? When you are about to die you start to wonder what mark you've made on the world. How are folk going to remember you?'

She smiled.

'I knew what I had to do, which was come home to my roots and find the best causes to leave my money to. Everywhere in the world there are people and organizations and causes in desperate need of money. No one person – not even a Bill

Gates – can help the whole world. You have your mantra, that lovely Vivien Leigh quote, and I have mine.'

'Which is?'

'No man made a greater mistake than the man who did nothing because he could only do a little.'

'That's beautiful. Reminds me of something I read a while back. "If you ever thought you were too small to make a difference, you've never shared a bed with a mosquito."'

'I love that! Maybe I should have it as my epitaph?'

'Stop talking about death, Paul!'

'Sure, sorry.'

He waited as their fresh drinks arrived, sipped his new Armagnac, then put the glass down. A warning voice inside his head was shouting, *Enough!* 'You know what I would love to do?'

She shook her head and sipped her fresh Zombie.

'You and I come from a very different Brighton. When I was a kid in the 1950s – brought up by my mum, a war widow – this was a seedy, tatty place. It was full of nasty people, violent gangs. It was a dangerous place. Now it's become the coolest city in the UK outside of London – one of the coolest cities on the planet. I'd love to take you on a tour of the Brighton I grew up in. Do you have any free time before I fly back to California?'

'Well,' she said thoughtfully, 'I need to defrost

my fridge. And I have some paint I need to watch drying. But I'm sure I could find a few minutes.'

He gave her a sideways look, and chuckled. 'Well, I wouldn't want to inconvenience you.'

'You wouldn't be an inconvenience. You'd be a very lovely distraction.'

He smiled. 'I've a busy morning tomorrow with my accountants and lawyers, but I've a clear afternoon.'

'Great,' she said. 'How about I pick you up here? I'm a very good driver and I have a nice car. I would be more than happy to be your chauffeur!'

He shook his head. 'I've arranged a chauffeured limousine through the hotel. I could pick you up from your home around lunchtime – we could get a bite to eat then do the tour. How does that sound?'

'Well . . .' She hesitated for an instant. 'Yes, that would be great, but I'm not actually sure where I'll end up tomorrow morning. How about I meet you here – what time would work?'

'Half twelve?'

'That sounds like a plan, if you're really sure it's no inconvenience?'

'I'd be grateful for the company.'

'I do have one condition for coming on this tour with you,' she said.

'And that is?'

'That you allow me to cook you dinner at my house tomorrow evening. That is if you don't have other plans?'

'Well, you know, it's a strange thing, but I don't have a goddam thing in my diary for tomorrow night.'

'So now you do!'

CHAPTER 104

Friday 13 March

Noah had been grizzly all evening. Finally, past midnight, after numerous trips to his room to feed and soothe him, Roy and Cleo had both fallen asleep.

Almost immediately, it seemed, Roy was woken by the rasping sound of his phone. He had left it on silent but vibrate mode, in the hope that if it did ring, it wouldn't wake Cleo, who was knackered.

He grabbed it, the display showing *No Caller ID*, slipped out of bed, went through into the bathroom, closing the door behind him, and switched on the light. 'Roy Grace,' he answered quietly. The time on the display was 12.43 a.m.

'Roy? It's Norman – sorry – Paul.'

Potting sounded pissed, his voice alternating between his Devon burr and his assumed Transatlantic accent.

'You shouldn't be calling me direct. It's all meant to go through your Cover Officer.'

'I know that, Roy, but I just wanted to let you know as well – cut the bureaucracy out.'

'It's not so much red tape as protocol, Norman. OK. I appreciate you calling, but it's dangerous, OK? This is a breach of procedure.'

'OK, chief, if you say so.'

'So?'

'I've made contact.'

'I've been informed from Surveillance.'

'Had a pretty interesting evening.'

'So it sounds.'

'Huh?'

'Boozy time?'

'Well, I had to keep up with her. I think she likes me. She's a fast mover. Our plan worked, I think she mus – must – have read the *Argus* piece and figured out who I was. You know?'

'Cornel.'

'Thash – that's – me!'

Alarm bells were ringing at the sound of his voice. 'Nice work, Norman – sorry – Paul. So?'

'I'm seeing her again tomorrow. She's suggested going to hers – she's cooking me dinner at home tomorrow evening, and you'll be able to pick the address up from my tracker when I get there.'

'Good, well done, but don't call me again.'

Grace ended the call feeling worried. Many officers in Sussex Police felt that Potting, with his non-pc attitudes – albeit less extreme these days – was well past his sell-by date. With the historic thirty-year service to retirement, few officers in Sussex Police were older than fifty-five. But with recent unpopular revisions to the pension scheme, working past the age of fifty-five was going to become the norm. And the DS, a late entrant to the police, would not be completing his thirty years until he was almost sixty. Another few years to go. As one of the officers to have worked closely with him over a number of years, Roy Grace saw qualities in the strange but kind character that eluded those who knew – or saw – only the old-school cop in him, and the values that came with that. Grace knew better and had fought Potting's corner several times in recent years, saving him from disciplinary action – and potential dismissal on more than one occasion – because he believed in him.

He hoped to hell that Potting wasn't going to let him down now. But even more importantly for the DS's personal security, he hoped he wasn't going to let his guard down. If Grace was right – and he was pretty sure that he was – Jodie Carmichael wasn't someone it was safe to get drunk with.

CHAPTER 105

Friday 13 March

T ooth rose at 5.30 a.m., adrenalin pumping, not wanting to miss what should be the big event of the day. He went over to his desk, opened his laptop and checked the cameras in Jodie Carmichael's house. She was still asleep in bed, just like most of her fellow reptiles. The only activity in that room was in two of the glass vivariums – the one containing the cockroaches and the other the mice. All of those crawling, wriggling, twitching, darting creatures, unaware that the sole reason for their existence was to be fed to their neighbours in the other vivariums all around them.

Just as Jodie Carmichael was at this moment unaware of what lay ahead for her in her garage.

Enjoy your last few hours on earth, sweetheart, he thought, squatting down on the floor to begin his regime of recuperation exercises.

When he'd finished, he showered and shaved, then began applying his Thelma Darby make-up. Shortly after 6.30 a.m., the breakfast he'd ordered

521

on the card he'd hung on the door last night arrived. 'Thank you, madam,' the young room-service boy said gratefully, palming his tip.

He ate whilst continuing to watch the sleeping woman, then packed his bag, slipped out of the hotel and headed over to his car. He didn't plan to return, but he didn't want the hotel to know that. Let them think he was still here for the three more days he had booked and paid in advance for. It all helped to cover his tracks from smartass Detective Grace. But, with luck, by the time the police came to the hotel looking for him, he'd long be back home with Yossarian.

Fifteen minutes later he drove along Roedean Crescent, checking out the stationary cars he remembered from last night. All of them had misted windows, including the Range Rover he had parked behind.

He continued past No. 191 to the end of the street, made a U-turn and parked up on the opposite side to her house, a couple of hundred yards away, with a clear view of the entrance to her driveway. He switched the engine off, moved his seat back, put his computer on his lap and logged on via his 4G phone connection, once more checking the cameras.

She was awake.

Good.

Jodie sat up in bed, sipping water, trying to resist taking some paracetamol for the hangover that seemed to be worsening by the minute, intending instead to go to the gym and do an hour's hard workout. She had drunk too much last night, far more than had been wise, and she was thinking hard for anything she might have let slip about her past to Paul Cornel. J. Paul Cornel. Julius Paul Cornel. But she reckoned she had it covered, and he'd had a skinful too.

And she couldn't believe her luck. Inside she was smiling. She had found him in the first bar she'd entered and they had got on so well. What a brilliant night, it had gone better than she could have possibly imagined! And the bonus was she actually did like him, a lot. He really could be the cash jackpot she had been hunting for for so long. All that money and no children alive! Her immediate task would be to prevent him from doing the stupid thing he had talked to the newspaper about, giving all his money away to charities. She needed to get that ring on her finger fast. Sometime during their evening yesterday he'd said he was intending to return to California next Tuesday. Which gave her just the weekend. Between now and Monday she had to have him invite her to go to California with him – and make him think it was all his idea. She did not want to risk any time apart. Not even a day.

He wasn't the greatest looker in the flesh – he'd seemed more attractive in his newspaper photograph – but he had a sense of fun that she liked. And hell, she had slept with a lot worse. She was going to give him the best night of his life. And the best morning in bed, too. By the end of the weekend he was going to be sated, and he was not going to want to be without her. No man she'd slept with since she had matured ever had.

Rays of sun were streaking through the window and, despite her headache, the day felt full of promise. She glanced at her clock. 7.05 a.m. She needed to get up and on it.

She was meeting Paul at the Grand at 12.30 p.m. He was going to take her for a bite of lunch, then on a tour of *his* Brighton, the Brighton he remembered from his youth. Then she planned to cook him a meal here this evening. He'd already told her his favourite foods last night. If she got up now she'd have time to go to the gym, get her hair and nails done, do the food shopping and be back in good time.

She pulled on her tracksuit and trainers, and went down to the kitchen, trying to remember the disturbing dream she'd had during the night, which she had woken from crying out for help, but it eluded her. She put it out of her mind, focusing on what lay ahead. She took a strawberry yoghurt drink from the fridge, shook it and swallowed it, then went upstairs and opened the entrance to the reptile room.

Everything looked fine. Pulling on her heavy-duty protective gloves, she removed a cockroach and dropped it into one of the vivariums containing a saw-scaled viper; moments later, she watched the snake pounce on it. She fed the other three vipers similarly. Next she took a live white mouse by the tail and dropped it into the emperor scorpion vivarium. Then she took out another mouse and carried it over to Silas the boa constrictor's vivarium, unclipped and lifted the lid, and dropped the wriggling, terrified creature in.

She knew the snake must be hungry as it had excreted the last food she had given it. But instead of instantly coiling itself around the terrified-looking creature, as it normally would have done, it did not move. Then she noticed the small bulge about a foot down its body, and frowned.

The bulge could only be caused by something it had eaten.

She felt a stab of panic. What was going on? She peered down into the foliage and saw, to her relief, the USB memory stick lying there. Then she stared back at the bulge. 'What have you eaten, Silas?' she asked, out loud.

Tooth, watching her on the screen in his car, smiled. *Nice to see you worried. Don't want you dying happy.*

Jodie left the reptile room, closing the secure door behind her, mystified. That looked like a food bulge – the kind made by the snake swallowing a rodent. But she had not fed it. Was Silas sick? Was it a tumour? How the hell could a rodent have got into the vivarium? She tried to think back to the rush she was in before leaving for the cruise. Was it a mouse she had left him in his tank that she'd not noticed, and which he had only just now eaten?

Fretting, she went back downstairs, took her Mercedes key fob out of the hall table drawer, then went into the kitchen. She opened the door to the integral garage, switched the light on and stared for a moment at the beautiful dark blue car. Although, if all went well in the coming days, she decided, maybe in time she would buy the car she had always really dreamed of, an Aston Martin.

She pressed a button on the fob and the doors opened with a clunk, the indicators all winking together. She climbed in, picked up the garage door clicker and pressed it. The door began to rise. She fired up the engine and watched the dials come to life, put on her seat belt, then let off the handbrake. She was about to move the gear shift to D when she suddenly noticed a distinct whiff of alcohol. She frowned, placed her hand in front of her mouth and exhaled. The smell of booze was on her breath.

Just how much had she drunk last night?

She tried to calculate. How many units? A lot, for sure. And she actually wasn't feeling that great, as if she still had plenty of the stuff in her system. She would feel a lot better after a good workout in the gym, she knew. She pulled an open pack of chewing gum from the door pocket, popped a piece in her mouth and chewed, enjoying the instant minty taste explosion. But as she put her hand on the gear shift her head swam.

Am I fit to drive? she wondered, thinking about the piece in the *Argus* yesterday, about the new police blitz in the city on morning-after drinkers.

That would not be clever, to be caught in one of those spot checks. Quite apart from the risk of blowing her date with Paul Cornel, the consequences of being arrested could be catastrophic if any of her alternative identities were uncovered. She switched the engine off, walked round to the rear of the car, opened the boot and took out a breathalyser kit she had bought a long time back. She read the instructions, clipped a mouthpiece into place, switched it on and blew into it as hard as she could.

The dial glowed red. It showed a reading of 51.

She cursed. The legal limit for a breath alcohol reading in England and Wales was 35 microgrammes per hundred millilitres of breath.

For the cost of a taxi, it wasn't worth the risk, she decided. She went back into the house and called Streamline.

Tooth watched her in impotent fury. Testing her breath? Over the goddam alcohol limit? Ordering a taxi? You bitch! Think you are being clever? I'll show you what *clever* is. *Get back in that goddam car!*

CHAPTER 106

Friday 13 March

Tooth had to wait nearly four hours for Jodie Carmichael to return. The neighbourhood was quiet. A few cars pulled out from driveways and returned a while later. He saw a man emerge in Lycra, on a racing bike, and pedal off. A red post van stopped at each of the houses in turn, the driver keying in gate codes and then running in with the day's mail. Around 11 a.m. he saw a vehicle that didn't fit, an old, beat-up-looking Volkswagen Golf driving slowly, the driver wearing a baseball cap low over his face.

With a stab of anxiety he wondered, for a moment, if it was an undercover police surveillance officer. But from the slow speed the car was travelling at, and the way he drove past his car without paying him any attention, he ruled that out. A burglar casing the area? he wondered.

Finally, shortly before 11.30 a.m., a taxi pulled up at the top of Jodie's drive. When she emerged, holding several grocery store bags, he noticed she'd had her hair done. Tooth followed her on the cameras as she entered the house. She emptied the bags, putting most of the stuff, including a bottle of champagne and a bottle of wine, into the fridge, then went up to the bedroom, dialled and ordered another taxi for 12.15 p.m. Then she began to take off her clothes.

Another taxi?

Drive your car, lady, drive your goddam car!

How long was he going to have to wait here before she drove anywhere?

Seething with anger and frustration, he watched her slip off her underwear. At least she was giving him a show. She had a good body. He'd had no sex for weeks and he was starting to feel aroused. Long, slender legs, a flat stomach, large but firm breasts.

She sat down naked, provocatively, theatrically, in front of her white dressing table. She was behaving almost as if aware she had an audience, and was deliberately flaunting herself.

His arousal was deepening. Rays of sunshine lay across her white flesh. He looked at his watch. 11.40 a.m. The last flight today out of this freezing shithole country and back to the US was in just under five hours. If he left soon he could make that flight. He could slip in through the front door now, up the stairs, fuck her, break her neck and be gone in ten minutes. In plenty of time to make the flight.

The bang on his window sounded like a gunshot. He turned his head, startled, his body instantly coiled for action, his laptop sliding on his dress and wedging against the steering wheel.

Peering in through the window he saw a severe-looking elderly lady in a tweed coat and a Tyrolean hat. He snapped shut the computer lid and hit the button to lower the window. She leaned in and said in a booming voice, 'I've seen you've been here for a while. You haven't noticed a small black and white dog – with pointy ears – have you?'

Tooth, gathering his composure, gave a sweet, Thelma Darby old-lady smile and shook her head.

'His name's Bonzo and he's a rascal. Just a puppy, you see. Must have got out of the hole in our fence – I've been on at my husband to fix it for ages.' The woman was looking at him oddly. Had he missed something with his make-up,? he wondered.

He gave her another sweet Thelma Darby smile.

'No, well, thanks anyway!' she said.

As he raised the window, there was another sudden sharp rap on it. He lowered it once more and she peered in again. 'By the way, I'm the local Neighbourhood Watch coordinator. I've had a few calls from people who have noticed you. It's a free world, of course, but we like to keep an eye on strangers. Just so you know.'

She walked on. As he raised the window once more he heard her call out, loudly, 'Bonzo! Bonzo! Come along! Bonzo!'

Angry at himself for being so careless, for not noticing her approaching and allowing himself to be startled like that, Tooth started the car and drove for several minutes before stopping again, this time in a lay-by on the main seafront road. He was angry that he'd fucked up.

He didn't do fuck-ups.

CHAPTER 107

Friday 13 March

A few minutes after the time they had agreed, 12.30 p.m., Jodie Carmichael stepped out of her taxi in front of the Grand Hotel into the bright sunshine and strong breeze.

She had been back home for less than an hour. It had given her time to shower and dress appropriately for a tour of Brighton with, potentially, her next victim, and she was in a good mood. Her hangover was gone after the workout in the gym, shopping for dinner tonight was complete and her worries about Silas were temporarily parked. Her hair had been done exactly as she liked it, her fingernails and toenails were manicured and varnished, and she was dressed elegantly in a leopard-skin coat over a grey sweater, leggings and high-heeled ankle boots. She looked great, she knew. She'd decided not to drive as she had a feeling that lunch and the afternoon with J. Paul Cornel might well involve more alcohol.

'Wow!' he said, striding along the lobby towards her. 'Wow!'

She smiled and stared into his eyes. 'And right back at you!'

He was dressed in a mandarin-collared black shirt, buttoned up to the neck, a beautifully tailored charcoal suit and expensive-looking black loafers.

'I think I just won the lottery!' he said.

She grinned. 'Me too.'

'I thought we'd have a light lunch here – I've a bottle of Moët on ice and two lobster salads up in my suite. How does that sound?'

'That sounds rather lovely,' she replied with a warm smile. 'You wouldn't be planning to seduce me by any chance, would you?'

'If my old wedding tackle was up to it, absolutely I would be doing just that, my dear. But I'm afraid my days of seduction are long behind me. So you are in safe hands!'

'Isn't that just too bad?' She grinned. 'But I'm sure there are other ways.'

An hour and a half later the silver Bentley threaded its way through the network of hilly, narrow residential streets. Brighton's Whitehawk Estate, on the north-east of the city, lined with post-war semis and bungalows, had some fine views to the south and east.

Jodie and Paul lounged back in the rear seats, her right arm linked inside his.

'So this is where you grew up?' she asked.

'Yep, it was pretty rough back then,' he drawled.

'There were plenty of good, decent folk living here, like my mother. But it was a haven for villains in those days, too, in the fifties. Cops wouldn't leave a car unattended here, because if they did, they'd find it jacked up on blocks with its wheels stolen!'

'But it looks nice now,' she said.

'Uh-huh.' He was peering intently through the window. 'Make a right here, please, driver,' he said. Then a few moments later he said, 'If I'm right – and it was a long time back – make a second left.'

'How does it feel being back here?' she asked.

'Strange. Like – like nothing's changed and yet so much has – there weren't so many cars back then. Or satellite dishes.' He gave a wistful smile and turned to her. 'I keep seeing familiar things and it's like . . .' He shrugged and fell silent.

'Like what?'

He shook his head. 'Maybe it was a mistake bringing you here. Maybe this is not the person I ought to be showing you.'

'Of course it is. I find you fascinating. I want to know everything about you. I think what you've achieved in your life is incredible.'

He reached forward and tapped the driver on the shoulder. 'Here! Stop! Stop!' he said, excitedly. Then he turned to Jodie and pointed through her window at a small, semi-detached house perched on a rise above them. The garden was a complete junkyard, stacked with busted furniture, rotted doors, a supermarket trolley, a rusted car engine, several tyres, slabs of concrete and old bricks, all lying amid a tangle of weeds.

'Interesting art,' she said.

'That house! That was where I grew up! My mum looked after that garden.' He shook his head. 'How – how does someone let it get like that?' He looked balefully at the neat lawns and flower beds of the neighbouring houses. 'Jeeez, I'm sorry, I guess I made a mistake. I shouldn't have come back.'

'No,' she said. 'I'm glad you showed me. Nothing stays the same in life, don't you think? It's good to be sentimental sometimes.'

He continued to stare, fixated. 'I can't believe what's happened. My mum was so proud of it.' He shook his head.

'The past is another country, they do things differently there.'

'Yep, it sure is. You know, I left here when I was eighteen. I wonder who lives here now.'

'Want me to go and knock on the door and find out?'

He smiled at her. 'I'm not sure it's gonna be anyone that you or I would want to have a conversation with. So why don't you tell me more about yourself?' he asked. 'You said last night you were from Brighton – where was your family home?'

Instantly he saw she looked uncomfortable.

'Oh, yes, originally, but we moved a lot because of my dad's work.'

'What did he do?'

'He worked for a bank and they moved him around the country. We were constantly uprooted – you know – it was tough as a kid, always changing schools. You just make a new set of friends, then you have to say goodbye to them and move on again.'

'Where in the city were you born?'

'In some maternity unit, I don't honestly remember where it was.'

'And what about your parents? Are they still alive?'

'No.'

'I'm sorry,' he said. He told the driver to move on, to take them to the Dorothy Stringer School, where he was educated. All the while, as they drove, he kept up a running commentary about the places of his youth. And all the while he fed Jodie subtle questions, trying to get her to talk more about herself. But she fielded each question either with a lie or by telling him that it was too painful to delve into her past.

By the time the limousine turned into the drive of her Roedean Crescent house, just after 6 p.m., he had gleaned virtually no more about her than he knew when they had started out.

But he did know his handler would now see from the GPS tracker their exact location.

'Nice home you have,' he said, as the car pulled up by the front door. 'I like the style. How would you define it – Tudor Revival?'

She laughed. 'Have you really been away from

England for that long you've forgotten? The style is *mock* Tudor.'

'Ah, right, sure, I get that. But your home seems more than just *mock*. Maybe that's your natural beauty enhancing it,' he said with a twinkle.

'Flattery will get you everywhere. If you have time, I'll give you the five-dollar tour.'

'I'll make the time! Hell, we have all evening.'

'Cup of tea and some of my homemade cake when we get in?' she asked.

'It would be rude to refuse.'

'It would be. *Very* rude. And you haven't changed your mind about staying for dinner, have you?'

'Well, I guess it would also be very rude to do that.'

She leaned across and kissed him on the cheek. 'I like you,' she said. 'I like you a lot.'

The driver opened the boot of the car and Cornel removed a heavy Butler's Wine Cellar bag. Handing it to her, he said, 'I got some champagne, red wine and white wine from this local wine store the concierge recommended earlier.'

'So you figured out I like a drink?'

'Judging by last night, and the amount of champagne we got through at lunch, I guessed.' He smiled. 'So what time should I tell my driver to come pick me up tonight?'

She whispered in his ear, 'How about around midday tomorrow?'

CHAPTER 108

Friday 13 March

'I have the address. Looks like 191 Roedean Crescent. Potting's gone into her house, sir,' the undercover monitor said to Roy Grace over the phone. 'Cake and tea and then she's cooking him dinner.'

'Lucky sod,' Grace replied. 'Thanks for the update. So the address confirms the location we thought. No other information?'

'Nothing significant, sir. He's doing a convincing job, but she's revealing nothing.'

'Keep me updated.'

'Yes, of course, sir. I'm going off shift at 8 p.m., handing over to Andy Clarke.'

'OK, thanks.'

'I'll be back on at 8 a.m.'

'Have a good evening.'

'Thank you, sir. It's my husband's birthday. I'll be drinking orange juice.'

'Enjoy!'

'Huh.'

Grace stood and looked at the map of Brighton

538

and Hove, and located Roedean Crescent. He knew the area. So now Norman Potting was there, with the target. And it was likely Tooth would know it by now, too. He rang the ACC, advising him that the UC might be in increased danger. With the knowledge that there could well be venomous reptiles in the property, he told Pewe he would speak to Nick Sloan, to discuss round-the-clock Armed Response Unit surveillance. He also added that if they were to attempt an entry to the house to rescue him, should anything go wrong, they would additionally need an expert on venomous reptiles to be present, and that was in hand.

'Roy,' Pewe said, 'you know how stretched we are. Do we have the resources to protect UC adequately? If not, you'll need to consider pulling him out – if you don't want anything that happens to him to be on your conscience.'

'Sir, so far everything has gone according to plan, like clockwork. I think he'll deliver. We just need to make him safe.'

'Was going into her home part of our plan?' Pewe questioned.

'Absolutely, sir.'

'You believe she might keep venomous reptiles there and you haven't already arranged for an expert to be on hand? Do you realize the conse-quences for Sussex Police if he was bitten?'

'I have arranged an expert, and I've a lot of faith in our officer.'

'Good to hear that, Roy,' he whined. 'I'm glad somebody does.'

Grace hung up. God, he hated that man. Why the hell hadn't he let him fall to his death over Beachy Head? It was a question he had asked himself so many times. He'd saved his life, and this was his reward.

One day Pewe would get his true comeuppance. But right now Roy's priority was Potting's safety, and arresting that bitch on murder charges that would stick. He vitally needed better evidence.

He called DS Tanja Cale and asked her to confirm that Dr Rearden, the snake expert from London Zoo, was on his way down to Brighton for the pre-search planning meeting. He then rang the on-call Gold Commander, to brief him on the current deployment of a UC at No. 191 Roedean Crescent, and the possible need for an ARV unit to attend in an emergency.

Grace was not pleased to hear that due to the shortage of manpower there might not be a surveillance unit available immediately. He knew that Potting should be able to take care of himself, and that he had a panic alert on his iPhone which would send a unit over at once, should he need it. The Gold Commander, Chief Superintendent Nev Kemp, told him he would talk to Silver and sort out the necessary resources.

Grace ended the call and sat, frustrated. Five years ago, if he'd needed an armed surveillance unit to safeguard Potting, there would have been one at scene within thirty minutes, and a rota of units would have remained there for as long as it took. Now it would take some while to arrange.

Great.

Grace stared down at the files on his desk. Updates on Crisp, Jodie and Tooth.

He glanced at his watch. 3.05 p.m. He frowned – it had to be later than that. Much later. He shook it and realized it had stopped. It was a chunky Swatch that Glenn Branson had made him buy some while ago when he had insisted on taking him fashion shopping for a makeover, when Grace had first begun to date Cleo. Probably needed a new battery. He glanced at his iPhone. 6.20 p.m. Then saw the date.

It was Friday the 13th today. *Paraskevidekatriaphobics* was the word for people who had a fear of this date. But it had never bothered him. The only superstition he had ever taken note of – if it could even be called a superstition – was a full moon. In his early days in the police, as a beat copper in Brighton, it always seemed there was a rise in violent incidents whenever there was a full moon. One of his colleagues, some years back, had actually made a study and had concluded that it was true.

He felt at this moment like a juggler holding a whole bunch of spinning plates in the air. He had a female killer on the loose in Brighton; a fugitive serial killer somewhere in France, or Europe, or anywhere in the world by now; and an American

541

killer for hire playing cat and mouse all over the city.

And a boss who would give anything to blame him for failing to lock all three up.

The only useful thing he had right now, thanks to Norman Potting, was Jodie Carmichael's address, and some rather flimsy circumstantial evidence against her.

He was relying heavily on Potting finding something with which they could nail her.

Friday the 13th.

Hell, it had to be a lucky day for someone.

CHAPTER 109

Friday 13 March

Tooth, munching a pulled-pork wrap and sipping a Coke in an almost-deserted golf course car park half a mile away, watched the afternoon progress into evening. Lemon cake and tea gave way to champagne and canapés. *Oh, Jodie,* he thought with grudging admiration, *you are a true pro.*

The tubby American was revelling in her attentions. Right now he was lounging on a sofa, stroking a cat and holding a freshly refilled glass of bubbly.

Meanwhile she was busy in the kitchen, swigging his champagne as she cooked.

She wasn't going to be driving that Merc anywhere tonight.

But the one bit of good news was that she seemed to have persuaded him to cancel his limousine for tomorrow, and to let her take him on a further drive around the Sussex of his youth in her car, instead.

Tooth decided he might as well abandon his vigil

for tonight and go find a hotel within easy striking distance, but outside of Grace's likely search area. He googled and found several in the vicinity of Gatwick Airport, where he'd stayed on his last visit.

There was a Hilton at Gatwick. Hiltons were pretty anonymous places. He checked online and booked himself a room.

Erotic flashes of Jodie Carmichael naked in front of her mirror returned to his mind. There'd be plenty of hookers he could find online who'd be willing to come to an airport hotel like the Hilton. The thought cheered him up.

But not as much as the thought of Jodie Carmichael driving herself and her fat boyfriend out of the garage tomorrow morning did.

CHAPTER 110

Friday 13 March

J. Paul Cornel stifled a yawn, enjoying the aroma of the massive Armagnac that Jodie had poured him, then puffed on the last few inches of the fat Cohiba cigar. Patting his belly contentedly, he said, 'Jeez, you spoiled me tonight. What a meal. Divine scallops and the most perfectly cooked steak – you know, I can't remember ever eating a better steak.'

Actually, he could. It was full of gristle and she'd overcooked it. But he wasn't about to tell her that. The high-backed Perspex chair at the glass dining table was cripplingly uncomfortable, but he wasn't about to tell her that either.

'You're a true genius as a chef. Apple crumble and custard – my favourite dessert.'

'Nothing's too good for you. I'm loving your company.'

'And me yours.' He yawned. 'Look at the time. Almost midnight – where did the evening go?'

'I had no idea it was so late.' she said. 'It's been such fun.'

'It has. Think I'm pretty much ready to hit the sack. I'm afraid my medication has that effect on me.'

'Your room's all made up.'

'A few years back and I'd have made love to you all night.' He raised his glass. 'My lovely Jodie, where have you been all my life?'

She raised her Drambuie.

'God, how I wish I'd met you sooner. I wonder how different my life might have been,' he said.

'It's never too late. Is it?'

'I'll drink to that.' He drained his glass, stubbed out the remainder of his cigar and stood up, unsteadily. 'I don't have a toothbrush.'

'I've got a spare one.'

'You're an angel.'

'True.' she said.

They both smiled.

'I wish – you know – that I could make love to you,' he said.

She kissed him on the cheek. 'Let's get you to bed.'

'Good plan.'

'What would you like for breakfast?'

'You!' he said.

'I think I can arrange that!'

Ten minutes later she led him upstairs. Cornel noticed her cat scratching a wall at the end of the corridor.

'What's he after?' he quizzed her.

'I think he's mousing. He keeps doing that – maybe there's a mouse in the cavity wall. Tyson!'

she shouted. The cat shot off along the landing and down the stairs.

There seemed to be a lot of scratches at the bottom of the wall, as well as a few shallow grooves. What, he wondered, was the other side of it? Her snakes? He would try to take a discreet closer look when he had the opportunity.

A few minutes later, with J. Paul Cornel safely installed in the guest bedroom with ensuite bathroom, Jodie went back downstairs to clear up. She was feeling pretty good about how the day had gone but, she knew, she needed to deepen the bond between them. He seemed to be a bit guarded, and she needed to break that down.

How?

He had confessed his impotence due to a prostate operation. Maybe, if she could arouse him despite what he had said, that would do the trick? Perhaps later she would slip into his bed, naked, and try.

She topped up her Drambuie, lit another cigarette and sat at the kitchen table. She liked him. Which was as well, she thought, if she was intending to marry him.

A copy of the *Argus* newspaper lay there. As she sipped her liqueur and smoked, idly flipping through the pages, her eyes were suddenly drawn to a story.

SUSSEX POLICE OFFICER TO RECEIVE POSTHUMOUS QUEEN'S GALLANTRY MEDAL

It wasn't so much the headline that caught her eye, but the photograph below.

DS Bella Moy with her Sussex Police officer fiancé,
DS Norman Potting.

An attractive brunette in her mid-thirties, with her arm round a large man of indeterminate age, mid- to late-fifties, at least.

She read through the article. The two detectives were engaged to be married. Then tragically, whilst off duty, Potting's fiancée had bravely entered a burning house to rescue a child and dog trapped inside. The child and her dog had got out, but DS Bella Moy had failed to emerge. Her body was recovered some hours later.

And now she remembered something that Paul had said to her over dinner last night.

I lost my soulmate in a house fire.

His whole expression had changed after he had uttered those words. Last night she had taken it as someone very private revealing too much about himself.

She stared back at the photograph, concentrating hard on the man. The shape of his face. The slightly bulbous nose. The thinning hair in a comb-over. The short bull neck.

Feeling a prickle of unease, she opened the lid of her laptop and googled 'Sussex Police – Norman Potting – Images'.

A whole raft of photographs appeared. Some were of total strangers. But others looked remarkably like a shabbier version of J. Paul Cornel.

Was she imagining it? Was he just a lookalike? Was she being too cautious after the Walt Klein fiasco?

There was one way she might find out.

She googled J. Paul Cornel and started to sift though his images, taking screen-shots of each.

CHAPTER 111

Friday 13 March

Norman Potting was in danger and there was no one immediately available to protect him.

Cleo was feeding Noah, and Grace sat up with her, thinking hard. Should he break with all the rules, drive down to Roedean Crescent and be on hand for Norman? He had confided the UC's identity to Cleo, which she knew she would keep secret.

Half an hour later, just approaching midnight, Noah was sound asleep and Cleo collapsed, exhausted, into bed.

'Try to sleep, darling,' she said. 'You won't be any use to Norman if you're too tired.'

He yawned. 'You're right.' He reached out and turned off his bedside light, but then after a few moments switched it back on. 'I'm sorry,' he said. 'I can't leave him exposed like this. I've got to go and check he's OK.'

'Do what you've got to do. Just be careful and get back as soon as you can, you have to have *some* sleep.'

He dressed, pulled on a warm coat, made himself a quick espresso and calmed Humphrey, who seemed to think it was morning. He wiped the mist off the Alfa's windows, started the engine and drove fast towards Brighton.

Fifteen minutes later he turned into Roedean Crescent and slowed, looking at the house numbers in the dark street. The odd numbers were on the left-hand side. He put the window down and shone his torch, driving slowly, passing a few parked cars with misted windows, indicating they had been there for some while, until he reached No. 191. He carried on. A cat shot across the road a short distance in front of him.

He cruised the area, turning down all the side streets, looking for any suspicious vehicle where Tooth might be lurking. Although it was quite possible that the hitman was having the same difficulties as they'd had in locating Jodie Carmichael's real residence, until Potting had established it. He drove back along Roedean Crescent, halted a good hundred yards from the entrance to the drive, switched his lights off, climbed out and walked back.

In case Jodie had night vision CCTV cameras, something he wouldn't have put past her, considering her form, he just ambled slowly past like any man out taking a late stroll, glancing down the driveway as he passed. He could see the silhouette of the house directly below, which appeared to be in complete darkness. Norman Potting was in there, somewhere, asleep, according to the latest update.

Grace crossed the road, and walked back along the other side, barely glancing at the driveway this time, then crossed over again and got back into his car, still looking around and thinking, wondering. Just what was going on in that house right now?

According to the duty handler, who was listening to every word that was exchanged between Potting and Jodie Carmichael, not much. Potting had gone to bed. Alone.

He looked at his watch. It was coming up to 1 a.m. Despite the espresso he felt leaden, and thought back to Cleo's words, that he'd be no use to Norman if he was too tired. He felt exhausted.

He drove home.

CHAPTER 112

Saturday 14 March

Jodie, wide awake, sat up in bed staring at her laptop, her room lit only by the dimmed headboard spots and the glow from her screen. For the past hour she'd been saving the few photographs of Cornel that she could find on Google and on other search engines onto her computer, as well as all the photographs she could find of Detective Sergeant Norman Potting.

When she had finished, she double-clicked on one image of Cornel. A window appeared, with a request for her to enter his name. She did so and instantly all seven newspaper and online photographs of Norman Potting showed up as a potential match, each with a blue tick against them, giving her the opportunity to confirm or reject any.

She stared at the faces. The computer confirmed her increasing suspicions that they were a match. That J. Paul Cornel and Detective Sergeant Norman Potting were the same person. But how the hell could they be? Cornel had a long history on the internet, a trail of stuff going back twenty years or more. Were there just uncanny facial similarities between the two men?

I lost my soulmate in a house fire.

Was Cornel perhaps talking about a girlfriend way back in the past who had died?

She heard the click of a door opening. Stealthily, she switched off the lights altogether, closed the lid of her laptop, tiptoed across the thick carpet to her door, in the darkness, and listened. She heard the creak of a floorboard. Then another. Cornel trying to walk along the landing quietly? She saw a streak of light, just for an instant. Then again.

Holding her breath, she opened the door and peered out. And saw him at the end of the corridor, crouched down, examining the scratches.

She watched him for as long as she dared, then slowly drew her head back into her room.

Her heart was thudding.

You want to know what's behind that wall, do you? Strange behaviour for a billionaire who professed a short while ago to be so tired. Maybe I should show you what's really behind that wall, Detective Sergeant Norman Potting, you bastard?

After a few minutes she heard his footsteps creeping back, another creak of a floorboard, then the click of his door once more.

She closed her own, silently, and switched her headboard spots back on. Then she checked and rechecked the faces of Cornel and Potting.

She gave it a while, then removed her clothes and put on her dressing gown. Holding her phone, she slipped out of her room. She crossed the landing and stood still outside the guest-bedroom door. He was snoring loudly. She opened the door, as quietly as she could, just a few inches. If he woke, her plan was to slip sexily into bed beside him, whispering that she couldn't sleep.

She switched on the phone torch and played the beam across the room.

There was no change in the snoring.

His jacket was hanging on the back of the dressing-table chair. Holding her breath, Jodie inched towards it, slipped her hand into the inside right pocket and felt the bulge of his wallet. She eased it out and turned back towards the door. As she did so she saw that his watch, on his bedside table, was lying on its side and there appeared to be an inscription on the back plate. She picked it up, not wanting to risk waking him up by shining the light too near his face.

Two minutes later she was back in her room, with the door shut. She switched on the overhead light, opened the wallet and began to rummage through it. There was an electronic room key for the Grand Hotel. American Express and Visa credit cards in the name of J. Paul Cornel, along with a Californian registered US driver's licence. There was nothing in it to confirm her suspicions.

She then examined the back of the watch and saw, in tiny engraved Gothic script, N, love B XX.

She stared at it, her hands shaking with anger. 'You bastard,' she whispered.

Her first reaction was to go storming into his room, confront him with the watch and kick him straight out. She had to calm down, she knew. Calm down and think this through.

You bastard.

She thought back on today, and to the previous evening. Had she told him anything incriminating? Almost certainly he was wearing some kind of wire or transmitter. The police would know her address now. What else did they know that they could pin on her?

She carefully replaced the contents in the wallet, in the order in which she had found them. Then, turning the lights off again, holding her phone, she tiptoed back out into the corridor and stood, listening, outside his door.

He continued snoring loudly.

Gently, she pushed it open. As she did so she heard a purring sound and Tyson brushed up against her right leg. She pushed the cat away and slid into the room, one step at a time. There was sufficient ambient green light from the glow of the clock radio for her to make out his jacket again.

As she reached it she heard the rustle of bedding, and froze.

'Eh?' he grunted. 'EH?!' he shouted out.

She didn't move a muscle.

There was another rustle, a loud snort, and then he began snoring again.

Shivering from the icy blast of air coming in through his open window, she waited several seconds, then slipped the wallet back inside his jacket. His snoring continued.

She placed the watch on the bedside table, edged towards the door, backed out and closed it. Down the end of the landing, Tyson was once again scratching noisily on the wall. She switched on the torch again and shone it at him. 'Tyson!' she whispered.

He gave her a sulky look and stopped.

She continued staring at the wall, thinking about what lay on the other side of it. Tempted. Oh, so tempted to teach this copper a lesson he would never forget. Because if she did what she was sorely tempted to do, he wouldn't live long enough to forget.

CHAPTER 113

Saturday 14 March

Norman was woken by his bladder, as he was most nights, and lay confused, trying to figure out where he was. The room was filled with an eerie green glow.

Green digits in the darkness said 3.03 a.m.

His head was pounding.

Where the hell—?

Then he remembered.

He swung his feet out of bed and his toes sank into deep-pile carpet. Steadying himself with his hands, he blinked, staring into the green-hued darkness. Heaving himself upright stark naked, he tottered unsteadily, feeling disoriented, worried he might fall backwards onto the bed.

Finally he trusted himself to take a step forward. Where were the light switches?

He reached down, groping on the bedside table for his phone. Then he found the lamp and the cord attached to it. A short distance along the cord he touched the switch and pressed it. Nothing happened.

The pressure on his bladder was worse now he was standing. The bathroom was dead ahead. He took a few steps and collided with something. A chair. The bathroom door was to the right. He groped his way forward, felt the door, pulled it open and went in, fumbling for the switch. It was to his left, he remembered. But his fingers touched cold, bare tiles. Was it on the right?

He eventually found it and pressed it, and instantly squinted against the bright light and the image facing him in the mirror. The tiny loo was through the door to the right. He pushed it open, went in, saw the light switch on the left and pressed it. Immediately a dim light came on.

He shut the door and lifted the toilet seat, and was about to relieve himself when he noticed what at first looked like a shadow moving down the wall.

Then when he saw what it actually was, he shook with fear.

A furry black spider, the size of his hand with orange markings.

It was staring at him. Creeping slowly down the wall, a thread unspooling behind it from the ceiling, as if it was abseiling. It was level with his face now. No more than a foot from his face.

Breaking into a cold sweat, he moved back as far as he could, his head pressing against the wall behind him, looking frantically for a weapon. Was there a toilet plunger?

All he could spot was the toilet-roll holder.

He could see bristles on the creature's abdomen. And its eyes. Eight black, shiny beads staring at him, fearless, hungry, angry.

He moved a hand to his right, towards the toilet roll.

Rivulets of perspiration ran down his body. He tried to call to Jodie for help. But no sound came out.

He tried again.

But his voice was paralysed by fear.

He stared into the eyes. His hand touched the toilet roll. Tried to free it but it wouldn't move. The spider crawled down another few inches. Instinctively he covered his penis and testicles with his left hand, and yanked hard on the toilet roll. Suddenly, with a loud clatter, it came free and dropped down between the wall and the toilet seat.

Then, like an acrobat, the spider swung on its thread away from the wall and straight at him, its hairy, spiky legs clamping onto his face.

He screamed. Shook in terror. Screamed again. Again. Again. Shook. Shook. Trying to shake the bloody thing off. A thousand pinpricks stabbed his skin simultaneously.

'HELP ME! HELP ME!'

Suddenly, all he could see was a weak green glow.

The dial of the clock. 4.07 a.m.

He lay back in the bed, the sheets sodden with his perspiration, gulping air. And bursting to have a pee.

For some moments he fought it off, still filled with stark terror from the nightmare. He reached out his hand, found the bedside lamp cable, then switched it on. Instantly the room flooded with light. He stared fearfully up at the ceiling and the walls. At a framed oil painting of a rainy Parisian street scene. At another framed painting of a Provençal village.

He slipped out of bed and crossed over to the bathroom, pulled the door open warily, found the light switch and turned it on. He peered around before entering, then, even more warily, pushed open the loo door. He took a step in, snapping on the light and looking up at the ceiling and around at the walls and the floor.

There was nothing in there.

All the same, he was as fast as he could be, then went back out, shutting the door firmly, before rinsing his hands and going back into the bedroom, shutting that door firmly, too.

He climbed back into bed, wide awake and too scared to go back to sleep.

It seemed only moments later that his alarm was beeping and the room was flooded with daylight.

He was too relieved to notice his head pounding from all the Armagnac he had drunk the previous night.

CHAPTER 114

Saturday 14 March

After a sleepless night, fretting about DS Norman Potting, Jodie Carmichael finally gave up on trying to get any rest, and went into her bathroom.

Standing under the jets of the shower, she was trying hard to think everything through. She was reasonably satisfied she'd said nothing to Detective Sergeant Potting that the police could use against her. What exactly was his game plan?

To try to take a look around her house for evidence? Good luck with that one! The only thing she had here that she could, in theory, be arrested for was the memory stick, and the stash of dollars she'd taken in New York. It made her smile that the dollars were sewn inside the mattress that he had spent the night sleeping on. She doubted very much that the owner of the memory stick and cash would have made a complaint to the police.

She thought about seeing the detective studying the landing wall last night. If he brought in a search team they would find the reptile room. And then?

So her first husband, Christopher Bentley, a reptile expert, had died from a snake bite. So had Rowley Carmichael – in India – from a bite from a snake that killed 158 people a day in that country.

So she kept saw-scaled vipers among other pets in her home.

So she didn't have a licence for them, here in Brighton. But she had inherited most of them from her late husband, Christopher Bentley, and still kept up a valid licence for them under his name, at the address of her London bolthole, a small flat in South Kensington. The police might rumble and bust her little secret Brighton address, her bedsit flat near the Seven Dials. But they'd find nothing there. She would always be one step ahead of them.

Were they going to try to show that she'd taken a snake with her in her luggage on the cruise?

No way, José.

Keep your friends close, and your enemies even closer.

Shrewd, she thought. For a few hours at least, with luck, she would have the jump on that fat oaf detective. Maybe if she was smart, and gave nothing away, she could glean information from him. Men were weak creatures. If his prostate problem was his cover – his lie – for not sleeping with her, then maybe if she could seduce him once, and record it, she'd have a hold over him. Men didn't reject her advances, they found her irresistible.

A plan began to formulate in her mind.

A couple of minutes later she stepped out of the shower, dried herself, brushed her teeth and sprayed on some perfume. She put on her dressing gown, activated her phone's voice recorder and slipped it into her pocket, then went out onto the landing, rapped once, softly, and opened the guest-bedroom door, ready to slip into bed with her guest, smother him with kisses and work him into a frenzy.

To her dismay he was standing up, fully dressed.

'Good morning!' she said breezily, recovering the situation. 'Just wanted to see what you would like for breakfast – as you forgot to leave your order hanging on the door!'

'So I did!' He laughed, then shrugged. 'Well, I guess I'll go along with whatever you're having.'

'Bacon and eggs, black pudding, fried bread, tomatoes and mushrooms? Would that hit the spot?'

'A full English? How could I resist? But I have a really important conference call booked to my suite at the hotel for nine a.m., which I have to be there for. So what I'll do is call a cab, go back to the hotel, take the call, shower and change while I'm there, and pick up a newspaper on the way – I normally get the Saturday *Financial Times* mailed to me every week in the US. Then perhaps we could have that breakfast when I'm back.'

'It'll be on the table, all ready. Oh, if you're getting papers, could you pick up a *Mail, Times* and an *Argus* newspaper for me?'

'Sure.' He looked at his watch. 'I could be back here in – say – an hour and a half?'

She walked up to him, placed her hands lightly on his shoulders and, looking into his eyes, said, 'That's too long, I'll miss you. I really enjoy your company. Try to make it sooner.'

He placed his hands on her shoulders. 'I'll do what I can to be as quick as possible.' She detected a faint change in his expression. 'The other option is we have breakfast back at my hotel. How would that sound? Save you the trouble of cooking?'

Why was he suggesting that? she wondered. Had he been making calls during the night? Testing him, she said, 'Hotel dining rooms are so impersonal. I think breakfast should be a very private occasion, don't you?'

'I've never thought about that.'

'It can be the most romantic of all meals – if you're with the right person. And best of all naked in bed.' She cocked her head and then gave him a light kiss on the forehead. 'You know how you can tell the difference in a hotel between lovers and old married couples?'

'No, how?'

'Lovers are the ones there talking to each other. The married couples are the ones sitting in silence reading newspapers while they eat!'

He nodded. 'I guess I'd buy that.'

'And mostly the true lovers are having their breakfast in bed up in their rooms.' She cocked her head again with a smile. 'I bought everything for a really nice breakfast, I'd hate it to go to waste. How about I drive you in the Merc? It's a glorious morning – we could put the roof down – and it would save you the cost of the cab. I can wait for you while you change, and get the papers, to save time.'

'Well, that's – that's a – you know – a very kind offer. But – ah – that would delay you getting breakfast ready. I'm already pretty peckish.'

'Good point. Hey, you told me last night how much you love cars. I have a very beautiful 500SL – take it. It'll save time waiting for a cab and you'd have fun!'

He nodded. 'Well, if you'd be happy with that?'

'Of course!'

'And you'd trust me not to run off with it?'

'I think I would!'

'Well, I guess it would be kind of fun to drive over here on the wrong side again.'

'The *wrong* side?' she chided. '*Wrong* side for who?'

He grinned then looked serious for a moment. 'Is there any issue with insurance?'

You don't need to worry, you're a police officer, you're probably insured to drive anything, she thought. 'No, any responsible adult can drive my car. Are *you* a responsible adult?'

He grinned again. 'I hope I never will be.'

'Don't be; there are far too many of those already in the world. It's one of the things I like so much about you, your naughty streak. You're still a kid at heart, aren't you?'

'That's how you make me feel. I don't think I ever met anyone who made me feel the way you do.'

'Me neither,' she said. She leaned forward and kissed him on the forehead again. 'Come downstairs, I'll get you the car keys. The sooner you go, the sooner you'll be back!'

'What do you say in this country about – you know – going home the next day in the same clothes you went out in?' he asked.

'*The Walk of Shame*.'

'Same in America. Guess that's what I'm doing right now, *the Walk of Shame*.'

'Been there, done that, didn't get the T-shirt though – was still wearing it from the night before.'

He laughed.

Tooth, dressed in his normal clothes, ready to catch a plane, was parked down a side street a few hundred yards from Jodie's house, hopefully safely off the dog-walking route of that nosy Neighbourhood Watch bitch from yesterday. He listened in growing horror to the conversation.

Nothing ever panicked him, usually. But he was as close to it as he'd ever been at this moment as, on his laptop screen, he watched Jodie walk down the stairs, followed by the American.

No. Shit, shit, shit. No.

He watched her slide open the drawer in the hall table and pull out the car keys.

He had seconds, he knew, to act.

Making his decision, he flung open the car

door, slamming it behind him and hitting the central-locking button on his key, then sprinted, uncomfortably, up to Roedean Crescent, turned right and raced, limping, along to No. 191.

Jodie kissed Potting on the lips, and said, 'Drive safe, Paul, hurry back!' She pointed at the door in the kitchen that led directly through to the integral garage. 'The garage clicker's in the car, right by the gear lever.'

'Thanks. It's an automatic?'

'Absolutely.'

'OK! I'll be right back!'

'*Hasta la vista*, babe!' She gave him another kiss on the lips.

As he reached the garage door, she was already halfway back up the stairs. She was going to use the next hour, or however long she had, to check out the reptile room and, in particular, Silas. Just how the hell had whatever he'd eaten got into his vivarium? Hurrying along the landing and into the spare room, she grabbed the remote and pressed the button, then opened the glass door and went straight across to Silas.

The boa constrictor was curled up, inside his vegetation, looking content.

'What have you eaten?' she asked. 'I need to know. Let's have a look at you, shall we? Are you going to be a good boy?'

The creature, now approximately twelve years old, was nine feet long. Her late husband,

Christopher, had warned her never to try to handle a boa on her own. He'd told her there should always be two of them in the room. If the creature became nervous for any reason, its natural self-protective instinct would be to wind itself round whatever it perceived to be the threat. When the snake had been younger and smaller he had demonstrated this by handing it to her and scaring it by shouting loudly. Before she'd had time to react, lightning fast the snake had coiled round her arms, pinning them to her midriff, then wound its body round her neck.

Within seconds it had begun to crush her neck, suffocating her. She'd tried, desperately, to free herself but the strength of the reptile had been too much. She was close to choking when Christopher had freed her by unwinding its head and tail.

'You bastard!' she'd spluttered as the pressure came off and he lifted the snake away, placing it back in its vivarium. 'Why the hell did you do that?'

He'd just laughed. She could still remember, years later, how he had looked into her eyes. 'I love you, my darling, I want you always to be safe. Now you've experienced the power of these creatures for yourself, you'll be safe around them. OK?'

It had been a good lesson. She lifted the lid carefully. 'Hi, Silas,' she said. 'So what have you eaten?'

Norman Potting pushed open the interior door to the spotlessly clean double-garage, he was scanning it for any obvious clues. He saw the gleaming blue Mercedes sports car, as well as a hybrid mountain bike and a helmet on a shelf above it, a stack of suitcases, a red plastic crate on a shelf piled high with newspapers, and a row of gardening tools on hooks.

To his surprise, the garage door was already up.

As Tooth, panting from his sprint, and in deep discomfort, reached Jodie's front door, he heard the roar of an engine and saw the blue Mercedes, with a man in a baseball cap behind the wheel, accelerate hard up the steep driveway. The car turned left and shot off down the road.

Shit, shit, shit. Breaking her goddam neck would have to do instead.

He looked into the kitchen, the dining room, the living room, but all were empty. Then he hauled himself up the stairs.

The reptile-room wall at the end of the landing was open.

Through the glass door, he saw her, facing away from him, peering into a vivarium.

Just as he rushed forward, he heard a massive explosion that shook the windows and doors in the house.

Jodie felt the floor of the house shake as she heard the deep boom somewhere close by. *Jesus, what the hell—*

As she turned, in shock, to run and find out

what it was, she saw a small, wiry, shaven-headed, furious-looking stranger, in an anorak, jeans and trainers, hurtling through the door of the reptile room towards her, holding a long, pointed blade.

She had no time to think. She just acted instinctively, in self-defence, doing the only thing she could think of. Finding almost superhuman strength from somewhere, in her panic, she heaved the heavy boa constrictor out of its vivarium and hurled it straight at him.

The creature hit him full in the chest, its weight halting him in his tracks, knocking him off balance, sending him stumbling backward against a wall.

'Yurrrrgggggghhhh!' the man yelled, as the snake instantly began winding itself round him and bit him on the hand. 'Yowwwww!' he yelled, trying frantically to shake the snake free, but it responded by wrapping itself tighter round him, pinning his arms to his sides, then continuing to wind round his shoulders and then neck. He could feel its strength crushing him. 'Get him off me, you bitch!'

Jodie grabbed a glass vivarium containing four tarantulas, raised it in the air and held it up above her head.

'Who the hell are you?' she shouted. 'Are you police?'

He looked up at the spiders, terrified. 'Who the fuck are you?' he shouted back. 'Jodie? Judith?'

'Both of them,' she replied, clearly. 'And more.'

'Get this thing off me!'

'Oh yes? And then what?' She raised the vivarium higher, as if preparing to hurl it at him.

'No. Noooooo! Please, I hate those critters, please. Look, lady, I'll go away, I promshhhh.' The snake was winding more tightly round his throat and it was getting harder for him to speak.

'Like I believe you. You know something? I've killed three people – two husbands and a fiancé – actually, four, if you count my stupid sister. You think I care a toss about some shitty intruder?'

'Plessshhhhh. Pleasssshss gerris off me.'

He was finding it even harder to gulp down air. He stared up, wide-eyed with fear, at the undersides and hairy legs of the spiders.

'Help you? Tell me who the hell you are!' she yelled.

His voice was coming out as a croak now. 'Get this thing off me and I'll—'

She slammed down the vivarium on his head, knocking him sideways and onto the floor. It shattered, freeing the spiders. She picked up another vivarium containing three light-brown-coloured deathstalker scorpions, and brought that crashing down on the floor beside his head. As it shattered, freeing the scorpions, she took several steps back towards the door, and saw, to her satisfaction, one of them crawling across his face.

'Helppsssshhhhhhhhhh!' he screamed, writhing in terror, his face bleeding in several places, as the boa increasingly tightened its grip.

'Who are you?' she said. 'Who are you?'

He stared back at her in silence, shaking.

She raced past him and through the open glass door, slamming it shut behind her, shaking with fear and relief. And confusion.

'Who are you?' she screamed again, through the door.

He just stared back, transfixed in terror.

Was he a police officer?

But he had an American accent. Couldn't be. So who was he?

His face was turning blue. A tarantula was crawling down his neck. A scorpion, its sting poised, was standing over his eyes.

The boa was coiling tighter and tighter round his neck.

'Help me please!' she heard him gasping. 'Helpppsssshhh haveshhhhh – plsssshhhhh, pleash-hhhh help.' His eyes were bulging as if they were going to pop, and stared at her, imploring: *Have some pity.*

She watched the scorpion crawling over his cheek.

Then she went into the spare room, picked up the remote and pressed the button. Instantly the false wall began sliding back into place, blocking the stranger from sight and blocking out his rasping screams.

She didn't do pity.

CHAPTER 115

Saturday 14 March

Norman Potting had just reached the top of the drive, racing after the car, when the blast threw him off his feet. He picked himself up and stared, in momentary numb shock and disbelief, at the scene in front of him a hundred yards or so along the road. It was like something out of a war movie. He saw the blazing, skeletal remains of the convertible Mercedes, and a Range Rover, that had been parked in the road, on fire beside it. A solid lump of a smouldering engine rested against a garden wall yards from where he stood.

Even closer, in the middle of the road just feet away, he saw a blackened human arm, wearing a wristwatch. Two wheels, attached to an axle, lay a short distance further on. Unable to help himself, and shaking uncontrollably, he threw up.

His confused mind was in turmoil. Was this Jodie's doing? Had she engineered him to be driving her car? Just who the hell was the shifty-looking character in the baseball cap, who'd been sitting in the driver's seat as he'd entered the garage and had raced away in the Mercedes?

His professionalism began to kick in. Pulling out his phone and giving his identity, his voice full of panic, he requested all the emergency services and, panting with exertion, ran forward as close as he could get to the inferno. Twenty feet away the searing heat was so intense he had to stop, impotently. All he could do was watch, transfixed. Thinking.

This would have been me.

He also called his handler, asking for urgent backup, and then Roy Grace.

'Stay where you are, Norman, don't go back into the house. We have armed response and a full team on their way.'

'Thank you, chief.' Then he began to shake uncontrollably once more.

Staring at the fireball, all he could think again was that person driving could have been him. Should have been him. He tried to piece the last few minutes together. Who the hell was the man driving the car?

People were starting to appear from every direction around him, some of them holding up phone cameras. He saw a woman with two small children, staring, frozen. As he heard the first distant siren, he began shouting at them, 'Police, keep back! Keep back!'

He saw another woman holding the hand of a small girl who was crying. 'You really want your child to see this?' he yelled in blind fury, as he noticed more charred human body parts everywhere amid the glass and debris from the car. All the time he was thinking more and more clearly.

Jodie.

That bitch had set him up. But who the hell was the poor sod in the car?

For some moments he stood, uncertain what to do. He needed to go back to the house to get Jodie. But he had to take charge of the scene. Were there any casualties other than the driver? He realized that the way he was dressed, he looked pretty improbable as a police officer. A woman was screaming hysterically. Only yards from him.

He saw her, with a large dog tugging on a leash, trying to restrain it from reaching a human head and part of a spinal cord only a few feet in front of her.

He looked over at Jodie's house. At a line of cars backed up down the street. *Christ. Christ.* Sirens were coming closer.

More and more people were appearing.

'Back!' he yelled at them. 'Stay back, there might be another explosion!'

There were also people gathering on the far side of the car, but the heat was too intense to run past it. To his relief he saw strobing blue lights. The first siren came closer and he saw a patrol car. He ran up to it as it halted, holding up his hands, and jabbered out a quick summary. As he finished, another patrol car, followed by an ambulance with a fire engine in its wake, were all approaching.

He broke into a fast, lumbering run back towards Jodie's house, down her steep drive and in through the open garage door. 'Jodie!' he yelled. 'Jodie!'

She came down the stairs, looking pale, in her dressing gown. 'What's happened?' she said. 'Paul, what's happened?'

'I'll tell you what's happened, young lady.' He strode over to her before she had a chance to move, grabbed her right wrist roughly, then swung her arm up behind her in a half-Nelson hold. 'I'm arresting you on suspicion of attempted murder. That's what's happened.' He was shaking like a leaf. But he wasn't going to blow this by putting a damned foot wrong, despite the state he was in. 'You do not have to say anything, but it may harm your defence if you do not mention when questioned something which you later rely on in court. Anything you do say may be given in evidence.'

Something valuable he had learned about over the years he had worked with Roy Grace was the psychology of the behaviour of suspects. Genuinely innocent people often tended to resist arrest vociferously, and sometimes quite aggressively. But most guilty suspects became like putty in your hands, almost as if relieved the game was finally up. She felt like putty, now.

'Attempted murder? What are you talking about?'
'You wanted me to take your car, didn't you?'
'Yes.'

'So who just drove off in it?'

'Someone drove off in it? Who?'

'You tell me.'

'I'm sorry, Paul, I don't know what you're talking about. What was that noise just now, that explosion?'

He wrenched her arm further up her back, so hard she cried out in pain. 'You little bitch,' he replied.

His phone rang. He answered with one hand and heard Roy Grace's voice. 'Norman, where are you?'

'In 191, holding my suspect.'

'Can you open the front door, there are officers outside.'

Potting frogmarched her across and unlatched the door.

'You'd better hurry, guys,' Jodie said with a smirk. 'One of your colleagues is upstairs and he doesn't have very long to live – if he's even still alive.'

CHAPTER 116

Saturday 14 March

With Jodie's hands cuffed behind her back, Potting was right behind, escorting her up the stairs and along the corridor, followed by several officers. She stopped beside a door and turned to Potting.

'There's a wardrobe just inside, to the left. If you open the door you'll find a remote. Press it.'

Potting did as he was told. Instantly the wall at the end of the corridor slid open to reveal the glass door behind it.

'Holy shit!' someone exclaimed in horror.

A small, shaven-headed man, in an anorak, jeans and trainers, his eyes bulging, lay on the floor, motionless, with an enormous brown-and-beige-patterned snake entwined round his body and neck. Crawling about on the floor were several large black hairy spiders as well as some light brown scorpions, one of which was on the man's neck.

'Don't go in!' said a voice behind them.

They all turned to see Detective Superintendent

Roy Grace, in a dark suit, shirt and tie, standing beside a man dressed like a bee-keeper in a hooded white protective suit, padded gloves and a large glass mask. 'This is Dr Rearden, a reptile expert from London Zoo. He'll deal with this.'

Public Order officers were a tough bunch, used to dealing with anything. Norman Potting had never seen them step away with such relief on their faces as when the reptile expert moved forward.

'Be our guest!' Potting said, as Rearden opened the glass door, went through and shut it rapidly behind him.

'Well, look who's in there! If it isn't our friend, Mr Tooth!' Grace said. 'What a surprise! All wrapped up for me – and it isn't even my birthday!'

CHAPTER 117

Sunday 15 March

'The time is 10.17 a.m., Sunday 15th March, interview with Jodie Carmichael in the presence of her solicitor, Clifford Orson,' DS Guy Batchelor said clearly, for the benefit of the video recorder above their heads. They were in the small interview room in Sussex House. Beside him, on another hard chair with little back support, sat DS Tanja Cale, who was also a trained advanced interviewer. The first interview had taken place on Saturday afternoon to establish certain facts and the background of the defendant and for her to give an account. This second interview was to challenge some of her previous answers in light of the information subsequently discovered by the police investigation.

Both Guy and Tanja were aware that Roy Grace was watching the live video feed in the tiny observation room next door. And they were also aware that they could only keep a suspect for thirty-six hours. To keep Jodie any longer they would need to go before a magistrate and present good reasons for an extension. She had already been in custody now for just over twenty-four hours. They had until ten o'clock this evening to charge her or else come up with grounds for seeking an extension.

Across the table, littered with glasses of water and mugs of coffee, sat Jodie Carmichael, quiet and sullen, dressed in a black top and blue jeans, toying repeatedly with the chain of the locket round her neck. Beside her was her brief, a tough, sharp London solicitor from a leading criminal law practice, suited and booted and with freshly gelled hair. He spoke with a strong Brummie accent.

The two police officers were expecting a fight.

'This is the second interview with Jodie Carmichael, née Danforth, also known as Jodie Bentley and Jemma Smith, among other possible names.'

'Other names?' the lawyer interjected. 'Would you care to specify them?'

'Not at this stage. We are carrying out investigations into your client's background and we believe she may have used other aliases in the past.' Then Batchelor looked at Jodie. 'You married Christopher Bentley when you were twenty-two. Is that correct?'

She glanced at her solicitor before answering, 'Yes.'

'And am I correct in saying that some years into your marriage, your husband died after being bitten by a saw-scaled viper snake that he kept at home?'

She nodded. 'Yes. It was terrible. He understood those snakes so well, and he knew their dangers.'

Batchelor went on. 'Am I correct also that your second husband, Rowley Carmichael, died from venom from the same snake – the saw-scaled viper?'

'According to the post-mortem report, yes.'

She pulled, theatrically, a handkerchief out of her bag.

'Would I be correct also in saying that you currently keep several of these snakes in a room at your house in Roedean Crescent, Brighton?'

'Yes, I do.'

'Are you aware just how deadly these creatures are?'

'Absolutely. You'd have to be a bit stupid not to be.'

'Are you aware that a licence under the Dangerous Wild Animals Act is required to keep these creatures?'

'I am.'

'You told us yesterday in interview that your late husband, Christopher Bentley, had such a licence. Despite his death, you maintained the licence in his name at an unoccupied flat in South Kensington, London. May I ask why you never transferred the licence to your own name and never notified any relevant authority that you had moved these reptiles to Brighton?'

She looked at her solicitor again, who nodded that it was OK for her to answer.

'I've been busy,' she said. 'I suppose I just haven't got round to it yet.'

'Busy for all those years?' Tanja Cale asked her, with a hint of sarcasm.

'I thought that if it was a valid licence, it didn't matter where they were actually housed.'

'You certainly have been busy,' Batchelor said. 'Let's go back in time a little. I understand that you were present when your older sister, Cassie, died. You outlined the brief details in yesterday's interview but could you tell us the circumstances in detail?'

'No comment,' her solicitor interjected.

'No, it's OK,' Jodie said. 'It was a terrible accident. Our parents had taken us over the October half-term to Cornwall. We were staying in Boscastle. Cassie and I went for a clifftop walk. She asked me to take a photograph of her at a particular high point. She stepped back right to the cliff edge. I was really worried and told her to move away. She told me I was being a wuss and instead she took a step further back. Then she stumbled and – she – she – suddenly—' Jodie closed her eyes. 'Oh God.' She opened them again. 'I'll never forget the terrible look on her face. One second she was there, then she – she—' Tears filled her eyes. Her voice broke. 'She just dropped out of sight.' She paused, apparently to compose herself, then sniffed. 'I crawled to the edge and looked, and I could see her body down on rocks, way below. I don't know how far. Two or three hundred feet.'

Tanja Cale passed her a box of tissues. Jodie pulled one out and wiped her eyes. 'I'm sorry,' she said, her handkerchief still clutched in her hand.

'How did you feel at that moment?' DS Cale asked her, gently.

'It was the worst moment – *the* worst moment of my life.'

Jodie then described what happened in the aftermath and the impact on her family.

Guy Batchelor pulled a sheaf of paper from his inside jacket pocket. He handed one sheet to Jodie, one to her solicitor and one to Tanja Cale. 'Jodie, search officers found a diary from your childhood in your house, yesterday. This is a photocopy of an entry from it. For the benefit of the tape it is marked exhibit GB/9, the first anniversary of your sister's death, after you had visited the grave with your parents. I'll read you the last part of what you wrote:

'*My family. My embarrassing family. The things they say. But this really made me laugh. Mum suddenly said she wanted to light a candle for Cassie, have it burning on the table with us during our meal. So my dad went up to the bar and asked if they had a candle they could light for his daughter. Ten minutes later the chef and two other members of staff appeared with a small cake, with a candle burning in the centre of it, and walked towards us, all smiling at me and singing "Happy Birthday to You"!*

'*I'm still laughing about that, even though it's nearly*

midnight and I've got homework to do for tomorrow that I've not even started yet.

'But, honestly, I have to say, I've not felt so great in a long time!'

He laid the sheet of paper in front of him. 'That doesn't sound much like a grieving sister to me.'

Jodie stared into his eyes as if she was looking right into his soul. 'Really? Have you ever lost someone you loved? I had a year of hell living with the guilt that I was somehow responsible. Sure, I remember that day with my parents, and the ridiculous mistake that pub made bringing a birthday cake. It did make me laugh, of course it did. The whole stupidity of it. It did cheer me up; for the first time in a whole year I actually smiled.'

'OK, Jodie, let's move forward to Christopher Bentley. He was an experienced reptile handler – one of the world's foremost experts in venomous snakes among other creatures. Yet he allowed himself to be bitten by a deadly saw-scaled viper. Can you tell us how you think that might have happened?'

Jodie and her solicitor exchanged looks. She gave him a steady nod and turned back to the detectives. 'I'm afraid that all experts get over-confident. To be honest, the way he treated some of his venomous creatures really worried me and I warned him several times. From the way he acted with them, he was starting to believe that he had somehow tamed some of them, and he was taking fewer and fewer precautions handling them.'

586

For the next fifteen minutes they asked a number of questions about the day it happened.

Batchelor studied his notes for some moments. 'We'd now like to ask you some more questions about Walt Klein. When did you meet him exactly?'

'In August, last year, in a hotel bar in Las Vegas – the Bellagio.'

'Can you tell us what happened about a month ago?'

Without looking at her lawyer, she said, 'Sure. We went skiing to Courchevel in the French Alps – he was a very keen skier.'

'What was the nature of your relationship?'

'We were engaged to be married.'

'And what happened while you were there in Courchevel?'

'Walt was a real – what we skiers call *powder hound*. He loved skiing fresh powder snow – they get a lot more in the US than we do in Europe. We'd been there several days and there was finally a really great dump of snow overnight. But it was still snowing heavily in the morning. He woke, raring to get up on the slopes. I tried to dissuade him, as the forecast was for the weather to improve later in the morning, but he was determined to get the fresh powder before it was skied out. So we went up together.'

She sniffed, and sipped some water. 'We got to the top of the cable car and I told Walt to follow me – I'd skied there before and he hadn't. I made several turns, then stopped to wait for him – and he never appeared. I figured he must have taken a different run – I'd taken a blue – the easiest – because of the conditions – but thought he might have taken a red or a black. After a while I realized he must have gone on, so I skied down to the bottom, to the place where we'd agreed to rendez-vous if we lost each other.' She shrugged. 'But he never showed up. And that evening . . .' She again raised the tissue to her eyes, hoping she wasn't overdoing it.

'What happened that evening?' Cale asked, gently again.

'A police officer told me he had been found at the bottom of a sheer drop.'

'You were engaged to be married,' Batchelor said. 'Did you know that Walt Klein had written you into his will?'

'No comment,' her solicitor said.

'It's OK,' she said to him, then turned to Batchelor. 'He was worried, he'd had some heart issues. He didn't get on that well with his two children, he said they were spongers and hardly ever bothered to contact him or come and see him. It was his idea – he wanted to stop them getting every cent when he died.'

'Very kind of him,' Batchelor said.

'What are you implying?' Clifford Orson said. 'I'm making an observation. Let's move on. Jodie, you say you were engaged to be married to Walt Klein?'

'Correct, yes.'

'Did Walt Klein ever talk to you about his financial affairs?'

'No, never.'

'Did you love him?'

'I was engaged to him, of course I loved him very much.'

'So was there a reason why you didn't attend his funeral?'

'No comment,' her solicitor said firmly.

Ignoring him, Jodie replied, 'Actually, there was. His son and daughter met me at the airport when I arrived back in New York and made it very clear I would not be welcome. I felt it would be extremely disrespectful to attend in those circumstances.'

The two officers then asked her a number of questions about the meeting at the law firm in New York and the circumstances of her stay at the hotels.

'OK, thank you, Jodie. Let's move on to your second husband, Rowley Carmichael. You told us yesterday that you first made contact with him through an internet dating site and had spent several months exchanging messages. When did you actually meet him?'

She reddened, then thought hard, and knew it was not going to look good. 'Last month,' she said.

'Can you remember the date?'

'February 24th.'

Batchelor studied his notes again. 'Tuesday, February 24th?'

'Yes.'

'Your fiancé, Walt Klein, was buried on Friday 27th February. So you were dating Rowley Carmichael three days before your fiancé's funeral?'

Jodie turned to her lawyer.

'My client would like to take a short break,' Clifford Orson said.

CHAPTER 118

Sunday 15 March

'The time is 11.35 a.m., Sunday 15th March, interview resumed with Jodie Carmichael in the presence of her solicitor, Clifford Orson,' DS Guy Batchelor said.

He repeated the question he had asked before and reminded her she was still under caution.

'I was feeling desperately low,' Jodie replied. 'I'd just lost my fiancé and his family made it clear I wasn't welcome at his funeral. I went out for a drink to my favourite bar in Brighton to try to cheer myself up – and I arranged to meet Rowley there. His wife had died a while ago and he seemed like a lost soul. We just sort of connected as we had done over the internet – it was as if we knew each other after our online chats.'

'Is that so?'

'We had dinner and then, later, he told me he was booked on a cruise and asked if I'd like to accompany him. I thought why not, what the hell. I had nothing else on, and I was feeling pretty distraught about Walt – I thought it would be good to have a total break.'

'You didn't know Rowley Carmichael well at the time you were dating – and engaged to – Walt Klein?'

She hesitated. 'No, not really, we had never met.'

'So you were in regular email correspondence with him for several months prior to going on the cruise with him – during the time you were seeing and dating and subsequently engaged to Walt Klein?'

She turned to her solicitor.

'My client has no further comment to make,' Clifford Orson said.

'We have a few further questions,' Batchelor responded. 'Jodie, can you confirm that you were registered with at least three different internet dating agencies for single ladies to meet wealthy men?'

Despite another warning glare from her lawyer, Jodie said, 'Are you married, Detective?'

'I'm asking the questions.'

'I'm thirty-six. I don't know if you are aware just how hard it is for a woman my age to meet a decent guy without baggage. My biological clock is ticking. All I've ever wanted is to be married to a man I love and raise a family. I'm getting increasingly desperate and I've registered with loads of dating agencies. Is there something wrong with that?'

Choosing men in their late seventies as potential life

partners and fathers is unusual, Batchelor wanted to say. But instead he merely shook his head. 'Not at all. But it's certainly at best unfortunate that your late husband, Rowley Carmichael, a very rich man, died within days of your wedding. But very fortunate for you that the ship's captain was a legally registered celebrant. So many ships' captains aren't, so although they perform weddings at sea, they are not recognized in law. But in your case, your marriage was completely legal.'

'What are you implying about my client, Detective Sergeant?' Orson demanded. 'She didn't book the cruise.'

'I'm merely making an observation. And of course I would like to point out the coincidence of the terrible tragedies, that both your client's first and second husbands died from the venom of saw-scaled vipers.'

'Precisely,' Orson said. 'Your words. She is completely innocent. You have no evidence at all. Everything you and your colleague have said is pure conjecture. Unless you have any real evidence, I want my client released immediately.'

Batchelor replied, 'At this moment in time that's not going to happen. The investigation continues as we speak and we believe your client is responsible for the deaths of at least three men and was possibly already planning to kill her latest victim, who narrowly missed being blown up by a car bomb yesterday morning. Your client's house continues to be searched and we are looking in detail into the exact circumstances of the deaths of Christopher Bentley, Walt Klein and Rowley Carmichael. The case may be circumstantial at present but we have many more questions for your client.'

Orson responded, 'Circumstantial and no more, she is entitled to be released.'

The door opened and Roy Grace, holding a laptop, entered the room. He introduced himself to the solicitor and to Jodie Carmichael, as well as formally for the benefit of the tape, then placed the computer on the table and said, 'I am about to show your client some material held on a laptop that has been seized from another suspect.'

He opened the computer's lid. 'Mr Orson, your client is probably not aware that her house was very elaborately bugged with cameras concealed in every room. We believe the person who fitted them had come to collect items he had been sent to recover, that he suspected your client had stolen from a person in New York.'

'Do you have any evidence to support this accusation, Detective Superintendent Grace?'

'Actually, I do. What I'm about to show you is from a clone of a hard disk taken from a computer we found in a car close to your client's residence in Roedean Crescent, yesterday morning.'

He tapped some keys on the laptop, then turned it so all present in the room could see the screen clearly.

The images were from a camera, positioned high

up on the wall of a room containing glass tanks filled with snakes, scorpions, frogs and spiders.

Jodie Carmichael was standing at one end of the room, lifting the lid from a tank containing a large snake. There was a loud boom, causing the camera to shake for some moments. Then a small man ran into the room. As he did so, Jodie lifted the snake from the tank and hurled it at him. The creature hit him full in the chest, sending him tumbling backwards onto the floor.

They all watched in silence.

'Yurrrgggggghhhh!' the man yelled, trying to get up, as the snake instantly began winding itself round him, as well as biting him, furiously, on the hand.

'Yowwwww!' he yelled, rolling over and over, as the massive snake wrapped itself round him, pinning his arms to his midriff, then continuing to wind round his shoulders. They saw him scream and shout out in pain and rage. 'Get him off, you bitch!'

Jodie grabbed a glass vivarium containing what looked like four tarantulas, raised it in the air and held it over him.

'Who the hell are you?' she shouted. 'Are you police?'

He looked up at the spiders, clearly terrified. 'Who the fuck are you?' he shouted back. 'Jodie? Judith?'

'Both of them,' she replied, clearly. 'And more.'

'Get this thing off me!'

'Oh yes? And then what?' She raised the vivarium higher as if preparing to bring it smashing down onto him.

'No. Noooooo! Please, I hate those critters, please. Look, lady, I'll go away, I promshhhh.' The snake was winding more tightly round his throat.

'Like I believe you. You know something? I've killed three people – two husbands and a fiancé – actually, four, if you count my stupid sister. You think I care a toss about some shitty intruder?'

Grace stopped the recording and looked down at Jodie, who was again toying with the chain of her locket, and then at her solicitor. 'Is that real enough evidence for you?'

'With respect, Detective Superintendent, this is my client, in fear for her life, shouting out a threat in self-defence.'

'Self-defence? Strangling her intruder with a massive snake? I don't think so. And that explosion you heard, for your information – that was a bomb placed in her Mercedes car, possibly with the intention of killing a police officer, and we are looking to establish if your client was involved.'

'Can you give us one shred of evidence that it was placed there by my client?' the solicitor asked. 'It's preposterous.'

Grace closed the lid and picked the computer up. 'We'll let you have a copy of this recording before you leave, Mr Orson.' Then he smiled. 'Oh, and by the way, the police team searching your client's house discovered the sum of one hundred and ninety-nine thousand, nine hundred dollars, in new bills, concealed in a mattress in one of the rooms. This may be entirely coincidental, but I've been informed by the New York Police Department that your client is a person of interest in the theft of two hundred thousand dollars from a hotel room in Manhattan on the night of Wednesday 18th February of this year. However, what your client doesn't know is that it is counterfeit money. As I say, this might be entirely coincidental or perhaps even circumstantial. I apologize for interrupting this interview. Please continue.'

Jodie, still toying with her necklace, glared at him.

About to walk out of the room, Grace hesitated suddenly, stared hard at her and took a step towards her with a frown. 'Could I have a look at your necklace and locket, please?'

'Why?'

'I'd like to see it.'

She removed it and handed it to Grace. He studied the locket for a second and then shook it. Something inside rattled. Looking back at Jodie, he noticed her face had paled a fraction. He opened the locket carefully and peered inside.

At what appeared to be a solitary snake fang.

He paused for a moment, thinking hard, then said, 'I'm taking this item into police possession as a potential exhibit in my investigation.'

'Would you please be careful with it?' she replied.

597

'It's sentimental. My first husband gave it to me. It came from a Gaboon viper that bit his best friend. Christopher killed the snake and managed to save his friend's life. He gave me this fang as a good luck charm soon after we met.'

'I apologize again for interrupting this interview. Please continue.' Grace left, closing the door behind him.

CHAPTER 119

Monday 16 March

Grace was in a pensive mood. 'The time is 8.30 a.m., Monday 16th March. This is the eleventh briefing of Operation Spider.' He scanned his assembled team. Everyone was present except for Norman Potting, who had left him a message that he was on his way.

'I'll give you the good news first,' Grace continued. 'Most of you here were involved in Operation Violin, the investigation last year into two revenge murders and the abduction of a young boy. Our prime suspect, an American professional killer known only by the name Tooth, vanished following a fight with Glenn on a dock at Shoreham Port. He was missing, presumed drowned, after jumping into the water, although a subsequent extensive underwater search never found a body. Then a short while ago we had a tip-off from Pat Lanigan from the NYPD that Tooth was very much alive and active again, and had returned to Brighton in pursuit of a memory stick and a sum of money that had been stolen from a hotel room in New York, allegedly by none other than our Jodie.'

He sipped some water, then some coffee from the mug in front of him. 'According to intelligence Lanigan had received, Jodie had links to a Romanian bagman for a Russian crime gang, who was found murdered in New York at the same hotel she had been staying in. She was seen in the bar with him by hotel staff one evening, a couple of days before he was found dead in his room. In what I suspect is not a complete coincidence, during a search of Jodie's house at 191 Roedean Crescent yesterday, the sum of one hundred and ninety-nine thousand, nine hundred dollars was found inside a mattress. Interestingly, a single one-hundred-dollar bill, matching the plate serial numbers of those in the mattress, was found in a holdall in Tooth's hire car, on Saturday, along with a USB memory stick. We've learned that the money was actually counterfeit.'

He sipped some more coffee. 'The contents of the memory stick are currently being examined by the High Tech Crime Unit. It appears to be some kind of ledger, containing names, addresses and coded transactions, within the US and some mid-European countries. We're sending a copy to the NYPD as it holds a number of names of persons of interest to them, we understand.'

'Do we know how Tooth escaped after going in the water?' Branson asked.

'Not yet. And I'm not sure that we ever will.'

'How come?'

'Video footage taken from Jodie's Roedean residence shows the unfortunate Tooth attempting to attack her with a stiletto knife. She defended herself by hurling a huge boa constrictor at him, which proceeded to wrap itself round his torso and neck in apparent self-defence – and constrict his airways. This charmer suffered severe oxygen starvation, as well as several bites and stings from various other creatures before the snake was removed. He's currently in the Intensive Care Unit of the Royal Sussex County Hospital, on life support. His score on the Glasgow Coma Scale – which measures responses – is not good. The only sound he has uttered since being admitted on Saturday morning is, apparently, the word "Yossarian".'

'*Yossarian?*' Guy Batchelor said. 'Yossarian was a character in that amazing novel, *Catch-22*. One of my favourite books.'

'Can you elaborate?' Grace said. 'Apparently he's repeated it several times, in a state about it.'

'He was the central character,' Batchelor said. 'Shit, I read it a long time ago. He was paranoid that people were trying to kill him, I seem to remember.'

Grace wrote down the name, *Yossarian*, in his policy book. 'It would be helpful, Guy, if you could look into this further.'

'Yes, boss.'

'Tooth is currently undergoing further tests and

601

I hope to have an update later today. Meanwhile he is under police guard in hospital.'

He looked down at his notes again. 'OK, now on to Operation Spider, where the news is not as good as I'd hoped. First, I'd like to commend DS Potting, who'll be here in a minute, for his bravery. None of you will be aware of this, but he was our undercover operative. He placed himself in great danger, and we have sheer luck to thank for him still being with us today. The unintended victim of the bomb was a suspected member of the car theft gang, and a known offender, Dean Warren. He has been identified from fingerprints on an intact arm recovered at the scene. From what we are able to establish so far, Warren appears to have decided Saturday morning was a good time to steal this car.'

'Didn't you say in an earlier briefing that Stonor and Warren are associated, chief?' Frowning, Guy Batchelor stood up and went over to the family tree pinned on one whiteboard, and pointed out the connection.

'Drinking buddies, they have been for years,' Dave Green said.

'Yes, you are correct, Guy,' Grace replied. 'My hypothesis is that Shelby Stonor attempted to burgle Jodie's residence on the night of Tuesday 24th February. This accords with information Jodie provided us with during interviews yesterday. Prior to, or during, this bungled burglary attempt, in which Stonor may have been fatally bitten by one of the saw-scaled vipers that Jodie kept, he saw this recent-model Mercedes and passed information on to his mate Warren.'

'That's what friends are for.' Guy Batchelor said.

'I don't want any of you to underestimate just how close Norman came to driving off in that car. It's by sheer luck he is still with us. Whilst we are here this morning to celebrate good news, I want all of us to reflect, for a moment, on the dangers that face us daily in our work. Something for which we all too rarely get any public recognition. I can talk openly about Norman being the undercover operative as he has decided that was his first and last deployment undercover – and I don't think any of us can blame him.'

He was distracted for a moment by Potting entering the room, clutching a sheet of paper, then went on. 'Jodie is still in custody – we were able to get a forty-eight-hour extension to keep her in, but frankly we need more evidence. She's so damned clever. All we've got against her is circumstantial at this moment, and it may be difficult to convince the Crown Prosecution Service to bring a case.'

'What about the theft of the two hundred thousand dollars and the memory stick, Roy?' Tanja Cale asked.

He shook his head. 'No one's reported the theft – the information we have from the NYPD is from one of their intelligence sources. It's probably drugs money – and we know it's counterfeit. I don't think anyone's going to be reporting it.' He gave a knowing smile.

'How strong is all the circumstantial evidence on her, boss?' Batchelor asked.

'Probably not strong enough. A sister who died, when she was with her, when they were teenagers. Her first husband who died from a snake bite. Her fiancé who died when she was with him, in a French ski resort. Her second husband who died from a snake bite in India. The Financial Crimes Unit are doing what they call *following the money*. The searches of all three premises linked to Jodie have revealed a number of passports, birth certificates and credit cards in different names. But it could be months before they come up with enough evidence – and even if they do, we're looking at minor fraud. We need to find something – I don't know what – some hard evidence.' He turned a page of his notebook.

'So we know Jodie was with her sister, her first husband, and her fiancé, when they died. She was on honeymoon with her second husband of just a few days when he died, also from an apparent saw-scaled viper bite. I have serious concerns about this latter death, but I have no substantial evidence to support these concerns, at this stage.'

'What concerns do you have, sir?' asked DS Cale.

'We've pulled in a number of experts to help us with this. Dr West, from the Liverpool School of Tropical Medicine, examined Carmichael's body, and had two major issues. Unfortunately, because it had been embalmed, any opportunity for an effective second post-mortem had gone. But he said he was bothered by the lack of any discolouration – ecchymosis – around the puncture mark on Carmichael's leg, which he would have expected to have been present following a bite from a saw-scaled viper. He also categorically said that the location where he was allegedly bitten by this snake is not the creature's natural habitat. He was at the Crocodile Park in Borivali East, outside Mumbai, according to what Jodie subsequently told the cruise ship's doctor. But James West said this snake typically lives in open, dry, sandy terrain – under rocks, at the base of thorny plants.'

He paused. 'West knows the Borivali Crocodile Park well – he's spent time there. He says the exact area of terrain where Carmichael was bitten is swampland, and that a saw-scale viper would not go near that.'

'Is it possible she brought the snake with her and planted it there?' DS Exton asked.

'Well, I think that stretches credulity – even by this lady's standards,' Grace said. 'They were on a minibus from the ship to the crocodile park, so she'd have had no opportunity to buy a snake anywhere en route. Prior to that they'd been at sea for several days. It's possible she had smuggled one out of England and had it in her cabin, hidden in a suitcase, but I think this is improbable – and besides, we have no real evidence. In reality the only charge she could be facing at this moment in time is killing Rowley Carmichael, and as you've heard we're not there yet.'

Norman Potting raised a hand. 'I think I may be able to help with that.'

CHAPTER 120

Monday 16 March

All eyes were on the Detective Sergeant. 'Whilst I was operating this past weekend as a UC in Jodie's house, I took the opportunity to look around late on Friday night while she was asleep. It was part of my brief.'

Far from looking shaken by his close brush with death, Grace thought, Potting seemed animated.

'I also had the chance of a bit of a snoop around while she was making me dinner – actually, I'm quite glad I won't have to endure another of her meals, she's not that great a cook.'

Several of the team laughed.

'I didn't find anything in the rest of the house, except her cat was very insistent on scratching the wall we now know was a false door to her reptile room, but I did notice a strange appliance in her kitchen. She told me it was a domestic freeze dryer, and that she had it because it was the healthiest way to preserve vegetables – flash freezing them. Later that night when I'd gone to bed, I googled freeze dryers, and saw the one she had was considerably more elaborate than a domestic one – it was a very expensive industrial-grade one.'

'What are they used for?' Exton asked.

'Flash freezing food of all kinds – and chemicals – in fact, almost anything. They remove moisture and are apparently a way of preserving not just food but the potency of drugs and chemicals,' Potting replied. 'In the morning when I heard her in the shower, I went down to the kitchen and had a snoop through the drawers of her freezers – she had two very large freezers, one in the kitchen and the other in a pantry. Most of the drawers were filled with frozen rodents – mice and rats.'

'Sounds like a suitable diet for this witch,' Batchelor said.

Potting grunted agreement. 'One of them would have been a lot tastier and less tough than the steak she cooked – or rather *cremated* – for me. Anyhow, I had a good rummage through, and beneath several layers of the things I found a stash of unlabelled, rubber-stoppered vials.'

'Containing what, Norman?' Grace asked.

'Amber crystals – I had no idea what they were, and I wasn't about to taste one to find out – luckily. They all looked identical, so I took one, wrapped it in a freezer bag I also found in there and pocketed it, intending to bring it straight here and have it sent for analysis. But in view of the subsequent events, I contacted the Head of Forensic Services in Guildford, told her my suspicions and asked if the analysis of the vial could be fast-tracked. To avoid any possible breach of chain-of-evidence argument by a brief in court, I drove it there myself on Saturday morning.'

'What were your suspicions, Norman?' Tanja Cale asked.

He held up the sheet of paper he had brought in earlier, and gave a broad smile. 'I was late for this briefing because I was waiting for the emailed result to come through. I have the full details from the lab here, if anyone would like to read them. But to cut through the technical jargon, the vial contained freeze-dried venom from a saw-scaled viper.'

Roy Grace's mind was spinning. There had been no ecchymosis around the puncture mark in Rowley Carmichael's leg. Which was strong evidence that however the venom had got into his system, it hadn't been through a snake bite. That had been confirmed by Dr West. He'd also confirmed that the geographic location where Carmichael was purportedly bitten was not terrain where this snake would be found. Grace stood up, balling his fists. He was so excited he could have hugged Potting. 'This is really good, Norman, well done. This is going to help us enormously.'

CHAPTER 121

Monday 16 March

An hour later, back in his office in a far happier mood, Roy Grace did not imagine today would get any better. But it was about to.

As he sat in furious concentration, hammering out his statement of facts to present to the Crown Prosecution Service for their consent to charge Jodie with the murder of Rowley Burnett Carmichael, his phone rang.

'Roy Grace,' he answered.

It was the London Interpol detective he had spoken to before, Tom Haynes.

'Sir,' he said, sounding more good-humoured than the last time they'd spoken, when the man had been rather stiff and formal. 'I have some information regarding your suspect Dr Edward Crisp that I think you will like.'

'Tell me?'

'Lyon police have him back in custody.'

'They do?'

'He was arrested early this morning.'

'This is brilliant news – how – what happened?'

'Apparently we have a French farmer to thank. His wife got up at her usual early hour to milk their cows, and saw a grubby-looking man stealing clothes off their washing line. Her husband detained him with his shotgun. I don't have all the details at this stage, but I understand he was filthy, exhausted, frozen and possibly relieved. He didn't put up any resistance.'

The image of arrogant Crisp spending the past week covered in excrement from his escape through the prison sewer system, and grubbing his way furtively around the French countryside, appealed to Grace. 'Excellent news, Tom. I'll notify the Extradition Service right away. Perhaps the French prison service can keep a closer watch on him than the last time.'

'They're pretty embarrassed by what happened, sir. I don't think he'll have a second chance.'

'Please thank everyone involved.'

'I think it was sheer luck that they got him.' He was silent for a moment, then he said, 'I guess we all need luck.'

'The harder I try, the luckier I get?' Grace said.

'Thomas Jefferson,' the detective replied. 'It actually goes something like, "I find the harder I work, the luckier I get."'

'That's it!'

'There's another, from Franklin D. Roosevelt, sir: "I think we consider too much the good luck of the early bird and not enough the bad luck of the early worm."'

Grace smiled. 'You're well up on your American quotes, Tom.'

'I am American.'

CHAPTER 122

Monday 16 March

Almost immediately after he had finished his conversation with Tom Haynes, Grace received an update email from Michelle Websdale confirming the findings of the toxicology report in Goa. Rowley Carmichael had definitely died as a result of venom from a saw-scaled viper.

At lunchtime Roy received the final piece of the jigsaw.

As soon as he had left the interview with Jodie, yesterday, with the snake fang locket, he had secured it in a sealed exhibit bag and then contacted Dr Colin Duncton, a Home Office pathologist who had developed an expertise in the interpretation of wounds and weapons.

He had spoken to the man over the phone, explaining what he wanted, and the pathologist had agreed to come down to Brighton Mortuary the next morning. He also informed the Coroner's Officer of his action.

He was about to call the mortuary to see how

Dr Duncton was getting on, when the pathologist rang him.

'Detective Superintendent, I believe I have the good news you were hoping for. I've carried out a microscopic examination of the puncture-mark wound on the right ankle of Rowley Carmichael, believed to have been caused by a snake bite – a saw-scaled viper?'

'Correct.'

'I can tell you first that that wound was not caused by an ordinary snake bite, and I can categorically state that the wound was caused by Exhibit RG4, the snake fang that one of your officers handed to me this morning. On examination of that snake fang, I was able to detect striation marks – in particular, a number of specific ridges, furrows and unique irregularities to the surface and point of the fang which are identical with the incision wound. In my opinion, this snake fang caused that wound. In addition, I have arranged for it to be examined in a forensic science lab, as I believe they will find minute fibre traces from the deceased's trousers. Do you have them?'

'Thanks, that is brilliant news! I'll try to track down the trousers.'

'As always, I will send you a full report outlining my findings in due course. But I will email you something you can use now.'

As soon as he ended the call, Roy Grace updated Pewe, the CPS and his team, and instructed

Norman Potting to prepare a murder charge against Jodie Carmichael.

His good mood stayed with him throughout the day. He arrived home earlier than normal, shortly after 5.30 p.m., with a beautiful bouquet of stargazer lilies for Cleo.

It seemed that even Noah sensed his good mood, and slept through most of the night. But Roy lay awake for much of it, running on adrenalin, thinking about the incredible turn of events this past day had brought. With Norman Potting's discovery of the vial and the subsequent identification of the contents, and the conclusive match of Jodie's snake fang and the wound to Carmichael's leg, they now had the evidence to nail this bitch. Tooth, whose disappearance had long been a thorn in his side, was now under police guard. Almost certainly, if he survived, he would be permanently brain-damaged. And tomorrow the Extradition Team, who had travelled back to France this afternoon, would be bringing Crisp home in custody, to face the overwhelming mass of evidence against him.

An added bonus was the phone call he'd received shortly before leaving the office from Pat Lanigan, who was close to ecstatic. The contents of the USB memory stick recovered from Tooth were pure dynamite, Lanigan said. It gave them names, links and associations that the entire NYPD Mafia-busting team had been working a long time to find.

Grace asked him if he would do him a favour and email his arsehole boss ACC Pewe, to tell him of their gratitude.

'You got it, pal, right away!' Lanigan had replied.

Finally, an hour of dreamless sleep claimed him before the alarm beeped.

Cleo had not stirred. But he was wide awake again. He went through to Noah's room and, without disturbing his son, sat in the rocking chair beside his cot, where Cleo sat when she was feeding him, thinking about the day ahead. And the weeks and months of paperwork that now lay in front of him to ensure, as best he could, the successful prosecutions of Crisp, Jodie and Tooth. On top of the rest of his workload of previous cases coming to trial. It would be months of pen-pushing, he thought gloomily, before he would be back as a fully operational homicide detective.

He slipped back to their bedroom, brushed his teeth, then pulled on his jogging gear, went down-stairs, grabbed Humphrey's lead and took him out into the early-morning dark, misty drizzle.

Forty-five minutes later, invigorated by exercise and a shower, he dressed and went down to the kitchen to make a cup of tea for Cleo, and to feed Humphrey. He entered the kitchen, switching the light on, and said his usual, 'Morning, Marlon!' to his goldfish. Then as he looked at the square tank on the work surface his heart sank.

'No!'

He ran across and peered in. The goldfish was

floating, motionless, on the surface. 'Marlon! Marlon!'

He dipped his cupped hand in the cold water and lifted the fish out. 'Marlon. Hey, old chap. Hey!'

As the water drained from his palm the small fish lay there, eyes glazed and motionless.

His heart heaved. 'Fellow!' he said. 'Hey, fella?' He blew on the creature, but there was no sign of any movement. 'Hey, come on!'

He slipped him gently back into the water. 'Come on, chap, swim! Come on!'

Then his mobile phone rang.

'Roy Grace,' he answered.

It was Marcel. His voice was sombre. 'Roy, I am sorry for calling you so early.'

'No, it's fine, I'm up.'

'I thought you would want to know. I'm afraid I don't have good news. I've just had a phone call from the clinic. Sandy was found dead in her room a short while ago at around 4 a.m. this morning.'

'Dead?'

Roy Grace felt as if the floor was sinking beneath his feet. As if he was in a lift that was plunging downward. 'Dead?' he repeated.

'I'm sorry to give you this sad news.'

'How – I mean – what – what happened?'

The German detective hesitated. 'Well, I'm sorry if this information is going to distress you. She was found by a nurse. I just went to the hospital to see for myself. She had hanged herself from a cord she attached to a light fitting.'

'Jesus,' he said.

The floor was still sinking and the whole kitchen seemed to be swaying. He gripped hold of the oak refectory table with one hand to steady himself. 'Oh God, Marcel, that's awful. Thank you – thank you – for – for telling me.'

'Roy, there is some more information I have for you. Sandy – her son, Bruno, yes?'

'Bruno. Yes, Bruno,' he said in a daze.

'Sandy left a letter in her bedside cabinet. It was sealed, but on the front was written, "To be opened in the event of my death."'

Grace said nothing. Kullen continued.

'I just opened it. Inside is a laboratory DNA report on Bruno, confirming from DNA samples from him, yourself and from Sandy that you are the father. And there is a letter, written to you, in her handwriting. Do you want me to read it to you? Or I can scan it and email it to your private address.'

Upstairs, he heard Noah crying. 'Yes,' he said. 'Please scan it and email it, and I'll call you back later this morning.'

'You will have it in a few minutes.'

Roy sat down bleakly at the kitchen table, staring at the tank, willing Marlon to suddenly start moving. But the fish remained motionless. He looked at his phone, waiting. Moments later, the email arrived from Kullen.

He opened the attachment and looked at the words, written in Sandy's familiar handwriting.

618

It was less neat than it used to be, but still clearly legible. Clearly hers.

Dearest Roy,

If you are reading this then you will know that I am gone. Where, eh? We used to talk about that, didn't we? All those long discussions about whether we just faded to black, oblivion, or whatever. Guess I'll find out now – or not.

I know you came to see me looking for answers, I'll do my best here in this letter. I made a mess of things, that's for sure, but I don't blame you for anything, and I don't want you blaming yourself. But your suddenly coming back into my life is too much. I've been happy, being anonymous. Now I've got a whole shitload of stuff dumped on me. All the people I'd have to tell – my parents, friends, authorities – I just can't cope with this – the shame and the embarrassment. I don't know how to start or where to go. I certainly didn't want you back in my life, I can't deal with it. I don't really think I can face anything, it's all too much. Like I've been living this past decade in some kind of a cocoon – some huge bubble – and suddenly the bubble's burst. We all make choices in life, constantly, every day, and sometimes they are the right choices and sometimes the wrong ones. I did a bad thing in the way I left you, but back then I really didn't want a future with a man married to his work. I didn't want to be the third party in that triangle. I discovered I was pregnant and I had some fast decisions to make. Either I stayed, in which case I would have been trapped by this child into remaining with you – for a while, at least. Or I had an abortion. But I didn't like that option, not after trying all those years to get pregnant, all the infertility treatments we endured. I was scared about my biological clock ticking – stupid, I know, because I was still young, but I was afraid that if I had an abortion, would I ever get a second chance? So the other option was that I leave, without you ever knowing I was expecting our child.

I don't really understand what was going through my mind at that time. You know I had never been happy about the hours you worked. I think it was that day, your thirtieth birthday, when we had planned a lovely, romantic dinner together, and then I got your call that yet again you were on a case and would be late. Something snapped inside me, and I made my escape – I'd been planning the possibility for some time, sitting on the fence, wondering if I would have the courage to actually do it. Simple as that. I don't expect you to forgive me. But I hope this, in particu-lar, will help ease your pain rather than worsen it:

You need to know I wasn't a saint, I wasn't the good person you always believed I was.

This may hurt to read, but you need to know that I wasn't always faithful to you – I had some one-night stands. I'm not making any excuses – nor am I going to name names. I've been in a dark place for years. Since long before you and I ever met. I thought being with such a strong, stable man would help me, that you would be my rock. But it didn't, not really. I hid things from you, like the medication I took for anxiety. You never knew that I was hooked on valium for quite a while – I managed to keep that from you. I kept a lot from you. I'm not a nice person, I never have been. I'm just a mess. My depression spirals. A guy I was going out with a few years ago got me into drugs and I spent two years, maybe longer, I don't remember exactly, hooked on heroin. I tried to clean up as much for Bruno's sake as anything. There's so much I wanted to tell you – and ask you – when you came here last. I don't know why I didn't. I was so shocked to see you, my head was all over the place. I guess I knew then I couldn't see any future. My face is going to be permanently scarred. I've got motor-control problems – the consultant neurosurgeon just told me that my head hit the road at a bad angle – the worst bloody angle it could have hit – all my grey matter is jumbled up inside the box that's meant to protect it. But hey, I'm rambling.

I never wanted you back, but seeing you

and Cleo – that was pretty hard. It drove it home that for me, you're gone forever.

The thing is, Roy, I just see the future as a long, dark tunnel with no end. There's no hope, no future. Especially now everyone knows the truth. I just can't cope, I don't want to go on. Many people could cope with that, but I'm not strong enough to.

There, you have it. You are well shot of me. But just one thing I ask you, and I know I don't really have the right to ask you anything – but this is not his fault. So please, when I am gone, take care of our son, Bruno. He worries me; you'll see what I mean. Don't give him to my parents, they'd never cope and it would be hell for him. I'm leaving you plenty of money for him, to pay for his education and set him up in life. I've also left you DNA proof that you are his father. You won't know this but I took some samples from our house when I visited Brighton last year.

I do still love you, even though it might not have seemed that way to you for all these years. Sorry, but this is really the end for me. I know I'm a coward, but then maybe I always have been.

Sandy

CHAPTER 123

Tuesday 17 March

'Darling, I'm so late, I've got to fly.' Cleo ran into the kitchen, then stopped. 'Oh God,' she said as she saw Grace sitting at the table with his face in his hands, then noticed the goldfish.

She walked across to the tank and peered in for some moments, frowning. 'No!' she said. 'Marlon!' She dipped her hand in the water and gently lifted the fish out, studying it intently. 'Awwww, Marlon. You poor little thing.'

She shot a glance back at Roy, lowered Marlon back into the tank, rinsed her hand under the tap and dried it. 'I'm so sorry.' She walked over to Grace, stood behind him and put her arms round his shoulders, giving him a squeeze. 'He lived to a pretty good age. He's outlived a lot of goldfish by years, and he had a nice life.'

Grace nodded.

'He won the jackpot having you as his dad!'

He gave a bleak smile. 'Thanks.' There was someone else who now had him as their dad. He

623

needed to break the news to her, but now was not the moment as she was dashing off. He would do it later – and that would give him time to think. Time he very badly needed. He needed to compose himself and sort this mess out.

On top of the shock of having it confirmed he had a ten-year-old son, he was still reeling from the news of Sandy's suicide. Shouldn't he have spotted the danger signals all those years ago? But what were the danger signals? Leaving him the way she had had made his life hell. By disappearing off the face of the earth, there were plenty of people, he knew, including Cassian Pewe, who had harboured sneaking suspicions that he had murdered her.

Another dark thought swirled through him. 'I wasn't always faithful to you.'

So who were you unfaithful with? How many times, how many people? Is there someone I know who you once slept with, who secretly smirks every time he sees me?

And what did you mean when you said about Bruno – 'He worries me, you'll see what I mean'?

Cleo hurried over to the door, glancing up at the kitchen clock then at her watch as if for confirmation. 'Shit, I can't believe the time! I'm so late – we've four post-mortems this morning and we're one short on the team. Look, darling, why don't we find something nice to put Marlon in and bury him this evening?'

He nodded. 'Yeah, good idea.' He could hardly

speak. In a way he was relieved by Cleo rushing out, it bought him more time to think. He heard the front door close, a car door slam, followed by the familiar sound of her Audi's engine firing up and being revved far too hard while it was still cold.

Kaitlynn arrived a few minutes later. He found a small plastic sandwich box in a cupboard, put Marlon in, wrapped in a folded bed of kitchen roll, and placed him on a high shelf. Then he left without eating anything; he had no appetite.

Somehow, Roy got through the morning at work. But he was unable to concentrate. He kept pulling out his phone and reading and rereading Sandy's letter. Even a call from an uncharacteristically friendly Cassian Pewe, congratulating him, failed to lift his mood.

It was ironic, he kept thinking. For almost all of the time he'd been with Sandy they'd been trying for a child. After she had vanished, for almost another decade he hoped desperately she would come back. Then when he and Cleo began seeing each other, all that changed. But there had always been the spectre of Sandy somewhere in the background. And he had always felt something would happen one day; something that would shake him to the core.

But never in a million years did he think she'd had their son. God, so much to think of that had suddenly landed on him. What was the boy like?

What were his interests? Could he speak any English? How would he feel about being uprooted to England? More irony, he thought, since he was conceived here.

And more important than anything, how would Cleo react?

At lunchtime he asked Glenn to come to the Black Lion, because he needed his advice. Sitting in a booth, while his friend hungrily ate his way through a plate of lasagne, Grace's sandwich lay untouched in front of him.

'Suicide?'

Grace nodded.

'You can't blame yourself. Her life sounds like one long train crash after she left you.'

'Maybe if I'd said to her I'd have her back, she'd be alive now?'

Branson stared him hard in the face. 'What have you got inside that skull of yours? Shit for brains or something? You've moved on – like – your life's moved on *a thousand miles*. You have Cleo and Noah. They're your life and your future. Having Sandy back was never an option.'

'Cleo, Noah and now Bruno,' Grace corrected him.

'Do you have any other options for the boy? Grandparents? They could look after him if it's too big a burden for you and Cleo right now. You told me Sandy's parents are still alive, living in Seaford, right?'

'They're toxic, I can't stand them. God, I

wouldn't entrust any kid to them, they're horrible people. When I phoned them last week, despite what Sandy said, to say she was alive and I'd been to see her, there was no thank you! Instead of being thrilled they had got their daughter back, it was almost as if they were disappointed that the focus of their misery for the past decade had suddenly been taken away from them. They didn't even seem that bothered about phoning her, or jumping on a plane and flying out to see her.'

'So you don't have a choice, do you?'

'No, I don't. But how do I start the conversation with Cleo? I feel responsible for Bruno, he's my son, we have to bring him up.'

'You just tell her. All the time you've been together she's lived with Sandy as a shadow – a ghost. We're all prisoners of our past in some way. Cleo's a kind and caring person. She'll understand.'

'Understand that she's got a German stepson, who probably doesn't speak a word of English?'

'Look, thank God she met Sandy – and she shares this with you. You haven't cheated on her, she loves you, Roy. How do you feel about the kid, Bruno?'

'I don't know. I've never met him. I guess I'll find out soon enough.'

'Remember Bette Davis?'

'Bette Davis? I know the name, but couldn't pick her out of a line-up.'

'Only one of the greatest movie stars ever. I

thought with your advancing years you'd be old enough to remember. *All About Eve. The Nanny. The Wicked Stepmother.* She won two Academy Awards.'

'Never saw them.'

'Yeah, well she once said, "The key to life is accepting challenges. Once someone stops doing this, he's dead."'

'True,' Grace said.

Branson patted him on the back. 'I'm sorry about Sandy and about Marlon. Shit, what a day for you.'

'When we should be celebrating.' He shrugged.

'I meant to ask you – how did you know about the necklace – the locket?'

Grace smiled. 'I've known for some time that when a person fiddles with their wedding ring, they're probably guilty about something in their relationship. I could see her fiddling with the necklace during her interview. It made me curious.'

'Nice one, I'll remember that. Oh, and I do have one bit of positive news,' Glenn said. 'Yossarian.'

'*Yossarian?*' Grace said blankly.

'The name Tooth kept repeating in hospital, yeah?'

'Yossarian, yes. What news?'

'Tooth apparently had a lucid moment yesterday afternoon. A nurse gleaned from him that he lives in the Turks and Caicos, on Providenciales Island. She called the Enquiry Team. Guy Batchelor remembered that Acting Superintendent Steve

Curry is friendly with a guy called Neil Hall – known as Nobby – who joined Sussex Police a couple of years ago, and was formerly Deputy Chief of Police in the Turks and Caicos. Hall apparently remembers a strange character who used to bring his dog, called Yossarian, along to a bar there. Guy's been in touch with the Governor's office, who's just emailed back that Tooth's housekeeper is going to take care of the dog. And whilst we're on that subject, Jodie's cat is in a cattery, and her reptiles are now at London Zoo.'

'Well, it's great to know that we at least have a few problems solved,' Grace said, and smiled thinly.

CHAPTER 124

Tuesday 17 March

At 7 p.m. that evening, in the dry, chilly night air, under the beam of a torch Cleo held, Roy Grace dug a grave in the soft, damp earth beneath an oak tree in a corner of the garden. He went several feet deep, determined that no sodding fox was going to dig Marlon up.

He had wound gaffer tape round the sandwich box, sealing it completely, then placed it inside a jiffy bag, and sealed that with tape, also. He held it up in front of him. 'Funny to think that all those years ago I brought you home in a plastic bag full of water from a funfair! You were never very chatty, were you? But you know what? For many years you were my mate.'

He stooped down and placed the little package at the bottom of the hole. 'Goodbye, my friend,' he said. 'Maybe you'll find the happy hunting ground you were searching for all those years of swimming round and round in your tank.'

Then he stood upright for some moments, leaning on the spade, staring down.

'Goodbye, sweet Marlon,' Cleo said.

It was strange, he reflected. In a few days they would be flying to Munich for Sandy's funeral. But right now he felt more emotional about Marlon than he did about Sandy. Was it wrong to be feeling relief that the rollercoaster nightmare with Sandy was finally now at an end?

He shovelled the earth back, and they went inside.

For some reason the words of the previous Chief Constable, Tom Martinson, suddenly came into his head. Martinson had said them to him some years back in his blunt Midlands accent.

'You know what I always tell my officers, Roy. Never try to be a copy of anyone else. Try always to be a better version of yourself.'

He'd never fully understood, then, what Martinson had meant. But now he did. Cleo had brought that home to him earlier this evening when he had shown her Sandy's letter.

'Something I've always believed in my heart, Roy, is the wagon train circle. That's what true love is. It's not about holding hands, or staring into each other's eyes, or staring in the same direction together. It's a bond of strength. A wall around you. When you decide to make a life with someone by marrying them or just living with them, you form a circle against the world. It becomes just the two of you, and for the rest of your lives you never let anything or anyone break that circle. From time to time you let certain people inside that circle with you, and they become part of you and part of that wall.'

She went over to the fridge and took out a bottle of wine. 'Fancy a drink?'

He did.